The Velvet Cloak of Moonlight

The Velvet Cloak of Moonlight

Christina Courtenay

Where heroes are like chocolate – irresistible!

Copyright © 2016 Christina Courtenay

Published 2016 by Choc Lit Limited
Penrose House, Crawley Drive, Camberley, Surrey GU15 2AB, UK
www.choc-lit.com

The right of Christina Courtenay to be identified as the Author of this Work
has been asserted by her in accordance with the Copyright, Designs and
Patents Act 1988

A CIP catalogue record for this book is available
from the British Library

ISBN 978-1-78189-320-3

Printed and bound by Clays Ltd

This book is dedicated to the memory of
Mai Cecilia Augusta,
my lovely Swedish grandmother who taught me so much!
(1909–2006)

Acknowledgements

I love old castle ruins and when I moved to Herefordshire and found Raglan Castle only a short drive from my house, I just had to go there. From my very first visit, I was inspired by the place and the tragic events that led to its destruction. I couldn't stop thinking about it and this novel was the result.

As well as numerous visits, I had to research what actually happened during that summer of 1646. At first, I had trouble finding any proper accounts, but an email to Cheryl Morgan of Raglan Local History Society soon changed that. I am extremely grateful to her for pointing me in the direction of lots of interesting reading material and only hope that I have done the place justice.

Thanks also to Gill Stewart for super-fast emergency read-through of my manuscript; Katrina Power for advice about Kiwi heroes and Maori customs; Zana Bell for helping me out with the hero's New Zealand accent at very short notice; Mark Thomson and Chris Hugo at Knocker & Foskett, solicitors, for answering questions about the inheritance of an entailed property and subsequent debts; and Frances Younson at Gwent Archives for pointing me in the right direction with regard to more research books.

As always, huge thanks to the lovely Choc Lit team and to my family for their support. Special thanks to the Tasting Panel readers who passed the manuscript and made this possible: Jenny M., Isabelle, Jo O., Lizzy D., Kate P., Rosie F., Elaine R., Betty, Lizzie R. and Joy S.

And last, but not least, thank you to Melvin and Will Jenkins for letting me have a go at shearing a sheep – I apologise to the no doubt traumatised ewe!

Author's Note

The siege at Raglan in the final months of the first part of the Civil War happened as I have described it. I have tried to stick to the real historical timeline and facts as much as possible, although for the sake of my story I have altered things a little bit occasionally.

My hero and heroine are entirely fictitious, as are their families and the villain, but some of the other inhabitants of the castle were real people, notably the Marquis of Worcester, Lady Glamorgan (whom I have mostly called Lady Margaret in the story), Dr Bayly, Mrs Watson and Lord Charles. The Parliamentarian commanders and their engineer Hooper were also real. I read many accounts of the siege and have tried to portray these characters as accurately as possible, sticking to their known traits, but most of what they say in this book is made up as obviously they never met my hero/heroine for real and had no such conversations.

I admire the marquis immensely for sticking to his principles, even though he must have known from the start that he was fighting a losing battle. Such honour and loyalty are rare these days and although King Charles may not have appreciated it as he ought, at least it seems his son rewarded the family later on.

The ruins of Raglan Castle are well worth a visit, a testament to the futility of war, poignant and still echoing with the memory of all that happened one long ago summer. I highly recommend it if you are ever in the vicinity – it's a magical place!

For anyone who would like to know more about the siege, I can recommend the following books:

Raglan – History of 1797 – Chas. Heath

Anglia Rediviva (or England's Recovery) – Joshua Sprigge, chaplain to Sir Thomas Fairfax, commander-in-chief of Parliamentarian forces, 1647

Raglan Castle – Horatia Durant

Raglan Castle & The Civil War – Anna Tribe

The Civil War Earthworks around Raglan Castle, an aerial view – J R Kenyon

And if you'd like to read an old-fashioned novel also based on the siege, try *St George and St Michael* by George MacDonald – it's a lovely story.

Prologue

The velvet cloak of moonlight settled over the ruined towers of Raglan Castle, and the shadows beneath them stirred. The souls of those who had once lived here were restless, their tales as yet unfinished.

Battles had been fought and the echoes of victory and despair lingered, imprinted into the very stones of the castle's foundations. When the Parliamentarians lay siege to their Royalist enemies within its walls, the conquerors thought themselves victorious, but their triumph was hollow, as fleeting as the shadows.

And yet, there were those for whom the events of that long ago summer siege had a different impact. With their legacy now under threat, the time had come to reveal all. But evil, not fully purged by the passage of centuries, had other ideas, and the old stone walls could feel another battle brewing ...

Chapter One

Tess hated driving along the A40 towards Raglan. It was an ordinary road, nothing special, except for one small fact – it was where her late husband's fatal accident had occurred. But if you wanted to go to Raglan Castle it was the quickest route and she was tired of hiding from the horror of what had happened.

It was time to start living again.

Had it really been six months since that awful day? The reality of what had happened had hit her hard. And it was real. Giles wasn't coming back, but he was everywhere at Merrick Court, the big country house he'd been so proud of. The echo of his footsteps, the whisper of his voice; they haunted her even if he didn't. And she was more alone than she'd ever been in her life.

Tess tightened her grip on the steering wheel. She was moving on, sorting her life out. She'd be fine, but right now she just needed to get away from the house, do something – anything – other than feeling sorry for herself.

The road was straight with double lanes and mercifully free of traffic. Her sight was a bit blurry and she blinked, trying to focus. As she did so, she became aware of something on the opposite carriageway. A few bits of old yellow tape flapping in the breeze, left over from a cordoned-off area of investigation. The crash site. Tess tried not to look as it flashed past, but it was all indelibly etched into her memory as she'd seen it that day: police cars, a flattened grass verge, skid marks and a mangled car. A beautiful white Porsche. Or rather, what was left of it.

'No!' She mustn't think about that any more.

But her brain supplied a lot of extra images she definitely didn't want – a car swerving dangerously in the rain-soaked darkness, perhaps hitting the barrier in the centre of the road before bouncing to the left and off into the trees. Screeching tyres, the crunching noise of metal hitting metal, then metal hitting wood, screaming ... And all because Giles had been driving too fast again. Drunk.

She knew why, but she didn't want to think about that either.

Tess's heart was racing, her breath coming in painful gasps. She felt her hands slipping on the steering wheel as she broke into a panicked sweat. The rational part of her brain told her she shouldn't be driving at all in this state, but there was nowhere to stop other than the hard shoulder and she'd be vulnerable there. She had to carry on.

A roundabout hove into view and she slowed down, passing the first turnoff, taking the next one. A slip road could be glimpsed only a short way down the road and, breathing a shaky sigh of relief, she drove onto a tiny lane leading up a hill. A sign told her she was on her way to Raglan Castle and, after a hundred yards or so, she entered the car park and the castle's outline appeared above her, silhouetted against the cloudy sky. As she parked under a tree, next to some other cars, the ancient towers seemed to offer temporary sanctuary, as they must have done to countless others in its time. She leaned her forehead on the steering wheel and tried to calm down.

She was safe.

When her heart rate had slowed and her limbs stopped shaking, she got out of the car and looked up at the castle. What was left of the buildings dwarfed their surroundings, a majestic, but sad sight. She must have passed these ruins hundreds of times while driving to and from London, but she'd never stopped to go inside. Yet something about it had called out to her today, tempting her to come and have a look at last.

'Why not?' she muttered. Anything was better than moping around Merrick Court.

A shop on the right doubled as a ticket office. She quickly paid the entry fee and followed the path to the castle, staring up at the two towers flanking the gatehouse. Making her way across the moat, Tess passed through the gateway and into what used to be a large courtyard. The cobbles were uneven, but must once have been a labour of love, covering a large area that sloped downwards at one end. Clumps of grass grew between the rounded stones where horses' hooves no longer kept any vegetation at bay. Tess thought this added charm and softened the look of the surface.

There was something calming about old ruins. Stones that had withstood the ravages of time to show a fraction of the grandeur that once was. There were echoes of past lives here too, but they weren't personal, like the shadows at Merrick Court. Tess relaxed and allowed the peace of the ancient walls to seep into her very core.

Wandering aimlessly, she explored for a while, finding empty, roofless shells of rooms and staircases that either led nowhere or to dizzying vantage points. Eventually she made her way to the hexagonal Great Tower. Seventy-eight steps of a circular staircase took her – out of breath and with burning thigh muscles – to the viewing platform at the top. Three hundred and sixty degrees of amazing landscape surrounded her; undulating fields and hills, trees, hedges and tiny rivers, with the Black Mountains on the distant horizon. It was beautiful, but Tess couldn't stay there. It seemed dangerous and a quick glance down into the courtyard five or six storeys below made her head spin. She stumbled towards the stairs and safety.

Down at the base of the tower she found herself next to what was left of the moat. There was a stone wall which had crumbled away in parts and Tess sank down onto the cool stones, careful not to lean over too much. She gazed at the tranquil waters and the gently bobbing water lily pads. Timeless beauty. Serenity. Stillness. She felt the tension leave her body again.

The sun came out from behind the clouds and cast a shimmer of light onto the dark surface. She leaned forward a bit, wondering what was hidden in the murky depths. Tiny wavelets stirred the water and she watched, mesmerised, until she felt almost as though the moat was rising up towards her in a surge of liquid. Her head spun again and she felt herself swaying. She put out a hand to steady herself; she was going to fall if she wasn't careful.

She stood up and was just about to take a step away from the moat, when a pair of strong arms grabbed her round the waist from behind and pulled her back.

'Whoa, mistress, don't do that. Nothing is that bad, trust me. There's always something left to live for.'

What the hell ...?

Tess twisted to look at her would-be rescuer, whose strange speech in a thick Welsh accent took a moment to register. Had he thought she was about to commit suicide? That almost made her smile as it had never even crossed her mind, despite the calamity of Giles's accident. But the smile died on her lips as she squinted into the rays of the sun and took in his appearance.

The man standing before her was dressed in an old-fashioned outfit with a long leather waistcoat, white linen shirt with a drawstring fastening and loose trousers tucked into big leather riding boots with the tops folded over. A hat with a somewhat bedraggled plume sat on top of an awful lot of hair, sort of in the eighties' rock band style – very long, dark and wavy. It suited him, she had to admit, but then he had the kind of face that would have looked great with any hairstyle. Handsome, in a rugged way, and with a 'bad boy' twinkle in his eyes. Tess wondered if he was wearing a wig as she guessed he must be a re-enactor working at the castle, but the long tresses looked real enough. Good grief. A hard core history buff, obviously.

'Please, come inside,' he insisted. 'It's not safe out here.'

'I'm sorry?' What on earth was he on about? Tess looked around, trying to spot any obvious dangers, but saw none. Instead she found that the moat had disappeared and she was standing next to some sort of lake. A shoal of large, brown fish were circling near the surface, some opening their mouths as if waiting for treats. How did she get here? Did the castle have a lake? Thoroughly confused, Tess turned back towards the man and pushed out of his grip, intent on getting back to the moat. She'd only taken two steps when she began to feel light-headed again. Her vision swam. What the hell was going on?

'Mistress? Are you all right?'

She heard the man's voice coming as if from a great distance, then everything went black.

***

Raglan Castle, 21st May 1646

Arabella Dauncey kneeled by the lake at its northern end where the water garden spread out to her right. She loved watching the greedy carp who came to the surface to see if she'd brought them anything. Pieces of bread were always welcome, sucked into their open mouths with a smacking noise. She tried to feed them slowly, aware that this might be the last time she'd be able to visit this beautiful spot. The war was coming closer to Raglan and she'd been told a siege was imminent. The poor fish would have to fend for themselves, just like everyone who would soon be locked inside the castle. Would they even survive?

She didn't want to acknowledge that the question might equally apply to the human inhabitants.

She shivered at these dark thoughts and stood up, staring into the water and bending forward for one last look. Just as she was about to take a step away from the lakeside, a pair of strong arms grabbed her round the waist from behind and pulled her back.

'Whoa, mistress, don't do that. Nothing is that bad, trust me. There's always something left to live for.'

Arabella twisted to look at her would-be rescuer and pushed at his chest to make him let go. 'I beg your pardon?'

Had he thought she was about to commit suicide? She must have looked more wistful than she realised. Still, it was none of his business and she was about to tell him so when she noticed his appearance. The words died in her throat.

He was dressed like a cavalry officer with a long leather jerkin, riding boots and jaunty hat. It wasn't his clothing that caught her attention, however, but the man himself. Long, wavy dark hair framed a face she found amazingly attractive. Tall and well made in every way, his broad shoulders filled out his shirt very nicely. She'd felt the strength and muscles in his arms during their brief contact and she found herself wishing she was still being held by them. And his voice, deep and smooth, with a Welsh lilt that caressed the ears, was the kind you could listen to for hours ... She gave herself a mental shake. No, what was she thinking?

'Please, come inside,' he insisted. 'It's not safe out here.'

'What do you mean?' Arabella frowned at him. There hadn't been any reports of soldiers approaching yet or orders to stay inside the castle walls. Although if she listened carefully she could hear what might be musket shots in the distance. Someone practising? And there was a strange smell of burning in the air. Perhaps he was right,

9

but for some reason that irritated her even further and she stepped away from him.

'Have you brought news? Why did you not say so?' She turned and headed for the nearest stairs up towards the terraced garden. 'I'll go and …'

But she'd only taken two steps when she tripped on the hem of her long skirt, which must have become wet while she knelt by the side of the lake and was therefore longer and heavier than usual. She stumbled.

'Mistress? Are you all right?'

The man's hand shot out and once again he steadied her. Arabella glared at him and pulled her arm out of his grip. 'I can manage. Thank you.'

It wasn't like her to trip on her own skirts, but the man's presumption that she'd been careless made her cross. She was never careless. Not to mention suicidal. She was made of sterner stuff and so far the horrors of this war hadn't daunted her spirits. Who was he anyway? She'd never seen him before.

As if he'd heard her unspoken thought, he belatedly remembered his manners and swept off his hat as he bowed to her. 'Rhys Cadell, at your service, mistress. May I escort you back inside? Please?' He indicated the stairs she'd been heading for with a flick of his hand and a lift of his eyebrows. They were uncommonly fine eyebrows, perfectly shaped and not too thick, above a pair of sharp, moss-green eyes surrounded by dark lashes.

She felt her cheeks heat up. What was she doing admiring the man's eyes? She'd only come outside for a little while to be alone, something that was almost impossible inside a castle crammed full of people seeking sanctuary from this wretched war. Perhaps she'd stayed too long? She squinted again at the setting sun and realised she had.

'I thank you, but I can find my own way. I will go inside directly.' She nodded a cool dismissal, but the man didn't budge. He merely held out a hand to help her up the nearby steps and with some reluctance she took it. It seemed churlish not to, but the moment her fingers touched his, she regretted it as it felt as though a current reverberated through her all the way down to her toes. What madness was this?

The green eyes, when she made the mistake of looking into them again, seemed to be glinting with amusement. Was he aware of the effect his touch had on her? She sincerely hoped not. As soon as she'd reached the top of the stairs, she let go of him. 'Thank you.'

She was about to walk away, when he spoke just behind her. 'May I know your name, mistress? I am new to this place so a friendly face would be welcome.'

Arabella hesitated, but it would be impolite to refuse to reply. 'Arabella Dauncey.' She gave him a quick curtsey and almost added 'unmarried ward of the Marquis of Worcester' but stopped herself just in time. Why would he need to know that?

'A pleasure to make your acquaintance, Mistress Dauncey.'

She nodded, not wanting to acknowledge that it had been a pleasure meeting him too. Then something he'd said registered belatedly. 'You have just arrived, you said? How can that be? I thought they weren't letting anyone in now.' The marquis had given orders that no one else was to be admitted, as the castle was full to bursting.

He smiled and shook his head. 'Now that would be telling, mistress. And it's not my secret to share.'

Arabella fought to quell her curiosity, which was well and truly piqued now, but she wouldn't give him the satisfaction. 'I see,' she managed to say calmly. 'Well, I hope your "secret" will help us all. We could certainly use a few miracles around here. Good day to you, sir.'

Before he could say anything else to upset her equilibrium,

she swept off towards the Bowling Green and the bridge to the South Gate. But although she didn't look back, she felt his gaze between her shoulder blades until she reached the safety of the vaulted entrance.

Who was he? And why should it matter to her?

Chapter Two

Raglan Castle, 21st May 2016

Tess came to when someone bumped into her shoulder on the way down the wooden staircase leading to the moat. She seemed to have passed out – or fallen asleep? – with her head leaning against the railing and now had a crick in her neck. The woman trying to get past sent her a glare, as if it was a crime to sit on Welsh National Trust stairs and doze off, but Tess ignored her. She was too busy wondering why she'd had such a strange – and very vivid – dream or hallucination and how she came to be sitting here when the last she remembered she'd been over by the moat.

No, by a lake? But there wasn't one here.

She stood up slowly and rubbed her neck with one hand. Glancing around, she could see that she was alone apart from Angry Woman. There were no handsome re-enactors in sight; in fact, no men at all. Had she dreamed him up? But he'd seemed so real. And what about the lake? She could see the greedy fish quite clearly in her mind.

No, impossible.

She shook her head. 'Get a grip,' she muttered, but inside her mind more images of the man kept playing, like an old reel of film, with snatches of conversation. The odd word here and there made sense – *Rhys, news, secret* … Had he told her his name before she passed out? She didn't think so. But he could have done. And why would he give her news or talk of secrets?

It was all so strange and she was gripped by a niggling sense of worry, an anxiety totally unlike the kind she'd been afflicted with in the months following Giles's death. This was different, more real somehow, as though there was something menacing she needed to be wary of. True fear. Her own worries about her future and what she should do with her life seemed very trivial in comparison.

What the heck was going on? What was there to be afraid of? She looked around again. Nothing. It was as peaceful a scene as you could possibly wish for. No dangers of any kind.

'You're seriously cracking up,' she murmured to herself and dusted off the back of her jeans before heading for the exit.

'Excuse me, but do you have re-enactors on site to give visitors a more authentic experience of the castle?' she asked the lady at the till by the entrance.

'Not today, no. Later during the summer, maybe. Too few visitors to make it worthwhile this time of year.'

'You're sure? Only I thought I saw a man in period costume ...' Tess trailed off and felt her cheeks heat up as the woman sent her a puzzled gaze.

'I haven't seen anyone like that, I promise. He would have had to get past me to go in.'

'Right, well, er, thank you.' Tess hesitated, then dared one more question. 'I'm sorry, but is there a lake near here?'

'No, not unless you count the moat. There used to be lakes at the back of the castle in the ornamental gardens. They're long gone though. Why do you ask?'

'Oh, no reason. Just curious.'

Tess left quickly, too embarrassed to even look at any of the souvenirs for sale. Seeing the crash site again had obviously messed with her brain. It was time to go home and face the empty house and the bitter memories. Time for more action. Maybe ditch the antidepressants completely, even though she'd already cut them down to an absolute minimum? They weren't helping, just numbing her thought processes. And giving her hallucinations?

Tess drove her little Mini carefully along the main roads, trying not to imagine what could so easily happen if you lost control of your car the way Giles had done. But she wasn't drunk, it was still light and there wasn't a raindrop in sight. No reason why she should have an accident.

She bumped along the smaller, winding roads towards Merrick Court and through the impressive wrought-iron gates, which were open. Bryn Jones, the old gardener, usually closed them before going home for the day, so he must still be around somewhere. Probably in his potting shed or in the greenhouse. The thought was comforting; Tess wasn't entirely alone. And he lived just down the road, in his small, neat cottage. Not far at all.

As she turned into the stable yard, she noticed there was another car parked where Giles's Porsche had always stood. It was also a Porsche, a Cayenne, the large Chelsea tractor variety, and Tess knew only too well to whom it belonged – her sister-in-law. She groaned out loud. 'Oh, hell! That's all I need.'

Taking a deep breath, she got out of her car, then made her way to the kitchen entrance. Her visitors were sitting on the back steps; Rosie and her two teenage kids – Louis and Emilia.

At the sight, it was as though a black cloud materialised around them, reaching into Tess's brain. She tried to shake off the anger that began to swirl inside her, but only partly succeeded. Why did Rosie keep visiting? When Giles was alive they never saw his sister from one Christmas to the next. Now she'd suddenly decided she had to keep an eye on the place and appeared at Merrick Court at regular intervals. She didn't even phone to ask if it was convenient, but then Rosie never thought about anyone's feelings apart from her own.

'There you are, Therese! Where have you been, for goodness' sake? We were starting to think you were never coming home,' Rosie began as soon as Tess was within earshot. 'I tried to call your mobile, but you didn't pick up.'

Tess resisted the urge to say, 'Lovely to see you too,' in a sarcastic tone of voice, and ignored the use of her full name, which Rosie knew she hated.

'I've been out.' Tess knew that made her sound like a defiant teenager, but really, did she have to account for her every move to Rosie? She had a life. Or she was supposed to have one, anyway.

'Well, we've waited ages! Actually, I think it would be a good idea if you gave me a key. You know, just in case.'

'In case of what? I lock myself out? Don't worry, I have that covered.' Tess walked past Rosie and up the steps, fishing out the keys from her back pocket. 'Hi, Louis, Emilia.' She managed a small smile for her nephew and niece by marriage, who had both stood up.

'Hey, Tess. You okay?' Louis, the only person in that family Tess actually liked, came and put his arms round her for an awkward teenage boy kind of hug. At nearly eighteen, he was starting to get over the teen stage, while his fifteen-year-old sister was in the very worst phase. 'Bet it's all still a bit tough, huh?'

'Yeah.' She hugged him back briefly. He was a nice kid, down to earth and not stuck up like his mother and sister. She noticed Emilia's face remained passive and the girl didn't look like she'd been mourning her uncle. Emilia was only ever concerned with herself, a spoiled little princess.

'Come on in.' Tess unlocked the door and didn't wait to see if they followed her into the large old-fashioned kitchen. It was like something out of a National Trust brochure and most people gawped when they saw it for the first time – faded grandeur with a large iron range, massive dresser, copper pots and pans and a black Aga. And scrubbed pine everywhere, together with enough blue and white porcelain for a battalion of servants, even though they were long gone, just like the money needed to pay for them. 'Are you staying the night?' she asked, trying to dredge up some politeness when really she wanted nothing more than to tell them to go away and leave her alone.

'Of course we are. It's a three-hour drive back to London and you know I don't like driving in the dark.' Rosie pulled the door shut with some force.

Tess closed her eyes for a moment, wishing she hadn't had to deal with Rosie today. Or any day, for that matter. 'Well, you can have your usual rooms but you'll have to make the beds up yourselves. I'm a bit tired. I'm sure you'll understand ...'

'Don't you have servants for that? We have a Filipina maid and she does everything,' Emilia piped up at last, while frowning at her iPhone. 'And why doesn't this work here? It's like we're in Outer Mongolia or something.'

Tess ignored the first part of the girl's sentence as Emilia knew very well there were no servants at Merrick Court. 'You need to log onto the Wi-Fi. It's the only way you'll be able to communicate with the outside world from here. We're in a sort of black hole, mobile-wise, remember?'

'Well, what's the password?' Emilia was stabbing furiously at the little keypad on her phone.

'Please?' Tess couldn't resist. The girl's attitude was just the final straw.

'What?' Emilia looked up and focused on her for a moment.

'She means they should teach you some manners at your school,' Louis put in, rolling his eyes. 'As in, what's the password, *please*.'

'Shut *up*, Louis.' Emilia glared at her brother, then at Tess, who decided the girl was too self-absorbed to even understand irony.

'It's Merrick123,' she said. 'I'm going to heat up some

soup and bread rolls – will that do for dinner? I'm sorry but I wasn't really expecting guests.'

Rosie sighed. 'I remember when this kitchen was always filled with cooking smells and the larder overflowing, just in case. People were forever visiting Mama and Papa, dropping in on the spur of the moment, so one had to be prepared.'

Tess heard the implied criticism but ignored it. 'Well, your parents could probably afford to feed the five thousand. I can't.' She headed for the walk-in larder, which was bigger than most normal people's kitchens.

'Soup sounds great to me,' Louis said. 'I'll help you. Why don't you and Em sort out the beds, Mum?'

'Yes, I suppose.'

'Don't call me Em! How many times do I have to tell you? It's Emilia, or Milla to my friends, so that's not you, obviously.' Emilia was looking daggers at her brother again and her mother wisely towed her towards the hall and upstairs, averting the inevitable row.

'Milla?' Louis trailed after Tess while imitating his sister's snooty voice. 'How pretentious can you get? God, she's so annoying.'

Tess put an arm round his shoulders and gave him another quick hug. 'Never mind. Siblings are always irritating. You've met mine, haven't you? Sarah would beat Emilia hands down in any annoying sister contest, trust me.'

Louis smiled, although Tess noticed the smile didn't quite reach his eyes. 'Hey, are you okay yourself?' she asked, while busying herself heating up soup. Was he still mourning his uncle? Shaken by the suddenness of it all? She hadn't seen the boy for a few months and although they exchanged the occasional email, that didn't tell her much.

'I'm fine. Lots of stupid exams coming up.' Louis shrugged.

'Oh, poor you, that's horrid.' Tess threw a packet of

frozen bread rolls to him. 'Here, catch and put those in the Aga, will you, please?'

'Yup, sure.' As if continuing their earlier conversation, he added, 'It was all a bit of a shock, wasn't it? Uncle Giles, I mean. Even though it was a while ago now, I keep thinking about it and it kind of freaks me out, the way these things can happen so suddenly. It's like ... my mind can't let it go.'

Tess nodded. 'Yes, me too.' She knew only too well that endlessly thinking about the 'what ifs' could really drag you down. Lately she'd been doing better on that front though.

'Aren't you scared, living here alone?'

'No, not really.' She had been frightened at first, jumping at every shadow, but that was when she'd gone to the doctor and been prescribed medication. The antidepressants deadened most feelings and she'd stopped caring. She added jokingly, 'Anyway, if the resident ghosts had wanted to get me, surely they would have done so by now?'

Louis cracked a small smile. 'I guess. Well, you don't have to stay much longer now – I hear the solicitors have finally found the heir.'

'Yes, although I haven't been told when he's coming.'

Merrick Court and the title that went with it – Earl of Merrick – were entailed in the male line. The solicitor had explained it all to Tess after Giles's funeral, and what it meant in practical terms was that she couldn't inherit anything other than the contents of the house, plus Giles's personal possessions. Everything else had to go to the closest male relative, descended in a straight line from father to son. Daughters apparently counted for nothing, so Louis couldn't inherit either. It was all very complicated.

It had taken the lawyers a while to locate the heir, a man who was descended from a younger son of Giles's great-great-grandfather or something, but Tess had been told just a few days earlier that he'd been abroad but had now been in touch. While the solicitors had been sorting things out, she'd stayed on at the house as a sort of custodian.

Louis was quiet for a while then said, hesitantly. 'Well, if you need support when he turns up, just say, okay? I could always come on a weekend.'

'Thanks, that's really sweet of you, but I'm sure it'll be fine.' She didn't anticipate any trouble with the heir. It was more a question of getting organised, selling off her part of the inheritance – the contents of the house – and finalising her plans for the future. She didn't need help with that.

Rosie and Emilia eventually came back to the kitchen and they all sat down to eat.

'Eeuuw, what is this?' Emilia muttered, wrinkling her nose.

Tess pretended she hadn't heard and instead looked at Rosie. 'So what brings you here? Again.'

Rosie's eyebrows rose in affront. 'Do I need an excuse to visit my childhood home? And there's so much to be done.'

'Done?'

Rosie waved her spoon around, gesturing towards the rest of the house. 'Yes, everything that needs sorting before you move out and—'

'I'm perfectly capable of arranging things myself, you know.' Tess gave Rosie a hard stare. 'I'm not an imbecile.'

Rosie flushed. 'I never said you were. It's just, you've been a bit down and we thought we'd help. Sorting out old stuff to take to charity, that kind of thing.'

Interfering, more like, and trying to appropriate things for yourself. But Tess didn't say that out loud. Rosie seemed to think that because some things at Merrick Court had sentimental value to her, Tess would let her have them for free 'as a memento'. She'd tried that tack a few times already, but Tess had had enough. If Rosie wanted something, she could pay for it. She had a rich husband after all.

'I'm fine now, but thanks for the thought. And I can

manage on my own.' She didn't give Rosie a chance to reply, just stood up and went to put her bowl and plate in the sink. 'If you'll excuse me, I'm going to bed. Louis, please will you make sure all the doors are locked?'

'No problem.'

'Thank you. Goodnight.'

Back in her room, Tess was too restless to sleep, and headed into her en suite bathroom. It was a lovely space, all bright white tiles, claw-footed roll-top bath and ancient sink with bronze taps. She'd added yellow towels and candles to give the room a warmer feel and now it was perfect for relaxing in.

Tess poured herself a bath, adding a liberal amount of rose-scented bath oil, and sank into the warm depths with a contented sigh. Leaning her head against a small, folded towel, she felt the heat of the water seep into her, beginning the process of unravelling the anxiety that still flowed through her.

She stirred the water slowly with her fingers, staring into its depths, and allowed her mind to drift …

Chapter Three

The castle gates were closed during mealtimes, with dinner strictly at eleven o'clock in the morning and supper at five in the afternoon. Arabella was at risk of being late for supper, having stayed outside for too long, and hurried to her room to wash her hands and tidy her clothes and hair.

Meals were rather formal affairs in Lord Worcester's household and everyone was allocated a specific place to sit, in accordance with their rank and duties. With around a hundred and fifty people to feed normally on a daily basis, this was necessary, and now that Raglan housed a huge garrison of officers and soldiers as well, it had become even more imperative to keep order.

His lordship, together with his daughter-in-law, Lady Glamorgan – usually called Lady Margaret by everyone in the castle – and the rest of their family and any visiting aristocrats, ate in a private dining room, while almost everyone else had a seat somewhere in the Great Hall. Arabella, although distantly related to the marquis on her mother's side, was merely one of Lady Margaret's ladies, so her place was in the housekeeper's, Mrs Watson's, rooms, where all the gentlewomen ate together with the chaplain and any temporary guests.

She made her way across the Fountain Court, afraid she'd be the last person to arrive. Just as she reached her chair, however, another latecomer slipped through the door and was ushered to the place next to her – Rhys Cadell, the man she'd met outside. Just her luck. She sincerely hoped he wouldn't mention anything about her loitering by the lake. There were probably other things she should have been doing instead.

'We meet again,' he whispered as soon as the chaplain had said grace and they all sat down.

'So it seems,' she replied, keeping her voice to a mere breath. 'But we're not supposed to talk during meals.' That wasn't strictly true, but it was mostly the housekeeper and senior ladies who made small talk.

The man by her side waited until the chaplain started to speak in a loud voice, then murmured, 'Are you certain that's not just an excuse to avoid talking to me?' He sounded offended, but when she risked a glance, his eyes were dancing with merriment. He was roasting her.

'No, of course not.' She was used to the men in the castle trying to court her, but they were usually scrupulously polite and rather serious. They were well aware they could be in trouble if they overstepped the mark with one of her ladyship's gentlewomen. This Rhys obviously didn't.

Arabella concentrated on her meal, a simple repast of cold meats, bread and cheese, washed down with cider. Dinner was always more elaborate, with numerous cooked dishes to choose from, but it was considered better not to go to bed with a full stomach so supper was lighter. Now there were so many people crammed into the castle – an additional eight hundred men if what she'd been told was correct – they needed to be more frugal with the supplies as well. Arabella couldn't imagine having to cook for that many. The poor cooks must be tearing their hair out.

'Did you hear what happened in the village last night?' the chaplain asked Mrs Watson, although everyone else at the table was clearly listening as well.

'No, but I was told musket fire was heard. And I saw houses burning this afternoon. Have you any news?'

'Yes, it would appear some Roundheads came after dark and killed at least five men, while taking others prisoner. The villagers tried to fight back, of course, and I believe some of the enemy were killed too, but not as many. And the scoundrels then had the temerity to steal some of his lordship's horses.'

'No – outrageous!'

'Indeed. His lordship has ordered that almost all the buildings in the village should be burned and even the church pulled down so that the Parliamentarians can't surprise us like that again. I believe his men were carrying out his wishes this afternoon.' The chaplain crossed himself and shook his head. 'These are evil times we live in, Mrs Watson, evil.'

Arabella felt a tendril of fear coil in her stomach. The English king and his parliament had been fighting for almost four years now, although the rift between them went back much further. Neither could see the other's point of view and neither would back down. What had happened in Raglan village was merely the latest in a long line of atrocities and conflict. Although the castle itself had so far been left in peace, only the previous month a group of about a hundred men from Raglan had been beaten in a skirmish with Sir Trevor Williams and his Parliamentarians. Many had been killed and about half the men taken prisoner. There were those among the castle inhabitants who had fled upon hearing that piece of news as things were looking grim for the Royalists.

They'd since heard rumours of fighting all around the Monmouthshire and Hereford area. Apparently only Raglan and Usk were still loyal to their sovereign. So far as anyone could tell, most other places in the country had capitulated, except Oxford, the king's headquarters throughout the war. But the king himself had left for Scotland and it was rumoured he had sneaked away in the night dressed as a servant.

'Any more news of His Majesty?' Mrs Watson asked, looking round the table to see if anyone was better informed than herself.

To Arabella's surprise, Rhys spoke up. 'I've but recently come from Oxford, mistress, and it is not looking good for our cause, I'm afraid.'

'Why? What's happened?' It was clear from the way her mouth was pursed that Mrs Watson didn't approve of anyone giving negative views unless they could back them up with proof.

Rhys appeared not to be fazed and answered in a calm manner. 'General Fairfax was heading that way and all the king's plans appear to have come to naught. There's no news from anyone on the Continent – no French, Dutch or even Danish troops on their way to help – and not a word from the Irish either.' He shrugged. 'And His Majesty is himself a prisoner of the Scots now.'

'Aye, a sorry business that,' the chaplain agreed.

Sympathy welled up inside Arabella. The poor king; he'd believed the Scots to be his allies and instead they had captured him, having made some sort of pact with Parliament. What whoresons. Surely they would see reason? The king was their sovereign.

'Well, we must hope our own Lord Glamorgan manages to bring the Irish over soon. If anyone can do it, he can,' Mrs Watson said stoutly, and no one dared gainsay her even if they privately thought it unlikely.

Lord Glamorgan was the Marquis of Worcester's eldest son. He'd fought tirelessly for the king's cause throughout the war and the previous autumn he had been sent to Ireland to raise more troops. Somehow things had gone very wrong. He had been taken prisoner over there and was, as far as they knew, still held captive. And the king had denied ever having sent Lord Glamorgan as an envoy after some of his private correspondence came to light. He'd lied in order to save his own skin, which had made the marquis extremely angry.

'It will be a mite difficult for him to bring anyone over if he's still incarcerated,' someone muttered, but Mrs Watson sent a quelling glance down the table. The king may have made an error of judgement, but everyone at Raglan was still committed to his cause. He was the rightful ruler of the country, no matter what.

'Formidable lady,' Rhys murmured to Arabella as fierce whispering broke out along the table.

'Yes, don't ever get on the wrong side of her,' she whispered back. She shouldn't encourage him to talk, but somehow she was drawn in by his charming manner.

'That sounds like someone who's learned from experience.'

She heard the smile in his voice and couldn't resist a glance at him. Those green eyes were sparkling with amusement and she had to drag her own gaze away. 'And how!' she said, speaking as quietly as she could. 'I once spilled red wine on one of his lordship's best linen tablecloths. Mrs Watson didn't speak to me for weeks.'

Rhys spluttered into his tankard of cider and turned the sound into a cough. Arabella helpfully slapped him on the back. 'Are you all right, sir? Did your drink go down the wrong way?'

'Thank you, I'm fine.'

The chaplain was complaining about something to the housekeeper so Arabella took the chance to ask Rhys a question.

'Have you really come from Oxford? Is that why you were so secretive earlier?'

'Yes and no.' He sent her a teasing smile when she bristled. 'Now don't be offended. I meant only that, yes, I did escape from Oxford before Fairfax arrived, but that's not where I've come from today. I'm here to report to Lord Worcester.'

'Oh, so you'll be leaving soon then.' Arabella berated herself for the instant surge of disappointment that flooded her. And for asking. It shouldn't make any difference to her. She shouldn't be taken in by a practised charmer like him, even if his smiles did make her innards flutter.

'Perhaps I'll stay for a while. There aren't many places of refuge left to people like us, after all.'

'You mean Catholics?' The Marquis of Worcester was proud of his faith and others like him had flocked to Raglan. Although she belonged to the Anglican Church herself, Arabella didn't mind anyone else's beliefs being different. They'd taken her in and given her help when she needed it so their religious views were unimportant to her.

Rhys shook his head. 'No, Royalists. I'm not a Papist.'

'Oh, right.'

'You do know there are very few places still loyal to the king, don't you?'

He sounded serious now and another tendril of fear snaked through her. The marquis never showed that he was afraid and seemed to have no intention of giving in. But if what Rhys said was true, then surely Raglan was doomed even before it was attacked?

'We're fighting a losing battle, aren't we?' she muttered.

To her surprise, he took her hand under the table and gave it a reassuring squeeze. 'All isn't lost yet,' he whispered. 'And even if Raglan falls, there are other places to go.'

'Overseas?' she guessed.

He nodded. 'Indeed. Let's talk about something else. Tell me about yourself. Have you always lived here?'

Arabella checked to make sure Mrs Watson and the chaplain were still chattering and hadn't noticed that everyone else was doing the same, albeit in hushed voices. They seemed to be having some sort of mild argument, so it was safe to continue her conversation with Rhys. Although why she was thinking of him by his Christian name, she had no idea. She really shouldn't.

'No, I've only been here for five years. The marquis very

kindly offered me shelter when … when my mother died.' That wasn't the whole story, but she didn't want to go into further details. Rhys was a stranger after all and she knew nothing about him. He might even be a Roundhead spy. Or a friend of her uncle Huw … She suppressed a shudder. She didn't want to think about *him*.

'He's a good man, obviously.'

'The marquis? Yes, very. Have you known him long?'

Rhys smiled. 'Never met him. I'm waiting to be called in to see his lordship. Probably after supper, I was told.'

'Oh, well I'm sure he'll receive you graciously. He always does.' Arabella lowered her voice even further. 'He was even kind to the king when he came last year and practically helped himself to Lord Worcester's wealth. Or what remained of it.'

Rhys's mouth twitched. 'Yes, I heard about that little episode. Tried to get the keys to the treasure room from a steward or something? Or so the gossips have it.'

'It was Dr Bayly he asked, actually, the marquis's friend and confidant. Of course *he* went straight to his lordship, who then went to offer the king the keys himself. Not how His Majesty ought to have behaved, according to some.'

'And you, what do you think?' Rhys looked as though he was really interested in her views, which surprised Arabella.

'Me? I don't have an opinion on such things. I'm merely here to serve my lady Margaret.'

'Hmm.' His eyes appraised her and appeared to like what they saw if the warmth in their moss-green depths was anything to go by. 'If you ask me, I think you have a great deal of opinions, but you are too clever to voice them. That's good.'

The meal was over and silence fell on the table as the chaplain bent his head to thank God for what they had received. When he had finished, Arabella heard Rhys whisper, 'I hope to see you again soon, Mistress Dauncey. In the meantime, I brought you this as an apology if I offended you by the lake. I obviously had the wrong impression of your intentions.'

From inside his jerkin, he pulled something out and put it in her lap under cover of the tablecloth. Arabella felt a stem and a flower and when she peeked there was a white rose, hardly damaged at all from its incarceration inside Rhys's clothing. Her eyes flew to his, but he didn't give her the chance to reply or even thank him. Which was probably just as well because what would she have said?

The truth – that she would look forward to seeing him too – was not an option.

✦

Merrick Court, 21st May 2016

Tess sat up abruptly, splashing water over the sides of the bath in the process. She blinked into the darkness, having forgotten to turn the lights on. That would explain why she'd dozed off. She had been asleep, hadn't she? The hallucinations had returned; not quite as vivid this time, just a sequence of unclear impressions. It had been almost like viewing a film through an aquarium, the images and sounds muffled. Very odd.

Rhys. She remembered him. He'd spoken to her, flirted with her, those extraordinary eyes sparkling.

No, she was fantasising. The man she'd met, whose name probably wasn't Rhys at all, didn't exist. Or if he did, she'd imagined him in the strange clothing. He was surely just another visitor to Raglan Castle, who'd thought she was about to throw herself into the moat. The sun, her agitation, the medicine she was taking, it all combined to scramble her brain. He *had* been very handsome and he'd obviously wormed his way into her mind, even though she hadn't been interested in men since … well, since Giles. Surely it was a healthy sign, an indication that she was returning to normal if she could feel attracted to someone? And who wouldn't have been dazzled by a man like him?

'Yes, a good sign,' she told herself, while getting out of the now cool water.

She stared into the bathroom mirror and wondered what *he* had seen when he met her. A nervous, defensive woman who must have looked sad or upset. Why else would he have assumed she was suicidal? A pale face stared back at her, but she was surprised to see that her eyes were more alive than they'd been in weeks, months. It was as though she was actually looking at herself properly for the first time in ages. Not through a pill-induced haze. She decided then and there to stop taking the antidepressants altogether.

'I don't need them.'

She was already on the lowest possible dose, but it was an unnecessary crutch. She was over the shock of Giles's death and no longer feeling depressed. Just a bit apprehensive about what the future would hold, but then who wouldn't be when they were starting on a new chapter in their life?

As she entered her bedroom, a different sort of apprehension washed over her for no discernible reason. She glanced around the room while trying to suppress a shiver. Someone was watching her, she was convinced of it, but there wasn't anyone here. Or was there?

She shouldn't have made that joke to Louis about ghosts. She'd spooked herself, literally.

'Giles?' she whispered, hearing the tremor in her voice. *Oh, God, what if he really is haunting me?* She hadn't thought he would actually do so, only through all the memories he'd left behind in the house. And it had been six months since he'd passed away. Why now?

She scanned the room again and her eyes were drawn to one of the two windows. It had a deep recess in the thick walls of this the oldest part of the house and she didn't normally keep anything on it as she didn't want to block the light. She jumped as she thought she saw a shadow flitting across the aperture, cutting off the moonbeams currently shining through the panes of glass.

'Go away, please,' she hissed. 'It wasn't my fault you drove like that. I never wanted you … d-dead.' She trembled all over, the horrible word making this so much worse. Giles *had* told her there were ghosts at Merrick Court, but she'd never seen one and thought it was just a joke. Now she wasn't so sure.

A draught stirred the air near her right cheek as if someone had caressed her and she twisted round, backing up towards her bed. But with the soft touch, a feeling of well-being flowed through her and for some reason her heartbeat calmed in an instant. '*Cariad.*' She thought she heard the Welsh endearment, a whisper so faint it could have been a trick of her imagination. Then the voice – one she vaguely recognised although she had no idea where from – flowed into her mind, stronger, repeating the word. '*Cariad.*' She sank down onto the bed and strained her ears for further sounds.

That couldn't be Giles. He hadn't spoken a word of Welsh and never called her '*cariad*' – 'darling' was more his style. But who then? A former inhabitant of this part of Merrick Court, perhaps?

'Who's there?' There was a faint shimmering over by the window, almost like a heat haze but more phosphorescent. Although she stared intently, she couldn't make out a specific shape, but she definitely wasn't alone and it would appear someone was trying to comfort her.

Tess just sat there for a while, until the feeling of being watched subsided and she was sure the ghost or spirit had left. Then she lay down, falling instantly asleep, sure that whoever had been there meant her no harm. She was safe.

Chapter Four

It was still very early when Josh Owens drove across the Severn Bridge. He was suffering from jet lag, but it had turned out to be a blessing in disguise as he'd escaped the London rush hour by leaving long before the city's inhabitants started waking up. Looking up now, he felt as though he was entering the gates of Mordor in *Lord of the Rings*, or some other magical country, as the bridge's pale green structure towered over him. And maybe he was – he'd heard a lot about Wales and now he was finally here it did seem a bit unreal.

As he turned off the motorway and headed up towards Usk and Raglan, the countryside became green and undulating, with dark hills brooding in the distance. The Black Mountains, he assumed. The scent of hawthorn drifted in through his partially opened window and a strange sense of homecoming rippled through him. It was almost like he'd been here before even though he knew he hadn't. But it was the homeland of his ancestors, so perhaps it was in his blood?

The sensation intensified when he passed the ruins of Raglan Castle, silhouetted against the bright morning sky. There was something oddly familiar about the view and his gaze was drawn to the ragged contours of its towers, which must once have been magnificent. A strange mixture of emotions assailed him: longing, apprehension, anger, fear and … attraction? He had to force himself to concentrate on the road, rather than turn and look back.

What was the matter with him? He must be more tired than he thought.

Following the satnav lady's instructions, he continued

on towards Abergavenny and the further into Wales he travelled, the stronger the sense of belonging became. He decided it had to be his grandpa's fault – his mother's father had hailed from somewhere near here and he'd filled Josh's head with stories of this magical place.

'You've Welsh blood in your veins, boy, don't forget,' Grandpa used to say every time he told him about his homeland. Josh wondered why the old man had stayed in New Zealand if he loved the country of his birth so much, but he'd never dared to ask.

Arriving at his destination at last, Josh climbed out of the rental car and stared up at the house he'd come to see. No, not house – mansion. Or castle even? Although he'd entered the stable yard and could only see the building side on, it was clear that it was a huge property. He'd have to follow the road round to the front to see the rest, but he was already impressed and not a little disconcerted.

'Bloody hell!' he muttered. This was not what he'd expected at all.

'Good morning! Can I help you?'

Josh turned to find a weather-beaten old man coming towards him from the direction of the gardens. He was still so dazed by the sight of Merrick Court – what he could see of it so far anyway – that he hadn't heard the man's footsteps. 'Morning. Yes, I've come to look at the house,' he said, closing his door and locking the car. It seemed easier to leave it here and walk round to the front.

'I'm sorry, but it's not open to the public. It's private. The gardens too.' The old man shrugged. 'But I can offer you a cup of tea if you like, seeing as you've had a wasted journey? Least I can do.'

Josh smiled. 'That's very kind, but I think you misunderstand. I'm not a tourist.'

'Sure sound like one, if you don't mind me saying.' Deep-set blue eyes crinkled at the corners. 'Australian?'

'Nah, Kiwi.' Josh swallowed a sigh. Why couldn't the Poms tell the difference?

'Ah, right. Well, if you'd like to come this way, please? I've got a kettle in the potting shed.'

'But I ... oh, all right then. Cheers.' Josh decided some tea would be nice after the long drive from London and he wasn't in any particular hurry. In fact, it would be great to have a bit of a breather while he recovered from the shock of seeing the property for the first time.

He followed the old guy into what looked more like a huge workshop than a shed. It was part of the stable block, next door to a greenhouse, and filled with tools of all kinds. The floor was made of old bricks laid in a herringbone pattern, swept clean, and the walls were whitewashed with implements hanging in orderly rows. Several workbenches lined the room and pieces of wood were stacked in one corner.

'Take a seat, please. I'm Bryn Jones, gardener yere.'

The old man's melodic Welsh accent put Josh in mind of his grandfather again. Bryn looked to be in his mid- to late-seventies and age was beginning to take its toll, but there was still a twinkle in the man's eyes and his complexion was a healthy colour. As it should be in a man who'd presumably worked outdoors for most of his life.

'Josh Owens.' He waited for Bryn's reaction to his name, but nothing happened, so he added, 'I'm the new owner of the estate.'

'Eh?' Bryn swivelled round so fast he almost dropped the mug he was holding. 'You're the new Lord Merrick?'

'Seems like it.'

'Well, I never! You should've said right off.' Bryn was still standing with the mug in his hand, as if shocked into immobility.

Josh smiled. 'You didn't really give me a chance. I did say I'd come to look at the house. I need to see what state it's in before I sell it.'

'S-sell it?' Bryn scowled. 'But ... there've always been Merrick lords yere, ever since the Conquest, like!'

Josh shrugged. He had no idea what conquest that might be and didn't really care. 'I wouldn't know. I only just found out I was related to them. Came as a bit of a surprise, actually.'

Bryn had recovered enough to continue with the tea making, but he was still frowning. 'You had no idea you was the heir?'

'No. My father never mentioned it so the letter from the solicitor arrived out of the blue. I didn't even know what an entail was.' He'd had to look it up – the whole concept of something being inherited only by males seemed outdated to him. Crazy. Only the Poms would cling to such an old-fashioned rule. Not that he should be complaining since he was profiting from it, but still ... He'd bet there had to be a female somewhere who was seriously pissed off.

'It was a bit of a shock to the people yere too, I can tell you,' Bryn muttered. 'And it took them lawyers ages to find you.'

'Ah, yeah well, that was my fault. I've been travelling non-stop for the last six months. I wanted to see the world before I got too old. I hadn't left a forwarding address so didn't get the letters until I came back.'

'Oh, right. So will you be going back to New Zealand then?' Bryn handed Josh his tea and offered him a biscuit from a well-worn tin. They looked home-made so Josh didn't hesitate to take one.

'Cheers. As for going back, I wouldn't have a clue. Nothing to go back to, really.' Josh had lived there his whole life, but it didn't feel like home any more. There were various, complicated, reasons for that which Bryn didn't need to know. 'I might travel some more first.'

Bryn looked as though he wanted to ask further questions, but either didn't dare or was too polite – probably the latter. For some reason that made Josh relent and tell the old man part of the story even though it was a painful subject.

'I inherited a sheep station from my father when he died recently, but I didn't want it because … well, we didn't get on.' That was the understatement of the year – he'd hated his father with a vengeance.

'A sheep station?'

'Yeah, kind of like a big farm or ranch just for rearing sheep and cattle. Fifteen thousand square kilometres of grazing land south-west of Christchurch, on the South Island.' It sounded like a lot, but there were bigger ones.

Bryn stared at him. 'Goodness! Not that I know how much a kilometre is, mind, but … you said no to that? Even though it was your da's?'

'Well, not exactly – I'm not that stupid.' Josh smiled. 'I accepted the inheritance but I didn't want to keep anything that had belonged to him so I sold it to a cousin on my grandmother's side – my father's mother, that is. Made me feel slightly less guilty for letting the family down.'

Not that there was anyone left to chastise him – they were all dead – but he'd sensed the disapproval of the spirits roaming the old farmstead and knew they weren't happy about his decision. His family had owned the land for over a hundred years. Fields, hills, valleys and streams, with brooding snow-capped mountains in the distance – it was a beautiful place, typical of New Zealand. But he couldn't keep it. Despite the blood ties, he didn't belong there.

True, he was the only son and heir, it was his responsibility to continue the line, but he didn't care. That was just old-school bollocks. He'd tried to settle there, he really had, but the memories of a childhood filled with violence and rows wouldn't leave him. And the hatred for his father, the man he'd inherited the property from, obliterated any feelings he might have had for the land.

'I see,' Bryn said, and Josh had the feeling the old gardener really did understand. His keen eyes saw more than most people's. He didn't voice the obvious – that it was ironic Josh had now inherited something even bigger because of his father. But Josh much preferred to think of this as coming from other ancestors further back.

He changed the subject. 'So do you have the keys to the house? The solicitor said they'd be here.'

'Er, no. Lady Merrick keeps them but I should think she's still asleep.'

It was Josh's turn to stare. 'Come again? The ... what do you call her? Dowager? She's still here? The lawyer didn't say anything about that. Only told me she'd inherited the contents of the house and I get the rest.' He hadn't been bothered about that as he wasn't planning on living here anyway and it seemed only fair the poor woman should have something.

Bryn shook his head. 'No, she's living at the Court. Hasn't been asked to move out, so far as I know.'

'Bugger.' This was a complication he could do without. And why hadn't the lawyer told him? Although to be fair, Josh had been in a bit of a hurry and hadn't given the man much chance to speak. He'd more or less just signed the documents and left with the directions on how to find Merrick Court.

'Uhm, I should perhaps tell you ...' Bryn looked away. 'The thing is, her ladyship is a bit fragile at the moment. She took it hard, you know, losing her husband so suddenly, like. Maybe you could ... go easy on her?'

'She's still grieving, eh? Of course, I understand. But she can't stay here forever.' Josh wasn't unfeeling, but he needed to sell the house. Surely the woman would appreciate that? He had no idea how old she was, but maybe she could go into a home for the elderly or something, unless she owned property elsewhere. Either way, it wasn't his problem.

'No, no, but if you could give her a little more time? And I'll need to find somewhere else to live too. My cottage comes with the job and I don't suppose any new owner would want to take on an old relic like myself.'

'Oh. Yeah. Right.' Josh was taken aback. He hadn't thought about the fact that he'd be doing the old man out of a job and a home. Not that Bryn ought to be working at his age ... Something else occurred to him. 'Is there anyone else employed here?' Was he turfing out a whole load of staff by selling up? It was becoming clear he hadn't thought this through.

'No, just me.'

'You look after this whole garden all by yourself?' From what Josh had seen, it was massive.

'I do what I can. There's no money for extra help. Hasn't been for years.' Bryn gave a small smile. 'And there's a fair bit to do, as you can imagine. In fact, I'd best be getting on with it.'

'So you reckon I should wait a while before going to see the house?'

Bryn checked his watch. 'Like I said, Lady M has been a bit delicate and I hardly ever see her until after lunch, but she's got visitors at the moment so she may be up earlier ...'

The thought of disturbing a grieving widow and a bunch of strangers dampened Josh's desire to see his inheritance. Besides, it was a beautiful spring day and here was an old man who very obviously needed some help. He made up his mind. 'Maybe I can lend a hand for a bit then? It'll be good to do some work for a change. I've been travelling for so long I've forgotten what that's like. I could do with some fresh air and a workout.'

'I can't let you do that!' Confusion flitted across Bryn's face. 'Although ...'

Josh grinned. 'Yeah – I can do what I want in my own garden and right now I feel like a bit of digging. Give me a spade and point me in the right direction.' He guessed tasks like that were getting to be too much for the old gardener.

An answering smile lit up Bryn's features. 'Well, if you insist. This way, my lord.'

'Josh, please! We don't do titles where I come from.'

'You might have to get used to it,' Bryn murmured.

'No way.' But Josh was starting to realise there were quite a few things he hadn't reckoned with and being called a lord was only one of them.

⁂

Raglan Castle, 22nd May 1646

'My lord, I regret to inform you that apart from Oxford there are only a handful of strongholds still loyal to the king at this time – Pendennis Castle down in Cornwall, Harlech up in north-west Wales and your own domain here at Raglan, plus Goodrich Castle. Unless help arrives from foreign shores, the king's cause seems rather hopeless right now.' Rhys tried not to sound too downhearted at the news he brought, but it was difficult to desist. As far as he was concerned, things weren't just hopeless – all was lost. It was only a matter of time.

It was just after midnight and he had finally been granted a meeting with Lord Worcester, after kicking his heels all evening in the Long Gallery. Beautiful though this chamber was, with its huge windows and intricately carved fireplace supported by sculptures at either end, he would have preferred to get the interview over with. The information he had was definitely not what the marquis would want to hear. Everyone was despondent and the best course for any Royalist would be to gather what riches he could and flee the country while it was still possible. Somehow he doubted Lord Worcester would agree though. From what he'd heard, the old man was as stubborn as they came and stuck to his family's motto – *'Mutare vel timere sperno'* meaning 'I scorn to change or to fear'.

As he'd gazed out the windows at the back of the Gallery while waiting, Rhys had seen the Black Mountains looming in the distance, a mere shadowy outline in the hazy light of the evening. A longing for his own home, in a valley on the other side of those hills, tore through him at the familiar sight but he suppressed it. He was never going back. His brother owned everything now and he'd made it clear Rhys wasn't welcome.

'Anyone who goes off to fight for that useless king is a fool,' Gwilum had shouted four years ago. 'What's he ever done for us Welshmen? He's never been interested in this part of the country. No, anyone with any sense will stay put yere.'

'That's not what Father would have said,' Rhys had pointed out. Their father had been an ardent Royalist and had brought up his sons to honour their sovereign.

'The old man was misguided, as are you,' was Gwilum's reply. 'So go if you want to, but don't expect to be given houseroom here when you return with your tail between your legs.'

Rhys had ignored his brother and followed a path his father would have approved of, though much good it had done him so far. All he had to show for it was a knighthood. There were no lands to go with it, no riches. Hell, he could barely feed himself and his horse. Suppressing a sigh, he steered his thoughts back to the matter at hand now.

'Hopeless, you say? Nothing is ever hopeless until the end,' Lord Worcester was saying as he winced and moved one foot slightly. Rhys had been told the old man suffered from gout, which wasn't to be wondered at. He was nearly three score and ten apparently, a great age. And if age wasn't the cause, then it was probably good living – his lordship was definitely a bit too stout for his own good.

Rhys bowed to acknowledge that the marquis was entitled to his opinion and he wasn't going to argue with him. 'You don't think perhaps the ladies of the castle ought to be sent away at this time? For their safety, I mean.' For some reason a particular lady's face came into his mind, as it had done at regular intervals ever since he'd first met her that afternoon.

Mistress Dauncey – Arabella – was a rare beauty, with big blue eyes and long brown lashes under fine brows, rich honey-coloured hair and a tempting figure. It wasn't just her outward attributes that had attracted him though, but the intelligence he'd seen lurking in those forget-me-not eyes. He'd enjoyed conversing with her; she caught on quickly and didn't simper or flirt. Very refreshing. Although he'd felt she was holding something back, a secret concerning her background perhaps, but this only intrigued him further. He wanted to find out what it was. Wanted to know everything about her ... He became aware that the marquis was speaking to him again and tried to concentrate.

'... and where would I send them? I can't spare any men for escort duty, they're all needed here. No, the ladies will be safe with us. I'll make sure of it.'

Again Rhys didn't protest. What could he say? It wasn't for him to point out that he doubted the marquis would have much choice in the matter if the Parliamentarians had their way, which seemed all too likely.

'Will you permit me to stay here and give what assistance I can then?' Rhys found himself saying. When he'd arrived earlier, he hadn't made up his mind whether to remain or not. Reason told him to cut his losses and try his luck in France or Holland as a mercenary, but somehow he couldn't bring himself to leave now. It seemed cowardly, even though the odds were definitely against them.

'Of course, we'd be happy to have you, young man.' Lord Worcester smiled for the first time. 'Make yourself at home. I'm sure the garrison could do with another officer. You've been fighting with the Prince Palatine's troops, you said?'

'Yes, I've been with Prince Rupert's cavalry since '42. He's still at Oxford, or he was the last I heard.' Rhys knew the prince had given up hope too so it was possible he'd already left the country. It made no difference now and Rhys wasn't going back. They'd said their goodbyes, parting as friends since they'd got on very well throughout their time fighting together.

'Good, good. We need all the experienced men we can find. Report to my son, Lord Charles, in the morning. He's in charge.'

'Very well. Thank you, my lord.'

'No, thank *you*. I appreciate you bringing me news.'

Rhys believed him and he couldn't help but like the irascible old man. There was spirit in him and a sincere trust that what he was doing was right. Rhys only wished he could be as certain, but he'd made his choice. Now all he had to do was see it through to the end.

That might be sooner than the marquis thought.

Chapter Five

Merrick Court, 22nd May 2016

'So, I'm going to make some lists ...'

Rosie came into the kitchen with a pad in one hand and a pen in the other. She was as immaculately made up as always, hair in a neat bob, and her only concession to country living was the fact that she was wearing flat shoes instead of heels. Everything else – the designer jeans, expensive tailored shirt and chunky jewellery – was the same as she would wear in London. Tess didn't know why this irritated her, but it did. She fortified herself with a sip of strong, very sugary, tea before asking, 'What kind of lists?'

'Of all the furniture and other items in the house. Anything of real value, that is.'

'I said I can handle that myself.' Tess frowned at Rosie.

'I know, but this is for my reference. Although, naturally, I would hope you'd agree to give most of the things here to Louis, I do understand that you'll want to be paid a little something for any proper antiques.'

A little something? Give most of it to Louis? Tess had to make a conscious effort not to let her mouth fall open. Rosie had a nerve.

The whole entail business had come as a surprise to all of them. Tess hadn't known anything about it, as Giles had never mentioned it; while Rosie had been under the impression that Giles had sorted it out in order to make a will in favour of her children if he didn't have any of his own. Apparently breaking an entail inheritance was a complicated process which would have involved the House of Lords and all sorts of legal procedures and, Giles being Giles, he'd simply put it off. He'd probably thought there

43

was no hurry. Rosie had been incandescent at first when she found that out, since she considered that the estate and title should have gone to Louis. But she soon rallied and had now come up with another idea – she and her husband would buy the estate from the new Lord Merrick and all would be well.

Tess found her voice. 'Why on earth would I give everything to Louis?'

'It all belongs in the family, surely you can see that? The contents are part of the house's history. And anyway, Giles always meant for Louis to be his heir if he didn't have children.'

'Rosie, Giles left me nothing apart from the stuff in this house and until my business is more profitable I'll need the money from selling it to live on. If you want anything, you'll have to pay whatever it's worth. I'm going to have it valued.' She should have done this already, but she'd been putting it off. With the heir's arrival imminent, it was clearly time to sort it out now.

Rosie's mouth tightened. 'You're being very unreasonable. Do you really feel you're entitled to any of it in the circumstances? Giles told me he was divorcing you because you didn't want children.'

That wasn't strictly true – she had wanted kids, but at first she hadn't seen the need to rush. And then once she'd been married to Giles for a couple of years she'd come to realise he wasn't the right man for her, and definitely not someone she would like to have children with. So they had been about to get a divorce, Tess couldn't deny that. 'Yes, but if we'd gone ahead, he would have had to give me a settlement. This is in lieu of that.'

Rosie was right in a way as Tess didn't feel entitled to receive a huge amount, but she was owed *something* and didn't feel she was asking too much. Besides, the woman was annoying her and Tess wasn't in the mood to give in.

Her sister-in-law had always acted as if she was superior in some way, but now Giles was gone, Tess didn't have to put up with that any longer.

'Well, perhaps I should ask the solicitor how much Giles would have had to pay you, then we can work from there.' Rosie attempted a wounded expression. 'Although I always thought you had a soft spot for Louis and would want him to be happy.'

Tess stood up and went to rinse out her mug. 'Emotional blackmail won't work. Go and talk to the lawyer if you want. Besides, you don't even know if the new owner intends to sell Merrick Court. He might want to buy all the contents from me himself. It's his family too.' And hopefully he'd pay the going rate, not some paltry family discounted price.

'Well, he's not exactly been rushing to claim his birthright.' Rosie made a face. 'He can't be very interested in it. No, I'm determined to secure it for Louis. The estate must stay in the family, as it has done for nearly a thousand years.' This was said with an accusing glare at Tess, who had, in Rosie's view, failed in her duty to provide Giles with an heir.

Anger and resentment made Tess's hands shake and she steadied them by gripping the edge of the sink. It wasn't as if she'd intended for Giles to die before having children. 'I never wanted it to be this way, Rosie.'

Rosie sighed. 'No, I don't suppose you did. Anyway, I'm only trying to help by moving things along a little. It's not as if you have anyone else here, is it?'

That was also true. Tess's parents and sister hadn't even come for the funeral. They all lived in France and Sarah couldn't possibly take the children out of school or nursery, and her parents had been needed to help Sarah, as always. Neither had they asked about her future plans. But she didn't want to acknowledge how useless her family was when it came to supporting her.

She calmed down. If Rosie wanted to make lists, what harm would it do? It wasn't as though Tess really cared – she just wanted it all over and done with. 'You're right. Perhaps it would be helpful to compare your lists to the valuer's as presumably you know more about the items here than they would. I wouldn't want to be cheated, after all.'

Rosie seemed mollified by this peace offering. 'Exactly.' Louis came into the kitchen and Rosie pounced on him. 'Louis, you can come and help me.'

'Eh? With what?'

'Lists. You'll be eighteen very soon, old enough to shoulder your responsibilities, although your dad will help, naturally. Running a big estate takes some getting used to.'

'I've told you before, I don't want this sodding house,' Louis muttered. 'You and dad have it if you like it so much.'

'Don't be ungrateful! It will be ours at first, of course, but you have to learn to look after it so you can take over. Come on, let's go upstairs.'

Louis rolled his eyes behind his mother's back and followed her out of the room.

***

Raglan Castle, 22nd May 1646

Arabella tried to tell herself she wasn't really looking out for Rhys as she dawdled by the entrance to the chapel after morning prayers. Everyone was expected to attend, no matter what beliefs they adhered to, and she couldn't see that it would do any harm listening to the chaplain, despite his Catholicism. They all needed to pray at this time as God's help was certainly necessary, judging by the rumours going round. She wondered whether Rhys would be there or if he'd left already?

The castle was teeming with people. It was a curiously built structure, more or less divided in half by the Great

Hall with the so called Pitched Stone Court on one side and the Fountain Court on the other. Buildings surrounded both so that they formed two quadrangles, although one was slightly lopsided along the outer edge. Only the higher-ranking members of the household and their guests were allowed on the fountain side, however. Everyone else stayed around the Stone Court.

No more than a fraction of the castle's present inhabitants would actually fit into the chapel and Arabella assumed the rest must hold a service of some sort elsewhere. Fighting men had come flooding in during the last few months, while the marquis prepared his domain for warfare. Trees were cut down in order to avoid giving the enemy the advantage of cover – even the beautiful avenue leading to the castle's main entrance – and fortifications built outside the walls. Accommodation had somehow been found for nearly eight hundred men, as well as a few of the neighbouring gentry who were afraid to stay in their homes. They were all crammed in, like pickles in a jar, with not an inch to spare anywhere. How, Arabella had no idea.

She was currently sharing her room with three of Lady Margaret's gentlewomen, two of them on truckle beds that were pushed out of sight during the day. It wasn't ideal, but she wasn't as bothered as some of the others who'd been muttering that it was beneath them to share in such a way. They all had to make sacrifices for the king's cause. Those who didn't want to had already left Raglan.

'Lovely day, is it not?'

The honey-smooth voice with its beautiful Welsh cadence made Arabella jump and her heart missed a beat. She looked up into the frank gaze of Rhys Cadell.

'Yes, indeed.' What else could she say? The sun was shining, summer almost upon them. The fact that she was enjoying this fine morning had absolutely nothing to do with the man standing beside her. Or so she told herself.

'A shame the sun can't dispel the storm clouds on the horizon though, wouldn't you say? And I don't mean that literally.' He smiled.

'No, we can but pray for deliverance.' Arabella nodded towards the chapel behind them.

'I don't wish to alarm you, but I rather fear that God may not be able to help in this instance. Forgive me for asking, but is there nowhere else you could go, mistress? It would be wise to leave now while you still can.'

'You think me a coward?' Arabella drew herself up to her full height, which was only average, and glared at him.

His smile grew and he held up his hands as if warding off her anger. 'Never! I was merely concerned for your safety. For that of all the ladies and children here, if I'm honest. This is not the place for any of you during the coming months. It will not be ... pleasant, shall we say.'

'I thank you for your concern, but we'll manage.' Arabella wasn't sure whether to be pleased or offended. It was nice that he cared – if he really did and wasn't just making small talk – but she had as much courage as the next person and if the marquis, to whom she owed so much, asked them to stay, then that was what she would do. 'Besides, I don't have anywhere else to go,' she admitted.

'I understand. Then we will see more of each other as I'm staying too.'

A strange kind of relief flooded her. He wasn't leaving and perhaps he'd help protect them. It looked like he was big, strong and capable, a man to depend on. She felt safe next to him, she had to acknowledge, which was ridiculous really as she didn't know him.

'Oh, I am glad,' she said, before she'd had a chance to stop the words. His immediate grin made her qualify this statement. 'I mean, we need all the help we can get, obviously.'

He bowed to her. 'Of course. I never thought for a

moment you'd be happy about me staying for any other reason. Good day to you.'

It was clear he believed the complete opposite and Arabella felt her cheeks become suffused with colour. He sauntered off to speak to Lord Charles, who was standing near the fountain in the middle of the courtyard. She wanted to run after him and tell him he was wrong, but that would be a lie and she never lied.

Damnation.

And she never swore either. What was wrong with her? She was afraid she had a very shrewd idea of what ailed her and she didn't like it. Not one bit. This was the worst possible time to develop any kind of feelings for a man, especially one she knew nothing about. And one who might be killed during the next few months.

But then, so might they all.

Chapter Six

At last the sun had made an appearance, after months of rain and gloom, and Tess decided she had to be outside on such a glorious day. It would get her away from Rosie and, anyway, she loved gardening. Or she used to, before her life was turned upside down. Today, she could really do with taking out her frustrations on something and the weeds, which had thrived on the constant showers, would be the perfect targets.

Merrick Court was a wonderful old house that practically oozed charm and Tess understood very well why Giles had been obsessed with it. She loved it herself, but the title and all that it entailed had always been more of a burden than a privilege to her. She'd be better off without it. The garden, however, was a different matter. She would miss that terribly when she had to leave. It was like something from a gardening magazine, laid out in large squares with different features. Two walled gardens side by side – one for vegetables, one for roses – an orchard with fruit cages next to it, some formal lawns, parkland and what was left of an intricate Elizabethan knot garden. The only parts that were currently in any proper state were the lawns, vegetable beds and fruit sections. And that was all thanks to the ancient gardener, Bryn Jones.

'Old Bryn's been here forever,' Giles had told her when he'd first introduced them to each other, but Tess could see the man wasn't *that* ancient. Mid-seventies, perhaps? He was certainly the old-fashioned kind of gardener though and did everything properly. During her four years of marriage to Giles, Bryn had taught Tess a huge amount about growing vegetables, pruning, thinning and generally encouraging everything to grow. She now felt she had a handle on what needed to be done when and although he did most of it, she'd always helped whenever she had a spare moment. Until Giles's accident ...

Well, time to get back into it as the May sunshine was making every part of the garden explode with greenery. She found the tools she needed and got stuck in.

An hour spent battling bindweed, brambles, nettles and their pestilential friends calmed her down and at the same time invigorated her. As she set off towards the compost heap with a full wheelbarrow she had an inner glow of satisfaction. With that to hold onto, she would cope with Rosie. She'd just have to stay out of the way and let her sister-in-law get on with whatever she was doing. Perhaps she'd soon tire of her lists and go home.

Deep in thought, she rounded a corner of the brick wall that enclosed the vegetable patch and almost rammed into a man who was bent over, pulling at a sapling that clearly shouldn't be there.

'Whoa!' Tess swerved, then stopped dead as the man straightened up.

Tall, with black hair that was shaggy and tousled, and with matching dark stubble, he had the kind of face that could sell millions of bottles of aftershave. Clear green eyes under perfectly sculpted eyebrows – Tess could picture them staring moodily out of an advert in a glossy magazine – and if he hadn't oozed masculinity, she would have sworn he was wearing mascara, so thick were his eyelashes. He was lean and rangy, but not too thin – his shoulders and arms powerful – and as he was shirtless she could see that his upper body was nicely defined under a stunningly deep suntan. There was some sort of tribal tattoo high up on his left arm and his faded and torn black jeans showed that his legs were as muscular as the rest of him.

'Who the hell are you?' she blurted out, then felt her cheeks heat up. Not exactly a subtle way to greet one of the hottest men she'd ever met, but he had no business being in her garden. Well, Merrick Court's garden. And she had no business finding him attractive – she was recently widowed, for heaven's sake, and the last thing she needed at the moment was a man to complicate her life.

His eyes reminded her of something – she'd been attracted to another green-eyed man the day before, the one at the castle who'd been gorgeous too, although in a different way. She frowned at the thought. What was the matter with her? And why was the county suddenly full of handsome men with emerald eyes?

'And g'day to you too. I could say the same, eh?' He leaned on the spade he'd been using to dig out the root of the sapling and regarded her with his head to one side as if he was wondering what *she* was doing there. His accent was Australian, or maybe New Zealand – Tess had had both Aussie and Kiwi friends at art college but could never tell which was which. Deliciously Antipodean in any case – she was a sucker for accents.

She ignored his greeting. 'I'm sure Bryn knows there's no money to pay for help in the garden at the moment.' Although in truth she couldn't actually remember the last time she'd talked to the old man. She had been kind of a hermit of late.

'Oh, yeah? Well, I don't need paying,' he said, with a smile that she found both infuriating and amazingly alluring. Yep, definitely model material. Was that why he didn't need to be paid? He was already rich? But he wasn't exactly dressed like a millionaire.

'I'll have to discuss this with Bryn.' She picked up the handles of the wheelbarrow and almost overbalanced it in her haste to get away from this man. He was disturbing her equilibrium and he shouldn't be in her garden. Damn it,

Merrick Court's garden. When would she stop thinking of it as hers?

'I'll come with you. I want to hear this.' The guy fell into step beside her, walking with long unhurried strides. 'Want any help with that?' Again, that annoying smile and his eyes were twinkling too as if he was amused by her efforts to stay calm.

'No, thanks, I can manage.'

She did, but only just, and she ended up panting with the effort of upending the barrow onto the compost heap, which didn't help. Nor did the stranger, who followed behind her but didn't offer assistance again. Instead he crossed his arms, making his biceps bunch up in the most eye-catching way. Annoying man, he was probably doing it on purpose so she'd look at him. She didn't want to but Tess had to force herself not to stare at the tattoo, which was strangely fascinating. By the time they got to the potting shed, where Bryn could usually be found if he wasn't outside, she was ready for some answers.

'Bryn, are you there?'

'In yere.' The old man's Welsh lilt was one of the things she loved about him. That and his ready smile. 'Just making tea again. Would you like some, my lovely?'

Tess walked into the shed, closely followed by the shirtless stranger. 'Yes, please, but Bryn —' She didn't have time to finish her sentence.

'Oh, there you are, er … Josh. Come and have a cuppa as well, won't you?'

'Sure, sweet.'

Bryn looked from one to the other. 'So you've met his lordship then.' It was a statement, not a question.

Tess swivelled towards the younger man. 'L-lordship? What do you mean?'

'The new owner of Merrick Court,' Bryn explained patiently. 'Josh, he says to call him, but I don't know …' He scratched his balding head.

But Tess wasn't looking at him. She glared at the newcomer. Josh, Lord Merrick? He couldn't be, could he? 'Why didn't you mention that?'

He grinned. 'You didn't ask.'

'Oh, for heaven's sake …' Tess stared at the man. Why hadn't he told her who he was instead of letting her think he was just some workman? But then she had been rather rude so perhaps he'd wanted to punish her a little? She felt her cheeks heating up, embarrassed now by her lack of manners.

'And who are you?' Josh said. 'I thought no one else worked here.' He raised his eyebrows at the old man as if they'd been discussing this earlier.

'Oh, didn't I say?' Bryn tutted at himself. 'This yere is Lady Merrick.'

'What?' Josh's eyebrows shot up even further. 'But I thought … oh, bollocks.'

'Er, would you care to explain that eloquent statement?' It was Tess's turn to cross her arms.

He looked a bit sheepish. 'Uhm, well, I was expecting what the lawyer called a "dowager". I mean …'

Tess cottoned on. 'Ah, an old-age pensioner? Sorry to disappoint you.'

'I wouldn't say I'm disappointed exactly.' Josh grinned briefly again as his gaze travelled the length of her body, lingering on her curves and long, honey-gold hair which was currently piled on top of her head and fastened with a clip. But then he seemed to recollect that he was talking to a widow and the smile disappeared. 'That's to say, your age doesn't matter to me. I was just surprised, is all.'

'I should hope not too.' Tess was annoyed to find that the warmth in his eyes as he'd given her the once-over made her hot and flustered. He was disturbingly handsome. How old could he be? Probably in his early thirties, although possibly younger as he was so fit. It was hard to tell.

'Come and have some tea and then you can get to know each other,' Bryn suggested.

'Good idea.' In truth, Tess had forgotten the old man was there, she was so focused on Josh. Which was totally wrong. She shook herself mentally and went to sit down.

'So you've been the lady of the manor then,' Josh commented, taking the mugs from Bryn and setting them on an old table surrounded by stools.

Tess loved it in here. It had been her refuge whenever things with Giles got too bad. Sitting in such timeless surroundings, breathing in the scents from the garden and chatting to the old man had always filled her with peace and inner strength.

Not today though. Josh made her all jittery and it annoyed her that he had this effect on her. She didn't like feeling wrong-footed and they had definitely not started off the right way. But he was nothing like she'd imagined he would be. Not that she'd thought much about it, but she too had envisaged someone older, so she couldn't really blame Josh for thinking the same about her.

'Yes, you could say that,' she replied. It was not a role she'd ever felt comfortable with but it was in the past, so no point mentioning that.

Bryn brought out his trusted old biscuit tin and put that on the table, together with a carton of milk.

'I'm sorry for your loss,' Josh said, his eyes showing that he meant it. 'Now that I've met you, I can see it's doubly tragic.'

Tess assumed he was referring to Giles's youth. 'Thank you. Yes, it was a bit of a shock, to say the least. An accident,' she explained, as Josh obviously didn't know what had happened. 'Didn't the lawyers tell you anything?' She tried to keep the irritation out of her voice, but she was still a bit cross about stumbling on him like this. Why hadn't he come up to the house? Or rung to say he was coming?

And why was he working in the garden? But maybe the solicitor had told her about his visit and she'd forgotten. The medication she'd been taking did make her lose track occasionally. Another good reason she'd stopped taking it.

Bryn answered the second of those questions as soon as he'd perched on one of the stools while Tess and Josh helped themselves to biscuits.

'Josh arrived a bit early so I persuaded him to wait before waking you. I didn't know you were up and about today. And he offered to help me with some of the heavy work while he was waiting. I hope you don't mind, Lady M?' He'd always called her that, as a sort of joke, ever since she'd told him not to be so formal with her.

'Well, no, of course not, but …'

'I'm sorry, I should have let you know I was coming,' Josh put in. 'But I was under the impression you'd moved out. I'm afraid I was in a bit of a hurry when I went to see Mr Harrison, the lawyer, in London and I must have missed the part about you still living here. I just wanted to come and have a look at the place.' Josh waved his biscuit to encompass the estate. 'He said the "custodian" would let me in. I had no idea that meant you.'

'I see.'

'Why *are* you still here? If you don't mind me asking.'

Josh's piercing green eyes made Tess want to squirm, but she had every right to be here at the moment. 'Mr Harrison felt that from a security point of view it was better to keep the house occupied and it took them rather a long time to find you, I gather.'

'I was travelling. The friend who was in charge of collecting my mail back home in New Zealand didn't think the envelope from Harrison looked important.' Josh rolled his eyes. 'Just because it wasn't a bill. He's not the sharpest tool in the box but he's a good mate.'

'Right. Well, anyway, Mr Harrison asked me to stay on

and so I did.' Tess had looked into renting a place nearby but hadn't wanted to start paying rent before it was necessary. That would have been a waste of money.

'Okay. I understand where he was coming from and I'm grateful to you for waiting so long. As I said, if I'd known I'd have come sooner. I'm sure we can come to some agreement now.'

'So are you wanting to move in immediately?' Tess held her breath, hoping he'd say no.

'Not exactly. I'll need a place to crash for a few days while I look at everything, but after that I don't intend to live here. I'm selling up. From what I've heard, that takes a fair bit of time in this country. Two to three months, right?'

'You're selling Merrick Court?' So Rosie had been right. Tess should be pleased the house might go to Louis after all, but for some reason she wasn't. This man had only just arrived and he hadn't even seen it yet. How could he care so little for what had turned out to be his birthright?

Josh sighed. 'Yes, that is my plan.' He glanced at Bryn. 'Although I'm getting the vibe you guys think I'm nuts.'

'No, no, it's up to you, of course. For now, I'm sure we can find you a spare room or two to sleep in.' It was meant to be a joke, but Josh's expression turned pensive.

'Hmm, yeah, that's a bit awkward, huh? I'm guessing you still feel this is your home so I wouldn't want to be an uninvited guest. Maybe there's a hotel nearby or something?'

'I don't mind, really.' Although that was a lie and Tess had a feeling he could hear it in her voice.

'How about you use my guest room?' Bryn put in. 'I'm only just down the road so you'll have easy access to the house.'

Tess and Josh answered at the same time.

'Are you sure?'

'Oh, Bryn, we don't want to put you out ...'

Bryn chuckled. 'It's no bother. You're more than welcome,

especially seeing as you own my cottage too.' The twinkle in Bryn's eyes told Tess he didn't mind and she wondered what Josh had done to get into the old man's good graces so quickly. Perhaps it had been the digging? Not exactly the behaviour expected of a lord.

'It should be me moving out,' Tess said, but Josh held up a hand to stop her protesting any further.

'No, it's fine. I stuffed up by not telling you about my arrival so I'll stay with Bryn. Cheers, mate,' he added and clapped Bryn on the back before grabbing his T-shirt which had been half shoved into his back pocket. As he pulled it on, Tess looked away, even though her eyes wanted to stray to that amazing torso. 'Have you got time to show me round the house now or should I come back later?'

'The house? Oh, yes, sure.' Tess stood up, dragging her thoughts away from the sight before her. Even with his T-shirt back on he was incredibly attractive, but it shouldn't matter to her.

'I saw Miss Rosie and the children arriving yesterday,' Bryn commented while he started clearing away the mugs. 'Come for a visit, have they?'

'No, she's just here to annoy me.' The words came out before Tess had a chance to think about it, but when Josh snorted, she realised she'd been a bit indiscreet. 'I mean ...'

Josh laughed, a delicious rumble that made something inside Tess stir. 'No, don't backtrack on my account. I love a good family feud. Had my fair share of them. I take it she's family?'

'Not mine. She's my late husband's sister. And it's not exactly a feud,' Tess started to say, but then wondered if it was. She and Rosie had been at loggerheads almost from the first time they'd met, since Rosie hadn't considered Tess anywhere near good enough for her brother. Presumably she'd have preferred one of her posh friends, not an art student from a very middle-class family.

'Miss Rosie never did learn any tact,' Bryn put in. 'Spoiled by her da', so she was, something rotten. Always demanding this, that and the other, and usually got it. I suppose it's the husband that buys it now.'

'Well, he can afford it,' Tess muttered. Besides having inherited a fortune, George was something important in the City and he seemed to give Rosie whatever she wanted.

'Are they staying long?' Bryn asked.

'No idea. I didn't even know they were coming, but they'll have to fend for themselves food-wise as I can't afford to subsidise anyone.'

Bryn smiled. 'Speaking of food, I've been offered a couple of hens. What do you think, should I take them? It would give you free eggs.' His smile faded. 'Although maybe there's no point now as I don't know where I'll be living in a few months' time. No, tell you what, I'll just borrow a couple from the farmer down the road.'

Tess swallowed hard and nodded. 'Yes, why not?'

He was such a sweetie, trying to help her out. He knew she was struggling to make ends meet. Without a regular housekeeping allowance, her only income was from the fledgling business that she'd started as a hobby. It wasn't making much profit as yet, but she was working on it so hopefully it would do soon.

'I'll see to that then. I'll keep them in my own garden.'

'Thanks, Bryn.' Tess turned to Josh. 'Shall we go?'

'Yep. Lead the way, Lady M.' He smiled at her and for some stupid reason she felt her cheeks heat up again. The way he said 'Lady M' in that wonderful Kiwi accent made her nerve-endings tingle, which was ridiculous. There was a whole nation of people who spoke like that, he was just one of them.

'It's Tess,' she said. 'Bryn only calls me Lady M because … well, it's a joke.'

'Okay, Tess it is.'

His green gaze fixed on her for a moment, filling her with confusion. Those eyes felt familiar, unsettling, but exciting at the same time. It was as though she knew him, but of course she'd never met him before today. Strange.

'Come on then.' She headed for the door. 'Thanks for the tea, Bryn.'

Chapter Seven

Josh followed Lady M – or Tess as she'd insisted he call her – out of the workshop and round to the front of the house, still reeling a bit from the discovery that she wasn't a little old lady. Instead she looked to be in her mid- to late-twenties and she was hot, no two ways about it – long golden blonde hair piled in a sexy mess on top of her head, beautiful blue eyes in an equally lovely face, and a great figure. The sadness he'd glimpsed in those big eyes had got to him though. She had been through a lot recently and he'd had an unexpectedly primeval masculine urge to gather her close and assure her everything would be all right. That he'd protect her, help her with whatever was troubling her.

He was an idiot.

It was nothing to do with him, obviously. He was only here to view his inheritance and had no reason to become embroiled in her affairs. Besides, she probably wouldn't thank him for interfering. She had shown some spirit, that was for sure, but he had a feeling it was only because he'd surprised her and jolted her out of her grief. Bryn had confided his worries about the mistress of the house and now Josh could see what he'd meant.

Lady M needed support.

But he wasn't the man to give it to her. He wasn't staying and he didn't want any ties or complications. And she would definitely mean both if he got involved. Much better to keep his distance.

As they rounded the corner of the house, he stopped to stare up at the imposing façade of the huge mansion that was now his. He whistled softly. 'Yo!'

The papers Harrison had given him had said something about 'an early medieval fortified manor house' that had undergone several transformations during its long existence. Josh knew a bit about English architecture and saw a Norman tower in one corner which looked incongruous next to a Georgian frontage, complete with imposing staircase leading up to the main entrance. A Tudor wing on the other side of the tower gave the house a lopsided feel, but its windows with thousands of tiny panes of glass glittered invitingly in the sunlight. On the opposite side was a Victorian wing, with huge Gothic windows that were probably draughty as hell.

You couldn't help but admire it. Despite the strange mixture of building styles, it was beautiful and he loved its quirks; a mullioned window here, a crenellation there, with a couple of gargoyles in between keeping guard. No thought to any symmetry whatsoever. The gargoyles weren't scary-looking and weirdly enough helped give a homely feel to the house. If he'd been looking for a permanent place to settle in the UK, this might have been worth hanging onto.

Tess had stopped over by the steps and was waiting for him, but he took his time, scanning the many windows. This may be a place you could call home, but there were shadows here too. Souls. Spirits, whatever you wanted to call them. Many more than he'd seen anywhere else, apart from when he'd visited old castles and monuments. He couldn't help but notice them.

Ever since he was a child he'd seen things that couldn't be explained – shadowy forms, not visible to anyone else but clear to him. He'd been frightened at first, especially when his mother told him it was only his imagination, but when he was ten, a visit to his Welsh-born grandparents helped as he'd found out he wasn't alone.

He'd been staring at a dark shape in the corner of the

room for some time when his grandmother Nerys came and put a hand on his shoulder. 'Don't worry, love,' she whispered. 'He'll not hurt us. He's just confused as he hasn't found his way to the light yet.'

Josh blinked up at her. 'Y-you see them too?'

She nodded and put her arm round him, giving him a reassuring squeeze. 'Yes. It's a gift, passed down through my family, but not everyone has it.' She glanced towards Josh's mother, who was talking to his grandfather, both oblivious to any spirits. 'I didn't know you did until now.'

'Are we ... psychic, then?' he asked, whispering too as he felt this was a secret only the two of them shared.

'No, we just open our senses more than most people. Ignore the shadows and they'll leave you alone.'

From then on, he'd accepted his 'gift' and tried to follow her advice. He wanted nothing to do with departed souls.

Through a large Gothic window on his left he glimpsed the shape of a woman in a crinoline, walking back and forth while seemingly wringing her hands. He'd bet hers was a sad story and she hadn't found the rest she'd sought in death. Suicide? Probably.

To her right, there was a huge bay window, and lounging on the window seats inside were several tiny blurred shapes. Josh swallowed hard. He hated it when he saw the spirits of departed children as it usually meant they'd suffered in some way. An epidemic? Nerys had told him little ones should never have got lost on the way to the light, but it happened. He turned away, not wanting to look at them or speculate about their fate.

Continuing his sweep across the front of the building, his gaze came to rest on the Norman tower. The windows there were mere slits for the most part, but up on the first floor there was a bigger one with a myriad of leaded glass panes. He'd read somewhere that medieval ladies usually had what they called a solar, a room with extra large windows to let in more light so they could work at their sewing or something like that. He assumed that's what had lain behind this window.

As he stared, he became aware of a shadowy figure staring right back at him and he almost gasped. The shape wasn't as blurred as they usually were. In fact, Josh could see the man clearly, something that had never happened to him before. He felt his eyes open wide when the spirit took off a broad-brimmed hat and swept it before him as he bowed.

Josh hissed out a breath in surprise, then looked quickly around to see if Tess had noticed, but she'd already gone in through the imposing front door. He was alone, so he was undeniably the only person the ghostly figure could be greeting.

Slowly, if a bit self-consciously, Josh bowed back, pretending to have a hat in his hand. He felt a drongo doing it, but imagined he caught a smile on the spirit's face as he straightened up. As if borne on the wind, he heard the words 'Croeso i Gymru'. He frowned, then understanding dawned – it was what it had said on all the signs near the borders of Wales: 'Welcome to Wales.'

He smiled and bowed again, but when he next looked up, the shadow was gone and he shivered. It was the first time he'd ever interacted with any of the entities he saw and he wasn't sure what would happen if he did. Grandma had told him to ignore them – were there consequences if you didn't? She'd never said.

But the exchange of bows left Josh with a strange feeling of belonging, as if the spirit had been telling him Wales was where he should be looking for his future home.

Perhaps he was right and he was being hasty in wanting to sell Merrick Court straight away? He'd have to think about that later.

He headed for the door, where Tess was peering out, no

doubt wondering where he'd got to. It was time to see the inside of the house.

'So this is the Victorian part of the house, with high ceilings, lots of cornicing and big marble fireplaces. No one goes in here in winter as it's absolutely freezing.'

Tess knew she sounded like a tour guide, but that was what she was, in effect. Despite Josh's consideration in not turfing her out immediately, she was acutely aware that what she was showing him was his. Apart from the contents, of course.

'Uhm, did Mr Harrison tell you that everything inside Merrick Court belongs to me?' She thought it best to ask since Josh didn't seem to have taken in much of what the solicitor had told him.

'Yes, he mentioned that. I figured it doesn't matter if I'm selling the place, but seeing it like this now I'm starting to wonder ...'

'What?' Tess noticed he'd said 'if' not 'when'. Was he changing his mind?

'It looks so much better as someone's home. If all the furniture was gone it would just be a big echoey house and might be harder to sell. You'd see all the faded bits of wallpaper and chipped paintwork.' Josh lifted up an old photo of some long-forgotten grandmother or great-aunt. 'Maybe we should work together? We could try to find a buyer who wants both the house and what's in it. That way you might get a better price too.'

Tess thought about it. She knew there wasn't much of actual value here, but someone who wanted a proper country house with the right style of interior might pay over the odds for the privilege. Everything at Merrick Court had been collected over the centuries so it was the genuine thing, not some interior decorator's idea of country chic. She thought of Rosie and what she'd said earlier. Tess wouldn't get much out of a deal with her. 'Yes, perhaps,' she said, not wanting to commit herself to anything at this stage. 'I could at least wait with selling the contents until you've had some viewings.'

'Sweet. I reckon that would help.'

They continued through the ground-floor rooms, with Tess explaining what they were for and how old each part of the house was. When they arrived back in the grand entrance hall, Rosie and Louis were just coming down the stairs.

'Oh, there you are!' Rosie started talking the instant she caught sight of Tess. 'I wanted to ask you about that little landscape by Hinton. It's a particular favourite of mine. Did you send it off for cleaning? Only, I can't find it and ... oh, you have a guest?'

Tess saw Rosie's eyes open wide as she took in the sight of Josh. She wondered what Rosie made of him but guessed from the slight frown on her sister-in-law's face that he didn't pass muster. It was probably the ripped jeans and T-shirt. Or possibly the stubble. Rosie's husband was never allowed to dress that casually, poor man. Pressed chinos and a polo shirt were required at the very least.

'Uhm, not exactly,' Tess said. 'Josh, this is Rosalyn Edmonton, my sister-in-law and her son Louis. Rosie, this is Josh, the heir.' She could perhaps have softened the blow a little, but Rosie was always so direct herself it felt good to get her own back for once.

'The what? No!' Rosie now resembled nothing so much as a bug-eyed frog as her eyes became even bigger. 'But ...' She turned to Tess and scowled. 'You didn't tell me he was coming.'

'I didn't know.' Tess shrugged. 'I found him in the garden.'

'Found him in the ...'

Josh stepped forward and held out his hand. 'Josh Owens. Nice to meet you, Mrs Edmonton.'

Rosie's frown didn't let up. 'Don't you mean Lord Merrick? If that's really who you are. I assume you've brought documentation to prove it?'

'Mum!' Louis hissed, entering the conversation for the first time. He looked like he wanted to be anywhere but here.

'Well, how do we know he's telling the truth unless he can show us some proof?' Rosie persisted.

Josh smiled at Louis and winked. 'No worries, mate, I can indeed. I'll go get the papers from my car later. But I'd rather not be called Lord anything, if it's all the same to you.'

'Well, really!' Rosie seemed to be having trouble with this concept and Tess could understand it. To the family, being an earl was a huge honour and something they were immensely proud of. Josh didn't seem to care at all. But then he wasn't English, they had to remember that. Presumably they saw things differently in New Zealand.

'Shall we continue the tour?' Tess suggested. It was clear that Rosie needed some time to digest this.

'Sure. Lead on.'

'Hold on a moment.' Rosie held up a hand. 'Are you intending to keep the house?'

Tess cringed. Rosie didn't hang around, did she?

'Nah, I don't think so.' Josh sounded less sure than he had earlier. 'Why?'

'My husband and I would like to buy it from you. For Louis. It's his birthright.' Rosie indicated an embarrassed Louis who tried to blend into the background while shaking his head. 'He's a bit young still and doesn't appreciate things quite as he ought, but he will, in time.'

Josh raised his eyebrows and fixed Rosie with those clear green eyes. 'His birthright? Funny, I was under the impression it was mine. As the "heir" and all.'

Rosie flushed. 'Well, yes, in a manner of speaking, but

what I meant was Louis has grown up expecting this to be his—'

'I have *not!*' Louis hissed, but his mother ignored him.

'—and I'm assuming you won't want to make your home here, so far from your own country.'

'The jury's out on that one,' Josh said. 'For now, I'd like to keep my options open. If and when I decide to sell, I'll let you know. You'd have to talk with the estate agents.'

Rosie attempted a smile. 'Well, I thought perhaps we needn't involve them. These things can be so costly and they're absolute sharks those agents. Better to keep it in the family, yes?'

'No. And like I said, I haven't decided anything yet.' Josh's blunt answer made Rosie blink, but he didn't give her a chance to say anything else. 'If you don't mind, I'd like to see the rest of the house now. Tess?'

Tess nodded. 'Yes, of course. This way.' She led the way up the grand staircase and tried not to giggle at the sight of Rosie's mouth opening and closing like a dying fish. It was very seldom anyone got the better of her and it was a sight for sore eyes as far as Tess was concerned.

'I see what you meant back in the shed,' Josh said as soon as they were out of earshot. 'Is she always like that?'

'Yes, but I don't think she means to be rude really. She's just forthright.'

'Is that what it's called over here?' Josh muttered.

When Tess had shown him everything he wanted to see, he thanked her. 'Now I'd better go check out Bryn's.'

'Are you sure? As you've seen, there's plenty of room here.' Tess felt this was all wrong.

'Really, I'll be fine. I was expecting to doss down on the floor in a sleeping bag so Bryn's guest room will probably be an improvement on that.' He smiled in a way that sent a tingle of awareness through Tess. 'I'll maybe see you later. I want to have a wander round the outside too.'

After he'd gone, Tess went to scrub her hands and nails in the butler's pantry as she was still a bit grubby from gardening. The water was a bit cold at first so she let it run, watching as it swirled down into the plughole, the vortex mesmerisingly perfect. Her mind drifted away and all she was aware of was a pair of very fine green eyes ...

Josh stopped on the gravel outside the front door and drew in a couple of huge breaths of fresh spring air, bending over to brace his hands against his knees. He felt as though he'd been through a fierce workout, both mentally and physically. His brain was all scrambled with too much information and a kaleidoscope of images jostling for space. The reality of Merrick Court had knocked him for six.

When he'd first been informed of his inheritance, he'd imagined a largish house in the countryside, but nothing like this. This was a bloody great big mansion. And old; ancient, in parts. Wandering through all the rooms behind Tess had been like touring some royal palace and he just couldn't take in the fact that it was his. Why had his father never mentioned being related to English aristocracy? It was exactly the sort of thing he'd have been proud of. But perhaps he hadn't known? Or maybe he'd been ashamed of the way they were connected. As far as Josh could make out from Mr Harrison, it was through a younger son who'd been such a black sheep he'd been sent to Australia as a condemned criminal. He'd gambled away everything he had, and more, stealing to fund his addiction, then ended up on one of the convict ships before later making his way to New Zealand after serving his sentence.

His father wouldn't have liked that, even though it was quite fashionable nowadays to have convict ancestors. No, he would have hated it. Which, conversely, made Josh like it.

'Thanks, Mr Black Sheep, I owe you,' he murmured, then

shook his head at himself. He was talking to thin air. Losing it big time. But was it any wonder?

He stood up straight and went to his car to retrieve a plan of the estate that Harrison had given him. He'd walk around some of the fields, clear his head a bit before finding Bryn again. There was an old stile not far from the gate where he'd come in earlier, so he climbed over that and set off along the perimeter of the nearest field. This was what he needed; some space to think.

It was a glorious day and the fields were edged with hedgerows where little birds hopped in and out, twittering away. Some of the bushes were full of blossom and their leaves were that amazing green colour only spring produced – clean and fresh. Josh took note of the soil, a rich dark reddish type that looked very fertile but heavy with moisture. Great for growing whatever you needed. In the fields used for pasture, the grass was lush, perfect for sheep and cattle. All round the edges trees grew – oak, beech and others he didn't recognise. Some of the oak trees looked to be hundreds of years old, their girth impressive. Josh had the sudden thought that his ancestors had seen them too, touched them, and had walked here for hundreds of years before him. It was an odd feeling. Emotional.

And nothing like he'd ever felt for his father's sheep station in New Zealand.

Not that you could really compare the two. The station had comprised mostly hills and wide open valleys, undulating tussock-covered land crossed by rivers and with high mountain ranges as a backdrop. It was a totally different environment, thousands of square kilometres to keep track of, necessitating the use of four-wheel drive vehicles for mustering the sheep and sometimes even helicopters. Here everything felt much smaller, enclosed, but not in a bad way, like he was hemmed in. Rather, it was manageable. He could see himself herding the sheep from one field to another with just the help of a trusted sheep dog. No quad bikes would be necessary. Nor big teams of helpers.

He stopped to lean against one particularly vast tree trunk and closed his eyes, letting the sun warm his face while he tried to process it all.

Did he really want to part with this?

Then again, how could he keep it? He didn't know the first thing about being a landowner and sheep farmer – or a lord for that matter – in the UK. But maybe it wasn't so different? A sheep was a sheep wherever it was in the world. And as far as he knew, there were no rules for how a lord had to behave, so surely that was up to him?

He sighed. This was something that would require a lot more thought than he'd envisaged.

Chapter Eight

Raglan Castle, 22nd May 1646

'Are you sure you want to do this for us? You're not afraid of the dark?'

'No, the darker the better as far as I'm concerned. It's the people that may be lurking in the shadows I have to look out for.' It was late in the evening and those shadows hid Arabella's face at the moment. She hoped Lady Margaret couldn't hear the fear in her voice. Of course she was afraid, but she owed the marquis's family a huge debt and she would have done anything they asked of her. She tried not to think about the treasures that had passed through her hands that evening, family jewels that were worth a fortune. All entrusted to her care. 'I'll try to be extra careful.'

'See that you are.'

She glanced through the cross-shaped arrow-loop in the wall of the Great Tower, checking one last time for movement. There was none. 'All clear,' she whispered.

Outside, the sheen from the sliver of a moon glistened on the still waters of the moat, but all was quiet. Not even a rat stirred; probably all sound asleep somewhere safe, as was everyone inside the castle. Lady Margaret led the way down through the family's private apartments to the Fountain Court, glancing around to make sure no one else was about once they were outside. The Court seemed empty and the two women hurried into the vaulted passage leading to the South Gate. A sleepy sentry sat in the guard chamber on the left, but when he saw Lady Margaret, he didn't protest and allowed her to unbolt the small door set into the larger gate doors. Just before Arabella slipped out, the lady gave her a swift, but fierce hug.

'Godspeed. I will pray for you,' she whispered, and pulled something out of a pocket which she placed in Arabella's hand. 'Here, this is for your trouble. Hide it well and sell it if you are ever in need, although it's supposed to bring luck to its owner so, if at all possible, do keep it.'

'But ... no! I couldn't possibly accept something so valuable.' Arabella knew what it was as she could feel the outline of a large cross in her palm with a long chain attached. It was a beautiful necklace Lady Margaret had often worn, the cross set in gold with pink and blue sapphires, and amethysts. Much too expensive a gift for her to accept. 'And if it gives good fortune, should you not keep it for yourself, my lady?'

'No. You are young; I want you to have a chance at happiness such as I've already found with my husband. And if you succeed tonight, it might bring us both luck.' Lady Margaret closed both hands around Arabella's. 'I won't take no for an answer. Now go and I hope to see you at dawn.'

'Very well. Thank you, my lady. I'll do my very best. And I will give it back if you ever need it, I swear.'

As she slipped outside, swiftly crossing the bridge to head down towards the Bowling Green and the former parkland beyond, Arabella shivered with fear and excitement. At last she was doing something to help and she would succeed.

Failure was not an option.

Rhys tried to delay going to bed for as long as possible. Sharing a small room with a group of snoring officers was not conducive to a good night's sleep and therefore the longer he could stay awake, the easier it would be for him to drop off once he finally tried it. There were others even more uncomfortable than him, probably crammed in like pilchards in a barrel, and he'd slept in many worse places himself, but right now he was wide awake and would only toss and turn. Far better to be outside for a while.

In the Stone Court there were others who were awake, playing cards or dice while waiting for their turn at guard duty, so he slipped through the servant's passage into the Great Hall and from there to the Fountain Court. Here, all was quiet and peaceful, and he settled himself on a staircase in the far corner, between the guest accommodation and the Long Gallery. The nearby walls threw shadows all around him and he doubted anyone would see him unless he moved.

The stone walls behind his shoulders were cool, but fairly smooth, the ashlar pieces hewn by a master stonemason. The soft night breeze brought the scent of fields and meadows beyond the castle's walls, and he leaned back and closed his eyes for a moment, letting the peace wash over him. It was rare to have any solitude here and it was all the more welcome for that.

He didn't know how long he sat there, but just as he was about to move and seek his bed, he saw two shadowy figures emerge from a door leading to the marquis's apartments on the other side of the courtyard, by the Great Tower. Two women, judging by their outlines, hurrying out with furtive movements. Rhys's interest was piqued.

When one of the two shadows stepped into a beam of moonlight for an instant, his senses sprang into full alert. Arabella, he'd swear to it. No one else had hair like liquid gold and the long tendrils snaking out from underneath her cap were unmistakeable. What was she doing creeping around so late at night? She should be in her bed. Was she a spy? And who was the other woman with her?

There was no time to ponder these questions. The ladies were undoubtedly heading out of the castle, as they went straight towards the South Gate. Rhys sprinted back to the Stone Court, as silently as he could, and walked quickly to a corner near the Library Tower where there was a small door set in the wall, leading to an enclosure outside where some of the horses were kept.

The door was guarded of course. 'Where you off to then?' The man standing there challenged him while suppressing a yawn.

'Need to check on my horse,' Rhys replied. 'Might have to change a poultice. He went lame earlier.'

'Oh, right. Pass then.' The man didn't seem bothered one way or another, which at any other time Rhys would have found irritating. Not to mention hardly reassuring, as an enemy could presumably pass the other way just as easily. For now, he just slipped through the gate, whistled for his horse, who came trotting obediently, and jumped onto the big stallion's back. He had no bridle or anything, but it didn't matter. Rhys had ridden bareback more times than he could count and his horse wasn't the nervous type; he'd never throw his master off.

Without making a sound, he set the horse at the fence and they jumped it easily. Once on the other side, they had to move slowly as it was dark beneath the walls of the castle. Rhys kept close to the bottom of those walls and circled round to the South Gate, regretting that he had to walk through some of the lovely flowerbeds in order to get there. He was just in time to see a shadowy figure disappearing down the hill and, after waiting for a moment, he followed.

Arabella seemed to be alone and walking with great purpose. But where was she going? He had to know.

⌖

Merrick Court, 22nd May 2016

Tess became aware of the sound of running water and blinked at the steady stream gushing into the butler's sink,

75

the water now so hot it was steaming. 'Ouch!' She pulled her reddening fingers away and turned on the cold tap to make it a more bearable temperature before washing her hands. How long had she stood there, daydreaming? She had no idea. Her mind had been lost in darkness and she'd seen herself in a shadowy courtyard. She'd sensed danger, her senses on high alert, expecting an ambush perhaps? But nothing had happened. And the man from the castle – Rhys? – had been absent this time. Strange how he was now inextricably mixed in her mind with Josh, the unexpected heir to Merrick Court. Both had green eyes that seemed to see all the way into her soul.

It was very confusing. Not to mention crazy.

She wandered into the kitchen, still a bit dazed, and almost bumped into Rosie who was making herself a mug of tea.

'I can't believe that man is the new earl! So rude. And an Aussie beach bum to boot. Honestly, it's got to be a mistake.' Rosie discarded her tea bag in the sink, a habit that drove Tess mad.

'We don't all have maids to pick up after us, you know,' she muttered, fishing the bag out and dumping it in the nearby pedal bin. 'And he's not Australian, he's from New Zealand.'

'Same difference.'

Tess was pretty sure Josh wouldn't agree, but decided he could fight his own battles on that score.

'So what are we going to do?' Rosie sat down at the table and looked up at Tess.

'What do you mean, do?'

'About buying the house, of course. Hello? Earth to Tess.' Rosie waved at her as if she wasn't all there. 'He can't possibly want to live here, especially if he's not interested in his title. Actually, maybe there'd be a way of having that transferred as well?'

'He said he hadn't decided. And if you want to buy the house, you'll have to bid for it like everyone else.'

'Oh, I heard him, but that's what I'm talking about – we have to make him see reason. We're family. Or I am, anyway; we must be some kind of cousins umpteen times removed. Once he learns about the history of Merrick Court and how we – or I and Louis at any rate – appreciate it so much more than he ever could, I'm sure he'll understand. Besides, if he wants to sell quickly, it's the best way. Why would he want all the extra cost of estate agents?'

Tess shook her head. 'Feel free to try, but I don't think he'll be that easily swayed. He struck me as the stubborn type.' Not that he hadn't been pleasant, but there had been something very steely in his eyes when he'd told Rosie no earlier. Tess was sure he wouldn't back down.

'I'll speak to Harrison, perhaps he can help. And maybe I should take him out to lunch?'

'Who, Mr Harrison?'

'No, silly, the heir.' Rosie put her mug down on the table with a bang. 'Honestly, you're not listening to a word, are you? You really need to pull yourself together. Are you still taking Prozac? It's time you stopped, if you ask me.'

'Thank you, Rosie, but actually I stopped ages ago,' Tess replied tartly. That was bending the truth a little, but God, the woman was such an interfering busybody. 'And for your information, I'm perfectly all right.'

'Well, good. Stiff upper lip and all that, eh?' Rosie smiled in what she probably imagined was an encouraging way.

Jesus. Thank goodness that soon she wouldn't have to see Rosie again. Once Tess moved out of Merrick Court and started a new life, there wouldn't be anything to bind her to Giles's family. Although hopefully she could still stay in touch with Louis.

'So you'll help me persuade him then.'

'I'm sorry?' Tess looked at Rosie.

'The *heir*. We'll have to think of something.' Rosie shook her head at Tess. 'Are you sure you're okay? Maybe you should go and lie down for a bit.'

'No, I'm fine. And as you said, *you* are related to him, I'm not, so don't involve me, please.'

'I would have thought you'd want to help for Giles's sake. Or Louis's.'

Tess only glared at Rosie.

'Fine, I'll see to it myself. Have you gone through Giles's papers yet?'

'What?' Tess was taken aback by the sudden change of direction.

'His papers. You *have* gone through them, right?' Rosie narrowed her eyes at Tess, as if she suspected her of procrastinating too.

'Er, most of them, yes. Why?' Tess didn't want to admit that she'd been putting off going through his things and, apart from a quick look for his will, just after he died, she'd left his desk alone. She supposed it was past time to tackle it now.

'They're private. We wouldn't want the likes of Mr Beach Bum to read Giles's correspondence. Do get on and finish, for heaven's sake. It's been months!'

For some reason hearing Rosie refer to Josh as a beach bum really riled Tess, although she had no idea why. It wasn't her job to defend him after all. But she replied with more force than usual. 'I'll finish off this week, although I hardly think Giles had any "correspondence" to speak of. He used a laptop like everyone else. Who writes letters these days?'

'I do.'

Yes, that figured, but Tess didn't say that out loud.

Rosie continued, 'And if you find that lovely family tree my father had someone draw up, you will let me have it, won't you? It will be great for Louis to see his illustrious ancestors.'

Tess almost snorted as they hadn't been anything special. Not that she'd ever been very interested in Giles's ancestors. She hadn't encouraged him to tell her about them, apart from the ones who'd done something exciting, like being a pirate for a while. Talk of genealogy would invariably lead to heated exchanges on the matter of having children and heirs, so she'd avoided that topic as much as possible. It was a subject she'd come to hate. Something they'd rowed about constantly during the last year or so. But Tess refused to think about that right now. Besides, what was the point? It was too late.

She changed the subject. 'How long are you all staying?'

'Well, Louis and Emilia are going back to London this afternoon, but I'll be here for a few more days.' Rosie sounded as though she was doing Tess a favour. 'I haven't finished my lists yet and I'll need to talk to the heir some more, of course.'

Something inside Tess finally snapped. 'Nice of you to ask if it's convenient.'

Rosie looked puzzled. 'Why wouldn't it be? It's not as if you're short of space here. It's a twenty-bedroom house, for goodness' sake. Do you begrudge me one of them?'

Talk about water off a duck's back. Tess gave up. 'Fine, but if you want any food, you're going to have to buy it yourself. I can't afford to feed you.'

'What do you mean?' Rosie put her mug in the sink, presumably for the invisible maid to wash.

'Do you mind washing that up, please? There's no one here to do it for you. And I mean I don't have any money so I'm not buying you food while you're here. The lawyers are only paying out running costs for the house and estate until everything is sorted out. Nothing for me personally.'

Rosie picked up the sponge with some distaste and gave her mug a quick wash. 'Oh, don't be so melodramatic. I'm sure Giles left you very well off. If not, you can always sell some of your little paintings.'

Tess resisted the urge to throttle the woman. She obviously had no idea that her sainted brother had gambled away every last penny and Tess had been lucky even to get a housekeeping sum during the final months of his life. Should she tell her? No, she'd promised not to. As for her 'little paintings' ... how many times did she have to tell Rosie she wasn't that kind of artist?

Really, the woman was unbearable.

Chapter Nine

Josh had to duck to enter Bryn's small cottage as the door seemed to have been made for midgets. It opened straight into a cosy sitting room with an inglenook fireplace and a low ceiling criss-crossed with dark oak beams. Deep rugs and lots of scatter cushions gave the room warmth and colour, and Josh guessed Bryn's wife must have added these as they were feminine touches. There was no sign of anyone though.

As if he'd seen the question in Josh's eyes, Bryn said, 'I live yere by myself. My wife passed away five years ago. Cancer.'

'Sorry to hear that. Took my mum too, way too early. Hate that disease.'

Josh dumped his huge rucksack just inside the door. It was dirty from months of travelling and he didn't want to ruin Bryn's rugs. He hadn't bothered to unpack it before leaving for the UK as Harrison's letter had seemed so urgent.

'Can I get you anything? Another cup of tea? Sandwich?' The old man walked over to a door that led into a tiny kitchen at the back of the cottage. Josh was starting to feel like he'd ended up in Snow White's house, only without the dwarves. At six foot two, he was going to have to watch his head around here.

'Something to eat would be great, thanks. Walking round that big old house took longer than I thought and then I went over some of the fields too.' He followed Bryn into the kitchen, ducking to avoid the low door lintel, and saw that a bathroom and laundry room had been added next to it, so at least there were some mod cons.

While Bryn busied himself slicing bread, he glanced at Josh over his shoulder. 'So you haven't got rid of your itchy feet then?'

'I don't know. I think I've seen just about everything I wanted to. I was in Peru two weeks ago and realised that Machu Picchu was the last thing on my bucket list.'

Josh had woken up in yet another unfamiliar bed and had had to think hard before remembering where he was. A faint feeling of breathlessness had reminded him – the ancient city of Cuzco in Peru was high up in the Andes where the air was thin and difficult to breathe. Still, it had been worth it. He'd been to see the glorious but eerie Inca hilltop town of Machu Picchu the previous day, something he'd longed to visit for ages, but that was the final item on his mental list of must-see places and afterwards he'd felt strangely restless and craving normality. Whatever that was going to be for him now. The only thing he was sure of was that he wanted to be among hills and fields full of sheep. He'd been dreaming about that for weeks.

'So that's when I went back to New Zealand to check on a few things and found the letter about Merrick Court.' He hadn't expected those hills to be in Wales, but now he was here he could see the landscape was very similar to that in his dreams. Was it a sign?

'Must have been a bit of a shock, as you said.' Bryn smiled and handed Josh a plate with a doorstep of a sandwich filled with ham, cheese and pickle.

'Cheers. Yes, can't say Wales was on my list of places to visit, although it should have been really. My grandparents on my mother's side were from around here. Plus, of course, my ancestors on the other side through whom I've inherited Merrick Court, although I knew nothing about that before receiving the lawyer's letter.'

'Ah, I thought you had the look of a Welshman about you.' Bryn smiled.

'You think?' Josh wasn't so sure. He decided to change the subject. 'Tell me a bit about Merrick Court. Why is there no staff other than yourself? I thought houses like that needed lots of servants.'

'Maybe in the old days, not so much now. No money, you see. The family spent it all.'

Josh frowned. 'But the land around here is good farm land and grazing, right? I thought the lawyer said the house came with hundreds of acres.' Small compared to the sheep station, but Harrison seemed to think it was vast.

'It does, but that doesn't bring in enough. Or not enough for some people.'

Josh read between the lines but wasn't sure if Bryn meant that Lady M or her late husband had been careless with money. He didn't want to ask. 'I'll have to look into it. And as I'll be here for a few days, maybe I can lend a hand in between seeing estate agents and things? I enjoyed digging this morning.' Josh grinned and the old man smiled back.

'Get away with you. You don't want to be doing that.'

'Sure I do. Too much leisure time can get a bit boring you know. I'd be happy to come and help.' He yawned. 'But maybe a bit later. I think the jet lag has just caught up with me.'

'I'll show you where the guest room is. Make yourself at home.'

'That'd be great.'

And he did feel at home. Almost like he belonged. Weird.

Raglan Castle, 22nd/23rd May 1646

Lady Margaret had said a horse would be waiting for Arabella where the trees started up again. Although most of the parkland had had to be cut down in order to prevent enemy soldiers from hiding there, once out of range of the castle's cannon some of the trees had been left standing. Here, Arabella found the horse and breathed a sigh of relief.

'There you are, my beauty,' she murmured, untying the reins from a sturdy branch. It wasn't much more than a pony, and a docile one at that, so she was able to clamber into the saddle with only a small amount of effort and soon she was on her way.

She stuck to the murky edges of the road, looking around continuously and trying to listen for any threatening sounds. She kept a tight hold of the reins in one hand while the other gripped a flintlock pistol. It was primed and loaded, but the safety lock was on. The marquis had showed her how to use it. 'But only in an emergency,' he'd warned. 'You have but the one shot.' She sincerely hoped she wouldn't need it.

She'd memorised the route she needed to take, sticking as much as possible to some of the smaller back roads and tracks which would take her to her destination faster. On horseback this was perfectly fine, whereas in a carriage she would have had to go via the main roads. The pony was sure-footed in the gloom of the late spring night, but whinnied a few times and pricked up its ears, making Arabella stop and glance behind her. She thought she caught the sound of hoof beats, but when she strained her ears there was nothing.

'I'm imagining things,' she murmured to the pony. 'And you're not helping. Let's go.'

A couple of hours later she stopped to dismount and tied the pony to a tree, leaving the reins long enough for it to be able to graze.

'You stay here and wait for me. I'll try to be quick.' She patted the horse's lovely forehead and slipped into a nearby copse of trees.

She was almost there and now stealth was of the essence. Her heart was beating triple time and she kept stopping to reassure herself there was no one about. But why would there be? It was the middle of the night. It wasn't just pursuers she was afraid of though, but the place she was heading towards – Merrick Court, her former home. Her own property, in fact, although at the moment it was held for the Parliamentarians by her uncle Huw. Her fists clenched at the thought of him. She almost wished he'd be the person to come across her as that would mean she could use her one and only shot on him.

Vile bastard.

As it wasn't entailed, Arabella had inherited the estate from her mother, Isabel, who'd been widowed at a young age. Huw – husband to her mother's sister – had been appointed as Arabella's guardian when Isabel died, but instead of protecting the inheritance, he'd exploited it for himself and tried to force her to marry into his family. It made Arabella's blood boil just to think of it. She took a calming breath. There was no time for such thoughts now. She had a task to perform and it had to be done quickly.

Huw didn't appear to be looking after her property particularly well as Arabella found a stretch of wall around the garden which was half falling down. This made it easy to climb over it and into the knot garden, exactly the place she wanted to be. She and her mother had spent many a companionable hour here during happier times. Sitting on a bench by the little fountain, which was in the farthest corner from the house, they'd chatted, laughed and taken the air, but Arabella didn't want to think about that now. Isabel was gone, and so were those carefree days.

The fountain no longer had any water in it but was overgrown with weeds, moss and lichen. Arabella knelt by the far side and took out a small spade from an inner pocket. She used it to prize up one of the paving stones that surrounded the fountain's rim. It took a bit of jiggling, but she soon managed it. After that, she dug a hole in the soft soil underneath, making sure that she shovelled the surplus soil into a small sack. Once the hole was deep enough, she began to retrieve various small packages from secret pockets on the inside of her skirt, depositing them in the cavity.

'These are all my best jewels,' Lady Margaret had told her. 'You'll be doing us a huge service by hiding these, thus hopefully keeping them safe. Then if we have to flee, we can retrieve them and at least we won't be destitute on the Continent, like so many others.'

'But why Merrick Court?' Arabella hadn't wanted to admit that it was the last place on earth she wanted to return to, but she was sure Lady Margaret knew that anyway.

'Where better? For one thing, it's your house so no one would think it odd if you were to be seen there. And for another, as it's now in the hands of the Parliamentarians, they won't think to look for *my* property there, will they?' She'd laughed. 'Hidden under their very noses, that's the best possible place.'

Arabella had to agree, it was ingenious, but it didn't make her happier about going there.

When she had put everything in the hole, she put back some of the soil, flattened it and replaced the paving stone exactly as it had been before. To make doubly sure no one would notice what she'd done, she pulled some of the weeds across. Then, after listening for a moment to make sure there was still no one around to surprise her, she repeated the process with another paving stone, slightly further away. This time it was quicker, as she only needed a very small hole for the necklace Lady Margaret had given her. For some reason, she didn't want it in the same place as the rest of the jewellery. Superstition, perhaps? She tore off a piece of her shift to wrap it in, even though the soil wouldn't harm it anyway.

'Oh, Mama, please watch over these treasures for me,' Arabella whispered, hoping her mother's spirit was somewhere nearby. There was no reply, of course, but she heard a breeze ripple through some nearby leaves and took that as a good sign.

When she was done hiding the cross, she made certain there was no sign of her having been here and once over the wall, she disposed of the surplus soil before hurrying back towards the pony. Now all she had to do was to return to Raglan before dawn.

Rhys waited behind a thicket, keeping his horse silent by rubbing his ears and patting the soft neck. 'Shhh, boy, I doubt we'll have long to wait,' he soothed in the lowest possible voice, although he had no way of knowing whether he would be kept kicking his heels for hours or minutes.

In the event, Arabella returned faster than he'd thought and he watched her climb onto her pony again, turning it to ride back towards Raglan. What on earth had she been up to in that garden? He knew well enough to whom it belonged; Huw Howell, a man he'd heard about. There was no doubt as to the man's allegiance and anyone associated with him was an enemy as far as Rhys was concerned.

Had she gone there to deliver a message? Report on the castle's defences and supplies? Such information would be invaluable to the enemy and if that's what she was doing, she would be putting all the stronghold's inhabitants at huge risk.

Rhys swore under his breath.

But what if it was the other way round and Arabella had been spying on Huw? Rhys decided he'd have to give her the benefit of the doubt for now, but he needed to keep an eye on her in future.

As before, she kept mainly to small roads and forest tracks, but closer to Raglan she followed a main road for a short way. Rhys kept his distance, trying to stay on the verges where he and his horse were in shadow and the grass muffled any hoof beats. As Arabella rounded a bend, Rhys suddenly heard voices and he pulled his mount to a stop. Now what? Another meeting?

'Stay,' he muttered to his horse, jumping to the ground. He had trained the stallion to obey such commands and trusted the animal would wait patiently.

He hurried through the bushes and trees by the side of the road until he had a clear view of what was happening with Arabella. She was still astride her horse, with two men on horseback facing her, although they were edging closer with an obvious view to hemming her in from either side.

'You expect us to believe you're out for a ride in the middle o' the night?' one man was saying. He guffawed. 'We weren't born yesterday, you know.'

The other man joined in the laughter. 'But we won't tell a soul, mistress, so long as you go with us. I'm sure we can come to some agreement, eh?'

Rhys swore again. So not an assignation then. There wasn't much moonlight but what there was showed him clearly that Arabella was petrified. Her eyes were wide open, her face paler than the moon itself. He clenched his fists, pulling a sharp knife out of his boot. He was good enough to hit one of the men at this distance and at the very least wound him, but that would give the other one the chance to grab Arabella.

'Cat got your tongue? Nothin' to say for yourself?'

As the men drew closer, Arabella was galvanised into action. Her hand came up and Rhys was astonished to see her pointing a pistol at the man nearest to her.

'Get away from me or I'll shoot,' she hissed, releasing the safety lock with an audible click. 'And don't think I can't do it.'

The man stopped moving for an instant, but then he laughed again. 'You can only hit one of us, so either way you can't win. Now be a good girl and put that down. We'll treat you right, see if we don't. There's no need for this.' He gestured towards the pistol.

'No! Don't come any nearer!'

Rhys had to do something. The men were edging closer once more and Arabella's gaze flickered from one to the other as if she wasn't sure how to handle the situation. He put his arm up to muffle his voice and hide his features with his sleeve. 'Shoot the right one, I'll deal with the other!' he shouted, throwing his knife with as much precision and accuracy as he could muster. It lodged deep in the left man's thigh and he gave a high-pitched squeal of pain and fell off his horse, clutching his leg.

Rhys ran towards his victim. 'Shoot, woman!' he yelled and Arabella pulled the trigger. There was a flash and a report, then the man to her right fell in his turn and landed with a thump. Rhys didn't look at him yet though. First he slapped the rump of Arabella's pony so hard it took off at a gallop. Then he bent to deliver an almighty punch to the man he'd thrown his knife at. The wailing stopped and Rhys retrieved his weapon. He doubted the man would die, but he'd be incapacitated for quite a while.

Glancing at the second man, he saw him struggle to sit up while clutching his side.

'Bitch! I'll get her! I'll—'

Rhys delivered another punch, knocking the man out flat. 'You'll do no such thing,' he muttered. He removed the man's hand and moved his jacket to one side. There was a bloodstain spreading across his shirt, but it didn't look like anything vital had been hit. A shame, but then Rhys had to be grateful Arabella had hit the man at all as she clearly wasn't experienced with weapons.

He made sure the two men were still unconscious, then went to retrieve his horse. The further away he was when they came to, the better. And he needed to make sure Arabella reached the castle without further incident.

Blasted woman ... If only he knew what she'd been doing.

Arabella was still feeling a bit shaky, despite having made it back to the castle safely. She'd left the horse where she had found him and slipped in through the small door in the South Gate. The gatekeeper must have been told to look out for her as he let her in without questions. She headed straight for Lady Margaret's rooms and knocked softly.

'Oh, there you are at last! I've been so worried. Is all well?'

Arabella was enveloped in a lavender-scented embrace and couldn't help a shiver from running through her. 'Y-yes, it is now,' she murmured.

Lady Margaret held her at arm's length and studied her in the pale dawn light seeping in through the windows. 'Now? What happened? Were you attacked? Robbed? My dear, if anything bad has befallen you, I'll never forgive myself ...'

'No. Well, yes. I mean ...' Arabella was having trouble stringing her thoughts together as the delayed shock of what had so nearly occurred set in. She took a deep breath and tried again. 'I went to ... the place you asked me to and performed the task as planned.' She didn't want to spell it out just in case anyone was listening. You never knew, there could be spies about. 'And then ...'

Lady Margaret nodded. 'Yes, and then ...?'

'On the way back, I was accosted by two men. I believe they were slightly in their cups, but they ... they wanted me to, er, go with them.'

Lady Margaret gasped. 'They forced you? Oh, my dear girl.'

'No, they didn't succeed, mostly thanks to my protector. I must thank you for arranging that. I thought I was on my own.'

'Protector? You must be mistaken. No one was supposed

to know about this venture apart from myself, you and his lordship.' Lady Margaret frowned. 'Someone helped you?'

Arabella nodded. 'Yes. I held up the pistol and was pointing it at one of the men, telling them to leave me alone, but of course I could only shoot one and they knew it. Before I had time to pull the trigger though, someone incapacitated the man on my left and shouted at me to shoot the other one. So I ... I d-did.'

She couldn't help the wobble in her voice as she thought about the fact that she'd shot a human being, possibly even killed him. Such violence was foreign to her nature and although it was happening every day all over the country, she had never thought she'd have to do any killing herself. Lady Margaret was made of sterner stuff.

'Good,' she said. 'They were probably the enemy. Think no more about it. I'm so relieved you are safe, but I wonder who your saviour was.'

'I have no idea. I didn't see his face and his voice was muffled.'

'Well, perhaps he was just an enemy of the two who waylaid you. I don't suppose we'll ever know. The main thing is that you're back.' Lady Margaret put an arm round Arabella's shoulders and led her towards a truckle bed in a small dressing room. 'And now you must have some rest. Sleep in here and I'll make sure you are not disturbed.'

'Thank you, you're very kind.'

'No, thank *you*. You have done us a great service and I won't forget. Neither will the marquis, I promise.'

Arabella lay down on the soft mattress, still shivering intermittently, but she was so exhausted from the long ride and all the nervous tension she'd expended, she soon felt her eyelids droop.

Thank the Lord she was safe, at least for the moment.

Chapter Ten

Tess was tempted to stay in bed the next morning, but now her time at Merrick Court was coming to an end, she needed to be more dynamic. Rosie's prodding was annoying, but even more irritating was that her sister-in-law was right – it was time to get started on Giles's papers.

Giles had used the library as his study and it was a lovely place, lined with old-fashioned bookcases, all glass-fronted and made of polished mahogany. Sitting down behind his desk felt all kinds of wrong, but it had to be done. She needed to put all his papers in order before the new heir took over. Josh. She wondered if he'd come over again today, maybe to look around some more? Well, he could tour the house by himself this time. She had things to do and being with him unsettled her. She didn't want to speculate as to why that was.

Taking a deep breath, she decided to start with the desk drawers.

Giles had never been tidy and Tess was appalled to find all manner of things just crammed in – bills, letters, receipts, old envelopes. With a sigh, she went to find some plastic bin liners and started to go through the bits and pieces one by one. Two hours later she'd reached the final drawer, the bottom right hand one, and found it difficult to open. This proved to be because it contained an absolutely massive old Bible with worn leather covers – it weighed a tonne, as she found when she lifted it out.

'Why on earth did Giles keep this here?' Tess muttered. He and his relatives weren't a religious family so it could have just been put on a shelf with all the other books. When she opened it to give the front page a cursory glance, however, she had her answer – there were a lot of handwritten notes; information about family births, deaths and marriages.

The records only went as far back as the early eighteen-hundreds, which was rather annoying as Tess would have liked to find some mention from the time of the Civil War. Merrick Court wasn't far from Raglan Castle, as the crow flew, and it would have been perfectly possible – even probable – that there was some connection between the two estates. And having seen the castle and read about its final stand against the Parliamentarian troops, her curiosity was piqued. Were the inhabitants of the Court on the same side as those of Raglan or were they enemies? Royalists or Roundheads?

Could there even be a link of some sort? That might justify the strange dreams she'd had since visiting. But perhaps it was just that she had somehow connected with a spirit or a person's soul from there when she was at Raglan. She had no idea if that was even possible, never having been interested in paranormal things.

'Or maybe it's the antidepressants?' she whispered. Even though she'd stopped taking them, she ought to go and see her doctor to ask if the medication had any lasting effects, like hallucinations.

She was about to put the Bible away when some of the bottom leaves folded in on themselves, refusing to lie straight. Tess flipped open the weighty tome again in order to straighten the pages, but gasped when she found why it wasn't closing properly – someone had carved out a hole inside the back part of the book, going through at least half an inch of pages. It seemed a terrible waste of such a beautiful old tome, but it was a perfect hiding place and nestled inside was a twist of silky material in a faded red colour. She took this out, carefully so as not to damage what looked like very old cloth, and peeled it back to reveal an earring.

'Oh!' It was small but beautiful. A thick gold hoop with a blue stone shaped like a teardrop hanging from it, also surrounded by gold. As she held it up to the light to admire the pure aqua colour, Tess could see it was an intaglio; an image was carved out of the back of the gemstone, like an indentation. It felt hollow to the touch while from the front the image was clear – a little lion with a crown on its head inside a very ornate letter C.

She couldn't resist trying it on. There was a mirror over a nearby marble fireplace and she carefully threaded the earring's fastening through one of the holes in her left ear. Tess had several on either side, usually just with plain gold hoops in each, so this one complemented them nicely.

'Gorgeous!' A thrill raced through her and it was almost as though she'd connected with the previous owner of the lovely jewel. One of Giles's long lost ancestors? No, she was being silly and fanciful. But someone who lived at Merrick Court had worn this and if she wasn't mistaken it had been a present from a king – either Charles I or II – which made it very special indeed. Why on earth hadn't Giles ever told her about it or shown it to her? It must have been extremely precious to him if he hadn't sold it when he was so desperate for money.

It occurred to her that as there was only one perhaps it was meant for a man? Charles I had worn a pearl earring. Tess had seen it for herself in an exhibition at London's Victoria & Albert Museum where it was claimed the king had still been wearing it when he went to his execution, a gruesome fact she wasn't sure she'd wanted to know. So maybe he'd owned this earring as well and given it to whichever one of Giles's ancestors was around at the time? And then it would have been passed from father to son, which could explain why Giles hadn't shown it to her.

She'd refused to give him that son.

Sadness made her lungs constrict and she sank into the nearest armchair. Giles was gone. He would never have children; the son and heir he'd wanted so badly. It wasn't Tess's fault as such – as they'd been on the brink of divorce he could easily have had them with someone else – but the fact that the house was now going to a stranger seemed wrong. However nice he may be, Josh obviously had no feeling for his inheritance and he'd be breaking the chain if he sold Merrick Court. Exactly what Giles had been trying to prevent. But Tess had thought there was still plenty of time for him. If it hadn't been for that stupid accident ...

'I'm so sorry it turned out like this, Giles,' she murmured, hoping he could hear her. 'You would have found someone else to give you an heir if you hadn't decided to drive home that night after drinking with your friends.'

Hopefully Josh would at least take over the burden of continuing the line. Even if he sold the house, he was still the Earl of Merrick and his descendants after him.

Tess took the earring up to her room for safekeeping, but before putting it in a drawer, she sat on the edge of her bed and stared at the pretty jewel. It felt right, as if it belonged in her hand, and she closed her fingers around it momentarily. She should probably give it to Josh, but as the current Countess of Merrick she was the rightful owner for now and she wasn't giving it up. Not yet.

She held it up to the light and admired the aquamarine colour, the exact hue of the water in a warm ocean lagoon. Crowding into her mind came images of other jewels, sapphires, rubies, strings of pearls, a magnificent cross ...

***

Merrick Cottage, 23rd May 2016

Josh woke to find that he'd slept round the clock and it was almost lunchtime the next day. He'd been in a deep sleep, but with the weirdest dreams of castles, people in strange clothing, talk of war and horse riding ... What was all that about?

He shook his head. Who cared? Jet lag sure did strange things to you. His stomach growled, reminding him he'd missed dinner. Time for a visit to the local pub – he'd treat Bryn to a meal and a pint as a thank you – and never mind the dreams.

Bryn had just returned from a morning's gardening and was happy to show Josh the way to the Merrick Arms. Situated in the middle of Much Merrick village, it wasn't a large establishment, but the food was home-cooked and the two of them were soon tucking into some pork sausages and mash.

'Mmm, great stuff. Haven't had spuds in ages,' Josh murmured. He'd been eating the food from so many different cultures during the last six months it was great to just have something familiar.

Returning to the subject they'd been discussing the day before, Josh asked, 'So Merrick Court's land, is it rented out?'

'Yes, to Fred Williams. He's up at the Home Farm.' Seeing Josh's no doubt bewildered expression, Bryn explained. 'Home Farm means it used to belong to the Court, producing everything they needed back in the day.'

'Oh, I see. So Mr Williams rents extra land now then?'

'Yes, for grazing his sheep and bullocks. The Home Farm is quite large, but he wanted to expand his herds and the late Lord Merrick wasn't interested in farming himself.'

'What was he like?' Josh was curious about what kind of husband had caught a woman like Tess.

'Like? Er, well, fairly easy-going, a bit used to getting his own way, but then people like him always are, eh?' Bryn smiled. 'No, he was nice enough, always treated me well.' He took a sip of his beer. 'He was a bit older than Lady M, ten years, maybe? Surprised everyone when he upped and married her.'

'Why?' Josh could see perfectly well why anyone would want to marry Tess – that wasn't rocket science. She was quite simply gorgeous.

'Oh, you know how these toffs are, they think things like what family you're from is important. Lady M wasn't one of them. She was just an ordinary girl.' Bryn lowered his voice. 'Between you and me, I don't think Miss Rosie ever took to her. A bit of a stuck-up one, she is.' Bryn winked. 'But you never heard that from me.'

Josh smiled. 'Heard what?' But Bryn had given him food for thought. 'So I'm guessing that's why Mrs Edmonton looked at me as if I was something the cat had dragged in.'

'Did she? Oh dear.' Bryn shook his head as if he despaired of the woman. 'Well, I will say this for her, she's very keen on preserving the family's inheritance and all that. She would've made a much better master of the house than her brother ever did. Don't get me wrong, he was proud of it all, but she'd have been more careful in looking after it.'

'I suppose you really do think I'm nuts for wanting to sell?' Josh could hear the unspoken words loud and clear.

Bryn looked away. 'No, no, it's up to you. Doesn't suit everyone and you obviously weren't brought up to expect it.'

No, but Josh had been raised to inherit his father's property, and although he'd never quite understood that obsession with passing it on to his heirs, maybe it wasn't so different from Merrick Court after all? It was the history of it, the fact that so many generations of the family had owned it before him. At least, that's what his father had always gone on about.

But Josh didn't want the bloody sheep station. No way. Not because he didn't like sheep farming, but simply because it had been his father's. Miserable old codger …

The last day, before leaving his father's former property for good, he'd shouted, 'Bastard!' hoping Robert's spirit could hear him, although he'd said as much to his old man face-to-face the last time he saw him alive.

Glancing towards the wrap-around porch that surrounded the homestead, he thought he'd seen movement on the old bench to the left of the front door. The one where Robert had always sat of an evening with a beer in his hand. The hazy outline of a human shape, undulating slightly in the afternoon heat? Josh had narrowed his eyes and stared intently, then smiled. 'So you heard me, eh? Good.'

The shadow had stirred restlessly and Josh didn't doubt it was Robert, but the old man was powerless now. Josh could feel it and it was clear the spirit understood that too, hence the agitation. 'I hope you're sent on your way to hell soon,' had been his parting shot to Robert's shadowy form. Or maybe having to watch his only son abandon the land he'd loved so much was Robert's own personal hell? The perfect punishment.

His mind returned to the present. Agitated ghosts or not, he certainly wasn't going back there. But did that mean he ought to hang onto this new inheritance instead? He was starting to feel torn.

'Why don't you stay yere a while, get a feel for the place, like?' Bryn suggested, as if he'd picked up on Josh's confusion. 'You're very welcome to my guest room for as long as you want. I'm not expecting any other visitors. If you ask me, you're making a very big decision in a hurry. That's never a good thing in my experience.'

Josh nodded. Bryn was right. 'Are you sure? I can always rent somewhere for a few weeks. I'm not short of funds.'

'No, it'll be nice to have the company. I get a bit lonely at times.'

'Thank you, I will then, but I insist on paying you rent. And if I sell the estate, I'll make it a condition that you get to stay in that cottage for the rest of your life. Deal?'

Bryn's weather-beaten features split into a huge grin.

'Sounds more than fair to me.' He stuck out his hand to shake. 'You have yourself a deal, boy.'

Merrick Court, 24th May 2016

Tess had had another look at the earring before going to bed the night before and woke to find that she'd fallen asleep clutching the little jewel so hard it had left a mark on her palm. A perfect imprint of the lion and crown motif. She had the ridiculous notion she'd been branded somehow.

'Idiot,' she muttered to herself.

But she was feeling unsettled as she'd had disturbing dreams. Raglan Castle had featured, she was sure of it, although there had only been shadowy outlines of the towers in darkness. They felt familiar, safe, and yet frightening at the same time – love and menace combined in a way that made her feel trapped. Why was she dreaming about it? She should never have gone there. The place had obviously cast some sort of spell over her.

She decided that perhaps if she found out a bit more about the castle the dreams would stop? What she needed was facts.

She dressed quickly and headed down to the library. Although she'd gone through most of Giles's effects now, there was still an old cupboard left. It was one of her favourite pieces of furniture in the house as it was a large chinoiserie style cabinet with lots of little drawers, shelves and pigeonholes. It occurred to her that it might have secret drawers too – didn't old furniture often have that? But her questing fingers didn't trigger any opening mechanisms and unfortunately most of the drawers proved to be empty.

'Damn!'

She'd so been hoping to find something exciting, but the

cupboard only contained one thing – a rusty metal box with a lock. Eventually she located the key for it on a bunch which had been kept in Giles's desk drawer. She lifted out a pile of documents, taking care not to damage them in any way, and then tried to decipher the old-fashioned swirly handwriting on the uppermost sheet. It took a while for her eyes to get used to it, but once she figured out what each letter looked like, they began to come together into words.

It was some sort of official deed with a seal attached on a ribbon and her heart beat a little faster when she saw the signature – Charles R. An actual original letter from the king? Surely not? It certainly had the appearance of something very old; dirty, faded and a bit creased, brownish in colour, with a few ink blobs and jagged edges that were flaking into dust. And that seal, hanging off a tatty ribbon of indeterminate colour.

Which king though? A quick check of the date – June 1660 – meant it had to be Charles II and although some of the ink was faded, she could make out that this was a letter confirming someone as Earl of Merrick, with lots of legal phrases about the estate and lands. Presumably the first earl then? But who was he? The name, unfortunately, was illegible, but it was still an amazing document.

'Damn it, Giles, why didn't you show me this? Explain your heritage in more detail?'

Instead he'd spouted a lot of crap about how being a lord gave him responsibilities and that, as his wife, she had to share them by producing children. That just made him sound pompous and selfish, as if he didn't care about her feelings on the subject, as if marrying a lord automatically carried with it the duty of getting pregnant as quickly as possible. Too old-fashioned for words.

She settled down to try to read a few more of the ancient letters, scanning them for any mention of Raglan Castle or the Civil War. The castle wasn't featured, but she did find one letter from someone who signed themselves *Marchioness of Worcester* in 1650. It was a short note thanking her '*dear Arbella*' for keeping her promise and returning '*what bellonged untoe me*'. Whatever that was? At the end, there was an intriguing sentence though: '*I pray you keepe the amythyst croʃs with my hartfelt gratitude – your loyalltie more than deserves it and I miss it not at all. I hope it brings you goode fortune.*'

Was that the Merrick treasure that was rumoured to be buried somewhere in the house or grounds? An amethyst cross? It certainly sounded grand, but not the sort of thing she'd envisaged when Giles went on about it. He'd made it sound like a chest full of gold doubloons or something, a proper pirate's hoard.

'Oh, what does it matter though?' she said out loud. Whatever it was, it was still lost.

Tess put the papers back inside the metal box and noticed a small black USB pen in one corner, which she'd previously missed. Presumably it had copies of important documents from Giles's computer, but she didn't have time to look now so she put it in a pencil pot on the desk. She carried the box up to her room for safekeeping. She wasn't quite sure why she didn't want it to stay in the library, but some sixth sense warned her to store anything she found in her own room for now. It felt right, like a sanctuary of sorts.

She remembered her original reason for going down to the library that morning – to find out more about the castle and the Civil War – and grabbed some old histories of the area to look at later. For now, she'd spent enough time indoors.

Rather than continue with the gardening, she went to her workshop, another converted stable. Her business was painting old furniture, 'up-cycling' as the interior decorators called it, and it was something she loved. She'd started to do quite well before Giles's accident, but lost heart afterwards.

It was time to get back into it as she'd need money to live off. She decided to finish some pieces so she could sell them on eBay or Etsy.

You're not just hiding out in the workshop in order to avoid Josh? a little voice inside her head asked. Maybe. She was afraid of the feelings he'd stirred up inside her so it was better if she didn't have to see him. After Giles's death, she hadn't thought she'd be attracted to anyone for a very long time, yet here she was only six months after the accident with her hormones running rampant. The mere sight of Josh's bare, tanned chest had been enough to unsettle her. It was ridiculous and it seemed wrong. Disrespectful, somehow.

But it shouldn't do, really. She and Giles had been over and maybe now it was time to move on?

Chapter Eleven

Tess had just gone inside to grab something for lunch when the front doorbell sounded.

'Hi, am I disturbing you?' Josh was outside, looking a bit hesitant which was ridiculous, considering he owned the place now.

'No, come in. You surprised me, that's all. We usually use the back door.'

'Oh, well you brought me in this way so I assumed ... but I'll remember for next time.'

His smile was disarming and Tess found herself smiling back. 'I'll give you a key. Sorry, I should've done before now.'

'Cheers. I promise I won't come in without knocking though. Wouldn't want to catch you in your undies or something.' He wiggled his eyebrows in comical fashion.

Tess felt her cheeks flame at the thought of him seeing her in her underwear, although that was silly. She turned away. 'I was just making a sandwich. Want anything?'

'No, thanks. I thought I'd have another look round, if that's okay?' He followed her into the kitchen. 'I'll need to get some local estate agents to come and give me an estimate so I at least know what figures we're talking about.'

'Local estate agents?' Tess stared at him, sandwich forgotten. 'Are you kidding?'

Josh frowned. 'Well, yeah, they'll know the area best, right?'

'No, no, what you need are the big London agents. The ones who advertise in *Country Life*.'

'*Country Life*?' Josh leaned against the Aga and folded his arms over his chest. Tess noticed he was wearing board shorts and flip-flops today, and a part of her couldn't wait to see Rosie's reaction to that.

She returned her thoughts to the matter under discussion. 'It's a magazine. Very posh. All the really big estates and expensive properties are advertised in there. That way they attract the richest buyers. No way are the little local estate agents going to be able to afford that.'

'Ah, I get that.'

'Here, have a look.' Tess went through a pile of old magazines on the dresser and found a copy. 'This is a bit out of date, but you'll see what I mean.'

Josh flicked through it, looking thoughtful. 'Hmm, interesting. Some of these are a tad pricey.'

'Mm-hmm.'

'Do you mind if I borrow this? I can make some calls later.'

'Sure, go ahead.'

'Great. I'll just go and make some notes then so I know what to tell them.' He took a small notebook and pen out of his pocket.

'Didn't Mr Harrison give you all the details?'

'Yeah, but I like to see for myself. His description was … er, a bit dry.' Josh grinned. 'Lawyer-speak.'

Tess laughed. 'Fine, well, you go ahead. Oh, and here are the keys.' She pulled out an extra set from a drawer and handed it to him. A warm feeling shot through her as their hands connected, but she steeled herself against it. He wasn't staying and, even if he was, she shouldn't be interested. She was the widow of his predecessor – could you get more complicated than that?

Rhys had followed Arabella all the way back to the castle the day before, making sure there were no other mishaps, but at the same time he'd debated whether he should have left her to fend for herself. After all, if she was a Parliamentarian spy, she didn't deserve his protection. But he couldn't be certain of her allegiance and didn't want to do her a disservice. The fact that he found her attractive had nothing to do with the matter, or so he told himself. He would have done the same for any lone female in need of assistance. It was the gentlemanly thing to do.

He needed proof before confronting her with any accusations.

He'd settled into the garrison and had been assigned a position by Lord Charles, the marquis's fourth son who was the governor. As he'd brought his own horse and equipment, Rhys didn't need to be outfitted in any way, which sped up the process considerably. He had simply been allocated a bed in a room with five other cavalry officers and told to join in the daily drills held in the Stone Court.

In his spare time, he set out to learn as much as he could about the inhabitants of the castle and to that end, he swiftly managed to charm some of the maids who looked after the nobly born ladies housed in the grand apartments around the Fountain Court. One, called Esther, proved to be a goldmine of information today, especially about Arabella Dauncey.

'Oh, a lovely lady, so she is. Not too demanding, you know, like some,' Esther confided. 'But then she's probably very grateful to be here, after all. She owes his lordship a debt.'

Rhys was intrigued. 'Really? He's lent her money?'

Esther laughed out loud. 'That's not what I meant at all. No, Mistress Dauncey came here to escape persecution, so she did.'

'Right. She's a Papist then, same as most people at Raglan?' Although he was sure Arabella had said she wasn't. Was she a liar as well as a spy? He supposed the two went together.

Esther shook her head. 'Not that kind of persecution, the family kind. I probably shouldn't be telling you this ...'

'I won't tell a soul, I swear.' Rhys gave the maid his best smile, hoping it was enough. It usually was, he'd found. There were very few ladies who weren't susceptible to his charming ways when he chose to exert himself, although he seldom did as he didn't like using his looks to deceive people into trusting him. He'd been disgusted by some of the fancy London gentlemen he'd met in Oxford who did just that in order to dupe poor, unsuspecting females into parting with not just their jewels, but their virtues as well.

'If I hear that you've told tales ...' Esther looked mildly threatening and Rhys opened his eyes wide to give her an innocent gaze.

'On my honour, not a word.' He put his hand on his heart for emphasis and Esther smiled. Wild horses probably wouldn't have stopped her gossiping, no matter what he'd said.

'Well, then ...' Esther crossed her arms over her ample bosom and leaned against a wall, obviously settling in for a long tale. Rhys tried not to show his impatience and continued to smile as she carried on. 'Mistress Dauncey has an evil uncle – though he might be an uncle by marriage I think as his name is Howell, not Dauncey like hers – and he wanted her lands for himself and his nephew. She's an heiress, you see, with a big estate over Bergavenny way, and the uncle thought to keep it in the family, as it were, by marrying her to the nephew. Well, she was no more than a slip of a girl, thirteen maybe fourteen or so, and not willing, but they tried to force her.'

'No!' Rhys acted shocked as Esther seemed to be relishing her story.

'Oh, yes, though really they should've asked the king for permission first, like.'

'The king?' Rhys was getting confused.

'Not personally, you know, but it was something to do with a Court of … Orphans?' Esther frowned, as if she was repeating something she'd heard but didn't understand.

'Ah, you mean the Court of Wards?' Rhys knew what that was. An official body that was supposed to look after the interests of rich orphaned heiresses, although from what he'd been told, its officials could be bribed to turn a blind eye.

'Yes, that's the one. The uncle should've asked them, but I think they'd expect payment and he weren't willing, so he tried to push her into the marriage by other means. She escaped one dark night and rode her horse all the way here, then waited outside the castle till morning and asked to speak to Lord Worcester. He was impressed by her courage and said he'd protect her until a better match could be found for her.'

'That's quite a story!' Rhys didn't have to pretend, he really was amazed. Not many fourteen-year-old girls would take matters into their own hands like that. He could see why the marquis might have been sympathetic. All women were supposed to have the choice to say no to a repugnant marriage, even if many were 'persuaded' by parents and guardians. Or perhaps his lordship had seen a potential match for someone in his own family? But no, Rhys didn't believe that as the old man he'd met with had seemed supremely honourable.

'Isn't it just?' Esther seemed pleased to have been able to relay all this gossip to one who'd never heard it before.

'But what if the uncle comes here to claim her? Isn't he her legal guardian? Or is that the Court of Wards?'

Esther shrugged. 'I've no idea, but I doubt he'd want to go against his lordship. Would you? And him not even a knight. No, he's kept his distance, probably enjoying the profits from Mistress Dauncey's lands for as long as he can, the knave.'

'Well, thank you for telling me, that was an interesting tale. Now what about everyone else? What should I know about the other inhabitants of Raglan?' Rhys didn't really want to know, but couldn't be seen to be too interested in only one particular woman.

Esther proceeded to regale him with more gossip than he'd ever wanted to hear in his life, but as he'd had the information he needed, he pretended to listen with the odd exclamation and smile. He might need the maid's help again so it was best to keep in her good graces.

While she prattled on, his mind turned over the information about Arabella. So Huw Howell was her uncle by marriage. Interesting. The man who was running the estate Arabella had visited last night – Merrick Court. Howell was a nasty piece of work by all accounts. Rhys had never met the man himself, but he'd heard of him.

'That's one Roundhead you want to keep away from,' someone had told him. 'Shoots Royalists on sight without asking their business if they come to his estate, or so I've heard. A friend of mine barely escaped with his life while his fellow officer was killed.'

This would tally with Esther's description, apart from the fact that the estate apparently wasn't Huw Howell's, but Arabella's. What if it was all a Roundhead plot and she was in cahoots with the uncle? Although Arabella had been at the castle for years, perhaps she was a spy sent here by Howell to infiltrate the marquis's household. With her beauty and those big, guileless eyes she looked appealing enough that anyone could be fooled by her supposed innocence and she would hear plenty of interesting snippets which she could pass on. Was her loveliness only skin-deep? Did she and her uncle pose a danger to everyone in Raglan Castle?

He wished he knew.

He had to admit he'd been taken in by her himself, if indeed she was acting a part. At first, it hadn't even occurred to him that she may be dissembling, but now he was on his guard. He'd be watching her to see if she really was what she seemed – a young woman who'd been wronged.

Angry with himself for falling under her spell so easily, he determined to keep an eye on her as much as his duties permitted.

<hr />

Merrick Court, 24th May 2016

Josh wandered round the house, making notes and drawing himself rough room plans. He needed them just to find his way, if nothing else, as Merrick Court was like some sort of giant puzzle. Had any planning gone into this at all? He was beginning to doubt it.

Sure, each part of the house had a layout that made sense in isolation, but it was as though the family had just kept tacking on new bits whenever they felt like it and none of it gelled properly. He had to admit it was quirky though. And charming.

Damn, he was really starting to like it.

'Oh, at last! Tess said you were around somewhere but I couldn't find you.' Mrs Edmonton – Rosie – came striding towards him down a corridor on the second floor.

Josh braced himself. What did the woman want now? Bryn's remarks had only confirmed Josh's instinctive dislike of her, although he couldn't quite explain why he felt so strongly about it. Normally he was very laid-back and loved meeting new people, accepting them as they were. Rosie, however, set his teeth on edge. 'I've been up here for a while now,' he said. 'It's easy to get lost.'

'Oh, one gets used to it.' She briefly eyed his board shorts and old T-shirt with a wrinkled nose, but seemed to force herself to concentrate on his face instead, schooling her expression into a polite mask.

One? Who did she think she was, the Queen? But Josh didn't say that out loud. 'So why were you looking for me?'

'I thought maybe we could do lunch?'

Do lunch? Was that, like, having sex and eating at the same time? Josh almost snorted out loud, then got his unruly thoughts under control. He wouldn't 'do' this woman for anything, even though she wasn't bad looking. 'Er, thanks, but I was about to head out into the garden. I promised Bryn I'd help him out for a while.'

Rosie frowned. 'I'm sure he can cope well enough with his job on his own. That's what he's paid for, after all.'

'Well, he's getting on a bit, you know?'

'I suppose, but then he'll be retiring soon, I expect.'

Her easy dismissal of Bryn riled Josh. 'Not unless he wants to,' he said firmly. 'I'll make sure anyone who buys this house keeps him on for as long as he likes. With assistance. For now, he and I need to make the garden more presentable since your family have let it go to rack and ruin. It might make it more appealing to anyone coming to view the house. Most people don't want a jungle outside their front door.' That was a bit harsh, but the garden was in a bad state, she surely couldn't dispute that.

Rosie glared at him. 'My brother had better things to spend money on. Houses like this practically eat cash – there's always something that needs repairing. And it's not cheap. With listed buildings you have to follow special regulations and use only proper materials and so on.'

'I'll keep that in mind if I ever want anything fixed. Now,

if you'll excuse me, I'm going outside.' Josh headed for the nearest staircase, which he hoped would take him down to the hall, or at least somewhere in the house he recognised.

Rosie called after him. 'Why don't you come back for tea and we can discuss the sale of the house a bit more? I really think you ought to consider your duty to the family.'

Jeez, she was a bulldog, this one. Josh turned just before setting his foot on the top step. 'So far I haven't been made to feel part of the family, so I don't think I owe you anything. You want to buy this place – make me an offer I can't refuse.'

Chapter Twelve

Tess had spent the rest of the day in her workshop and hadn't seen Josh again. She assumed he'd finished his notes and was now busy ringing estate agents. Why that thought upset her, she didn't know. It wasn't as though she'd expected him to stay on so what did it matter who owned the house? But somehow it did, because it would have been important to Giles.

Rosie had gone out in a huff, muttering something about stubborn Aussies, so Tess was surprised to hear the front door bell again. Had Josh lost his key already? But when she opened the door she found a man standing outside looking up at the façade of the house. She reckoned he was mid-forties or so and some sort of businessman as he was dressed in a very sharp suit with matching silk tie. Ginger hair, cropped very close to his head, glinted in the sunlight. The look suited him, the way it did the actor Bruce Willis in an action hero kind of way. There wasn't an ounce of fat on him, as far as Tess could see, so he obviously kept himself fit as well.

'It really is a lovely old place you've got here, isn't it?' he commented, then held out his hand. 'Marcus Steele, friend of your late husband's. We met when I came here to stay for a weekend.' He smiled and just like the movie star he resembled, this man had dimples that made his smile appealing.

Tess couldn't recall having seen him before, but didn't want to be impolite. She shook his hand briefly. 'Oh, right.' Whenever Giles brought friends she'd stayed out of the way, especially if they didn't bring wives or girlfriends. They invariably came for long weekends of poker, which wasn't her thing at all.

'I'm really sorry to disturb you, but I've come about a business dealing I had with Giles. Do you have a moment? I've written to you several times but you haven't been in touch.'

'Er, I suppose so.' Tess didn't really want to let the man in. Something about him made her wary, although she couldn't say why. He seemed harmless enough, suave and charming, so there was no reason for her to take against him. And he'd been a friend of Giles's. 'This way, please.'

She didn't remember reading any letters from anyone called Steele, but until recently she'd only been opening envelopes with red on the outside. Everything else had seemed like too much of an effort and probably junk mail. Maybe she should have checked? Damn that medication. She'd let everything slip.

She led him through the hall and down the steps into the kitchen. 'Tea? Coffee?' she asked, even though she'd rather he just stated his business and left.

'A coffee would be great, thank you.'

He took a seat at the big table and waited while she prepared two mugs. She saw him looking around, as if he was trying to put a value on everything in the room. Was he a high-class burglar, casing the joint or whatever it was called? A shiver of apprehension ran through her, but then she shook her head at herself – she really was letting her imagination run riot at the moment. He was probably just admiring the grandeur, like everyone else did the first time they came here.

She noticed he also gave her the once-over and wished she'd been wearing more than a T-shirt and shorts. His gaze lingered far too long on her bare legs for comfort.

'Here you go.' She put the mug in front of him and sat down, hiding her legs under the table. 'Now, what was it you wanted to discuss, Mr Steele?'

'Marcus, please.'

'Right. Marcus.' Tess didn't know why, but she definitely didn't want to be on first name terms with this man, but again it felt churlish to refuse.

'Well, *Lady Merrick* ...' The way he emphasised her name made it sound like he was waiting for her to tell him to use her first name, but she pretended not to notice. 'I'm afraid to tell you that you owe me a lot of money. Or rather, your late husband did, but as he's no longer with us, his debts have become yours. I've waited a while out of consideration for your ... emotions. It can't have been easy for you, losing him so young. But I'm sorry to say I really can't wait any longer. As I said, I've already written several times but rather than call in the debt-collectors, I thought I'd come and discuss it in person.'

'Debts?' Tess's heart sank. What had Giles done? But she could guess, even before Marcus confirmed it.

'Gambling. I own a casino in Bristol – The Black Rose – and Giles was a frequent customer there in the months leading up to his, uhm, demise. I extended him credit, in return for IOU's, as a favour, because I'd known him for quite a while, but his luck didn't seem to be in.' He shrugged and spread his hands. 'I'm sorry, but I have no option but to claim it back from you. It should have been paid months ago, actually.'

Tess was reeling from the disclosure that she apparently owed this man money, but mostly from the fact that Giles hadn't told her the truth. He'd promised he wasn't gambling and had never mentioned The Black Rose. As he'd said, what was there to gamble *with*? Nothing. But instead he'd signed IOU's? *The stupid, lying bastard ...*

Her thoughts drifted back to the first time she'd seen Giles. They'd met in a casino, where she was working as a croupier to help pay for her art college tuition fees, but she'd thought then that he was only there with friends.

It wasn't until much later she learned that he was an inveterate gambler, playing anything from roulette, to black jack, poker or whatever. Gambling fever, that's what they called it, and he'd been unable to stop. Until he had to, or so she'd thought.

More fool her. She should have known he'd never quit.

She considered how to reply, but then remembered that she wasn't in a position to pay anything at the moment. And perhaps the money owed would come out of the whole of Giles's estate, not just her portion? She'd have to check with Mr Harrison. Josh wouldn't be pleased if that was the case. 'I'm afraid I can't help you right now, Marcus,' she said, trying not to show how shaken she was. 'You will have to contact my late husband's lawyers.'

'What, you haven't had probate yet? But it's been months!' Marcus looked shocked, then added jokingly, 'I'd sack your solicitor if I was you.'

She shook her head. 'No, no, we have, but I haven't inherited all this.' She waved her hand to indicate the house. 'In fact, I'll be moving out soon. The house is entailed in the male line so there's a new owner.'

'Entailed? Never heard of that.'

'It means only the men of the family can inherit in a direct line from father to son, not widows, daughters or sisters and their children. So you may have to lodge your claim on the estate.'

He frowned. 'I don't have time to mess around with lawyers. I was given to understand that Giles had assets other than this house and it can't all be entailed, so you'll have your share.'

Tess shook her head. 'A few bits and pieces, but nothing much of value.'

'There must be something – jewellery or such like? I'm sure your husband bought you a diamond necklace or two. You can give me that on account for now and I promise to be patient for a while longer until you can come up with the rest.'

Tess stood up and glared at him. 'If you must know, Giles sold all my jewellery so he'd have money to gamble with. You've probably already had the proceeds if it was your establishment where he was hanging out. Now, please, take the matter up with the estate's solicitors.'

She'd expected him to stand up as well, but he stayed where he was, looking up at her through slightly narrowed lids as if he was considering whether to believe her or not. 'Well,' he finally said, and got to his feet, pushing the chair in slowly. 'I can see this has come as a bit of a shock to you, and I'm sorry about that, but I would much rather we sorted it out between us, just you and me, without involving the law. I'll contact you again when you've had time to think it over a bit. There has to be another way.'

Tess felt the blood drain from her face. Another way? She didn't want to even think about what that might mean. She took a deep breath. 'Just out of interest, how much are we talking about?'

'Five hundred thousand pounds, give or take a penny or two.'

Shock reverberated through her. 'I don't believe you.'

He walked round the table and stopped in front of her, a little too close for comfort. The look he gave her was sympathetic. 'I'm afraid huge sums are won and lost every night at The Black Rose. Giles was well aware of that and it was his choice to carry on playing. I'll send you copies of the IOU's. I'm sure you're familiar with his handwriting.' He stuck out his hand. 'Lovely to meet you again, Lady Merrick, even though it's under such sad circumstances. I really am sorry for your loss.'

She took his hand reluctantly and felt his large fingers enclose her delicate ones. Bracing herself for them to be crushed, she was surprised at the gentleness of his grip, almost as though he wanted to caress her hand, which was somehow worse. She snatched it away and was just about to answer him when a cheery voice from the back door forestalled her.

'Hey, Tess, where do you want these?' Josh had come in without knocking, carrying a small basket of eggs. 'Oh, sorry, didn't know you had visitors.'

Tess breathed a secret sigh of relief. Thank goodness for Josh. Marcus had backed off and was now staring at Josh instead, no doubt taking in the muscles on display as the man was shirtless yet again. This time Tess was glad of it.

'Marcus was just leaving,' she said. 'Perhaps you wouldn't mind going out the back way? We don't use the front much.'

The man hesitated for a fraction of a second, then nodded. 'I'll be in touch.'

As soon as he'd gone, Tess's legs gave way and she sank down onto the chair and buried her face in her hands. 'Jesus!' she exclaimed.

'What did he do? Did he hurt you?' Josh came over to crouch in front of her and looked up at her with an expression that was part worry, part anger. 'Do you want me to go after him? Make sure he doesn't come again?'

'No, thanks, it's okay. He was perfectly pleasant. I'll get the lawyers to sort him out.'

Josh took the chair Marcus had vacated. 'Want to tell me what that was all about? I know, it's none of my business, but he looked like a smarmy bastard.'

'Oh? I thought it was just my imagination. He was very polite and ...' Tess drew in a deep breath, still quaking inwardly after the unpleasant revelations of Giles's debt. 'He owns a casino in Bristol. Said that my late husband owed him five hundred thousand pounds. And he wants me to pay him back.'

'Bloody hell! Five hundred grand?'

'I know, right? Crazy. I told him I didn't believe him so he's going to send me proof. Or so he said. I'll just pass it on to the lawyers.' She gave a hollow laugh. 'I may live in a stately home right now, but I'm not rich. And I really don't think the contents of this house will fetch anything like that sum. So this Marcus guy will have to get his money some other way.'

'Five hundred grand?' Josh still seemed stuck on the enormous sum. 'Did your husband have that kind of money to spend on gambling?'

'No, of course not. He wasn't supposed to even *be* at Marcus's casino. We had agreed ... but obviously I shouldn't have believed Giles.' She shrugged, tamping down on the anger that surged through her again at his perfidy. 'I think it was an illness, you know? He just couldn't stop.'

'Yeah, I know what you mean. I had an ancestor like that apparently, but he came good in the end. Come to think of it, he was your husband's ancestor too. Maybe it runs in the family? Seems like I dodged a bullet there.'

'Yes, well, Giles never got as far as beating it. I did tell him to get help, but that just made him annoyed. He said it wasn't a problem and I should "lighten up".' She snorted. 'Not sure how that would have helped.' She leaned her forehead on the table. 'And, hell, why am I telling you all this? I don't even know you really.'

'Because I'm a good listener and I'm family, according to your sister-in-law? And I swear I can keep it to myself, don't worry.'

Tess sighed and looked up at him. 'Thanks, I'd appreciate it.' He looked sincere and she believed him. Somehow she knew her secrets were safe with him.

'Besides, it explains a lot. I had been wondering about the poor state of the garden and some of the rooms.'

'Yes, no money left for such boring things.' Tess tried not to sound bitter, but she'd tried to reason with Giles about it so many times, it was a sore subject. 'Anyway, thanks for the eggs,' she added with a small smile. 'Bryn's new hens laying already?'

'Er, no, the chooks are still settling in. I bought these.' Josh smiled back, his eyes twinkling.

'What?'

'I didn't like the look of that bastard when he arrived in his sleek, black BMW. Saw him outside. I just wanted to check and make sure you were okay and the eggs were the only thing I could come up with at short notice. I'd just been grocery shopping this morning.'

Tess couldn't help it, she laughed. 'That's the dumbest thing I've heard in a long time.'

Josh chuckled. 'Isn't it just? Sorry. I'll try to come up with a more plausible excuse next time.' He stood up. 'Right, better get back to the garden or Bryn will wonder what's happened to me. Later.'

'Okay. Thank you, Josh. Really.'

'No worries.'

'Let's hope there isn't a next time,' she muttered after he'd gone. She never wanted to see Marcus Steele again.

Taking the coffee mugs over to the sink, she had the urge to scrub them until every trace of the slick bastard was gone. It was ridiculous, but she actually wanted to throw away the mug he'd used as it would always remind her of him now. That was a bit of an overreaction though, so instead she filled the sink with water and loads of washing-up liquid to leave the mugs to soak. 'Kills all known germs' proclaimed the washing-up label. 'I certainly hope so,' Tess said out loud.

She stared into the foaming water as the sink filled up and forgot about Marcus as in her mind's eye she saw a pair of gorgeous green eyes staring at her with real concern in their depths. Josh, her knight in shining armour ...

* * *

Marcus Steele floored the accelerator and left the stately pile in a shower of gravel and stones. 'Damn it!' He banged his hand on the steering wheel, needing an outlet for the fury surging through him in uncontrollable waves, but it wasn't enough. He wanted to hit something, shout and curse, throttle the woman ... although really he was mostly angry at himself for being attracted to her and for being conned by her late husband.

He tried taking a few deep breaths to calm down but couldn't stop his hands from shaking with suppressed violence. '*Aaargh!*' He let rip with an almighty shout of frustration and that helped a little bit.

He wasn't quite sure why he was so unbelievably angry. He normally had more control over himself than that, but the moment he'd stepped into that bloody great house it was as though someone had lit a fuse inside him. Invaded his brain and planted a grenade in there. He'd had a hard time acting calm.

It was supposed to have been so easy. Wait a couple of months until probate had been granted. Send a few threatening letters. Show her copies of the bits of paper her husband had signed and hey presto – lots of cash. But from her vacant look when he mentioned the letters, he guessed the stupid woman hadn't even opened them. What was the matter with her? Was she on drugs? One of those society women who snorted cocaine? It wouldn't surprise him. He'd met his fair share of those.

Included in his plan had been the possibility that she would need a man to lean on in her grief, a man who was prepared to write off a small part of the debt in exchange for her spending a bit of time with him. Although, naturally, he wouldn't have put it quite so bluntly. That man would have been Marcus if he'd played his cards right. Instead he was leaving empty-handed, without even having had the opportunity to ask her out for a drink. Damn that handyman or whatever he was. She was supposed to have been alone and vulnerable.

Shit. She was a looker and no mistake, and Marcus wanted her as well as the money. Actually, no, he wanted her more. His obsession with her had begun during his one and only stay at Merrick Court the previous year and he'd been unable to let it go. He had no idea why as there were plenty of women in the world, but from the moment he'd set eyes on her at that country weekend of Giles's, he'd fallen in lust. One way or another, he'd have her.

Giles. 'Weak tosser,' Marcus muttered.

He'd had him pegged as a good source of income from the first time he'd seen him. Giles always had that fanatical look on his face that only a true gambler had, even when sober. And he was a rubbish player, no matter what game he attempted. Marcus had befriended him and watched the man win and lose over the course of a year, sometimes allowing him a large win just to lull him into a false sense of security. Then the real losses had started, ending in IOU's, which would hopefully force Giles to sell the country mansion he so frequently mentioned. His pride and joy.

The man had proved uncommonly stubborn though. 'There's no way I can sell the place, it's been in my family for generations,' he'd protested. 'I'll sell something else.' But he didn't and Marcus eventually lost patience and threatened legal action. That should have been that, but Giles turned the tables on him.

The bastard.

Marcus couldn't believe he'd been duped. Giles may have been a moron when it came to gambling, but he'd had a cunning streak that appeared when he was cornered. Instead of selling his house and paying up, he'd secretly filmed one of the croupiers on his mobile. How he'd guessed that the croupier was cheating in Giles's favour, Marcus would never know, but the evidence was irrefutable.

'So now we're quits,' Giles had told him. 'Tear up those IOU's or I go to the police.'

Marcus did, although he kept duplicates. He wasn't stupid. And he made Giles throw away his iPhone, plus he had the man's computer hacked to make sure there weren't any copies of the short film. Giles died shortly afterwards and Marcus's forethought should have paid off today. How was he to know the woman couldn't inherit the house? Damn, but he should have checked. It wasn't like him to be so sloppy, but the possibility of an entail had never occurred to him. Why would it? He'd never heard of such a thing.

Who the hell left stuff only to male heirs these days? It had to be illegal in this age of female equality and all that. Bloody aristocrats, still stuck in the Dark Ages. And why hadn't Giles mentioned it? Stupid git.

'Ah, to hell with it!'

His fury ignited further the more he thought about what she'd said. *Lady Merrick*. Hadn't even told him her first name, although he knew it already. He honked at a slow driver, just to give further vent to his frustration. He still didn't quite believe her. A trophy wife like that; she had to be lying about her own wealth. Her sort – beautiful, expensively glossy and much younger than their husbands – were canny as hell and he was sure she'd have a stash somewhere. Switzerland probably.

Well, he'd wait a bit and maybe pay her another visit. In the meantime, he'd have her watched. Let her stew for a while, then hopefully she'd be more amenable. And next time he'd come when the handyman wasn't around. He wanted his money and he'd waited long enough.

And he wanted her.

Chapter Thirteen

Raglan Castle, 25th May 1646

'Mistress Dauncey, are you well?'

Arabella looked up, her cheeks heating in a guilty flush. She was sitting on some steps at the base of the Great Tower, next to the moat, neglecting her duties. Had Rhys come to find her and tell her off on behalf of someone? She hadn't thought she'd be missed.

'Er, yes, very well, thank you. I was just—' She started to rise.

'No, no, don't stand up on my account.' He waved her to stay seated. 'May I join you for a moment?'

'If you wish.' The Great Tower could only be reached via the family's private rooms in the castle, so strictly speaking Rhys shouldn't be there either. 'How did you get here?'

'I was on my way back from delivering a message to the marquis when I spotted you through one of the windows.' He pointed up at the beautifully arched windows of the private apartments that overlooked this part of the tower. 'Took me a while to find you though. I had no idea there was a kitchen down here.'

The Great Tower had its own kitchen and water supply on the lowest floor of the building, which meant it could be used as a final refuge during a siege. The thick walls ought to withstand even the worst bombardment, and the moat helped too, of course, keeping the enemy at a distance. Arabella privately doubted anyone would last very long even so – it would be a matter of how much food was left and whether help was on its way. No point making a stand here otherwise.

'Yes, I suppose it will be needed soon with so many more mouths to feed. I believe we are upwards of eight hundred people in the castle now.' It seemed like madness and yet the soldiers were necessary for their defence.

'You keep track of such things?' Rhys regarded her with a smile, but she sensed there was more to his question than polite conversation.

She shrugged. 'Not really. It was just something I heard others speak of. Why, is it a secret?'

'No, not here, but there may be those who would be interested in finding out the exact strength of the marquis's garrison.'

Was he accusing her of being a spy? That was rich, coming from someone who'd only just arrived from the-Lord-only-knew-where. She glared at him. 'Well, I'll not be telling anyone, if that is what you're implying. I won't be setting foot outside the castle until the war is over, I can assure you.'

Although she *had* been outside so recently, she wasn't planning on repeating the journey. Not if she could help it, anyway.

He held up his hands, as if surrendering. 'I wasn't implying anything. Just commenting. We can't be too careful.'

'Indeed.' And that reminded her that she ought not to be sitting here with a strange man all alone. 'Now I had better return to my duties. Will you find your way out again or do you need assistance?'

'Thank you, but I think I can manage. I'll just stay here a while longer. It's such a peaceful spot. Thank you for leading me to it.'

She almost snorted – as if that had been her intention. But she contented herself with giving him a curt nod before going inside because his smile told her he knew what she was thinking. That man saw far too much and who was to say *he* wasn't a spy? It was an unsettling thought.

Following another bad night, this time filled with nightmares about menacing casino owners, Tess spent the day painting in her workshop while considering what to do about Marcus Steele. The promised copies of the IOU's had been emailed to her as scans and Tess had printed them out. They did indeed appear to be signed by Giles, but without seeing the originals, she couldn't possibly tell whether they were fake or not. She supposed Marcus could have heard about her bereavement somehow and decided to scam her as he'd thought her a wealthy widow. But there seemed to be more to it than that – his visit had been personal somehow. Why?

The email had contained a reminder for her to keep the matter between them. 'I think we're alike that way, you and I,' he'd added. 'We prefer to keep our business private.'

Damn right. But there was no way she could pay him. She had phoned Mr Harrison to ask his advice, in general terms.

'I just wanted to know who would be liable for any of Giles's debts, should they come to light. Me, the heir of the Merrick estate, or both?'

'I'll have to look into it,' he'd said. 'Leave it with me.'

Late afternoon, she returned to the house and sat in the kitchen nursing a tension headache. Thankfully Rosie was out with friends, so the house was quiet. Tess was pleased to be spared having to make conversation, but she had to admit it had been reassuring to have Rosie in the house the previous evening when she'd felt a bit shaken.

A knock sounded at the back door and Tess jumped. Had the annoying man come back already? Surely he'd give her more than twenty-four hours to come up with half a million pounds?

'Who is it?' she called out. She'd taken the precaution of

locking the door earlier when she came in, something she wouldn't normally have done until evening.

'Josh. Got a sec, Lady M?'

Relief surged through her and she opened the door. 'I thought we agreed it was Tess,' she scolded to hide the quiver in her voice, but she was smiling to show she could take a joke.

He grinned back. 'Lady M sounds much more ... exotic.'

It certainly did when he said it in his delicious accent. She wondered what he'd been going to say instead of 'exotic' but decided not to ask. And in the next moment she forgot anyway, as she spotted a dog lurking behind his legs. 'You brought a dog from New Zealand?'

Josh laughed out loud. 'No, I wouldn't wish that flight on any animal, it's bad enough for us humans. This here is Vincent. He's from the local rescue centre. Can we come in?'

'Er, sure. Vincent? What kind of name is that for a dog?' Tess stood back to let them pass and the dog threw her a wary look as he slunk in behind Josh. She was glad to see the man was wearing a T-shirt today, although it didn't make much difference as it stretched tight across his chest and arms in a way that emphasised his physique even more. His jeans were the old and ripped black ones he'd worn the first time she saw him, and she caught herself checking out his bum as he passed her. She almost shook her head at herself. What was the matter with her? She wasn't a teenager, for heaven's sake.

'Sit. Good boy.' Josh leaned on the old dresser while Vincent obediently sat by his side. 'He's been well trained, but sadly his owner died recently. The rescue place was looking for someone to foster him for a while and maybe take him on permanently if they like him. I was wondering if you'd like to have a go?'

'M-me?' Tess stammered. 'Why would you think I'd want a dog?'

Josh's eyes became serious. 'They're great for guarding people.'

'What? Oh.' The penny dropped. Josh had obviously figured she should have some protection against men like Marcus Steele. A warm feeling surged through her at the thought that someone cared about her well-being – although why Josh did, she had no idea – but if she'd wanted a dog she would have bought one herself. 'Well, it's very kind of you to think of me, but I couldn't possibly take on a pet. What would I do with him when I have to go out? And I have no idea where I'll be moving to. Could be a flat where pets aren't allowed.' She could always rent a small cottage with a garden, but she didn't mention that.

'No problem. Bryn will have him, I asked.'

'But ...' Tess was feeling as if she was being bulldozed here. He could at least have consulted her first.

As if he'd read her thoughts, Josh gave her a mischievous smile. 'I thought I'd just bring him. That way you might fall in love with him and not be able to take him back to the centre.' The smile turned into a teasing grin. 'Think of him, sitting in a cage with his little bundle of possessions, waiting for someone to love him again and watching as all the families with kids go straight for the puppies while ignoring him and—'

'Okay, okay, stop! You are so not guilt-tripping me into this. If you feel so bad for him, *you* have him.' But he'd already planted a vivid image in her brain and Tess almost groaned out loud. She looked at Vincent, sitting there so patiently, his big eyes watching her every move. It wasn't difficult to picture him in a kennel at the rescue centre, waiting day in and day out for someone who never came. Oh, hell ...

'But I don't need a guard dog. You do.' Josh's smile said

he knew his logic was faultless. And it was, damn him. 'The alternative is I move in here with you, but I still don't feel right about that.'

Tess didn't want that either. Or so she told herself, although the thought of having Josh in the house was rather appealing. She kneeled on the floor and held out her hand for Vincent to sniff. 'Hey, Vince, are you a good boy, like this guy says? Have you been having a rough time?'

Vincent's eyes said a definite 'yes'. He sniffed her and then lay down, letting her pat him on the head and scratch behind his ears, before moving onto his stomach. He seemed to be desperate for affection, but at the same time a bit shy. Tess continued to murmur to him until he relaxed and she could see he'd accepted her as a friend. He really was beautiful, black and white, some sort of Collie cross – big enough to be dangerous if he had to, but soft enough to be cute. And he was cute. She couldn't resist those melting brown eyes. Double damn. Tess was sure Josh would have been aware of that when he chose the dog. But how had he known that she liked them?

Bryn, of course. She'd often talked to the old gardener about the dog she'd had as a child, a lovely Lassie type.

She sighed. 'Fostering, you said? That's, like, not permanent, right?'

'Nope. Not unless you want it to be.' Josh's eyes were dancing, as if he was pretty sure he'd won. Possibly he was also fully aware that if she took this dog into her home, Tess would never be able to let him go. But if Bryn was there to help, what was to stop her? Giles hadn't wanted any pets, but he was gone. And Tess was lonely.

'All right, he can stay,' she said. 'But if I have any trouble, you're the one who'll be taking him back. Deal?'

'Deal.' Josh held out his hand for her to shake. She took it and felt reassured by the solid, warm feel of it. She wasn't completely alone. Someone had her back, at least for now.

'Want to stay for dinner?' she asked, without thinking. 'I've made ratatouille and rice.' She'd made a big pot, thinking she could save money by freezing it in portions, but what the heck ... Josh had done her a kindness. He deserved to at least be given dinner, if he wanted it.

'Sure, thanks. That'd be great. Let me just pop out to my car to get Vincent's stuff. I bought some tins of dog food while I was out.'

'Oh, right, thank you.' Tess felt stupid. She hadn't even considered that she'd have to feed Vincent as well. How would she afford that? But maybe dog food was cheap. As Josh came through the door again, she could see that she didn't need to worry about it for quite a while. He'd obviously been to a cash and carry as he had two whole trays full of tins and a sack of some kind of biscuits too. Vincent thumped his tail on the floor at the sight and Tess smiled at the dog. 'So you know what that is, huh? Okay, we'll feed you in a minute.'

Tess went to the dresser and collected plates, glasses and cutlery. She was slightly regretting the invitation now, as she didn't really know Josh that well and she hadn't had dinner alone with a man since ... well, since Giles.

'Here, give those to me and I'll lay the table.' Josh held out his hands for the crockery. 'Then you can sort out the food.'

Tess nodded and tried not to look at him as their fingers met under the plates. She ruffled Vincent's ears on the way to the Aga, where the ratatouille had been simmering in the oven. She took it out and put in on the table, together with a bag of grated cheese and some rice from a rice cooker. She'd bought one ages ago as it kept the rice warm for up to two days, which was ideal when you lived alone and only wanted small portions.

'Wine? Beer?' She had a bottle of red somewhere and a crate of beer that Giles had bought but never had a chance to finish before the accident happened.

'Beer please, if that's okay?'

'Yup. Er, do we feed Vincent first or …?'

'Well, strictly speaking dogs should really wait for their masters to eat but personally I think that's mean so he may as well have his dinner at the same time. I'll sort it.'

He'd brought two dog bowls, one of which he filled with cold water, and he emptied the contents of a tin into the other, together with some dog biscuits from the sack. No sooner had he put the bowls down than the food was gone. Vincent ate in about five seconds flat.

'Good grief! Did they forget to feed him at the centre?' Tess blinked at the dog, who was now eyeing the table.

Josh chuckled. 'Nah, I think he just wanted to make sure no one else got to it first.'

'Not much chance of that! They wouldn't even see it.' Tess sat down and gestured for Josh to do the same. 'Please, help yourself. And sorry, Vince, but you are *not* having this as well.'

They ate in silence for a while, but it wasn't the strained kind, more of a companionable one. Tess had missed having someone to share meals with and it was lovely not to be alone for once. The massive kitchen felt warmer somehow. And once they started to talk, she discovered that Josh was good company.

'Bryn told me you're a sheep farmer,' Tess commented. 'Have you left your flock with family?' She was curious about him, but didn't want to ask outright. He wasn't wearing a wedding ring, but for a working man, that wasn't unusual. It would probably just get in the way.

He shook his head. 'That's not exactly right – I've worked with sheep on and off all my life, but I only recently, uhm … acquired a sheep station. Before that I worked for other people. Anyway I sold it. The whole shebang. High country stations aren't as lucrative as they used to be and I had itchy feet. I've been travelling for months all over the world, visiting all the places I'd always dreamed of seeing. I just wanted to be free for a while, before I decided what to do next.'

'You travelled alone?'

Josh smiled as if he knew exactly what she was asking. His eyes took on a teasing glint. 'Well, yeah, I couldn't afford to bring my wife and ten kids so they had to stay behind and fend for themselves.'

'Ten?' Tess felt her eyes widening and Josh laughed.

'No, just kidding. Do I look old enough to have ten kids?'

'Er, I don't know ...' Tess didn't want to offend him, but she had no idea how old he was. Again, he second-guessed her.

'Okay, maybe I do. I'm thirty-four, so technically I could've had them, I guess. But there's only one, a daughter, and my ex-wife has sole custody of her so it wasn't a problem.'

Ex-wife. For some reason that word made Tess want to smile, but she suppressed it. 'I see,' she said. 'You must miss her though. Didn't you want to bring her over to see your new inheritance? Before you sold it, I mean.'

Josh's expression clouded over and he looked away, taking a swig of beer as if he needed to think about the answer. 'Yeah, I'd have loved for her to come with me, but Isla, my ex, and I don't get on too well.' He made a face. 'No, understatement of the year, actually. She hates my guts so I don't think she'd let me take Shayla out of the country. Maybe when she's older ...'

'That's a shame.' Tess didn't know what else to say. It seemed selfish of the woman to deny her child a holiday with her dad, just because you didn't get on with your ex. But it wasn't for her to comment.

'So what about you? What's your story?' Josh was very obviously changing the subject and Tess sensed he'd said more than he'd intended to.

'You mean, how did I end up here in this ancient pile?'

Josh smiled again. 'Yeah, that.'

'Short version – I was studying art, working as a croupier on weekends to help pay my way, Giles came in with a group of friends and that was it. We got married six months later.'

'Whirlwind romance, huh?'

'I guess you could say that.' She'd been young and in love, or so she thought. Giles was the dream boyfriend – rich, titled and with this amazing house – but she'd fallen for him because of his easy charm. A shame he'd stopped using it on her as soon as she no longer fell in with what he wanted.

'So how long were you married for?' Josh's question snapped her out of the regrets.

'Four years.' She sighed. 'Anyway, no point thinking about it now. Although it's kind of hard not to, as I'm still here.'

'Don't you like this house? I'd have thought it was every woman's dream home.' Josh glanced around the kitchen, which admittedly *was* probably most people's dream even though it was so shabby now. She'd always thought it the best room in the house; warm, cheerful and cosy despite its size.

'Yes, of course I do, but it's not mine, is it? Never has been, really. Somehow I never felt as though I belonged. Silly, maybe, but there it is.'

'Guess you're not going to kill me for selling it then, the way your sister-in-law wants to do.' Josh sent her a mischievous smile.

'Hmm, you know what? I actually might.'

'What?' His smiled turned into an expression of surprise. 'Why?'

'As Giles kept telling me, this house has been in his family – *your* family – since the Norman Conquest. That's 1066, in case you don't study that kind of thing in New Zealand, so nearly a thousand years – and it would be such a shame if it had to be sold to someone who'd never appreciate that heritage and had no connection with it. How many houses do you think have had that kind of continuity? I should think it's very rare. And you're about to break it.'

She really didn't want the chain of inheritance from father to child to be broken, now that she finally understood why it had mattered so much to Giles.

'That does sound awesome when you put it like that,' Josh agreed, looking thoughtful.

Before he could say anything else, Vincent startled them by jumping up suddenly to bark at the door. Tess put a hand on her chest. 'Jesus, he nearly gave me a heart attack but at least it proves he's a good guard dog. What is it, boy?'

Josh grabbed the dog's collar just in time as he began to bark even more when the door opened and Rosie walked in. 'Shh, easy boy. Quiet!'

Vincent obeyed, but he kept his eyes on Rosie, who glared back, but she only looked at the dog for a short while before transferring her gaze to Tess and Josh. 'What's going on here? Entertaining men already, Therese? And Giles barely cold in his grave.'

Tess gasped. 'For heaven's sake, Rosie, do you have to say things like that?' Talk about insensitive. But Rosie's cheeks were a bit flushed and Tess guessed she'd had a little too much to drink. She probably shouldn't even have been driving. Honestly, what was it with members of this family? They all thought they were above the law.

She tried not to show the anger that threatened to choke her. 'Why shouldn't Josh be here? It's his house. And he very kindly brought Vincent for me.' She indicated the dog.

'You've bought a dog? Whatever for? I thought you said you couldn't afford food for yourself, never mind a mutt.'

Even though that had been Tess's own reaction, she didn't

want to hear it from Rosie. 'I'll manage,' she answered between clenched teeth. 'And he might only be staying for a while.'

'Well, keep him away from me. I don't want dog hair all over my clothes, thank you very much. I hope he's sleeping in the stables. Papa's gun dogs always did.'

'Actually, he's sleeping on my bed.' Tess hadn't even thought about it, but decided this on the spur of the moment. Where better to protect her, after all?

She saw Josh's eyes flash with amusement, but he quickly looked down, finished his beer and stood up. 'Thank you for dinner,' he said politely. 'And I hope Vince behaves himself ... on your bed.' The twinkle was back, but thankfully Rosie didn't see it as she was busy making tea, yet again dumping her tea bag in the sink. Tess counted silently to ten. One of these days she was going to go and put the damn thing in Rosie's handbag.

'You're welcome.'

She followed him to the door and whispered, 'Thank you for Vincent. I'll let you know how we get on.'

'You'll be fine. Goodnight.'

Tess decided to forget the washing up and just head straight for bed. She let Vince out to lift his leg and then called him in. He came immediately, as obedient as Josh had said, and trotted after her when she headed for her room.

Rosie couldn't resist having the last word though. 'I hope you realise how disgraceful it is, you disporting yourself with that Aussie when you're so recently widowed. I suppose you're hoping he'll let you stay on permanently.' She laughed, then hiccupped. 'I doubt he'll want Giles's leftovers. And what will the neighbours think?'

'Sod the neighbours,' Tess snarled. 'And for the umpteenth time, he's from New Zealand and he was just eating dinner, that's all.'

She stalked up the stairs and only calmed down when

she had cooled her flaming cheeks with water. Damn Rosie. Did she expect Tess to live the rest of her life like a nun? Okay, so maybe six months wasn't very long, but it wasn't like she'd been sleeping with Josh. They'd been having a civilised meal, nothing more. And the thought of charming Josh into letting her stay on – as his mistress was what she assumed Rosie had meant – had never so much as entered her head.

The sooner Rosie went home, the better.

Chapter Fourteen

Raglan Castle, 3rd June 1646

'May I help you with that, Mistress Dauncey?'

Arabella peered round a mountain of bedding to find Rhys with his arms outstretched, ready to help her.

'Thank you, if you're sure you don't have something better to do?'

'I'm off duty for the moment.' He flashed a smile at her. 'There's only so much drilling we can do in one day and there isn't room for all of us at once in the Stone Court.'

'Very well.' Arabella tried not to show that his smile made her feel as if the day was suddenly brighter. That was a ridiculous notion and she really mustn't let herself even think such nonsense. She was grateful for his offer of help though and offloaded half the pile – several heavy woollen blankets, some sheets and a bolster. Her arms relaxed as she readjusted the rest of the bed linen she was carrying. 'I'm not going far, but there are a number of stairs to negotiate.' She headed towards the south-east range of rooms, situated to the left of the South Gate, and entered via a private staircase just inside the entrance passage to the gate.

A door stood open on the ground floor, showing that the room inside was luxuriously appointed. A huge fireplace with red stone surround dominated one wall, and the room was panelled in gleaming dark wood throughout. It wasn't where Arabella was headed, however, and she continued up the stairs.

'To tell you the truth, I was glad to escape,' Rhys told her as they made their way up to the second floor. 'The company of so many men can become very wearisome and over on this side of the Great Hall seems like a haven of tranquillity.'

'Yes, well, from what I hear, it won't be for much longer. I doubt the Parliamentarians will care which part of the castle they attack.' She hesitated. 'Is there any news? Do you know when they will be arriving to besiege us? It's only a question of time, isn't it?'

Most of the men in the household refused to discuss such things with the women, perhaps in the misguided belief that they shouldn't scare them more than was necessary. But Arabella felt that it was better to know – the uncertainty made her more nervous. She was therefore grateful when Rhys replied truthfully.

'They'll be here soon. No one knows exactly when, but his lordship's scouts have seen them approaching.' He looked around as they entered a rather grand bedchamber with windows overlooking the moat. It too was covered in gleaming oak panelling and had window seats and beautiful wall hangings, but the fireplace was smaller than the one downstairs with a simple carved stone surround. 'Who lives here?'

'Family members usually, although at the moment there are guests staying in this room.' She indicated the extra mattresses on the floor and two truckle beds peeping out from under the frame of a large half tester bed. 'As I'm sure you've heard, quite a few of the marquis's neighbours have come to seek shelter in the castle and everyone is having to squeeze in wherever they can.' She left the pile of bedding on the bed and indicated that Rhys should do the same.

He deposited his load and sent her a teasing grin. 'Well, it's not often I am taken to a sumptuous bedchamber by a beautiful young lady. I'm blessed indeed today.'

Arabella drew in a sharp breath. He may be jesting, but his words hinted at things no lady should even think about and she felt her face grow hot. Belatedly it dawned on her that she shouldn't be in here alone with him, even though the door was open, but despite the appreciative glance that accompanied his words, she didn't think he'd take advantage of this opportunity the way other men might. She sensed he was a gentleman.

'You asked to come along,' she replied somewhat tartly and went over to one of the windows in order to put some distance between them. 'I didn't invite you.'

'True. Still, now that we're here …' He chuckled and she turned to give him a frosty glare.

'Behave, Mr Cadell.'

'It's Sir Rhys, actually, but you can just call me Rhys if you like.' He followed her to the window but he was looking at her, not the view.

'Oh, I beg your pardon, I didn't realise.' How had she missed that? She must have been so intent on the man himself when he first arrived that she hadn't heard any introductions. 'But I can't be that familiar with you. We barely know each other.'

'I'm sure we could do something about that.' His lovely Welsh accent washed over her and for a mad moment she almost nodded agreement, but then sanity returned.

'Sir Rhys!' She pretended an outrage she didn't really feel.

He laughed. 'I only meant we could get to know one another by having conversations, like we are now.'

'Oh. Right.'

'Why, what did you think I meant?' The teasing note was back in his voice and she sent him another glare.

'Nothing.' Glancing out the window, she decided it was safest to change the subject and watched the work that was still ongoing outside. 'Have they many more trenches to dig?'

She heard Rhys step closer to stand behind her and although he didn't touch her, she could feel his nearness. It sent a shimmer of awareness down her spine, which she tried to ignore.

'I think it's more or less done,' he replied. 'Trenches,

ramparts, bastions, it's all in place. Now they're just carrying more supplies out there – muskets, bullets and so on.'

Lord Worcester had ordered outworks to be built all along the south-east and west of the castle which was the most vulnerable. On the other side lay the fishponds and a hill, plus more earthworks.

Rhys sighed. 'It won't hold them off forever though. We'll have to hope for reinforcements or assistance from elsewhere if we are to be victorious.'

Arabella turned and found herself so close her nose almost touched the top part of his leather jerkin. She took a step back and looked up at him. 'And is there any likelihood of that?'

He hesitated for a moment, then shook his head. 'I doubt it, unless there's a miracle of some sort. I'm afraid I don't believe in those.'

'Lord Glamorgan …?'

'Is still incarcerated in Ireland, or so I've heard. Even if he were to be freed, I don't think the Irish would follow him to England. Most people can feel when something is a lost cause and there's no money left. With the king a prisoner of the Scots and no pay, where's the incentive to fight? I'm sorry. I wish I could give you better news.'

'Don't be. Truly, I appreciate your honesty. And now, I had better carry on. I'm sure Mrs Watson will have more work for me. Thank you for your help.'

He stepped aside and gave her a slight bow. 'It was my pleasure. Perhaps we can continue our conversation some other time.'

Arabella couldn't help but smile at his persistence. 'We'll see,' she said, but she wasn't fooling herself. She was counting on it.

Just as she reached the door she heard him swear softly and then the clanging of a bell started echoing round the courtyards. There was a lot of shouting and the sounds of running feet. She turned to stare at Rhys, her heartbeat speeding up. 'What is it?' He was staring out the window, scowling, so she crossed the room to join him again. 'Tell me, please.' But she could see for herself what was happening.

To the left, just coming into view, were a huge number of men marching into some of the fields surrounding the castle and village. Wisely, they were staying out of range of any cannon or musket fire, but they were still close enough to be clearly visible.

'The New Model Army, curse them,' Rhys muttered. 'This lot is under the command of Colonel Thomas Morgan, if the scouts are right.'

There were hundreds of enemy soldiers, if not thousands, or so it seemed. As Arabella and Rhys watched in silence, they just kept coming in a never-ending stream. Most of them were wearing identical red coats which made Arabella think of blood. She put a hand to her mouth to stop a gasp from escaping. No, she must stay calm and block such irrational thoughts. The colour of their coats didn't matter – perhaps the vivid scarlet would even be of help to the garrison inside the castle as they'd make it easier to spot the Parliamentarians.

'We are vastly outnumbered,' Arabella whispered. How could Lord Worcester ever have thought that they would withstand a siege by so many? But perhaps he'd known all along that it was hopeless and it was just that his honour forbade him from surrendering without a token fight.

'Perhaps,' Rhys said quietly, 'but not by much as yet. We'll have to try to fight them off before any more arrive.'

'You think that's possible?' She looked up at him, wanting reassurance but at the same time the truth.

He nodded. 'Right now, yes. We have eight hundred odd men and can make sallies and surprise attacks. With a bit of luck, who knows what we can achieve? But it will have to be soon.' He took her hand and pulled her away from the window and the frightening sight of the besiegers. 'I must go back and get ready. Please, stay away from any windows and be careful whenever you cross the courtyard. And keep a weapon of some sort with you at all times.'

'A ... a weapon?' Arabella swallowed hard. He thought she might have to fight?

'Just as a precaution.' His voice was calm, reasonable. 'Nothing should happen to you, but in case you ever need to fend someone off, it would be good if you carried a small knife or something. Do you have one?'

'No.'

'Then I'll find one for you.' He squeezed her hand, then guided her towards the door with a light touch on her elbow. 'Don't worry, I'm sure you won't need it but I'm a great believer in being prepared for the worst.'

Arabella pulled herself together and nodded. 'Yes, you're right. Thank you.' There was no point panicking. The siege hadn't even properly begun yet and she should have thought of this herself. It was only common sense. But it was all so overwhelming, now that she'd seen the army massing outside. It had been easier to think straight when it was all merely a probability, not reality.

Just before they reached the bottom of the stairs, he stopped her by putting his hand on her arm. 'Mistress Dauncey?'

'Yes?'

'God keep you safe.' He bent down and gave her a soft kiss. 'I will see you soon.'

He disappeared before she had time to reply and she just stood there, one hand raised to touch her lips, the other clutching her ribcage. She found that she didn't mind him taking such a liberty – she was more afraid that he'd never have a chance to do it again.

'Dear God, please watch over him,' she whispered.

She wanted him to stay safe too.

Rhys cursed himself for a fool all the way across the Fountain Court. Why on earth had he kissed the woman? He'd meant to keep up a light flirtation in order to lull her into a false sense of security when she was around him. It was the only way he'd ever find out whether she was playing a dangerous double game or not. But those forget-me-not eyes, so wide with fright as the reality of their situation finally hit home, had made him oblivious to anything but the need to touch her, kiss her.

He was an idiot and he'd have to stay away from her until he could trust himself not to be beguiled by her.

Not that this would present much of a problem. Under the circumstances, he'd probably be lucky if he ever saw her again. *Damn the New Model Army!* But it was time to take a final stand against them and whether they succeeded or not was immaterial because the die was cast.

He went in search of Lord Charles to receive his orders.

<hr>

Merrick Court, 3rd June 2016

Tess's words had had more effect on Josh than he'd let on. If she'd been hoping to guilt trip him, she'd certainly achieved her aim. In fact, she'd done a much better job than his old man ever had, making him feel a part of something much bigger than himself. A family chain, unbroken for a thousand years. Did he really want to be the one who messed it up? And as if what she'd said hadn't been enough, the house itself was starting to get to him. Whenever he came into the yard, he looked up at the imposing façade and felt a twinge of something that seemed very much like belonging. But he didn't want to belong here. Or did he?

It wasn't like he had anything specific to go back to. Apart from Shayla and some of his friends, of course. But he hardly ever saw his daughter and the friends had become more distant during his long months of travel. He hadn't missed them all that much.

He sighed as he headed up the kitchen steps and put his key in the lock. There were four sets of estate agents coming from London today to look round and give him their estimates, and although he was curious as to what they'd say, he no longer felt the same urgency to sell and get the hell out of here.

Why shouldn't he stay? At least for a few years. Maybe see how it went? He could always sell at a later date. And he could get a better price if he fixed things up a little – painting, plastering, making good and replacing rotten woodwork. It wouldn't be difficult as he'd worked in the building trade during the times he wasn't needed on the sheep stations and knew his way round most tools, a jack-of-all-trades.

In the hall, he ran into Tess.

'Oh, hi,' she said. 'Was it today the London agents were coming? I did try to do some hoovering, but I'm afraid I didn't get very far.'

Josh smiled. 'I can imagine. It probably takes a week to get round the whole house and then the dust is back where you started, right?'

'Something like that.' There was an answering smile in her lovely eyes and Josh had to tear his gaze away. He was extremely attracted to her, no doubt about it, but he couldn't let that influence his judgement right now. That would just muddle his thinking. And it had been obvious from their conversation at dinner that she was still grieving for her late husband.

'Well, don't worry about it. I'm sure most estate agents have seen worse. Anyway, the only thing they'll be interested in are dollar signs. Or pound ones, in this case. Will you be around if they have any questions I can't answer?'

'Yes, I've got a valuer coming too, in about half an hour. He's going to look at the furniture and stuff.' She headed for the kitchen. 'I'd better put some coffee on – make the place smell good. Bring them all to the kitchen if you want to offer them some.'

'Okay, will do.'

The truth was he'd rather they weren't coming at all now, which was an unsettling thought. What was it about this place that was getting under his skin? He glanced into the Victorian sitting room and glimpsed the lady in the crinoline standing by the window. Maybe that was it – the spirits were helping Tess bind him to his ancestors. If so, he had no idea how to stop them.

At the end of the day, he headed to the kitchen, his head whirling with figures. Large sums, but for some reason they'd made him want to hang onto Merrick Court even more. Weird.

Tess was sitting by the table staring into space while Vince lounged by her feet.

'Hey, what's up?' He took a seat next to her and scratched the dog's ears.

'Huh? Oh, I was just thinking about what the valuer said. And Mr Harrison rang.'

'And?'

'It's not good news. Harrison says that as Giles's widow I owe Marcus Steele the money Giles promised him.' She glanced at him, her gaze flickering a little. 'I'd been wondering if maybe you, as Giles's heir, would be liable too, but apparently not as it was a personal debt that has nothing to do with the estate.' She sighed. 'Anyway,

144

the valuer told me there's nothing here that's worth a great deal. Nowhere near half a million. More like thirty thousand or thereabouts for the lot. So that means I'll have to sell what I can, give Marcus the proceeds, then declare myself bankrupt. Not great when I'm hoping to continue my business.'

'Business?'

'Yeah, I do up old furniture and sell it on.'

'Right. Bummer. How about I buy the contents of the house off you? I'll give you half a mill.' Josh had no idea where that had come from. His mouth spoke before his brain had time to catch up. But he could afford it and somehow it felt like the right thing to do.

She swivelled round to stare at him. 'Are you mad? It's not worth anywhere near that much. I told you. It's mostly junk.'

'Doesn't matter. It belongs with the house. And despite all the numbers the agents threw at me today, I'm kind of thinking of staying for a while. I'll need furniture.'

'Yes, but … No, I can't let you do that.' She shook her head. 'That's just crazy. And besides, even if Giles did owe Marcus that much, I wouldn't want to give it to him. This way he'll only get a fraction of the amount, which is what a shark like him deserves.'

'He'll try to get it one way or another. Think about it for a bit? No need to decide today. Bryn's said I can have his guest room for as long as I want and you guilt tripped me into giving some thought to my ancestors. Let's talk about it more another day, eh?'

She frowned but nodded slowly. 'If you say so. I still think you're nuts.'

He was beginning to think so too.

Chapter Fifteen

Rosie finally went back to London, having outstayed her welcome by at least a week. Following their latest disagreement, she'd kept a low profile, not going so far as to apologise to Tess for her insinuations, but nor had she made any further snarky comments. It had obviously been the drink talking, as Tess suspected. The two women had tiptoed around each other, an uneasy truce between them, which neither had been inclined to break.

'At last!' Tess shouted out loud after she'd watched Rosie's car speed out of the gates. Vincent joined in with a bark, no doubt wondering what was going on. It made Tess laugh and she ruffled the top of his head. 'At least I'm not alone now, thanks to you. What do you say, shall we go out in the garden for a bit?' She knew she ought to be looking into finding somewhere else to live, but it was such a glorious day and Josh hadn't seemed in any hurry for her to move out. She could help make the gardens more presentable instead.

Vince tilted his head to one side, as if he was trying to understand her, but he seemed to recognise the word 'garden' as that made him bark again and swish his tail back and forth.

Tess collected the wheelbarrow and her gardening tools, plus an old tennis ball, which had been lying around in one of the stables. She spent some time throwing it for Vincent on the lawn in a never-ending game of fetch, which he seemed to love.

'Boy, you have a lot of energy, don't you! Enough, I need to do some work now.'

She had finished with the roses and decided to try and do something about the Elizabethan knot garden. It was a project she'd been meaning to start for ages but somehow never got around to. Now was as good a time as any while she waited for Josh to make up his mind about whether to sell or not. Perhaps he'd appreciate her efforts? He and Bryn had made good progress everywhere else.

The box hedges that formed the patterns in the knot garden could still be seen, although most of them were way too tall and sprouting in all directions. Tess would have to prune them severely and hope they didn't die in the process. She was drawn to the far corner first though, where there were the remains of an old fountain. Right now it was covered in brambles and ivy and it was difficult to see if there was anything left underneath except a pile of stones.

'Only one way to find out,' Tess muttered. She pulled out her trusted fork and some shears and set to work.

A bark from Vincent alerted her to the arrival of company. The dog had been lying next to her, happy to doze in the shade of a large bush while she worked. Now he stood up, his tail wagging furiously as Josh approached. Tess was pleased to see him too, but tried not to show it.

'Hey, Lady M, need a hand with anything? Hello, Vince, helping your new mistress, huh?' He bent down to make a fuss of the dog, who licked him wherever he could reach.

'Hi, Josh. Well, there's some seriously stubborn ivy here, but it's Saturday. Wouldn't you rather do something else? You should see a bit of Wales now you're here.'

Tess wasn't sure she wanted him to help her. Despite what she'd said to Rosie, she was attracted to Josh and her sister-in-law was probably right. She shouldn't be, not so soon after being widowed. At least he was wearing a T-shirt again today, although the board shorts were back and that intriguing tattoo peeped out from under his sleeve. His dark hair was tousled, making Tess's fingers itch to run through it, and he had some serious stubble going on. Giles, having been very fair, had never looked quite so ... piratical. Dangerous. It was amazingly distracting and, yes, sexy.

'Nah, not today. Bryn was a bit crook earlier so I think I'd better stay close, just in case.'

'Crook?'

'Yeah, slightly dizzy, although he didn't want to let on.'

'Oh, no, I hope he's okay?' Tess knew Bryn worked harder than he should but he refused to be told.

'Probably just overdone it. Stubborn old bugger.'

'Okay, well, as I said, ivy ... be my guest.'

With Josh's help things moved a lot faster and after half an hour or so they had the entire fountain uncovered. It consisted of a round base, about eight feet in diameter with a foot-high edge, and with three tiers of smaller basins above it like a wedding cake. At the top was a rounded shape with a hole in the middle.

'Wow, cool! That's going to look heaps better with some water in it.' Josh pulled off his T-shirt and wiped his face. 'Could sure do with some right now. She's a scorcher today, huh?'

'Er, yes.' Tess had a feeling the heat surging through her had more to do with the sight of his naked torso than the weather. She forced herself to study the fountain instead of the gorgeous man next to her. 'It looks basically sound, don't you think? I can't see any cracks anywhere.'

'Yeah, it's amazing it's survived so well. If there had been cracks the ivy would've burrowed inside and made them worse. But maybe it hasn't been covered up for very long?'

'I don't know. It's been like this since I came here anyway.'

'I'll go get some water then we can see if it holds tight.' Josh left his shirt on a nearby bush and set off while Tess watched his retreating back. It was a very impressive back and she couldn't help but admire the way his muscles gleamed in the sunlight. And that tattoo on his arm – she'd never realised a tattoo could be so enticing, but it definitely added a certain something. Like a 'bad boy' stamp. The thought sent a shiver shooting through her. She'd always secretly wanted a 'bad boy' boyfriend but had settled for the safer options instead. Was that why she'd fallen for Giles? Although he'd turned out to be more boring and staid, than safe.

'Get a grip, woman,' she muttered. Vincent raised his eyes to her and she shook her head at him. 'No, me, not you. You're allowed to like Josh as much as you want, but I shouldn't.'

Josh returned with two watering cans full to the brim, then went back for more, repeating his journey quite a few times. Tess watched closely for leaks as he poured water first into the base of the fountain, then into each tier in turn. She walked slowly round the rim, then shook her head. 'Nothing. It all seems okay.'

'Excellent.' Josh smiled. 'We have ourselves a fountain, although how we're going to get that to spout anything, I'm not sure.' He pointed to the ball at the top. 'Wonder how it worked back in the Dark Ages?'

Tess laughed. 'I don't think it was quite *that* long ago, but you're right, I have no idea how it would have worked. Never mind, it will be pretty even if it's only filled with water that doesn't go anywhere.'

Josh looked around the immediate area. 'These paving stones will need to be taken up and reset,' he said. 'The grass has pushed them all out of place and someone could trip on them and fall.'

'Hmm, yes, but I think that will have to wait. I'd like to get some of these hedges trimmed first. They're so out of control, the path might be underneath them too.'

'Good point. Okay, let's start here and see what we find. How high do you think they should be?'

'Not sure. How about knee-height to begin with? Then

maybe they can be trimmed down more later. We don't want to kill them off completely.'

They both had shears and for the next hour or so, the only sounds to be heard were the snipping and sliding of metal on metal as they hacked away at the box and pulled out the weeds in between. An intricate pattern began to emerge and the more they worked, the easier it became to see what the pattern should be.

'Hell, this is killing my back.' Josh straightened up and stretched his arms over his head.

Tess followed suit and pushed both hands into the small of her back as she arched it. 'Yes, it's a real pain, isn't it? Let's leave it for now. I think we've done enough for one day. It must be lunchtime anyway.' Vincent immediately raised his head from where it had been resting on his paws and looked interested. Tess laughed. 'Vince certainly thinks so anyway. He knows that word.'

'I'm sure he'd eat any time of day, given the chance, but you're right. Let's put everything away and go check on Bryn.'

As they gathered up the tools and trundled the wheelbarrow over to the compost heap with all the cuttings, Josh tried not to remember the sight of Tess's chest in a tight strappy top as she'd arched backwards to stretch her muscles. Nor her bum in a pair of minuscule jeans shorts and the endless legs beneath. She had a fabulous figure and he could totally see why her late husband had fallen for her, even though according to Bryn she hadn't been in his league. Who cared these days? Only people like Rosie, he'd bet.

'Not upper-class enough for the toffs his lordship was friendly with,' Bryn had told him again the other day when speaking about Tess. 'I think that's why she spent a lot of time with me yere in the garden, like. They didn't exactly make her feel welcome, his friends and family. Except the boy, of course. Nice lad, that Louis.'

Josh thought this was ridiculous. A person should be judged on merit, not on what family they'd been born into. But he supposed if your ancestors had owned a place like this for a thousand years, maybe you got some strange ideas instilled in you from birth. Good thing he hadn't grown up here.

Tess was beautiful in every way though, as far as he could see. Apart from the obvious, she was kind and gentle, not at all up herself and very fair, as witness her desire for him to think a bit more carefully before making up his mind about this place rather than mourning the fact that she had to leave it herself. He didn't think she had an avaricious bone in her body and seemed not to have aspired to being a titled lady at all. And she was nice to old people like Bryn, as well as animals – Vince had taken to her straight away.

He shook his head. If he wasn't careful, he might fall for her and then he'd be stuck again. Trapped, like when he was married to Isla. That wasn't what he wanted. In fact, he didn't know what he wanted. Not yet. He was still thinking about it.

As they left the knot garden, he caught movement out of the corner of his eye and glanced back towards the fountain. Yet another bloody shadow, this one a lady sitting on a small stone bench which was still covered in ivy and brambles. Josh smiled to himself – of course, that wouldn't bother a spirit. From what he could see, the woman was wearing wide skirts and a bodice with puffy sleeves down to the elbows. A crinoline? He wasn't an expert on women's fashion, but had a feeling the dress was much older than the Victorian era.

He watched as her face lifted and although he couldn't see her expression, he thought she was waiting for someone. A secret lover? Was this an assignation gone wrong? Josh had no way of knowing, but he hoped whoever it was had come to her and she wasn't still waiting, hundreds of years later. That would be too sad for words.

'Josh, are you coming?' Tess's voice and a bark from Vincent made the shadow fade.

'What? Yeah, I'm right with you.'

He shook his head. This place was too full of shadowy souls for his liking, but at the same time he was intrigued. If only there was some way of finding out why they were still hanging around. He wished he'd asked his grandmother, but he never had and now it was too late.

Maybe he could do some experiments on his own though, try to open his mind more and see if that would tap into the thoughts left behind by those shadows? But did he really want to know? He needed to think it over before doing something he might regret. And he would have to be alone.

Tess went back outside after lunch, Vince happy to follow in her wake, but without Josh's help the work on the knot garden seemed boring. He'd gone back to Bryn's cottage, saying he'd probably take the old man out for a pub lunch to get him away from the garden for a while.

'You're welcome to come with us,' he'd added, but Tess declined. She didn't like going to the Merrick Arms; everyone always stared at her so.

'Maybe we should leave this for another day,' she said to Vince now. 'I'm running out of energy and it's too hot. Although you're okay, lying there in the shade.'

He tilted his head at her as if he was trying to understand the words, but when she perched on the edge of the fountain he put his head down on his paws and closed his eyes. Tess trailed her hand in the shallow water. It was cool, despite the strong sunlight, and she wondered if the stone the structure was made out of kept it that way. As she stared at the little waves her fingers were stirring up, she had that odd sensation of having the water rise up towards her again. She recognised it from her visit to Raglan Castle and quickly averted her gaze.

'No!' She'd fainted that time and been dizzy for a while, not an experience she wanted to repeat. But that was when that man had appeared, the one who'd thought her suicidal. Or rather, she'd thought he had appeared, but of course it wasn't real.

She began to wonder – she'd had so many strange dreams lately and they had all started after that day at the castle. Was her mind somehow trying to connect her to a different time? Was that possible? Thinking about it further, most of her hallucinations – for want of a better word – had come in connection with her looking at water. Did it have a calming effect on her brain, freeing it to receive messages from a bygone era? Perhaps it was a bit like meditation?

It seemed too crazy for words.

There was only one way to find out. She'd have to deliberately recreate the right condition for her thoughts to free themselves. She had to be brave. And why not now? She was all alone, no one would disturb her or think her mad.

'No, this is stupid.' Tess closed her eyes. She hadn't even believed in ghosts until she'd seen that shimmering haze in her room. But she *had* seen it. And heard it – him? – say '*cariad*'. She had to do this, had to find out if it was just her imagination.

She took a couple of deep breaths and tried to calm her heartbeat. Then, staring intently at the water, she stuck her hand back in and began to swirl it slowly with a circling motion. Tiny wavelets appeared, creating a series of vortexes. Perfect circles, rippling outwards. Pretty. At first, nothing happened, but then she experienced a strange sensation of weightlessness, of falling towards the water at the same time as it rose to meet her. And then the voices and images came ...

Chapter Sixteen

Raglan Castle, 4th June 1646

'Colonel Morgan had the temerity to send a summons for immediate surrender yesterday. As if we would give up that easily!'

Rhys saw Arabella hide a smile at the chaplain's words as if she very much doubted he'd be doing any fighting. She had a point.

'Lord Worcester refused, of course?' Mrs Watson asked, but it was a rhetorical question really. They all knew the marquis – and Rhys was beginning to feel he did too, although by hearsay only – and once his mind was made up, nothing moved him.

'Of course. Said he's not giving up the castle without permission from the king.'

A stalling tactic, it had to be. Lord Worcester was a wily old man and Rhys was sure both he and Colonel Morgan were well aware there was no chance of consulting His Majesty now that he was a prisoner of the Scots. The Colonel must be fuming. Well, it served him right.

'So what are we doing?' Mrs Watson, ever practical, sounded as though she wanted action rather than words. Rhys silently agreed and he could tell Arabella did too by the way she nodded slightly.

He was very aware of her sitting next to him and had noticed her glance his way every now and then. Really, he ought not to be here – he should be eating with the other men over in the Stone Court – but after his encounter with Arabella the day before he'd felt the need to spend more time with her. He had to keep her under observation, or so he told himself. Nothing to do with the fact that he just wanted to be near her.

'Making sallies, what else?' the chaplain was saying now. 'We can't let them get too close.'

Mrs Watson took a sip of her wine, her demeanour as calm as always. Not much appeared to ruffle her, a trait which Rhys admired. Some ladies could be every bit as formidable and courageous as men, this war had taught him that, if nothing else. 'I was told there are over a thousand men encamped outside. In fact, I've been *hearing* them all day.' The housekeeper's mouth turned into a sour grimace. 'Their foul language is beyond belief.'

'More like fifteen hundred, I'd say, and, yes, they are very coarse,' the chaplain agreed. 'We must close our ears to such filthy speech. I'm sure they are doing it deliberately in order to goad us.'

As outraged comments broke out around them, Arabella murmured, 'I've heard them too. Foul they most definitely are.' She sounded very offended.

As well she might be, Rhys thought. The enemy soldiers had been shouting curses and vile epithets such as 'Royalist whores' and worse, their jibes very obviously targeted at the women of the castle.

'The chaplain is right,' Rhys whispered back, while others round the table weighed in with their opinions. 'They are just trying to intimidate the inhabitants and it's best to ignore their taunts. They *want* you to care, to take it to heart. It's part of the strategy. Don't let them succeed.'

'Easier said than done,' Arabella retorted, then sighed. 'I still find it difficult to believe that the castle can withstand a siege, but it gives me some hope that his lordship was so adamant in his refusals. Surely he wouldn't be unless he thought there was some chance we could prevail? And you did say the castle garrison could overpower the enemy if we acted swiftly, did you not?'

'I did.' Rhys didn't want to share his misgivings with her. Far better to allow her some hope for now, even though he was under no illusions. They were fighting a losing battle, he'd bet his last groat on it.

She dared a question to the chaplain, who was known to be a kind man. 'Have the sallies begun, sir? There was a lot of commotion outside earlier.'

'Indeed. I believe our men fought Colonel Morgan himself, is that not so, Sir Rhys?' Rhys nodded, but didn't elaborate further, so the chaplain continued, 'At least the man has the bravery to lead his men from the front rather than cowering behind them. I suppose we must give him his due.'

Mrs Watson snorted, as if she'd rather not give anyone in the enemy camp their due. 'There were casualties, were there not?' At the chaplain's nod, she continued. 'We should set up a makeshift infirmary somewhere. I will speak to her ladyship about it. Perhaps in the Great Hall?'

'That sounds eminently sensible.'

'I'd be happy to be of assistance,' Arabella put in, as some of the other ladies offered their help.

Rhys thought it an excellent idea and guessed that having something to do of a practical nature would help Arabella and the others keep the fear at bay. Although they were trying not to show it, they had to be terrified, having now heard the sounds of battle and seen the huge number of men encamped outside. The siege was no longer something they were preparing for – it was upon them and very real.

Arabella glanced at him and sent him a determined little smile. 'I ... I pray we won't see you in there, Sir Rhys. I mean, that you're not one of the wounded.'

'Thank you, you may be sure I'll be praying for the same.' He smiled back and gave her hand a quick squeeze under the table to reassure her. 'Trust me, I'll try to keep out of harm's way.'

'See that you do.'

But he could be wounded. In fact, it was more than likely

he would be either hurt or killed. He saw Arabella swallow hard and wondered for the thousandth time how things had come to this pass. Why was this happening to them? Why couldn't everyone just have lived in peace with their neighbours and the king and Parliament have seen reason? It all seemed so senseless and unnecessary.

He looked round the table and saw the fear in the other ladies' eyes too. They were all helpless, trapped inside the thick walls, which had been bombarded throughout the day. So far the damage was slight, but for how long could the ancient stones withstand the enemy's ordnance?

They would have to wait and see.

'We will all take turns,' Mrs Watson decreed, breaking the fraught silence that had descended upon the table. 'I'm sure every woman will be needed and it's the least we can do to support the men.'

'Indeed, but let us pray for deliverance,' the chaplain said and everyone, whether Papist or not, willingly bent their heads. They needed God's help as never before.

***

Merrick Court, 4th June 2016

Tess was brought back to the present with a thump, literally, as she felt her bottom hitting the ground. When she opened her eyes, squinting in the sunlight, she found that she was sitting on the ground next to the fountain, the rim digging into the small of her back. She must have fallen off.

'Ouch.' As Vince came over to lick her chin, probably in the belief that he was being helpful, she rubbed at her backside, but she didn't really care about any possible bruises. They faded into insignificance compared to what had just happened.

'It worked, Vince! It really worked!' She caressed his ears

and he gave a short bark of joy, although he obviously had no idea why she was excited.

She could hardly believe it, but this time the scenes she had witnessed – no taken part in, as she'd been in the mind of someone called Mistress Dauncey – had been much clearer. Although she'd still experienced the fish tank effect, she'd heard snatches of conversation, smelled the beeswax of the furniture, the leather of Rhys's jerkin, the scent of him … No, *Sir* Rhys, he'd said, although she hadn't caught the rest of his name. It was magical.

And frightening.

She shivered as she remembered the sight of the New Model Army, arriving outside the walls of Raglan Castle. That made it clear which year she'd gone back to – 1646, the time of the final siege. Exactly three hundred and seventy years ago. Spooky. Tess had read a few snippets about it on the signs at Raglan, but she hadn't really paid attention. She'd need to go back again, find out more.

The scene had changed to a more intimate one, a dinner of some sort, and she'd felt the fear around the table, but also the determination. Whoever those people were, it was clear they were prepared to stand up for what they believed in. She admired such courage.

There had to be some way of connecting what she was experiencing with real events. If only she had more details, proper facts … but it was all so hazy.

She'd have to experiment again, but not today. It was too much to take in.

⁘

The Merrick Arms, 4th June 2016

'Have you met Fred Williams? He's up at the Home Farm, as I told you. Fred, this yere's his new lordship.'

Josh stuck out his hand. 'No, Josh Owens,' he said with a smile. 'I don't hold with all that title stuff. Pleased to meet you, Mr Williams.'

He'd been to the bar and came back to find Bryn in conversation with a man who looked to be in his late sixties or early seventies. He had the kind of ruddy complexion you only get from spending most of your life outdoors in all weathers. And his clothing – jeans, checked shirt and mud-spattered wellies – told the same story.

'Oh, Fred'll do then. We're neighbours after all and I've known the family up at the Court all my life.' The man cracked a smile.

'I understand the Home Farm used to belong to Merrick Court.' Josh had by now walked the boundaries of his own land and he'd seen the old farmhouse in the distance.

'Yes, but I own it now, like. One of my ancestors was allowed to buy the Home Farm when the then Lord Merrick was a bit short of funds.' Fred grinned. 'Lucky for us, you might say. Got it for a good price.'

'Yeah, real lucky.' Josh smiled back.

Fred's expression turned grim. 'Problem is, my son, Andrew, he doesn't want to be a farmer, so I'll have to give it up soon. Can't carry on by myself for much longer and there's not much point, is there? The wife wants us to go and live by the sea, retire like, and I'm starting to see the appeal myself so I've put the property on the market.'

'Already?' Bryn looked startled.

'Yes, but who knows? There mightn't be anyone wanting a farm these days. Anyway, you'll not be getting rid of me completely. My brother-in-law and his wife live in the next village, remember? We'll visit them regular, I'm sure.'

'Oh, well that's all right then.' Bryn smiled and clapped his friend on the back. 'Wouldn't want to be losing touch.'

'It's a shame you have to sell. Lovely area this.' Josh felt for the man, but farming was a hard life and he couldn't blame the son for wanting out. You had to have a passion for it in order to carry on. A passion he himself possessed. Although he'd never got on with his father, he *had* loved the life of a high country farmer. Even working for other people had been enjoyable. He was itching to get back to it now, just not in New Zealand. Maybe this was another sign? With the Home Farm lands plus those of Merrick Court, he could have quite a large flock.

Something made him hesitate though. He still wasn't sure he was ready to commit himself to anything. Josh decided he'd make some discreet enquiries, find out which estate agent was handling the sale of the Home Farm and the asking price. Perhaps he could go and look around as well, walking the perimeters of the fields to gauge exactly how many sheep it could support.

'Come over any time, young Owens,' Fred said as if he'd been reading Josh's thoughts. 'The wife'll be pleased to meet the new owner of the Court. She used to work there in the kitchens, back in the day, so she'll have some tales to tell you.'

'Thank you, I'd love to hear those so I'll definitely do that.'

Fred turned back to Bryn. 'Don't suppose you know anyone who's good at shearing? Andrew and I had a big argument and the idiot went off in a huff. I've no idea if he intends to return to help me out. Hasn't been in touch, not even with his mother. I have one shearer booked, but it'll be hard to find another at such short notice. It'll be slow going with just two of us and no one to help get the sheep into the pens.'

Fred was looking genuinely worried. Josh knew that the sheep had to be sheared at a certain time of the year and it was hard work. 'I can do it,' he offered. 'Hired myself out every year back home.'

'Really? You sure?' Fred peered at him, hope lighting his deep-set eyes.

'Of course. I'm pretty quick, I promise.' And it wasn't a boast. Josh had taken part in sheep-shearing contests and could fleece a sheep in under a minute with an electric cutter, although when not competing he took a bit more time than that in order to do it carefully.

'Well, I never.' Fred stuck out his hand again and Josh shook it. 'I'd be very grateful to you. We start Monday the week after next.'

Josh found that he was looking forward to it immensely.

Chapter Seventeen

Tess didn't see much of Josh during the next week as she was busy in her workshop. She'd had a couple of orders through the internet and wanted to finish them as soon as possible. The more satisfied customers she had, the easier it should be to spread the word about her business.

By Saturday morning she'd run out of pieces of furniture to paint and sell on, so it was time to buy more stock and today happened to be auction day at the local auction house. She needed a steady supply of new items, so after a quick breakfast she left Vincent with Bryn in the potting shed and set off to see if she could pick up some bargains.

It was a small, family run firm that seemed to specialise in house clearances and they sold everything from garden gnomes to proper antiques. There were outside lots, usually consisting of things like flower pots, garden tools and bicycles, while inside there were pieces of furniture, fine china and glass, antiques, paintings and books, plus much more besides. Tess loved it.

'I don't know why you want to go rooting around among this smelly old stuff,' Giles had said, the one and only time she'd taken him with her. 'Just go into the attics at Merrick Court if you want old things.'

But Tess didn't want to do that. Everything in his attic belonged at Merrick Court, whether it was in use or not. What she needed were bits of furniture she could do whatever she wanted with. Sand them, paint them, polish them or a combination of all three. It would have seemed wrong to take any of Giles's family possessions and sell them on. They were just on loan to the present generation, or that's how she saw it.

She arrived early and bought a catalogue, marking the lots she was interested in before the bidding started. There were a couple of milking stools outside, slightly the worse for wear but salvageable, and inside she found a wash stand, two mirrors and a lovely pine table. On closer inspection, she also found an old chest, which would look fabulous painted she decided, and a set of four chairs in the Shaker style.

'Isn't there enough furniture at Merrick Court already?'

The voice behind her made her jump, but at the same time sent a tingle down her spine. She just loved that sexy Kiwi accent, it was irresistible. She straightened up from where she'd been checking that the old chest wasn't riddled with woodworm and tried not to let the sight of him affect her. Every time she saw him, though, her heart beat a little faster. It was ridiculous. 'Josh! What are you doing here?'

He smiled and shrugged. 'Bryn told me you'd come here and I can never resist a good auction.' He glanced around and chuckled. 'Not that I'm sure this is any such thing, but still ...'

'It's okay. You can get some bargains, but it depends who you're bidding against.' There were dealers who came from some of the larger towns, even London sometimes, and they would pay silly money as they could easily charge more for things in their shops. Tess never bid against them as they would always win.

'I guess we'll see. You buying that?' Josh nodded at the chest.

'If I can get it cheap, yes.'

'You can never have too many chests, eh?' he said, looking at it as if he couldn't see its attraction.

'It's not for me. It's for my business, *Much Loved*. I buy stuff like this, do it up and sell it, and this will look great once I've tarted it up a bit.'

'Ah, I see. Bryn said something about you being an artist.

I didn't realise that included painting furniture. Canvases not good enough for you?' he teased.

Tess punched him on the arm, which made her knuckles smart as it was like hitting a stone wall. 'It's different. I add things like flower decorations or if it's for a child's room, for example, maybe some cute animals or something. This would make a great toy chest.'

'Okay, I get you. Sounds like a good thing to do and this old box could sure do with "tarting up".'

'What about you? Are you buying anything? Maybe you could make a killing in New Zealand with some English antiques?'

'Don't know. We'll see if anything catches my eye.' He waved a bidding card at her. 'I got one of these just in case.'

'Good plan. I'm just going to have a quick look in the other room.'

'I'll come with you. If that's okay?'

Tess liked that he asked and didn't just assume. She nodded. 'Sure.' It was nice to have company for once, someone to point things out to and discuss them with. *Someone who doesn't take the mickey*, a little voice inside her added, but that made her feel disloyal. Giles hadn't exactly done that, but he'd also never made her feel as though her furniture sales were anything worthwhile since she didn't earn any huge sums. He would probably have preferred her to deal in proper posh antiques.

In the next room there *were* some serious antiques – mostly brown furniture and old sofas and chairs, but Tess had no intention of buying those. There were also several tables full of china, glass and porcelain figures.

'Please tell me you don't collect those,' Josh whispered and pointed at some figurines of girls in ball dresses. 'I can't stand stuff like that. Totally useless crap.'

'But they're so beautiful,' Tess said, pretending to be

164

entranced by them. 'And they're worth a lot of money. That's why they're kept in these glass cases instead of on the table. I wish I could afford one.'

'Seriously?' Josh looked horrified. 'People pay good money for those?'

Tess laughed. 'They do, but I was pulling your leg. I hate them too.'

'Thank Christ for that!'

'These, on the other hand, I would love to collect.' Tess had stopped by a pair of Staffordshire Foo dogs, or 'mantle spaniels' as the catalogue called them. 'Aren't they just adorable?'

'Er … I wouldn't say that exactly. Funny, maybe. Ugly, definitely.' He studied her expression. 'You joking again? Or do you actually like them?'

She made an apologetic face. 'Sorry, but, yes, I really do like them. I can't explain why; they just appeal to me. But don't worry, I can't afford to waste money on stuff like that right now. I have to eat.'

'Hmm.' Josh threw a final glance at the Foo dogs and followed Tess into the last room where the paintings for sale were displayed.

'Oh, look at this frame,' Tess whispered and held up an old oil painting of a vase of flowers. The painting itself was fairly ordinary, but the frame was spectacular with curly rococo bits and faded gilding. She could turn this into a gorgeous mirror.

'Yep, nice. Why are we whispering, actually?'

Josh had bent towards her ear and Tess felt his cheek brush hers, making her supremely aware of how close they were standing. She had an almost irresistible urge to lean back towards his broad chest, but forced herself not to. What would he think? *Desperate widow throws herself at first available hot guy* … And her husband's heir, on top of everything else. Rosie's accusation flitted through her mind. No, she wasn't going there. She concentrated on his question instead.

'Because I don't want other buyers to know I'm interested, otherwise they might want this too.'

'Oh, right. Okay, I won't tell a soul.'

Tess sent him an exasperated glance and had a hard time tearing her gaze away from his twinkling eyes. They were so green, even in the slightly dim light of this side-room. And as for those long lashes, they really shouldn't be allowed on a man …

She noted down a couple more possible paintings with frames that could be embellished in various ways, then they made their way outside where the auctioneer was just starting. He had hundreds of lots to get through, but some went for just a few pounds and he made short work of the long list, stopping occasionally to joke about some of the items.

'He's good,' Josh whispered. 'But it still takes a long time, huh? I'm going to go inside and get a snack. Want something?'

There was a small cafeteria selling sandwiches, cakes, crisps and chocolate bars. Tess hesitated, then gave in. 'Yes, why not. A Kit Kat please?'

'One Kit Kat coming up.'

He gave her that supermodel smile as he took her order and Tess thought it was a good thing *she* wasn't made of chocolate or she'd be a puddle on the ground by now. She shook her head at herself. What a sad case. But he was seriously hot and she had noticed quite a few of the other ladies present checking him out. So it wasn't just her.

She eventually got her milking stools for four pounds. 'Excellent,' she muttered and made a note on her catalogue. She looked at Josh, who was munching his way through a Mars bar. 'There's nothing else I want out here. Do you? If not, we can go and bag some chairs in the inside saleroom.

This auctioneer will be heading in there when he's finished here.'

'Fine with me.'

Other people had had the same idea, so they ended up sitting on an old church bench together. It wasn't very wide and Tess tried not to notice how she was squashed up against Josh from shoulder to knee, but every time he moved, little arrows of heat shot through her. She couldn't get up though as that would have meant having to explain why. And truth be told, she found it exciting being so close to him.

They didn't have to wait long and it seemed to be her lucky day as she managed to get all the items she wanted. Most were bargains too. 'You must be some kind of good luck charm,' she told Josh. 'This is amazing! I should bring you every time.'

'I don't know about that, but I'm glad you're getting the stuff you want.'

'What about you? Anything caught your fancy yet?'

He glanced at her, deliberately looking her up and down, then grinned. 'Yee-es ...'

'Very funny.' Although her heart made an extra somersault at the thought that he might mean it, she knew he was just joking. He'd travelled the world, probably met some stunning women. And she was sure he could have pretty much anyone he wanted. No reason why he'd want her.

'Well, okay, I'm waiting for some lots in the other room,' he told her. 'Are you going home now or do you want to keep me company?'

'I don't mind staying a bit longer. It's fun to watch.' And it was even more enjoyable spending time with him, but she didn't add that, just followed him towards the other room.

In the doorway Josh narrowly avoided colliding with

someone and as Tess peered round him, she couldn't stop a small gasp from escaping. 'Marcus!'

'Well, hello, Lady Merrick! Fancy meeting you here.' Marcus stood blocking their way. The dimpled smile was in evidence, although it faded somewhat when he glanced at Josh. 'And you've brought the handyman to carry the heavy stuff, I see. Very sensible.'

Something about the man's smile made Tess suspect the meeting wasn't accidental. But how had he known she'd be here?

She felt Josh bristle at being called 'the handyman' and rushed in with a reply. 'Uhm, yes. Are you into antiques?'

'Of course. I'm quite the connoisseur.' Marcus laughed. 'I'm surprised I haven't run into you before.'

Tess wasn't as she was sure this was his first time here and he didn't look like he belonged in such a provincial auction room. He'd swapped his flashy suit for smart casual, but his clothing was still in sharp contrast to everyone else's jeans and T-shirts. A goldfish in a pond of brown carp.

'We need to get on. I think they're nearly at the right number.' Josh stepped to the side to allow Tess past him and she was grateful he refrained from commenting on Marcus's words.

'Yes, sure. Bye, Marcus.'

He just nodded, flashing his smile again, but she felt his gaze on her as she walked into the next room and soon afterwards she noticed he followed them, sitting down near the door. It was as though a shadow had been cast over an otherwise lovely day for Tess, but Josh pretended Marcus wasn't there.

Tess watched as the auctioneer went through a couple of lots, a photo of each one appearing on a screen so that even the people at the back could see what was on offer. After a while, the Foo dogs came up, and she couldn't help a wistful sigh from escaping. They were so cute, with their funny little faces and spaniel ears. She'd have to get a proper job in order to afford things like that though.

The bidding started, and there were only two bidders, neither of which seemed particularly enthusiastic. When the auctioneer got to twenty pounds, one gave up and the other one obviously thought she'd won. Then Josh put his card up.

'Josh! What are you doing?' Tess stared at him.

'Nothing.' His card went up again. Twenty-four pounds.

'Seriously, you don't want those.' She grabbed his arm and gave it a little shake.

'No, but you do.' He smiled at her as the auctioneer's gavel fell. 'Great, I got them. It will be an early birthday present. Or late, maybe? When's your birthday?'

'What? August, but really—'

'Early then. Hey, you'll be doing me a favour taking them off my hands. I wouldn't give them houseroom, honestly. Now shhh, here comes something else I want.'

Tess gave up arguing for now. It wasn't as if she could make the auctioneer take the Foo dogs back. Once the gavel fell, the deal was done. But why had Josh bought them for her?

She watched as he bid on a beautiful walking stick with a silver top in the shape of a ram's head. To her surprise, Marcus also started bidding and the price skyrocketed. 'Josh?'

'Yeah, I know what he's doing,' he said between clenched teeth. 'But I don't care.'

In the end, Marcus gave up, but the smirk he sent their way showed that he'd never actually wanted the walking stick. He'd just been bidding in order to make Josh pay more than the actual value.

'Stupid bastard,' Josh muttered.

'Why did you want a cane? Do you have a gouty foot or something?' Tess joked to try and break the tension.

'No, I'm not *that* old. Jeez, first you think I have ten kids, now this ...' But he was smiling again so she could see her ploy had worked. 'It's not just a walking stick,' he explained. 'It's one of those cool ones that has a sword inside it. I've always wanted one of those. And what better for a former sheep farmer than one with a ram's head?'

'True. So is that it? Sure you're not buying that porcelain lady too?'

Josh pretended to shudder. 'No, thanks, but I'm waiting for one more lot.'

It turned out to be an old hat and Tess wondered what on earth he wanted with one of those, but decided not to ask.

'Right, that's it.' Josh headed for the foyer. 'We'd better go and pay.'

He manoeuvred her into the queue in front of himself. Just then, Marcus came out of the saleroom and he smiled at Tess as he passed her on the way to the door. 'I'll see you very soon, Lady Merrick,' he whispered, but loud enough for everyone around them to hear. Tess didn't reply. It sounded like a threat and if he'd been trying to unsettle her today, he'd succeeded. She tried to shake it off. She wouldn't allow him to ruin the day.

Josh glared at Marcus's retreating back, but didn't comment. He turned back to Tess. 'Just out of interest, how are you planning on getting all your booty into your Mini?'

'One thing at a time. The back seats come down and I'll just have to drive back and forth.'

'Not today. I brought Bryn's Landrover. I'll take the bigger pieces of furniture.'

'Really? Thank you, that's very kind. Are you sure?'

'Yep, on one condition.'

'What? You can smash the Foo dogs?'

Josh laughed and drew the gazes of several ladies nearby, but he seemed oblivious to their admiring glances. 'No, you can do that yourself if you want to. Here, you'd better carry them.' He handed her the two porcelain canines. 'No, the condition is you come to the pub with me for a meal tonight. Please?'

'What, the Merrick Arms?'

'No, I was thinking of some other place Bryn mentioned. The Stag something-or-other.'

'The Stag and Hunter?'

'That's the one. So what do you say?' He tilted his head to one side and gave her a look that reminded her of Vincent. She didn't think she could withstand either of them, although she was sure it was probably a bad idea to go anywhere with Josh. They'd already spent almost the whole day together.

'Why not?' she heard herself reply. Yes, who was she kidding? She couldn't pass up on that offer. 'It would be lovely to eat a meal I haven't had to cook. Thank you.' And she meant it.

She'd just have to guard her heart against his charm. How hard could it be?

Chapter Eighteen

'Arabella, please will you fetch me a tisane? It's so infernally warm today, it's giving me a megrim.'

'Yes, of course, my lady. I'll go to the kitchen directly.'

Arabella had been taking her turn to sit with Lady Margaret, who was a kind and undemanding woman, but one who didn't like to be on her own. Arabella didn't think it was the heat that was giving her ladyship a headache, rather it was too much crying. Not only had the siege begun properly now, with cannonballs and artillery fire making a fearsome noise every so often, shaking the very foundations of the castle, but the poor lady had lost her only child, a daughter called Lady Mary, not so long ago. The sorrow sometimes became too much for her and with the terror of everything going on around them at the moment, it was no wonder her ladyship felt ill.

Hurrying across the Fountain Court, which was eerily silent in between the bursts of cannon fire as the fountain itself had been turned off, Arabella walked quickly through the Great Hall and down to the end. Mrs Watson hadn't been allowed to set up her infirmary in there, but was making do with some smaller rooms elsewhere so it was empty for now. Through a doorway she entered the buttery, then a passage from there leading past the pantry directly to the kitchen, which was situated on the ground floor of an enormous tower in the north-east corner of the Stone Court. One of the cooks immediately set about making a tisane for Lady Margaret.

'Won't take more'n a few minutes,' he muttered. 'You might want to wait outside, mistress?'

'Thank you, yes.' The kitchen was as hot as she imagined hell might be, with two big fireplaces heating an already warm room to unbearable temperatures. No doubt it was better in winter, but during a scorching summer's day like now it must be a terrible place to work.

Arabella didn't want to go into the Stone Court, where hundreds of men were milling about; some grooming horses, some polishing weapons, while others rushed to and fro carrying gunpowder, cannonballs and other military paraphernalia. Instead she lurked in a small entrance area next to a wide serving hatch, through which she could observe the frenetic activity in the kitchen without being in the way. She could also see the Stone Court through the open door and scanned the area without acknowledging to herself that she was looking for one man in particular, but every time she saw someone with long, dark wavy hair, her heart skipped a beat. Unfortunately, it was never Rhys.

She'd seen him twice since he'd helped her carry the bed linen the day the besiegers arrived. Apart from at supper the night before, she'd also caught sight of him that morning. He'd been loitering outside the chapel and had followed her inside to stand next to her during the service. They hadn't spoken, but just having him so close gave her a sense of security, even though she knew that was ridiculous. He was only one man. Still, it was as though he was trying to imbue her with his strength and she'd felt calmer afterwards when he melted away into the throng of people spilling out of the chapel.

She closed her eyes and sighed. This was foolish. She should stop daydreaming and concentrate on the here and now.

'Ah, so there you are. At last I've found you!'

Arabella's eyes flew open as her thoughts were interrupted by a voice she'd hoped never to hear again, one which was nowhere near the melodious Welsh lilt she'd been wishing for. Her heart began to beat a rapid tattoo of fear as she blinked in disbelief at the person standing before her. Although handsome, in a rough sort of way, he was as far from Rhys in looks as he could possibly be, with reddish gold hair and pale blue eyes. 'Glyn?' she whispered, not wanting to believe her own eyes. 'How ...? Why ...?'

He laughed, but it wasn't a joyful sound. 'I'm glad to see you too,' he sneered.

She felt as though she'd just swallowed a large quantity of snow as her insides went numb. How was this possible? Uncle Huw's nephew, the man he'd tried to force her to marry, here? Surely they hadn't turned Royalist? Huw had always been violently opposed to the king.

'What are you doing here?' she asked, moving a step to the side as he was standing much too close. She was breathing in the smell of him, which was a bit rank, as was his ale breath.

'Defending the castle, of course, same as everyone else.' He smirked, very obviously enjoying her discomfort. 'And I thought that as I'm here anyway, I could claim my bride while I'm at it. Two birds with one stone.' He reached out and grabbed her by her upper arms, shoving her against the stone wall behind her roughly. 'I've been looking for you. And don't think you're getting away this time. There's nowhere left to run.'

'Let go of me!' she hissed. 'I'll scream and tell everyone you're a Roundhead spy. I don't believe for a moment you and uncle have turned Royalists. For one thing, he'd never back a losing cause.'

'Hah, so you admit your refuge is going to crumble around you soon? I'm counting on it. But we can leave any time, just say the word. After we marry first, if they have a minister here who isn't a Papist. Breathe so much as a word about me being a Parliamentarian though and I'll kill you with my bare hands.'

'For the last time, I'm not marrying you. Ever. The marquis won't allow it.'

'Oh, yes, you are. Promised to me, you were, and his high-and-mighty lordship has no say in the matter. He won't be long for this world, Colonel Morgan'll see to that.' He shoved her against the wall again so that the back of her head connected with the smooth stonework.

'Ouch! I never was. Uncle Huw was lying. He had no right ...' Arabella tried to glance around him to see if there was anyone who could help her, but he was blocking her line of sight.

He moved in even closer until his face was only an inch away from hers. 'You'll leave here as my wife or not at all. Hide over there with the fancy ladies for now if you want, but sooner or later this place will fall and you'll have to come out. I'll be waiting. In the meantime, we can have some sport now that I've caught you ...'

He bent to kiss her, moving one hand towards her left breast, but Arabella had had enough. She wasn't a skinny fourteen-year-old any longer; she was nineteen and stronger. Turning her head away from his mouth, she kicked at his shin as hard as she could. Her shoes were made of leather and quite worn, but she still managed to hurt him enough for him to let go of her momentarily.

'You little bitch ...' He tried to grab her again but she shot away from him and cannoned into something solid. A male chest clad in a leather jerkin.

Looking up, she came face to face with Rhys, who lifted one eyebrow while glaring at her. 'Mistress Dauncey. Having a lover's tiff?' He slanted a look at Glyn, who smirked and tried to reach for her again.

'That's right,' Glyn said. 'Now if you'd just let us—'

'No!' Arabella ducked under Rhys's arm and headed off into the kitchen. 'Leave me alone.'

She heard Glyn's hateful chuckle which seemed to echo

round the sweating walls, but the cook had the tisane ready and Arabella escaped back to the safety of the Fountain Court via the covered walkway as fast as she could. Fortunately, Rhys had stayed put, acting unwittingly as a buffer between herself and Glyn so he couldn't catch hold of her again.

But was she safe there? Could Glyn follow her? She had no idea, but from now on she would have to be on her guard at all times. He was a conniving bastard who'd stop at nothing.

How had he managed to inveigle himself into the garrison? She should tell someone, but she didn't doubt Glyn's threat had been real. He would kill her.

She shivered. Best to keep quiet for now. No one would believe her anyway.

⁕

Merrick Cottage, 11th June 2016

Josh was pleased he'd managed to persuade Tess to have dinner with him that evening. He'd really enjoyed spending the day with her and although his conscience told him he shouldn't be flirting with her, he silenced it. It was just a meal, two friends eating together. That was all.

As for that bastard Marcus, Josh wondered what the man was playing at? Had he been spying on Tess or was it a coincidence that he was attending that auction? Josh would bet his last dollar it was no such thing and he decided to keep a closer eye on Tess from now on. He hadn't trusted the look in Marcus's eye one bit and the way he'd turned the bidding over the walking stick into some kind of competition still rankled too. Josh hadn't wanted the item that much, but neither had he wished to be beaten by Marcus so he'd continued until the stick was his. It felt like a minor victory, although what he was going to do with it, he had no idea.

Back at Bryn's cottage, he found it deserted and guessed the old man was still in his beloved potting shed. Josh ran up the stairs to the small guest bedroom – one of only two bedrooms on the second floor – and put his newly purchased cane under the bed. He'd look at that later, but first he wanted to try the hat.

He'd smiled to himself when he first noticed it in the saleroom. It was just like the one the shadowy figure in the Norman tower had flourished at him. Well, now he could return the gesture properly, provided no one else was around, of course. He picked it up and turned to the small mirror above a chest of drawers while he positioned the hat at a jaunty angle. It had a wide brim and a long feather, which had definitely seen better days as it hung down on one side in a lopsided kind of way. A bit rakish; Josh liked it and thought it would suit him.

However, when he looked at himself in the mirror, he froze, still holding onto the brim of the hat. He couldn't just see his own face, but another as well. It was as though it overlaid his own, the two alternating, almost jostling for space. He swallowed hard and blinked deliberately to see if that helped. It didn't.

Instead, the other face became clearer and took over entirely, while his own features faded away. The eyes that stared back at him were similar to his own, the green colour perhaps a tad darker; the facial features had a more weathered look, like Bryn's, with skin that had been outdoors a lot. The gaze was wary, watchful, the eyes slightly narrowed. Josh received the impression that this was someone who didn't trust easily, who perhaps lived off his wits and his strength.

He felt his own eyes widen as the implication of what he was seeing hit home. An arrow of fear shot through him, but before he had time to think about it properly, his own thoughts faded altogether and other images crowded into his mind ...

Raglan Castle, 11th June 1646

Rhys glanced once more at the smirking face of the man who'd been all over Arabella, about to kiss her and obviously not caring if everyone in the courtyard saw him. He wanted to smash his fist into that mouth. Instead, he took a deep breath and walked away.

He soon found out the man's name – Glyn Howell – and it wasn't difficult to put two and two together. It made him angry as hell that he'd been right. She was playing a dangerous double game and so must her lover be doing. They were Parliamentarian spies, the pair of them. Had to be.

So the story about her not wanting to marry her uncle's nephew had been a lie. There had been something very intimate about the way they'd stood together, hinting at more than just collaboration. Perhaps they were already married? If so, Arabella's innocent air had fooled everyone in the castle.

'Why do you want to know?' Matthew Emrys, one of the men Rhys was sharing a room with, was the one who'd told him Howell's name. 'He has a vicious streak, that one. I've seen him in his cups, picking fights for the sheer joy of hitting someone.'

Rhys shrugged. 'Oh, just something someone said. Hinted that Howell might be a spy, but he doesn't look like he has the brains for it.' He didn't want to let on that it was his own suspicion.

'You never know. Could be playing the fool on purpose,'

Emrys replied. 'Perhaps it's worth keeping an eye on him? In secret, of course. Or should we tell the commander?'

'Maybe not just yet. We have no proof. Let's watch him, just you and me?'

'Very well, for now.'

Rhys was glad to have a reason for watching Howell, but deep inside he couldn't care less if the man was a spy or not. He was only interested in Arabella.

Damn her for a traitorous bitch.

* * *

Merrick Cottage, 11th June 2016

'Jesus!'

Josh blinked and shook his head, leaning heavily against the chest of drawers. What had just happened?

He dared another look into the mirror, but this time only his own features were visible, his eyes green pools of uncertainty as they stared back at him. A sharp pain shot through his skull, but soon dulled to a normal headache. Slowly he pushed himself away from the chest and sank onto his bed, lying down with his hands above his head.

'So I guess that answered my question then,' he whispered into the silence. One of the shadowy ones had communicated with him, although not in the way he'd imagined. If anything, Josh had thought perhaps he could talk to them, maybe not with words but with an exchange of thoughts. Telepathy? He hadn't envisaged someone's spirit actually going inside his head, using his eyes to see themselves and his brain to relive events. 'Thanks, whoever you are, but you scared the shit out of me!'

He glared around the room, then closed his eyes. There was no one here now. Whoever he'd been, he was gone.

What was it the shadow had wanted him to know?

The images were jumbled – a conversation about a spy and anger while watching some man with a woman. He'd wanted to hit someone.

'Okay, so you wanted me to hear about a war … Sir Rhys?' Josh was pretty sure someone had addressed him by that name and it felt right now he said it out loud. 'A siege. So what? Something happened there? Something bad?' Unfinished business, it had to be. Or did some spirits just want to continue their existence somehow? Who knew?

Josh waited to see if there was any reaction to his question, but felt nothing. Not so much as a stirring of the air.

He glanced at his watch and noticed the time. 'Okay, mate, we'll have to continue this some other time. I've got to go.' Not that he was sure he ever wanted to experience this again, but it wasn't as if he'd had a choice. That spirit had come to him unbidden, he could do it whenever he wanted, that was clear. Unless Josh could find a way to block his thoughts? But he had no idea how to do that.

He'd think about it later. It was time to get ready for his date, which wasn't a date. Not really.

'Yeah, yeah, keep telling yourself that,' he muttered. He had a gut feeling he wasn't fooling anyone, least of all himself.

On the way out, at the last moment, he grabbed the hat and crammed it onto his head. He refused to be intimidated by a shadowy spirit who'd been dead for probably hundreds of years. And it was *his* hat.

'So what d'you think? Be great if I ever get invited to a costume party, right?'

Josh had arrived to pick Tess up wearing his new hat and she almost gasped out loud at the sight. It was a broad-brimmed one with an old ostrich feather in faded blue dangling forlornly to one side, but it wasn't the hat as such that made her blink. It was the way it looked on Josh, as if he'd been born to wear it. *As if it was his right.*

For a moment her vision swam and she saw another man in a similar hat – a man with long, wavy hair and laughing eyes. She thought she heard someone whisper '*cariad*' and her heart gave an extra kick while she glanced around. As before, there was no one there and she'd probably imagined it. She swallowed hard and tried to concentrate on Josh as he swept the hat off and made her a deep bow. 'My lady, your carriage awaits.'

'Er, so what would you be going as?' she managed to ask as she followed him over to Bryn's Landrover. 'A Cavalier?'

'Nah, I was thinking Musketeer, you know, D'Artagnan kind of thing? "All for one, one for all."'

'Oh, right.' Tess had forgotten that Josh probably didn't know much about English history, having been brought up in New Zealand. 'A Cavalier is—'

He held up a hand. 'It's okay, I know what they are. My grandad used to tell me stuff about them when I was a kid. He had books about castles and things too.'

'I see. Well, good.' Still feeling a bit shaken, she took her seat in the car and was relieved to see Josh throw the hat onto the back seat. She hoped he wouldn't put it on again.

Chapter Nineteen

The Stag and Hunter, 11th June 2016

The Stag and Hunter turned out to be right next to a meandering river and as it was a balmy summer evening, they decided to sit outside. Josh liked that better as inside you couldn't hear yourself think, let alone have a decent conversation. And he wanted to talk to Tess, very much so.

He really had enjoyed the day at the auction. It was something he'd indulged in occasionally in New Zealand, but always alone. When he'd still been married to Isla, he hadn't dared confess to spending any money that was just for him. And later there hadn't been anyone he wanted to go with. Tess was great company and their tastes had been remarkably similar.

Apart from those awful china dogs. But, hey, no one was perfect.

They chatted about general things like music, films they liked and books they'd read.

'Not that I had much time for reading until I went travelling,' he told her. 'Working on a sheep station is hard work. Well, any kind of farming really. You get up at the crack of dawn and you're lucky to finish by ten thirty at night. But it's a great life nonetheless.'

'You miss it.' Tess's blue gaze was sympathetic. She'd obviously heard the slightly wistful tone of his voice.

'Yeah, I guess I do. Maybe I should start over here? The countryside is perfect, although if I stayed at Merrick Court I'd need to buy more land for grazing as your late husband's family seem to have turned a lot of their acres into woodland.' He decided not to tell her about Fred yet.

'That was Giles's doing. He discovered that he could get

some kind of grant if he planted lots of trees. Rosie tried to talk him out of it, but he wouldn't listen.'

'Hmm, don't mention that woman, please. She's called several times and left me messages saying we should have "a little family discussion". Not happening. I haven't even rung her back.'

Tess smiled. 'Oh dear, she'll be getting so frustrated. But about buying more land, can you afford that?'

'Sure. As I told you, I sold my station in New Zealand and I didn't blow it all on travel.' He gave her a lopsided smile. 'I'm not a complete moron.'

Her cheeks turned a pretty shade of pink. 'I didn't mean … Of course you're not. It's just, well, I wouldn't know how much money you've got, would I? Land isn't cheap.'

'You're right, but don't worry. I think I could get what I needed if I want.' He didn't tell Tess that potentially he had plenty of money as he'd also invested in rental properties as soon as he was old enough to do so. If he sold them all, he'd make a tidy profit. The Auckland market had rocketed in recent years.

'But what about your daughter?' Tess was frowning and he wanted to reach across the table and smooth out her brow. 'You won't get to see her if you stay here. Or not very often anyway.'

'No, but maybe she doesn't want to see me? To tell you the truth, I don't think I'm flavour of the month with her either.'

'Why? Did your ex poison her against you? I've heard of that happening.' Tess seemed concerned on his behalf and it gave Josh a warm feeling in the pit of his stomach. This woman, who'd only just met him, was already on his side and in a battle she knew nothing about.

He sighed. 'Yes, I think she did, but it's also partly because she's a teenager and I refuse to buy her all the things she wants.' He ticked them off on his fingers. 'An iPhone, iPad, laptop, Wii, Playstation, clothes ... you name it. I'm sorry, but I figured spoiling her wouldn't make up for not seeing her a whole heap. And besides, Isla would've killed me.'

'I can see why.' Tess smiled now. 'That would have made me mad too, if I was her. So how old is ... Shayla, was it? ... exactly?'

'Sixteen.'

'Sixteen? I thought you said you were ...'

'Thirty-four, yes.' He shrugged. 'She was a teenage mistake. I was eighteen when she was born and had just got married.'

'Wow, that's a bit young! Shotgun?'

Josh wasn't sure if Tess was shocked or amused, but she didn't look too bothered by his carelessness. 'Sort of. Isla's dad was a Methodist minister and mine was ... not there, but my mum was and I realised I'd let her down. Kind of made me grow up overnight, I guess you could say.'

'Hmm, yes. Quite a responsibility for an eighteen-year-old. So is that why things didn't work out with Isla? You were both too young?'

'Yes. That and the fact that we're very different. She likes living in a town, I like the countryside. She wanted flashy cars and clothes, I couldn't care less ... and so on. A match made in hell, really.' He smiled. 'But let's not talk about that any more. As for Shayla, once she grows up a bit, I hope she'll come to see I'm not the bastard she thinks I am.'

They finished their meal and went for a walk along the river before driving back to Merrick Court. Josh wanted to take Tess's hand, but resisted the impulse. He could sense her reserve. She probably wasn't ready to jump into any relationship yet, let alone a casual fling, even though he was sure there were sparks between them. And he wasn't ready for anything serious. He'd give her time and who knew, something might happen? In the meantime, perhaps he could at least give her a quick kiss goodnight?

As his car drew up by the back door of the Court, however, Josh could see that this plan was doomed to failure. On the steps sat a teenage boy who looked extremely pleased to see Tess. Louis.

'Oh my God!' Tess exclaimed. 'What's he doing here?'

'Looks like you're about to find out.'

Josh tried not to feel disappointed that it wasn't quite the end to the evening he'd envisaged. But he really didn't want an audience if and when he kissed Tess, so he left her to sort out the boy. Kissing could wait.

Tess didn't know whether to be pleased or annoyed to find Louis sitting on the kitchen steps. She'd had a lovely evening with Josh and had spent the entire car journey back to Merrick Court wondering if he'd try to kiss her goodnight or not. He hadn't taken her hand as they walked along the river – a romantic opportunity if ever there was one – so she'd come to the conclusion he probably wasn't interested, but she'd still been on tenterhooks.

Now, she'd never know.

As Josh drove off, she hurried over to her nephew with Vince in tow. They'd picked him up from Bryn on the way home, but he hung back a bit at the sight of Louis, as always wary of strangers. 'Louis? What on earth are you doing here? Has something happened?'

Louis stood up and allowed her to hug him. Instead of responding in that awkward teenage way of only half leaning into it, he threw his arms around her and almost crushed her, which made Tess conclude there was something very wrong.

'Let's go inside then you can tell me what's up.'

He nodded and bent to hold out his hand for Vince to sniff. 'Who's this?'

'Vincent. He's a rescue dog and I'm fostering him for a while. Come in.'

While Louis and Vince got to know each other, she made two cups of hot chocolate, even though it was really too warm for drinks like that. It was soothing, and as she sat down at the table opposite Louis she saw him put his hands round the mug as if gathering strength from it.

'I finished my exams already,' he finally said, not looking at her but studying the table as if his life depended on it. 'I'll get shit marks, even though I tried. I really did. But the dyslexia … I just can't see the words, you know? They … it doesn't work.' He shrugged. 'So school's out and I decided to spend my summer holidays with you. If that's okay?' He looked up at last and Tess almost melted. There was no way she could have resisted the pleading in his eyes.

'Of course you can stay here if you want. You're always welcome, you know that, although I'm not sure how much longer I'll be here myself. Still, we'll worry about that later. But what did your parents say? Are they okay with this? And surely school can't be totally finished. It's only June.'

'I didn't tell them. Mum and Dad, I mean. I had some savings so I just took the train and the bus. That's why I arrived so late. And then you weren't here …'

'Sorry. I was just out for dinner with Josh. The heir, remember? He's still here sorting things out.'

'Yes, 'course I remember.'

'So your parents think you're still at school?' Louis attended a very expensive boarding school somewhere in the Home Counties so Rosie and George wouldn't necessarily know that Louis was gone, unless the school had informed them.

Louis nodded. 'I'll text them tomorrow.'

'And the school?'

'They've given us leave. As soon as the exams were done us sixth formers could do what we wanted. I'll just have to go back for the official end of term and maybe a party or two. I told them I was visiting you and left your address and phone number.'

'Oh, good.' At least he'd had the sense not to just run away.

They drank their chocolate in silence for a while, then Louis sighed and started talking again. 'Mum and Dad want me to go and study accountancy – I'm okay with numbers. But it's not what I want. I'm done with studying. I just can't handle any more. And even if it's mostly numbers, there will be essays and shit to write, then I'll get bad marks again and they'll be disappointed …'

'What *do* you want to do then? What's your dream?' Tess had heard his unspoken plea for support and she gave it to him without hesitation. She'd thought for quite a while now that his parents didn't seem to understand what a struggle school was for Louis. They thought that if only he worked harder, he could overcome the dyslexia and do better. To a certain extent, it was possible to learn to cope with it, but she sensed that Louis wasn't the studious type anyway.

'I want to be a gardener.' Louis almost whispered the words, but Tess heard him.

'Okay. What kind? Parks? Landscape? Or do you mean like a garden designer?' she asked.

Louis stared at her as if he couldn't believe she was taking him seriously. 'Er, I don't know. Any, I guess.'

'Well, whichever one you choose, presumably you'll still have to study somewhere. Or maybe you can get an apprenticeship? Have you looked into it?'

'No. I've been so busy filling in stupid uni applications, I didn't think to … but, yeah, I guess I should have a look.' His expression showed a flicker of hope. 'You think they'll buy it?'

He was talking about his parents, of course, and Tess's first instinct was to say no, because she was sure they'd be furious. And not just with him, but with her for interfering. She decided to be honest with Louis. He deserved to be treated like an adult now he was almost eighteen.

'Probably not at first,' she admitted. 'But if you come up with a proper plan for how you're going to become a gardener and ultimately that it leads to a job, they'll realise you're serious. And maybe hint that you're aiming to start your own business eventually, that'll make it sound even better. It's going to be tough, but you have to stick to your guns if this is what you really want to do. It's your life, Louis, you decide. And I'm here for you if things get tough.' She gave him a small smile. 'It's not as if your mum and I get on all that well anyway.'

He smiled then, a smile that again melted Tess's heart. Even though she'd only known him for five years, she loved this boy as if he was her own and she wanted him to be happy. She would back him, and to hell with Rosie and George.

'Thank you. You're the best.'

Tess didn't think that was true, but she wanted to be, for Louis' sake.

'Go for it, Louis. Now we'd better go to bed as it's late. Come on, I'll give you some sheets. Want your usual room?'

'Yep, that'll be fine, thanks.'

He stood up and without her asking, took both mugs over to the sink to rinse them off. *Not his mother's son, obviously*. But she'd known that already.

***

Raglan Castle, 11th June 1646

'You're in an uncommonly good mood this evening, Howell, how come?'

Matthew Emrys was playing a game of dice with

Arabella's lover and a few others, while Rhys lounged against a nearby wall. He and Matthew had been watching Howell all day between them, but so far he'd gone about his business like everyone else. Although the man was slow to obey orders, he did as he was told, and he hadn't slipped outside to sneak off for any assignations with the enemy.

Rhys wished he had, as that would have given him an excuse to pound the man and haul him before their superiors. But obviously Howell was cannier than that.

For the last hour or so, he had been drinking copiously though. Where he'd obtained so much ale, Rhys had no idea, as they were all on short rations, but Howell had been winning so perhaps the man had bribed someone to provide him with extra. The only good thing about it was that it was starting to loosen his tongue.

'I had some good news recently,' Howell replied to Matthew's question, looking so smug Rhys had to put his hands in his pockets to stop himself from punching the man. 'About an inheritance.'

'Oh, aye? Won't be much use to you in here,' Matthew commented.

'Well, I don't know about you, but I'm not planning on dying just yet. I doubt this siege will last long. The marquis will have to surrender fairly quickly and then we'll all leave.'

Matthew shook his head. 'You don't seem to have much faith in his lordship. It's a wonder you're here at all. Are you sure you're on the right side of the walls?'

'No, no,' Howell blustered, 'I didn't mean that. It's just that I've heard ... well, sieges don't normally last long.'

'Hmm, we'll see, won't we?' Matthew took his turn to roll the dice. A pair of sixes, which made Howell swear as he peered at them.

'I'll beat you yet, see if I don't.' Howell rattled the dice in his turn, then smirked. 'Not that it matters. I'll have more than pennies soon ...'

Rhys had had enough. It turned his stomach to hear the man brag like that and the thought of Arabella with this coarse bastard ... How could she have chosen someone like him? He pushed away from the wall and went out into the courtyard, taking deep breaths of fresh air. He couldn't stand to be in the same room as the man. May he rot in hell.

Chapter Twenty

Josh found Tess in her workshop, accompanied by Vincent and Louis.

'Good to see you again,' he said to the boy. 'You were here briefly when I'd just arrived, weren't you?'

'Yep, with my mum.'

Louis was using an electric sanding machine to get old paint off some of the furniture Tess had bought the day before so Josh waved her outside for a moment. 'Can't hear yourself think in there,' he said.

'Yes, it's deafening.' Tess leaned on the bottom half of the stable door, which was the entrance to her workshop.

'Nice stuff you have in there.' Josh smiled. 'Now I see what you meant about the "tarting up".'

'Thanks. It does seem to sell well.' Tess's cheeks turned pink.

'And why shouldn't it?' Josh tilted his head to one side, wondering why she was embarrassed.

'I ... er, no one's ever actually said they liked it before. To Giles it was only ever a "little hobby" and I don't think he saw the beauty in the pieces I'm creating. Or the hard work that goes into it.' She shrugged. 'Art wasn't his thing.'

The guy had obviously been a moron not to appreciate his wife's talent, but Josh refrained from saying so. 'Well, I think it's great. You have real talent, for sure.' He decided to change the subject. 'So was there an emergency?' Josh kept his voice down, just in case Louis could hear them. He'd been wondering what had brought the kid here so late and uninvited.

'Not really. He's finished his exams and he was a bit

down because he doesn't think he did very well.' Tess went on to explain about Louis's dyslexia, his parents' hopes for him and his own dream. 'So he wants to spend some time here with me. Do you mind? He'll have to leave if you decide to sell, of course.'

'No, that's fine.' Josh was glad Tess wouldn't be alone in the house any longer. Despite the presence of the dog, he'd wondered about her safety.

She added in a whisper, 'We're hiding out in my workshop because he's sent his mum a message to tell her and she's bound to be on the phone immediately. Only, we can't hear the house phone out here and as you've probably found out already, mobiles don't work at Merrick Court.'

'Er, wouldn't it be better to talk to her?' Josh was sure Louis's parents would have more than a thing or two to say about him having come here without permission, but the boy seemed like a nice kid and if he had genuinely been struggling, Josh agreed it seemed cruel to make him study just for the sake of it.

'I think she needs to calm down a bit first or she won't even listen to what Louis has to say.' Tess made a face. 'Much better to wait until at least lunchtime.'

'Right. Well, if he wants to be a gardener, shouldn't he be outside working with Bryn?'

'He would be normally, but he spotted you earlier so I think he figured the old man had enough help.'

'You can never have enough help in a garden. Want me to take him with me? I'm sure Bryn would love to see him.' And maybe that would give Josh more time to spend with Tess. Not that he should really, as he was getting much too addicted to her company, but was that so bad? He enjoyed being with her, talking to her and ...

'Would you?' Tess's eyes lit up and looking into their blue depths he would have done anything for her at that moment.

Oh, shit, he was in trouble.

He was definitely starting to feel at home here and if he got to know Tess even better, he wasn't convinced he'd ever be able to leave at all. But maybe he wasn't meant to? He had to put down roots somewhere; why not at Merrick Court? In fact, since arriving here he hadn't once experienced the 'itchy feet' sensation he'd had so often before leaving New Zealand.

And hell, he'd even been welcomed by one of the spirits. Well, invaded more like, but still ...

'Sure.' He returned his thoughts to the matter at hand and waved in the direction of Tess's workshop. 'Maybe later when you're done here we could do some more work in that knot garden?'

'I'd like that. I've just got to get the first coat of paint on some of these items then I'll come and find you.'

'I'll look forward to that.' *Yeah, a little bit too much maybe.* But Josh decided to ignore the voice inside his head. You only lived once and wherever this ... friendship was heading, he'd enjoy it while he could.

Tess's plan backfired big time. Just as she and Louis were sitting down to a lunch of toasted cheese sandwiches, they heard a car speed into the yard and brake hard as if it had been travelling a little too fast. The two of them looked at each other.

'Uh-oh.' Louis put his sandwich down, his face going pale. 'Shit. I should have known Mum wouldn't wait patiently by the phone.'

Tess reached across the table and gave his hand a squeeze. 'Just stand up to her. You're old enough to decide about your own life. I'm not rich, but you can always stay with me if you need to. And if you decide to do that course you were talking about this morning, you can apply for a student loan. Okay?'

Louis nodded and she saw his mouth tighten with determination. He'd apparently been up early and had already looked into degree courses in gardening. There were a couple of possibilities if he got his skates on and applied soon, so they'd been discussing his options over breakfast. A proper qualification seemed the best way, even if it might mean the odd essay or two.

'I can always help you with those,' Tess had said. 'If you just email them to me I'll check for typos. No big deal.'

The kitchen door was thrown open now and Rosie stormed in without knocking, followed more slowly by George. Rosie's face was twisted with fury, while her husband merely looked resigned. He raised a hand in greeting and opened his mouth to say something, but Rosie didn't give him a chance. She launched into speech immediately.

'What the *hell* do you think you're doing, filling my son's head with stupid ideas and encouraging him to play truant? Let me tell you, you have absolutely no say in Louis's upbringing and I'll thank you to keep your nose out of our business.'

This tirade had, of course, been directed at Tess, who didn't even bother to reply. Better to allow Rosie to let off some steam first. The woman turned on her son next.

'And as for you, what do you mean by behaving in this way? We pay an awful lot of money to that school and you can't just up and leave when you feel like it! I'll be calling the headmaster later to find out why they are allowing their students to disappear without informing their parents. And you're coming home with us now. Go and get your things, please.'

Louis stood up. 'Actually, I'm not, so you've had a wasted journey. I've finished my exams and I have leave. I told the school where I was going, so don't blame them. Unlike you, they consider Tess an adult who it's okay for me to stay with.'

'How dare you speak to me like that? You are grounded for the rest of the summer. And you can forget about those driving lessons we promised you and—'

George held up a hand to interrupt his wife. 'Rosie, darling, perhaps we should sit down and let Louis speak?'

'I'm not sitting at the same table as this ... this traitor!' Rosie glared at Tess, who raised her eyebrows at her sister-in-law.

'Excuse me? Are you saying you'd rather I'd have thrown your son out, late at night and possibly with no money to go anywhere else?'

'Tess is right, darling.' George put a hand on Rosie's arm. 'As I told you in the car, let's be sensible about this and find out what's going on before jumping to conclusions.'

Rosie shook off his hand. 'Don't you "darling" me. Why are you taking her side? This is our son we're talking about. He's nothing to do with Therese.'

'Hello? Could we get back to the point here?' Louis raised his voice and Tess inwardly applauded him. Good, he was standing up for himself.

'Which is that we're leaving now. Therese doesn't need to be part of this discussion.' Rosie's mouth set into a mulish line, but Louis matched her for once and didn't move.

'I told you, I'm not going anywhere. If you'd just listen for five seconds, I'll tell you my plans.'

'Your "plan" is to go back to school until term ends and then—'

'Rosie! Let Louis speak, for God's sake.' Tess had had enough of the histrionics.

Rosie gave her a dirty look, but said, 'Go on then,' to Louis, rather ungraciously.

So Louis told his parents he was determined to study horticulture or landscape and garden design, and that he'd been looking into suitable courses. 'I'm *not* studying accountancy, whatever you say. It's boring and I don't want

195

to spend my life stuck in an office. And I'm going to help Bryn in the garden here all summer. He's the best teacher ever and it's good practice.'

'No,' Rosie said. 'This is ridiculous. Gardening isn't a proper job. You think we've spent all that money on your education just so you can fritter away your life pottering around with plants like some … some labourer? Think again. You'll need a well-paid job in order to afford all the maintenance on this house when it becomes yours one day.'

'You haven't bought it yet. And stop going on about how much money you've spent on my school,' Louis snarled. 'That was your choice and fat lot of good it did me, eh? I still can't spell and I'm going to get crappy grades in my A-levels.'

Rosie looked to her husband for support. 'George? Say something! You're the one who's always going on about how expensive the school fees are.'

George shrugged. 'Actually, it sounds to me as though Louis has thought this through and he's right, it's his life. It's not like he's saying he's going to become a traveller or something.'

'Well, if that's all the support you're going to give me, I could have come by myself. Thanks a million.' Rosie sent George a death glare, but he ignored it.

'Come on,' he said. 'I have a meeting this afternoon I need to get to and you've seen for yourself that Louis is fine.' He turned to his son. 'We'll see you at the end of term celebrations. You'll return for that, won't you?'

Louis nodded. 'Of course. Thanks, Dad.'

'I'm not leaving him here.' Rosie crossed her arms over her chest. 'Therese is filling his head with a lot of rubbish.'

'I am not,' Tess stated firmly, glaring at Rosie until the woman looked away.

'Mum, I'm not a moron,' Louis added. 'I can think for myself, you know. The only thing Tess has done is treat me like an adult. It would be nice if you could do the same.'

'Well, really!' Rosie looked like she'd swallowed a lime, whole.

George took her arm and steered her towards the door. 'Let it go, Rose. Accept defeat, for once in your life, and think about something other than what *you* want.'

'Bastard!' Rosie hissed, but she preceded him out of the door, leaving without saying goodbye to either Tess or Louis. Tess didn't envy George the journey back to London.

When the door had slammed shut behind them, Tess and Louis looked at each other and both let out a sigh of relief. Then Tess held up her hand for a high five. 'Go you!' she said. 'Well done for staying cool.'

Louis smiled and high-fived her back. 'And you.'

They both burst out laughing, giddy with relief. They'd won that battle.

Raglan Castle, 12th June 1646

Arabella didn't see Glyn the next day and thought she could probably avoid meeting him by the simple expedient of never venturing into the Stone Court. The soldiers weren't allowed in the other quadrangle unless they were on duty in one of the towers on that side, so all she had to do was make sure she looked carefully before going outside. That way, if he was crossing the Fountain Court on his way to a post, she would see him and could wait until he was safely out of the way.

She'd forgotten about the pantry. This was situated at one end of the Great Hall and towards evening she was sent there to fetch some wine for Lady Margaret. Just inside the door, she almost cannoned straight into Glyn, who was standing with a tankard of ale in one hand. He was with another soldier, but grabbed her arm as if to steady her, then bent to hiss, 'Don't think you can avoid me forever. I'll find you, I promise.'

'Just leave me be.' She wrenched her arm away from his grip and because the other man was watching he let go. But the smirk on his face told her he hadn't given up, quite the opposite. Her avoidance tactics would just make him more eager to find her, but what else could she do?

Unfortunately, she didn't see Rhys either, except in the distance. He hadn't come near her in the chapel that morning and the few times she'd caught his eye he was scowling at her something fierce. She could only surmise that he had the wrong idea about her and Glyn. Admittedly, they had been standing very close to each other, with Glyn trying to kiss her, but why hadn't Rhys noticed that she wasn't willing?

A lover's tiff, he'd called it, and that was obviously what he thought. It made her both furious and downcast at the same time. She wanted to explain to him, but if he wouldn't even give her the benefit of the doubt and talk to her, how could she? Honestly, men were so obtuse sometimes.

All the men were kept busy though and she felt guilty for thinking of herself when all the castle's inhabitants were in such dire straits. The garrison made several sallies a day against the troops camped outside, with cavalrymen such as Rhys leading the way, and the besiegers had to fight hard to force them back into the castle. But their cannon continued their onslaught on the castle's walls and the formerly neat Fountain Court was now strewn with debris – stone, mortar, glass and bits of lead. Arabella tried not to jump every time she heard a bang, but it was hard not to.

'Are the sallies having any impact on the enemy numbers at all?' Arabella ventured to ask the chaplain, who was a great friend of the marquis and therefore knew all about what was going on.

He shook his head. 'Not enough, I'm afraid. There are just too many of them and much as I'm loath to admit it, Colonel Morgan is an able leader.'

'I heard tell a command arrived from the king yesterday.' There had been much talk and rumour about it throughout the castle, but Arabella wanted to know the truth and the chaplain could be trusted to give her that.

'Yes, well, it was a message purporting to come from His Majesty, asking any remaining garrisons to lay down their arms, but Lord Worcester refused. After all, how do we know it wasn't just a ruse on the part of the enemy?'

From what Arabella had gleaned, Raglan was one of the last places to hold out so she thought it entirely possible that such a command could be genuine. After all, the king was in no position to do anything other than surrender, being a prisoner himself. But she couldn't help but admire the marquis for his staunch support of the monarch. He'd decided on his allegiance and he was going to stand by it, come what may. That was true honour, wasn't it? Or just sheer stubbornness in the face of insurmountable odds?

She peeked out of the windows occasionally when she was with Lady Margaret, as that room had views over the Leaguer Fields where the enemy had set up their camp. It seemed to her their numbers were swelling, rather than lessening, and her hope dwindled with it. Still, Lord Worcester had been kind to her and she owed it to him to try and be as courageous as he was. As long as he refused to surrender, she would support him in any way she could. She could only hope that God would protect them all somehow.

Chapter Twenty-One

Home Farm, 13th June 2016

'Either of you guys want to come and help shear sheep?'

Josh came into the kitchen on the Sunday night, asking this strange question, and Tess just stared at him. 'What?'

'I've promised to help Fred Williams up at Home Farm and I'm sure he could do with a few more pairs of hands if you're interested.'

Tess wondered if Josh was winding them up, but he didn't look like he was joking.

'I'll have a go!' Louis was all for it, smiling at Josh.

Tess wasn't so sure. 'I doubt I'll be of much use, but sure, we can come. How do you know Fred?' She'd only met him herself a couple of times, mostly when he came to pay Giles for grazing.

'Bryn introduced us down the pub. Anyway, all good, I'll see you tomorrow then. Come over any time after seven.'

Tess and Louis agreed that seven was a bit too early for any sane person, so they bumped down the lane to the Home Farm at just before nine. They parked in the yard and made their way towards the huge barns as a lot of noise was coming from that direction. In between two buildings, under a roof, a makeshift shearing station had been set up, with stacks of hay either side and several small pens in the middle. There was one set of electric shears on a metallic arm on either side of the smallest pen, and six or seven sheep were crammed into it waiting their turn to be shorn. They were bleating incessantly, some clearly worried while others were taking it all in their stride. Tess soon gathered the animals had to be tightly confined so they wouldn't jump out. The whole area was strewn with little bits of wool and there was dust flying around.

At first, no one noticed their arrival so Tess and Louis stopped to watch the proceedings. Josh and another man were doing the shearing, while Fred seemed to be herding more sheep towards the central pens with the help of two sheepdogs. The dogs had big grins on their faces as if they were really enjoying their task.

Tess couldn't take her eyes off Josh. He was quite clearly an expert at this and in his element. Grabbing a sheep from inside the pen, he brought it out and more or less turned it over, clamping it against his legs, belly up. The sheep's bottom was still on the floor and its head just above Josh's knees. It seemed docile enough as Josh took hold of the shearing device and started under its chin, working his way down the stomach, but Tess guessed it probably took quite a lot of strength to keep the animal in place. As she watched, he continued with the inside of the back legs, then the outside up towards the animal's backside before going back to the head, front legs, round the shoulders and along the back down to the other side. Working in quick, sweeping motions, Josh soon had the whole body clear of wool and finished off around the sheep's neck and face. The entire task took less than two minutes, probably more like a minute and a half, the fleece coming off neatly all in one piece.

Tess was astonished and must have let out a noise of some sort, as Josh looked up and spotted them. He let go of the shorn sheep and it took off, doing little leaps like a gazelle, either for joy or in fright, Tess wasn't sure which. It joined other equally naked-looking animals that were milling around. Josh smiled. His handsome face was, as always, covered in stubble, his green eyes shining as though he was truly enjoying himself. Tess couldn't help but admire the confident way he moved, comfortable in his own skin, so sure of his abilities here but totally without the need to be cocky about it. It was incredibly sexy, that innate self-confidence, and warmth flooded her entire being as he came towards them. She hoped it didn't show on her face.

'Ah, the new recruits have arrived. Fred, want to put Tess and Louis to work?'

Fred, who'd just finished pushing more sheep into the middle pen, came over, giving them an assessing glance as if he wasn't sure Josh was serious. He took in their attire – jeans, wellies and old T-shirts – and they must have passed muster. 'Sure, we can always do with an extra pair of hands. Er, would you mind folding up the fleeces and putting them in those bags over there?' he said to Tess, indicating a pile of enormous white bags that were slowly being filled with wool. 'Here, I'll show you.' He seemed slightly embarrassed, as if it was somehow not right to ask the lady of the manor to do something so menial, but Tess gave him a big smile and followed his lead.

'No problem.'

The fleeces turned out to be quite heavy and extremely oily.

'Lanolin,' Fred said. 'You get used to it.'

There was a table at one end of the pens and he showed Tess how to put the fleece on there and fold it into a tight bundle. It was dirty on the outside, clean on the inside, and not at all smelly, contrary to what Tess had expected. The bundle was stuffed into a sack and once this was full, it had to be sewn together with a large needle and twine. 'Rough stitches are fine,' Fred instructed, demonstrating on the nearest one, before turning to Louis.

'Can you help me herd more sheep towards the pens, please? The older ones know what to expect, but the young ones get a bit panicky.'

'Sure.' Louis was soon hard at work chasing sheep, trying to get them to go in the right direction.

They were all working together as a team. It felt good. No, better than good. For the first time in ages, Tess was doing something really useful and she realised she'd missed that. Being a housewife had never been her ambition and she'd hoped to develop her business further in time. Giles, however, had wanted her just to raise their children and perhaps have the furniture painting as a small hobby. She knew now that would never have worked out for her.

The hours flew by and Tess was surprised when Fred's wife, Mair, came to tell them it was lunchtime. The woman did a double take when she caught sight of Tess and Louis, but smiled when she noticed what they were doing. 'How lovely,' she said in her beautiful Welsh accent. 'Everything goes so much faster with more helpers. Come and have a bite to eat.'

'I'm sure you hadn't reckoned on having to feed us all,' Tess protested. 'Louis and I can go home and have lunch, then come back later.'

'Rubbish! There's plenty for everyone.' Mair beckoned for them to follow her, and soon the six of them were seated at a long wooden table in the farmhouse garden. The weather continued warm, but with a cooling breeze that was particularly welcome after the hard work. 'Help yourselves, everyone. I'll just get some more plates and cutlery.'

Mair had set out what appeared to be a veritable feast on the table – quiche, potato salad, bread, cheese and cold meats. And huge jugs of beer and lemonade. Josh slid onto the bench next to Tess and offered to pour her some beer.

'Thanks, but I think I prefer lemonade. Better when you're thirsty.' She helped herself.

'No way. Nothing beats a cold beer.' Josh grinned at her and added, 'Sorry about the dirt. Hope I won't put you off lunch?'

Tess pretended to sniff and wrinkle her nose, then laughed. 'Nah, it's fine.' He was very dirty and sweaty, but she found she didn't mind at all. She wasn't exactly clean herself.

'How many sheep can you shear in a day?' she asked, curious about the whole process.

'Two hundred, maybe more. I'm helping out for free here, but normally you get paid per sheep so the more you can do, the better, obviously.'

'Two hundred? Wow!' That sounded like a lot to Tess.

Mair came back with plates for her and Louis, and everyone tucked in.

'Thank you for coming, Lady Merrick.' Mair, seated at one end of the table near Tess, passed her the butter. 'It's very kind of you.'

'Not at all, I'm enjoying it. And please, call me Tess. I'm not really Lady Merrick any longer.' She bumped her shoulder into Josh's. 'This here's the new lord.'

Josh rolled his eyes. 'I wish everyone would stop saying that. Have you ever met anyone less like an aristocrat? No, plain Josh Owens, that's me.'

The people round the table all laughed at that, but Tess silently disagreed. He may not be posh or talk with a cut-glass accent, the way Giles had done, but he had an air of authority about him. He was a born leader, someone who got things done, just not in an overt manner. She could definitely imagine him as a medieval lord, managing his estate in a good way, fair to tenants and servants alike.

Surely that was worth a lot more than just being born into the role?

After lunch, Josh gave Tess a lesson in sheep shearing, finding a smallish ewe for her to have a go at. He stood behind her, his chest against her back and his legs braced behind her in case she needed a helping hand. The feel of her body moulded to his like that was exhilarating. So much so that he had to concentrate really hard in order to teach her rather than just hold onto her.

'Look, you grab it by the head, like this.' He demonstrated, wrestling the animal onto its back. 'Clamp the head against your thighs with your elbow and put your foot under its front hoof. You need both hands for the shearing as you have to pull the skin tight against the shears in order to cut properly.'

He placed his hand on top of her smaller one and guided her movements along the sheep's belly, where the shears left little ridges after the fleece came off. For him, it was just routine, but he knew it could be scary at first. It took a lot of practice to get it right.

'I don't want to hurt her,' Tess murmured. 'What if I cut her skin?'

'You won't, don't worry. I'll help you.'

He kept his hand on hers all through the task. It took much longer than if he'd done it on his own and he wondered if the poor sheep was getting traumatised, but it seemed calm enough. And Tess got the hang of things, even if she went about it slowly and carefully.

'Great! You did good,' Josh said as they let the animal go. Tess leaned forward and breathed deeply, as if all the air had gone out of her. He pulled her back up and against his chest, folding his arms round her middle. 'Hey, wasn't that fun?'

She let him hold onto her for a short while, as if she didn't want to break the contact between them either, but then she stepped away and faced him. Shaking her head, she gave him a tremulous smile. 'Not sure that classifies as "fun" exactly, but it was certainly interesting. Thank you for being so patient.'

'No problem. It's a pleasure.' And he meant it. He could have stood there showing her how to shear a sheep for hours. He was a sad case, obviously.

'Please can I have a go?' Louis had come over and was looking at Josh expectantly.

Teaching him wouldn't be nearly as much fun, but Josh liked the kid and could see he genuinely wanted to learn. 'Sure, mate. Let's get you a sheep.'

As he taught Louis the same things he'd just showed Tess, he was operating on automatic, his gaze on her half the time. Even folding fleeces she was lovely and he had a vision of them working together like this for years to come. But would she want that? Today it was an adventure, something new to try, whereas for him it was a way of life he loved. Could she learn to like it too?

That was the million-dollar question.

Merrick Court, 18th June 2016

'I've put some more water in the fountain. What d'you think?'

Tess had asked Josh to meet her in the knot garden. A whole week had gone by without them finding the time to work on the hedges. He'd been busy helping Fred, with Louis as their assistant. She'd done her bit there too, but part of the time she'd had to be in her workshop finishing a couple of orders that had suddenly come in. The hedge cutting had been put on hold, but now they were finally free to continue.

It would seem he'd arrived a lot earlier than her today though and he had been busy. She glanced towards the water, feeling a strange pull as though it was wanting her to come closer. Tess gave herself a mental shake – she was getting too fanciful for words. Water couldn't *do* anything to her, it wasn't alive. Sure, it seemed to act as some sort of facilitator for her dreams, but now she knew that, she was the one who decided when and if that happened. She turned to Josh.

'Very pretty. I don't understand why this was allowed to get so overgrown. It's a beautiful spot. Let's get on with the hedge trimming, shall we?'

'Sure.'

After a while, Tess ventured to ask him about the house. 'Have you heard any more from the estate agents? Are they putting Merrick Court in *Country Life*?'

'No, not yet. I can't seem to make up my mind.' He stared over towards the old stone bench they'd cleared and frowned. 'Something's holding me back.'

'You like it here?' Tess could understand if that was the case. The house was lovely and she'd been enchanted with it the first time she'd come here. How much more intense must that feeling be if you actually belonged?

'Yeah, I do.' Josh looked troubled. 'I just don't know if it's me. Lord Merrick and all that.'

Tess smiled. 'You'd still have the title even if you went back to New Zealand.'

'Yeah, but I wouldn't use it and I could forget all about that. Here it seems to go with the house. It's like everyone's going to see me differently because of it. Not the real me. Know what I mean?'

'I think so. But maybe you just have to change their perceptions or pre-conceived notions of what an earl should be like?'

'Yes, maybe.'

'Is Rosie still hassling you about buying the house?' Tess had heard via Louis that his mum hadn't given up hope yet.

Josh sighed. 'Yeah, but every time I think of her owning it instead of me I see red. No idea why. Like she says, at least she's family, sort of.'

Tess laughed. 'She has that effect on people. Either way, you will let me know when you've decided, right? I've made some enquiries and there are a couple of places to rent round here but I need a bit of notice to pack my stuff.'

Josh frowned. 'Of course. No rush. I think I'll stick around at least until the end of the summer to give me time to think things through.'

'Well, you should be living at the Court so I'll see if I can move out by the end of July. It's all wrong, you camping out in Bryn's little cottage when you own a huge house.'

'No worries. I think Bryn's happy to have me there and I'm enjoying it too. He's a nice guy. Reminds me of my grandpa.'

A few hours later they were more or less done. 'I think that's as good as it's going to get right now.' Josh stood up and stretched out his back.

Tess noticed his tan had deepened even more and, as always when working in the garden, he was without a shirt. He didn't appear self-conscious about showing off so much of his body, but then why should he be? It was superb. She'd had a hard time concentrating on her shears, rather than Josh. She sat down on the rim of the fountain, with her back to the water, and stretched out her legs in front of her. The weather continued hot and she was getting quite a respectable tan too.

'Yep, that's definitely enough, I'd say,' she agreed. 'Wish this water was drinkable. I'm dying of thirst. I suppose I'd better ...'

Josh held up his hand. 'No, stay right there. I'll go get us something cold from Bryn's little fridge in the shed. He doesn't just keep milk in there for tea, you know.' He grinned. 'Or at least he doesn't when I'm around. I stashed some beer and Coke in it earlier.'

'Sneaky.' Tess smiled back. 'Okay, I'll just rest for a bit then.'

Without thinking she stretched out a hand behind her and stuck it into the water, which was now lapping the rim of the fountain behind her. Again, she had the sensation of being drawn towards it.

'That's ridiculous,' she muttered, but this time she couldn't resist. She turned around and stared into the clear liquid that filled the basin. The compulsion became stronger, almost as if it was sucking at her innards. Tess swallowed hard, scared now but unable to move away. She knew what was going on, but wasn't sure she wanted it to happen. But maybe she didn't have a choice? That made her angry, and in consequence, braver.

'Okay, I get it. There's something else you want to show me, Mistress Dauncey.' She glared at the fountain, as though the spirit of the dead woman was in there. 'Fine, bring it on, but be quick. Josh'll be back soon.'

She concentrated on the water surging round her fingers as she slowly stirred the little waves, and the sounds of the garden faded into the background. Instead, there was only darkness and menace ...

Chapter Twenty-Two

Arabella was deep in thought as she headed for her own room late one evening and didn't see the shadow that detached itself from a corner until it was too late. Glyn had grabbed her and put one hand across her mouth before she had time to utter so much as a squeak, and although she fought him with all her might, he half carried, half dragged her towards the pantry.

'We have unfinished business you and I,' he muttered, huffing with the effort of keeping her from clawing at him and kicking him. 'You're a little hellcat, but it won't do you any good. I'm your master and the sooner you learn that, the better it will be for you.'

She bit his hand. 'Never. I'll never be yours—' But with an oath, his hand returned to her mouth and pressed even harder, almost cutting off her breathing.

Arabella noticed they were heading for the stairs down to the wine cellar. Where was everyone? Had they all gone to bed? Why didn't someone come and help her? She made as much noise as she could behind Glyn's hand, but only muffled squeaks came out and it made her even more breathless to the point where she thought she might faint.

He forced her down the circular staircase and into a dark tunnel that led to the cellar, but then stopped halfway. There was a window embrasure in the wall, almost as thick as a full-length man, and here he pushed her onto her back, launching himself on top of her. Again, she managed to free her mouth and screamed. The sound echoed off the damp stone walls, but she doubted anyone would hear. A sob of both fury and fear tore out of her, and she thrashed her head from side to side to avoid his disgusting mouth, which seemed to her to be slobbering all over her face and throat.

'Lie still, bitch!' He slapped her hard and Arabella's head buzzed.

She tried to blink to clear her head and continued to fight him, but he had her pinned down and his hands were working their way up underneath her skirts, bunching them up beneath her. As he fumbled with his breeches, she screamed again. 'HELP! Someone, please, help m—'

'Shut *up*!' Glyn hit her again, this time so hard she blacked out for a moment.

When she came to, she found the weight of him lifted off her and heard a crunching sound. She looked up and in the faint light from the window behind her, she saw Rhys bashing Glyn's head against the stone wall.

'Don't. Ever. Touch. Her. *Again!* You whoreson!' he snarled, hitting Glyn once more for good measure. The man sank to the floor like a sack of grain, his eyes rolling up into his head.

'Is-is he dead?' Arabella whispered, her voice hoarse with fear and shouting.

'Unfortunately not, but he will be if he tries to force you again.' Rhys held out a hand and pulled her gently off the ledge. 'Are you hurt? Can you stand?'

'I ... no, not hurt. And yes, I th-think I can.'

But she was shaking so much that in the end he just picked her up and carried her up the stairs and into the Great Hall. There was still no one about, so he headed for the big oriel window where there were some seats. No one would see them there unless they came in through the doors at this end of the room.

Now that the ordeal was over, Arabella found that tears were coursing down her cheeks. She couldn't stop them, but felt foolish to be crying now that she was safe. 'I'm s-sorry. I can't seem to ...'

'Shhh, it's all right, *cariad*.' Rhys pulled her onto his lap and just held her close, rocking her like a small child. 'He won't hurt you again, I'll see to it. I'll report him to Lord Charles and he can deal with him. He's firm when it comes to discipline.'

'No, don't! He'll find a way to hurt *you* after he's been punished. Trust me, I know him. It's not worth it. As long as he can't g-get to me again …'

'Are you sure? I can look after myself.'

'No, please. Everyone will gossip about me and they'll think … they'll think the same thing you did the first time you saw us together. And once people begin to suspect something, no matter what you say the doubt will always remain. No smoke without a fire they'll say. Really, I couldn't bear it.'

'Very well, I won't say a word, I promise.'

Arabella relaxed and leaned her head against his shoulder. She was safe.

Merrick Court, 18th June 2016

'Tess? Tess! Are you okay?'

Josh dropped the cans onto the grass and sank down next to her. She was slumped against the fountain, half lying on the ground, and appeared to have passed out. Thankfully she was breathing; the sight of her chest rising up and down went some way towards tamping down his first panicked reaction. He touched her arm. 'Tess, talk to me.'

'Josh? Oh, ow …' Tess blinked at him, her eyes unfocused and the pupils dilated, almost obliterating the blue irises around them.

'Did you faint? Too much sun?' He looked up but the sun's rays weren't as strong now and there was a tree partially shading the area around the fountain. Perhaps she'd just worked too hard.

'Mmm, maybe ... don't remember,' she muttered, but she kept her eyes down and he had a feeling she was lying.

'Can you sit up?' He helped her into a more upright position. 'You want your drink? Beer or Coke?'

'Coke, please.' She held out a hand that was visibly shaking and sipped from the can he opened for her.

'Seriously, what happened?' he asked, not believing for a minute that she didn't remember.

'I don't know. I guess I got dizzy and ... I-I'm sorry, but I can't explain.'

Her eyes were bright with unshed tears and Josh felt his heart melting. Without pressing her for any more answers, he sat down next to her again and pulled her close, holding her until she stopped shaking. They sipped their cold drinks in silence and Josh stared with unseeing eyes at the beauty around him, feeling confused.

What the hell was going on?

After a while, her regular breathing told him she'd fallen asleep and he closed his own eyes. He became aware of a faint noise, a sound which was growing into something recognisable. A single word, repeated over and over again.

'Listen, listen, listen ...'

The admonition, insistent and cajoling, was carried on the wind, a susurration passing from leaf to leaf in the bushes and branches around him. It invaded his brain and Josh blinked into the setting sun. To his right, he noticed a shadow under the trees, agitated, restless. It was fairly obvious it was trying to communicate and, as far as he knew, Josh was the only person there with whom it might actually work. Adrenaline raced through him and his pulse rate went up several notches. It had happened before with the mirror; it could work again. But did he want it to? Yes, definitely. He focused on the shape, addressing it in his thoughts.

'*You want to tell me what's going on? Does it have something to do with Tess?*'

The shadowy form seemed to nod. Josh took a deep breath, preparing himself mentally. After a lifetime of ignoring the lost souls he wasn't sure he was ready for this, but if it would help Tess, he'd go along with it.

'*Okay, I'm listening.*'

He closed his eyes and tried to free his mind from all other thoughts, waiting for the voice until it rang out again. '*Listen.*' And then the images came too …

Raglan Castle, 18th June 1646

Rhys felt like a cad. 'Forgive me. I shouldn't have doubted you, I see that now, but I have to admit I thought you might be a Parliamentarian spy and … well, I believed you were a couple, perhaps even married.' He didn't want to tell her he'd been jealous, but that was the truth. The green-eyed devil, pure and simple, because he wanted her for himself.

'A spy? Me? Whatever gave you that idea?'

Rhys took a deep breath and decided to be honest with her. He had been a fool to doubt her, but he'd been justified to a certain extent. The fact that he'd let his liking … no love, for her, and consequently his jealousy, blind him to her possible innocence was something he regretted now. He winced. She'd come so close to being raped tonight by that bastard Howell. If he hadn't been watching the man and heard Arabella's screams, things would have ended very badly for her.

He couldn't bear to even think about it and suppressed a shiver.

'Very well, I'll confess. I followed you to Merrick Court one night and I put two and two together, obviously coming up with the wrong answer. But you must admit it was a bit suspicious, you going there of all places.'

Arabella gasped. 'That was you? Oh no! But—'

'Don't worry, I won't tell a soul, I swear. I have no idea what you were doing, but your secret is safe with me and whoever you were meeting. Was it someone dear to you? An old retainer perhaps or a relative?'

She shook her head. 'I wasn't meeting anyone. I was hiding something. But you definitely mustn't *ever* tell anyone about that.'

'I won't, I promise.'

'And that means I owe you my thanks twice over – you saved me from those men that night too, didn't you?'

'I only helped a little. It was nothing.'

'It was! I would never—'

'Shhh, let's forget that night as well.' He felt absurdly relieved that she hadn't been going to Merrick to see anyone, but he'd think about that later. For now, he needed to calm her down and reassure her. 'Are you sure you're not hurt, *cariad*? He didn't …?'

'No, just a few bruises and my head hurts, but you came in time. Really, I can't thank you enough.'

He pulled her even closer and she buried her face in his shoulder. 'No need for thanks. I shouldn't have had to rescue you. That man is a menace, but perhaps you're right. I won't report him. I'll just continue to watch him. And I will ask some of the others to help.'

She raised her head. 'You were spying on him?'

'Just keeping an eye out for anything suspicious. I thought he was in cahoots with you, remember, but now I know he's likely here for his own purposes. I've heard of your uncle and I doubt very much any nephew of his will be a Royalist.'

'No, never. He admitted as much that day outside the kitchen, but he said if I told anyone he'd kill me. And he means to marry me so he can get his hands on Merrick Court. He's welcome to the estate, but I wouldn't wed him if he was the last man on earth!'

'Oh, Arabella, I'm so sorry …' Rhys felt that he'd failed her spectacularly, but he would make up for it now. 'And I never gave you that knife I promised you. If I had, you could have defended yourself better. I'll see to it as soon as possible.'

Her hand came up to cup his cheek, her fingers stroking his soft stubble. 'Thank you, Sir Rhys. I am in your debt.'

He took her hand and held it. He was very tempted to kiss her, but sensed that this was not the right time. Not with the memories of what Howell had tried to do so fresh in her mind. 'No "Sir", just Rhys, if you please, at least when there is no one else around. And you're not indebted to me at all. Just promise me you'll be more careful from now on. Don't go anywhere in the castle alone.'

'Very well.'

'As I said, we'll be watching Howell, so if he tries anything else, just scream.'

And he'd be keeping an eye on Arabella too, as much as he could in between his duties fighting for the garrison. He'd never let Howell hurt her again.

＊

Merrick Court, 18th June 2016

Josh opened his eyes and shivered. The sun was going down and the grass was beginning to feel cold and damp underneath them. He pulled in a deep breath, then looked around for the shadow. It was gone.

Sir Rhys had shown him what had happened to Tess, although it wasn't really her. It was some woman the man had been in love with, a long time ago. Arabella. She looked a bit like Tess though – same golden hair and big blue eyes – so had Sir Rhys mistaken her for his woman? And had he shown her the images too? That would explain why she was so shaken.

Josh had heard about people becoming possessed by spirits, but he'd thought it all a load of rubbish. Now he knew differently. But Sir Rhys didn't appear to be doing it with any evil intent, he was just relaying events that had happened. The question was why? What did these things matter now? Damned if Josh knew. He just had a very strong urge to protect Tess, even though he had no idea what she needed protection from.

It was all scary as hell.

'Tess? Wake up, time to go inside.'

'Hmm? Oh, sorry, did I nod off?' She stretched and Joss guessed she was stiff from the awkward position she'd been sitting in.

'Want to tell me more now?' He regarded her with his head tilted to one side, blocking her way.

'Er, just some stupid dreams I'm having. Honestly, it's not a big deal,' she murmured.

Josh hesitated for a moment, wondering whether to push for more answers, but she obviously wasn't ready to share yet so he'd wait. Dreams. Or visions? He'd been right – she *was* being shown things by Sir Rhys, probably the same events he'd seen himself. But at least she seemed okay now. And Arabella, whoever she'd been, was fine as well.

The mystery of why this was happening would have to wait for another day.

Chapter Twenty-Three

Merrick Court, 19th June 2016

Tess was woken in the middle of the night by Vincent's frenzied barking. She hadn't gone as far as to let him sleep on her bed, but he had an old duvet on the floor next to her so the racket he was making had her sitting up in seconds.

'What is it, Vince?'

She scrabbled for the light switch and scanned the room while trying to focus in the sudden brightness. Vincent was by the door, pawing at it, and she got out of bed and opened it. He raced off down the stairs, still barking, and Tess heard a crash somewhere. She ran after the dog.

On her way to the nineteenth century part of the house she almost collided with a bleary-looking Louis who came shooting out of his room. 'What's happening?'

'No idea. Burglars maybe?' She threw the words over her shoulder as she ran and was glad when Louis sprinted after her. She'd rather not confront anyone on her own, guard dog or not.

They found Vincent in the library, barking at an open window. The catch at the top appeared to have been sawn through and the sash raised high enough for someone to climb in. A small lamp lay on the floor, knocked off a side table, its bulb in a thousand pieces. Tess's gaze was immediately drawn to the open safe which had been hidden – rather predictably – behind a painting on one wall. It was like something out of an Agatha Christie novel, old and cumbersome.

'Quiet, Vince! I think whoever it was has gone now. Shush!' She patted the dog. 'Good boy. Well done for waking us. Now, please sit, over here, out of the way of the shards of glass.'

'Shit!' Louis breathed, coming to a stop next to her. 'All your valuables! There's nothing left.'

Tess couldn't help it, she snorted, then shook her head. 'No, I'm afraid whoever got that open had a wasted evening. It was empty already.'

'What?' Louis blinked. 'But the family jewels and all the important papers! Uncle Giles showed some of them to me last year and said they were irreplaceable. He kept them in a special box with a lock.'

'The papers are safe upstairs in my room – I found the box in another cupboard last week. As for the jewels, there aren't any. They're all gone. Giles sold them.'

'Why?' Louis was nothing if not direct, a trait Tess liked normally, but it wasn't easy to have to explain to him that his uncle had squandered the family's wealth. And all because he'd had a compulsion he couldn't control and refused to seek help for. Still, she'd have to tell Louis now.

She sighed. 'Your uncle was a gambler. And not just the odd flutter on the horses – a serious gambler at the really up-market casinos. It was one of the reasons he and I weren't getting on so well towards the end. He'd lost every penny we had and was starting to sell anything of value he could find here. The jewels, the silver, even some copper stuff, although I managed to hang onto most of that. Sadly, there weren't any Rembrandts or anything, but he found some Chippendale chairs upstairs and they fetched quite a lot. Plus that painting your mum was asking me about. The Hinton.'

'Jesus! If he was still alive, Mum would kill him. She's always going on about the Merrick jewels and how she thinks she ought to be allowed to wear them and not just ...' He stopped and flushed as he seemed to realise what he was about to say.

'Not just me,' Tess finished for him. 'I know. And believe me, I would've been happy to share them with her, but I couldn't because there aren't any.' She didn't mention the earring she'd found – perhaps she would show him later.

Louis scowled. 'And there was Uncle Giles telling Mum you wanted them to yourself "as was your right". What a bastard! Mum was so pissed at you.'

Tess put a hand on his shoulder and shook him slightly. 'He only said that because he was desperate for her not to find out. I think he was ashamed of what he'd done. I had agreed he could tell her that because he'd promised me he was going to stop gambling and one day buy them back, at least some of them.'

'That's still a shit thing to do.' Louis threw himself down in an armchair. 'He should have been man enough to fess up.'

'Yes, well, I don't think it was easy. Your mum can be quite ... er, formidable, when she wants to.'

'Don't I know it,' Louis muttered. He looked around the room. 'So what else did he sell? I haven't noticed any gaps on the walls or anything.'

'As I said, he didn't find much of any great value. He looked everywhere and had some specialist dealer come in as well, but short of selling all the furniture at once, he wasn't going to raise any great sums. I think he must have been getting pretty desperate, because he started looking for some old family treasure he thought was buried in the cellars. He didn't find anything.'

'Oh, yeah, I've heard of that. Mum told us about it too but I think it's just a bunch of bull. Apparently they used to hunt for it when they were kids, but if there was such a thing, it would've been found ages ago.'

'That's what I told Giles too, but he wouldn't listen.' She swallowed hard, determined to tell Louis everything now. 'Actually, it seems he found a different solution to his problems, although a temporary one. He didn't tell me but he'd started signing IOU's.'

'No!' Louis's eyes opened wide. 'How do you know?'

'Some casino owner came to see me and he emailed me copies. Said Giles owed him half a million pounds.'

'Half a m—! What? How the hell did he lose that much?'

'It's easily done at places like The Black Rose. I should know. I used to work in a casino, remember?'

'Yes, but … half a mill? That's insane.'

'Gambling is an addiction. A form of insanity, you could say, so, yes, it is pretty crazy.' Tess paced the floor, thinking. 'Maybe this break-in had something to do with Marcus Steele?'

'Who?'

'The guy who came to see me. He didn't seem to believe me when I told him I didn't have any money at all. Perhaps he sent someone to check?'

'Yeah, well, I guess he knows now.' Louis nodded at the empty safe. 'Unless he thinks you keep your jewels under your mattress?'

'He'd better not try and look there or he'll have Vince to contend with.' She made a fuss of the dog again. 'You really are a good boy, aren't you? The best. I think this deserves a treat. I can't sleep now anyway, not with a broken window. Want some hot chocolate?'

Louis cracked a smile at last. 'Is that your answer to everything?'

'Yes. Well, chocolate in one form or another, I'm not fussy. Come on.'

Bristol, 19th June 2016

'The safe was one of them old ones, easy as hell to find and open, but you didn't say nothin' about no dog, boss. I don't do jobs where there's dogs. Hate the mutts.'

Marcus stared at Archie, one of his best employees when it came to more nefarious duties, and tried not to shout. Who cared if there was a dog or not? You could just kick the mangy creature and get the hell out.

'You're saying there was nothing in the safe? Nothing at all? Not even computer disks or something?'

'Nope. A bunch of dust bunnies, tha's all. Looked like it hadn't been used for years.'

'Then it must be a decoy. You'll have to go back and find the real one.' Marcus didn't like being led on a merry chase and he had the feeling he was being played right now by that glossy widow. He wasn't having it.

'I told you—'

'Yes, yes, I heard you.' Marcus waved away Archie's protest. 'Take someone with you next time with a baseball bat or something. Hit the mutt over the head, whatever. I don't care. Just. Get. It. *Done!*'

Archie's expression turned mulish, but he'd known Marcus a long time and finally sighed and capitulated. 'Okay, fine. But not for a while. They'll be on their guard now so we'll 'ave to let them get over it first.'

'Well, don't wait too long. I want this finished soon. Understood?'

'Yes, boss.'

Marcus watched him leave and drummed his fingers on his desk. He couldn't tell Archie the real reason he was so impatient. That he wanted the woman herself. No, that would seem like a weakness and if there was one thing he disliked above all else, it was to appear weak in front of his employees.

He clicked open a document on his laptop and stared at a photo of the beautiful Lady Merrick – Therese – and a streak of lust shot through him, making him instantly aroused. He really ought to go and see her again, but he wasn't sure he could trust himself not to give the game away. No, better to just send her a little reminder and then wait a bit until he could be sure she'd been lying. If he could prove that she was as wealthy as he thought, he'd have her exactly where he wanted – at a disadvantage and dependent on his goodwill.

Actually, if she wasn't she'd be even more in his debt. He smiled.

Yeah, that would work too. Perfect.

Merrick Court, 19th June 2016

Josh knocked on the back door of Merrick Court with a nagging feeling of unease. Tess had phoned Bryn to let him know what had happened the night before and asked for Josh to come and help fix a window. He'd brought a toolbox as he didn't quite know what she'd meant. He wasn't a glazier but anything else he could manage. But he didn't like the fact that there had been a burglary. Not one bit.

A woman alone in a huge house like this – his house – with only a dog and a teenage boy for protection, anything could have happened. Shit. Now she wasn't just having weird 'dreams', as she'd called her experience of the day before, but people in the real world were hassling her and all.

'Josh, hi. Thank you for coming so quickly.'

Tess didn't look too upset and Josh couldn't understand why. 'Are you okay?' he asked, before greeting Vincent and nodding to Louis, who was munching his way through a big bowl of breakfast cereal.

'Yes, thanks to Vince. He's my hero, aren't you, boy?' She bent to kiss the top of the dog's head and Josh exchanged looks with Louis as they both made a face.

'Eeuuw, do you know where he's been?' Josh teased.

'What? He's clean,' Tess protested. 'I gave him a bath myself recently, so there.'

'Yeah, right.' Josh wished she'd kissed him instead. Jealous of a dog – how pathetic was that? She was looking stunningly beautiful this morning though, despite being a trifle pale from lack of sleep. Her blue eyes were outlined with a little bit of make-up, but in truth she didn't need it as she seemed to have naturally dark lashes. She was wearing those micro-shorts again, which showed off her tanned legs, and her feet were bare with delicately painted lilac toenails. How the hell could toenails be sexy, for God's sake? But they were.

He followed her to the library. 'Are you sure you're all right? Yesterday …'

'I'm fine, really. And I'd rather not talk about that, okay?'

Josh had hoped she'd be ready to open up, but he didn't feel he had the right to push her so he nodded.

She pointed to the window. 'Can you nail some bits of wood to the sides, please, so it can't be opened more than a couple of inches? Most of the other windows have side locks on them, but for some reason this one doesn't.'

Josh could see what she meant. It was an old-fashioned sash window and if you inserted a small saw it was easy to break off the catch, then the window could be raised high enough for someone to climb in. By adding blocks of wood they would act as a brake so the window couldn't be opened much even with a broken catch. An easy job.

'Isn't there an alarm though?' Josh couldn't believe anyone would live in a mansion like this and not have a burglar alarm.

'Yes, but it can only be turned on when I go out, not when someone's in the house.'

'We should have that fixed. Can you call the alarm company? I'm sure they can make it so the ground floor alarms can be on when someone's upstairs.' Josh didn't want to think of her here on her own when any burglar worth his salt could virtually stroll in without her knowing. Thank God for Vincent.

Tess nodded. 'I will.'

'What about the police?' Josh added. 'Have they been already?'

'No, I wouldn't bother contacting them.'

'What? Why? Surely we need to report this.' He couldn't believe she'd be that blasé about it.

Tess nodded towards an empty safe and shrugged. 'There wasn't anything in there so no theft to report. And I doubt the burglar would have been stupid enough to leave fingerprints. Everyone knows to wear gloves these days, don't they?'

Josh could see her point so he didn't argue.

He fixed the window and checked all the others, just to make sure. He only found one more without side locks and added bits of wood to that one too. Then he made his way back to the kitchen where Louis was busy washing up. Well-trained kid, obviously. Josh was impressed. It wouldn't have occurred to him to help out at home at that age.

Tess came into the room with the day's post in her hand and sat down at the table to open the envelopes. 'Make yourself some coffee or something if you want.' She waved a hand towards the kettle.

Josh didn't really want a hot drink, but he didn't want to leave yet either so he took a mug from a nearby mug tree. He almost dropped it when Tess let out a loud curse and banged something down on the table. He spun around to see what was the matter. She was staring at a letter, which had 'By Hand' typed on the envelope.

'For fuck's sake!' she huffed. 'What is his problem?'

'Who?' Louis was staring at her in surprise, but took the letter from her after a polite, 'May I?' She nodded, crossing her arms and frowning. 'Marcus Steele?' Louis read the signature first. 'Is that the guy you said, er ... wanted you to pay him a certain sum?'

Tess nodded. 'It's okay, Josh knows about it.'

'Him again?' Josh frowned, remembering the look in the guy's eyes at the auction house as he played his little power game, bidding against Josh. That had obviously just been a start.

'Yep. He just won't give up. Honestly, what am I going to do? There's no way I can raise that kind of money. And I really don't want to give him anything. It wasn't me that gambled at his stupid casino.'

Louis was still reading. 'He says he hopes you're ready to do business with him, but he's willing to give you a bit more time to "liquidise some assets" – what?'

'He means, sell something. He thinks I own a bunch of diamond jewellery. Hah! As if.'

Louis continued to quote from the letter. 'Then he's coming to see you.' He looked up, his expression troubled. 'It doesn't say what he's going to do when he gets here if you *don't* have the money.'

'No, but I can guess. He hinted that ... well, he was looking at me like ... er, you know.' Tess blushed.

Josh guessed what she meant. Steele had wanted her. Well, what man wouldn't? Her voice was still taut with frustration, but Josh heard the wobble in it too. She was getting scared which was understandable. That man was clearly devious. Who knew how far he'd go? And the thought of Steele having Tess was one that sent shafts of fury through Josh. No way.

'Not if we can help it,' he said firmly. He took the letter from Louis and read it for himself. 'He's still asking for half a mill. Did you tell your lawyer?'

'Yes, and he promised to "communicate" with Mr Steele to tell him he'd get the proceeds of the sale of the house contents, but nothing more.' Tess stood up and shoved her chair in, hard. 'I'd better go and ring the lawyer. There has to be a way of sorting this.'

Josh put the letter on the table. It very carefully didn't say anything specific about what would happen to Tess should she fail to pay, but the implication was definitely there. The utter bastard. Josh clenched his fists.

Tess was blinking away tears – whether of anger or fear, he didn't know. Without thinking, he went over and wrapped his arms around her, pulling her close. 'Hey, it'll be okay. We're here for you. He can't do anything to you with other people around and you can't pay him with money you don't have. He's probably made it all up.'

She was shaking, her hands splayed against his chest. When she buried her head in his shoulder, she seemed small and fragile and the thought that someone would want to hurt her in any way – whether physical or not – made white-hot rage surge through him again. *The way Sir Rhys had felt when holding Arabella.* Was this what the spirit had meant? That Tess was in danger from Steele? It could be.

'It'll be fine,' he repeated, rubbing her back. He breathed in the scent of her shampoo and stroked the long, straight hair rippling down almost to her waist. She was so precious and he was afraid he was getting in over his head here. But how could he fail to protect her?

After a while, she disentangled herself slowly and mumbled something about calling the lawyer. Josh saw that she was blushing again, as if she'd only just remembered who she'd been cuddling up to. But he didn't say anything, just watched her leave the room.

He turned to the boy, who had watched the embrace without commenting either. Josh could tell the kid adored Tess, and no wonder if she was taking his side in the battle for his future. But he guessed there was more to it than that. The two seemed to have a rare bond and he was sure Louis would do anything for her.

'Will you help me keep an eye on Tess, please?' he asked. 'I don't like the sound of this.'

'Sure.'

'If there's anything or anyone you don't like the look of, call me or come find me, okay?'

'Will do.'

'Thanks. See you in the garden later, then.'

He'd have to watch Tess carefully from now on and keep her safe.

Chapter Twenty-Four

Raglan Castle, 19th June 1646

Arabella picked her way across the debris that littered the Fountain Court until she reached the chapel. There, pretending to be enjoying the morning sun as if it was just a normal day, stood Rhys on the short flight of steps leading to the door. The whining noise of a cannonball flying through the air, then the resulting crash when part of an outside wall took the hit, didn't seem to affect him. She envied his sangfroid. As she reached the top, he stepped close to her and pressed something into her hand under cover of her skirts.

'For your protection,' he murmured. 'Make yourself an inside pocket to hide it in and if he ever ...' He left the sentence unfinished but Arabella heard the unspoken words. Stab Glyn with it if he tried anything again. She certainly would.

Touching the small dagger with great care, she could feel that it had a very sharp blade and a smooth handle of either bone or wood. It was light but deadly. 'Yes, thank you,' she replied as quietly as she could, grateful for his support.

If truth be told, she was still quaking at the thought of what had so nearly occurred the night before. If it hadn't been for the intervention of Rhys ... She owed him more than she could say. The bruises would fade, but not the memory of Glyn's hands, hard and insistent, inflicting pain and enjoying it. His hateful words, the weight of him on top of her ... She shivered and tried to put it out of her mind.

Rhys followed her into the chapel and they stood at the back of the crowded space. It wasn't surprising that everyone felt the need to ask God for help and deliverance from the besiegers, to pray for their very lives. It was impossible not to be afraid with the constant bombardment all day, every day. Consequently, in an area that shouldn't hold more than a maximum of fifty people, there were probably at least half as many again. Definitely too many, and the air was thick and hard to breathe. Smoky clouds of incense wafted up towards the vaulted roof. It was surrounded by corbels in the shape of human heads and Arabella had the nonsensical notion that they may be choking. The smell of guttering candles added to the fug and she had to stifle a coughing fit. With a light touch on her elbow, Rhys guided her towards the back wall. He leaned on it and with a couple of soft nudges encouraged her to use him as a support in turn. She allowed herself this luxury as no one would notice in such a throng.

He was like a solid buffer between her and any threats and she felt safe, comforted and also strangely exhilarated. The sleeve of her shift was thin and she could feel the warmth of his chest through the material of his shirt where his leather jerkin had fallen open in the middle. His nearness wasn't threatening in the way Glyn's had been, but somehow right. She wished they could stand like this forever.

But he had duties, as did she, and after the service he melted away after giving her fingers a squeeze and whispering, 'Look after yourself.'

'And you. Be careful out there,' she breathed back. A swift nod to acknowledge her words, then he was gone.

Merrick Court, 20th June 2016

'So did you say you'd found Uncle Giles's papers?'

'What?' Tess was once again in the library, sitting in the chair behind the desk. She was supposed to be making sure she hadn't missed any important documents and putting the ones that needed to be kept in labelled envelopes for Josh. Instead, she'd been looking at the beautiful earring, which she'd brought down to show Louis. And somehow, staring into the aquamarine depths of the jewel, she'd been drawn into another vision.

Damn.

'The papers?' Louis repeated as he sauntered in, munching on an apple.

Tess tried to marshal her thoughts and drag them away from a chapel full of smelly incense. And a knife? She was sure there had been a knife, which seemed an odd thing to bring into a holy place. She focused on Louis. 'Yes, they were in a locked metal box, like you said, which he'd put in that Chinese cupboard for some reason.'

'Seems weird.' Louis glanced at the painting behind which the safe was located. Tess had closed it and put it back as it was before the burglary. 'When he showed them to me he said they had to be protected for future generations of the family. He was going to pass them on to his son and barely let me touch them.'

'Well, perhaps he'd been looking at them and then he drank too much and forgot about putting them away?' Tess shrugged. Giles had done a lot of drinking during the last few months of his life, mainly because he didn't have that son. She was tired of thinking about that though. 'I guess we'll never know, but it's lucky he did so the burglar didn't find them at least.'

'Could I have another look at them, please? I didn't get much of a chance last time.'

'Sure, I'll go and get them now.'

When Tess came back down from her room, she also showed him the earring. 'Look, I found this as well when I was tidying up Giles's desk. It was hidden inside an old Bible.'

Louis whistled. 'Nice! He didn't show me that. I thought you said there weren't any family jewels, that he'd sold them?'

'Yes, all except for this apparently. And I think I know why he couldn't bear to part with it. Look at the carving.' Tess held it up so Louis could look at the blue stone properly.

'A lion and … is that a letter C?'

'Yep. And it's not just any lion, he's wearing a crown. So my guess is this belonged to King Charles.'

'As in the one who had his head chopped off?' Louis stared at her in surprise.

'Or his son – I don't know which. Either way, if it was a gift from a king I don't think Giles could possibly sell it. It would have meant a lot to him, to the family.' She shook her head. 'I wish he'd shown me.'

'I guess he would have done once you had kids. Isn't it the kind of thing you bring out at christenings and stuff?' Louis took the box she handed to him. 'Did you find anything good in here?'

Tess told him about the document creating some ancestor of his Earl of Merrick and the letter from the Marchioness of Worcester. 'I haven't had time to read the rest properly. You have a go if you like.'

She'd had the box for ages now and could have looked at it up in her room, but she'd been reluctant to touch anything old because of the strange things that kept happening to her. She wasn't sure she could cope with any more, but then it seemed as though she couldn't avoid it anyway, what with water and the earring repeatedly drawing her mind back in time.

Louis settled down with the box while Tess got on with her own tasks. Eventually he looked up. 'I can't read most of these. They're either faded or in some illegible handwriting. Jeez, did it have to be so complicated?'

Tess laughed. 'It looks beautiful though, don't you think?'

'I guess. So was that all you found in that Chinese cupboard?'

'Yes, unless you can locate any hidden drawers. I couldn't.'

That was a challenge Louis couldn't resist and to Tess's surprise he did find one eventually, behind another drawer right at the back.

'Oh, brilliant! Anything in there?'

Louis groped around and came out with a miniature painting. After blowing the dust off it, he laughed. 'It's a picture of you in a funny dress.'

'What? Let me see.' Tess tried not to show that his words had scared her, but her hands shook ever so slightly. 'No, it's not,' she said firmly, 'although I admit there is some similarity.' The woman in the picture had the same colour hair as Tess, but in a topknot and with little ringlets framing her face and a longer curl caressing her shoulder. She was wearing a lovely blue dress with big puffed sleeves and a low neckline. The outfit matched the lady's eyes, which were the colour of cornflowers.

'She's pretty,' Louis commented. 'Apart from that horrible hairstyle. I wonder what year it was painted?'

There were no clues on the back and the miniature wasn't signed. 'Let's google female fashions,' Tess suggested. 'Then maybe we can see approximately how old it is.'

They did and the woman's clothing seemed to match those worn by ladies at Charles II's court. 'That fits with that document about the first earl, right?' Louis said. 'Maybe this is his countess?'

'But who were they? It's so frustrating – I can't read his name on that paper.'

'We'll have to do some research. Or maybe look at other paintings in the house. Did Uncle Giles ever tell you about those?'

He had, but Tess had long since stopped noticing them. They were just part of the decor. She remembered being shown around when she'd first visited Merrick Court and Giles giving her some lecture or other about the ancestors that stared down at them from every wall. But she couldn't recall much about it and definitely not him saying anything about a first earl. 'Let's go and look,' she suggested. 'Maybe this woman features in a larger painting?'

'Yeah, or maybe someone will be wearing that earring?'

But although Tess and Louis checked every room in the house, they didn't find any portraits that looked like the woman in the miniature. Nor did they come across anyone wearing the royal earring.

'That's really strange.' Louis frowned. 'You'd have thought if you owned something like that you'd be proud to show it off.'

'Not if it wasn't the fashion for men to wear earrings any longer. And hang on – after Charles the Second died, his brother took over but was deposed and replaced by William and Mary. So it probably wasn't a good idea to show off a gift from a Stuart king if you wanted to be in favour with the new royal couple.'

'Yeah, I guess. There should still be a painting of the first earl though. I mean, come on!' Louis waved his arms around. 'He's, like, the most important guy this family's ever had if he got us the earldom.'

Tess sighed. 'There aren't any portraits here older than early seventeen-hundreds, but you're right. If I'd just been made an earl, I would definitely have wanted my picture on the wall. So where is he?'

'What about in the attic? Em and I used to play hide and seek up there when we were little.'

Tess shuddered. 'You and the hundreds of spiders?'

'Don't be a wuss.' Louis laughed. 'Come on, let's have a quick look.'

'Oh, all right then.'

Tess had only been to the attic once before and hadn't been keen to go back, but she followed Louis now and let him lead the way. At least then she wouldn't get spider webs in her face.

They rooted around for a while, half-heartedly peering into all the nooks and crannies. The light up there wasn't great – just a few dormer windows interspersed with bare bulbs that barely lit up the corners – but they could at least see the outline of the old junk. Mostly it was broken furniture and trunks or boxes full of clothes and other items. On the way back to the door Louis stopped abruptly. 'Look! I can see some old frames.'

Tess almost collided with him. 'What? Where?'

'Over here.' Leaning against the wall near the door were several paintings of different sizes, their backs facing out. When Louis turned the first one round, Tess drew in such a hasty breath she almost choked on it.

'Jesus!'

She was staring into the face of the man she'd seen at Raglan, the now familiar features of Sir Rhys.

'What's the matter? You've gone all pale.' Louis took Tess's arm. 'You want to sit down or something?'

'No, no, I'm fine. It was just … so much dust up here.' It was a feeble excuse and Tess's pretend cough probably didn't fool Louis, but she really didn't know how to tell him she'd met the man in the painting in her dreams. He'd think she was losing it. 'Uhm, does it say who that is?'

'I can't see up here. We'd better take it downstairs. I'll just quickly check the other paintings first. Oh, bloody hell, here she is!'

'Huh?' Tess looked up to see another face she recognised, but thankfully it was only the woman from the miniature and not someone she'd met. 'Oh, good. Bring her as well. Anything else?'

'No, just boring landscapes with holes in them.'

The two paintings were quite heavy and they ended up having to go down twice, working together to carry them. But once they had them leaning against a wall on an upper landing, where daylight shone in through the windows, they were able to study them more closely.

Louis peered at the woman's portrait. 'No date or anything, but she's even prettier in this one and she's wearing the same kind of dress.'

'Mmm.' Tess was busy studying the other painting which interested her far more. 'This one's ripped at the top and the writing is gone, but it looks like the paintings were done by the same artist so they must be connected. Could he be the first earl and she his countess? Look, he's wearing the earring.'

'Oh, yeah.' Louis bent forward to study the portrait closer.

Looking at him – at Rhys – made something like an electric current shimmer down Tess's spine and if she closed her eyes she could still hear his voice, beautiful Welsh accent and all, asking her to be careful and not fall into the lake.

It was impossible, insane.

And how had he ended up at Merrick Court?

'We'll have to do some family tree stuff, find out their names. You know, like in that TV programme? Tess? *Tess.*' Louis lightly bumped her shoulder with his fist.

'Hmm? Oh, yes.' Tess was having trouble tearing her gaze away from Rhys's mesmerising moss-green eyes. She took a deep breath and tried to pull herself together. 'Yes, we definitely need to find out more. Let's leave these here for now, but turn them towards the wall. They're obviously in need of some serious restoration which is probably why they're not hanging downstairs, but we don't want the light to ruin them even more.'

Both canvases were in a bad way and Tess guessed there

hadn't been any money for restoration. Nor would anyone have wanted to buy them in this state. *Thank God for that!* If they had, she'd never have seen them and she was very glad she had. At least it proved the man had existed somewhere other than in her imagination, even if she still didn't understand how she could possibly have talked to him or why she saw him in her visions.

The very idea was crazy.

Chapter Twenty-Five

Merrick Court, 21st June 2016

'Hello? Anyone in?'

The knock on the stable door made Tess's hand shake and a blob of paint dropped off the tip of her brush and onto the floor as Josh came into her workshop. 'Jeez! You scared me. I didn't think anyone would be around today, in this weather.' It was pouring with rain and she hadn't heard anything other than the pounding of water on the roof. She frowned over at Vince, who jumped up to greet their visitor. 'Some guard dog you are.'

'Sorry, didn't mean to make you jump. Hey there, Vince. You okay, mate?' He made a fuss of the dog, then closed the door and leaned back against it, crossing his arms over his chest. For once he was wearing a proper shirt in a green check, although the sleeves were rolled up to the elbows, displaying his powerful forearms. His black hair was damp and even messier than usual, but that just made it look sexy as hell. 'Are you okay? Haven't seen you for a few days.' Josh's laconic Kiwi accent had a slight edge to it.

'Why wouldn't I be? Louis and I have been busy. We found these old paintings in the attic and we think they might be of the first earl and countess of Merrick, but we can't find out their names. You'd think there would be a family tree or something, wouldn't you? But there's nothing which goes that far back. So we've been doing some research ourselves, but we probably need to go to a record office or something.' She didn't want to tell Josh she was sure the earl was called Rhys as she couldn't explain how she knew that.

'I see.' Josh didn't look very interested in the earl or

his countess. He pushed away from the door and came to sit on a stool next to Tess. He stared into her eyes, his eyebrows raised, and she could see that he wasn't going to leave without answers this time. 'Enough with the family tree stuff. Talk to me, Tess, please. I need to know what happened the other day. You didn't just faint, did you?'

She sighed. 'No, but I can't explain it. Not really.'

'Try me.'

'But you're going to think I'm nuts. Seriously!' He just raised his eyebrows a fraction higher. 'Okay, fine. So I've been having these strange dreams, or maybe hallucinations or visions is a better description, I don't know. I … experience things, which I think might be someone else's memories. Someone who lived in this area a long time ago.' She glanced at Josh, but he wasn't showing any signs of surprise or looking at her like she was crazy. 'It's like I'm reliving things that happened here. Nothing's clear. I see images, hear snatches of conversation, feel someone else's emotions. Honestly, I can't explain it.'

'And when I found you by the fountain?' Josh prompted.

'I'd just seen a lot of events that happened to the woman I'm channelling.' Tess almost laughed as that sounded ludicrous, but that was what she was doing, wasn't it?

'You're seeing things through a woman's eyes, not being shown them by a man?' Josh was staring at her intently, as if her reply was important.

Tess shrugged. 'No, why would I be a man?'

'No reason.' Josh was silent for a while, then he just said, 'There are lots of things we don't understand. That doesn't mean they can't happen. I believe you're telling the truth.'

'You do? Thank you!' His words brought a sense of relief. Tess hadn't realised how much it would mean to her for him not to think she was making all this up. 'You seem to be remarkably chilled about this. I have to say, it's been freaking me out.'

He shrugged. 'My gran was a bit psychic and I've experienced a thing or two myself in the past.'

'Well, I'm glad it's not just me then.' She tried to smile but it was probably a wobbly effort because Josh leaned forward and pulled her in for a hug. Without thinking she put her arms round his middle and leaned into him. Her body fit perfectly and she didn't want to let go.

'I'm scared,' she murmured into his shirt and his arms tightened around her.

'Maybe there's a way to stop it happening?' he suggested.

'Well, it sounds silly, but it seems to have something to do with water and certain items, old ones from that time. They make me feel drawn towards them, like they're sucking me into the past, and that's when the visions come.'

'What sort of items?'

'An old earring, mainly. I'll show you later. I think it's probably yours anyway as it has to do with your ancestors. Even if it's part of the house's contents, it wouldn't feel right for me to keep it.'

'I'd love to see it, but maybe you should try to avoid old things then?'

'I'll do my best.' And she would. No more baths or washing up in the sink. Showers and the dishwashing machine might be safer. The earring could be locked in a drawer.

They sat close together for a while but eventually Tess let go. 'Thanks for your support. Makes me feel a bit better.'

'Any time.' He stood up. 'I'd better go. Do you fancy a drink or another meal some time?'

Tess appreciated his effort to change the subject. 'Uhm, sure.'

'How about tonight?'

'Yes, why not. I think Louis said he was meeting up with some friends.'

It would be nice to spend an evening not thinking about

anything to do with Merrick Court or its inhabitants, dead or otherwise.

'So let me get this straight – you sold your sheep farm in New Zealand ...'

'Sheep *station*. We don't call them farms.'

'... whatever, because it wasn't very profitable, but now you're considering trying over here instead? Isn't it even harder in Wales? I thought New Zealand was *the* place for sheep.'

Tess was trying to talk about normal things, nothing to do with the past or the house she lived in. Tonight she wanted to be a normal woman, out on a date with a man who made her feel very alive.

Josh smiled and took a sip of his beer. 'Maybe. It's hard anywhere, but if you love it, what does it matter? As I told you, it's a very satisfying job, despite the crazy hours.' He hesitated, then added, 'And I didn't quite tell you the truth. The reason I sold my property was mainly because I hated my father and he so wanted me to keep it on. Revenge, pure and simple.'

'Oh, I see.' Tess was intrigued and remembered he'd said something about knowing a thing or two about family feuds. 'May I ask why? Although don't answer if I'm being too nosy.'

'It's not a secret. My father, Robert, was a bastard, that's all there is to it. He drank, he was a bully and he was violent.'

'That sounds awful.' Tess reached out and covered his hand with hers. He turned his palm up and twined their fingers together. She loved the sensation of that.

'Yeah, it wasn't exactly a great environment for a little kid to grow up in. Robert – I can't even make myself call him Dad – drove my mum almost insane with his abuse. As soon as I was old enough, I managed to get her away from him and we went to live in the city, she and I, but she never quite recovered. At least, not mentally. And then she died …'

'Oh, no! From … from what he did to her?'

Josh made a face. 'No, I can't blame that on him. It was cancer. Just bad luck.'

'How dreadful!'

'For sure.' He gave her a lopsided smile. 'But it's in the past and now I'm determined to only look forward. You know, when I sold that station it was as though I'd been let out of prison after years of darkness and misery. I was free. Free to travel the world. Free to forget about Robert, because he didn't deserve anyone remembering him. And I swore I wouldn't settle again until I found a place that really felt like home. Then I got that letter …'

'And now you think this is it?' Tess tried not to infuse her question with too much hope. She was beginning to realise how much it would mean to her if he stuck around.

His fingers tightened on hers. 'It just might be, yes.' He hesitated, then asked, 'What about you? Are you coming to terms with what happened? I'm sure you must still be grieving.'

Tess nodded. 'Yes, of course, but perhaps not in the way you think. What happened was desperately sad, but Giles's death didn't really affect my future. We were about to get a divorce when … when he had the accident. So I would have been leaving Merrick Court either way.'

'Oh, I see.' Josh looked thoughtful. 'I didn't know.'

'I thought maybe Bryn would have told you. It wasn't a secret that we'd been having problems. Giles could be very stubborn and he liked to have things his way. He was older than me, ten years almost exactly, and I guess he was used to deciding everything before he married me. He'd been a confirmed bachelor for years, apparently. Anyway, things weren't working out between us so we'd agreed to call our lawyers, but the very next day...' She shook her head. 'No point thinking about it now. It's in the past too and you're right, it's time to look forward.'

And for the first time in ages, Tess actually felt positive about the future.

They took a walk around Merrick Court's gardens when they got back, since it was still fairly light. Josh was happy that Tess had agreed to extend the evening a bit longer as he didn't want to leave her just yet. He was enjoying spending time with her, holding her hand, inhaling the scent of her beautiful hair which was hanging loose down her back. Everything about her appealed to him. She was special. Just like this place.

'What's your favourite part of this garden?' he asked.

'I think you can guess – the knot garden, of course.' She smiled up at him. 'And not just because we've worked so hard on it. The whole symmetry of the planting appeals to me, it's so orderly.'

'I know what you mean.' Josh had loved that part of the garden right from the start too, but he had a feeling it might have more to do with the time spent there with Tess. 'Let's go and look at it in the moonlight. Not that you can see the moon much as it's still so light.'

They walked in silence along the gravel paths, past the walled gardens and over to the secluded corner tucked away behind everything else.

'It's so beautiful.' Tess stopped and regarded the neatly trimmed little hedges spread out before them.

Josh stood by her side and admired the view too. It was a peaceful scene, the tiny leaves on the box glinting silver in the half-light. He scanned the edges, checking for shadows that didn't belong, but couldn't see any this evening. Hopefully the spirits wouldn't bother them and if they tried, he'd do his utmost not to give them entrance to his mind.

He figured the best way of shutting them out would be to concentrate on the here and now; on the lovely woman whose fingers felt so right twined with his. He looked down at Tess. 'We've done a great job, even if I say so myself.' He chuckled. 'Mind you, cutting hedges isn't rocket science.'

'Hey, it's not that easy.' She punched him playfully on the arm and he captured her fist, then brought it up to his mouth to kiss her knuckles. She stilled and tilted her head up to stare at him.

'It is when you have a beautiful helper,' he murmured, looking down into her eyes. They were huge pools of deep sapphire in the semi-darkness and Josh could have drowned in them. The urge to kiss her was overwhelming and he gave in to it, lowering his mouth to hers slowly so as to give her time to pull away if it wasn't what she wanted. She stayed right where she was.

He kept the kiss light and playful. He figured she might not be ready for anything full on just yet as she was so recently widowed. Although she had said she'd been on the brink of divorce – that must mean she'd been about to move on. He wasn't sure though as there was a slight hesitation in the way she reciprocated, as if she wasn't convinced she ought to be doing this. He ended the kiss and put his arms around her, drawing her into a soft embrace instead.

'You *are* very beautiful,' he whispered, 'but then I'm sure you don't need me to tell you that.'

She burrowed closer and he tightened his hold. He thought he heard her say, 'Oh, but I do.' But she didn't elaborate, so he kissed her cheek and stood still, savouring the moment.

After a while she was the one to withdraw, taking his hand to pull him in the direction they'd come. 'I think I'd better get back. Vince will wonder where everyone's gone.'

They'd left the dog at home guarding the house and Josh agreed he should probably be rescued now. But it was a wrench to leave the knot garden. Josh had wanted to stand there forever with Tess in his arms.

⌑

Raglan Castle, 25th June 1646

'Can you meet me down in the stables after supper?' Rhys managed to whisper the question to Arabella as they filed out of the chapel.

She nodded without looking at him and he breathed a sigh of relief. He had to see her today or it might be too late.

After the meal he made his way into the stables which were temporarily located in a large cellar underneath the marquis's private apartments. The poor horses had to go down a set of stairs and it was probably a far cry from what they were used to. Cold and damp, even on a balmy June evening, with hard earth floors, the horses stood crowded into three rooms – about twenty or thirty of them in the largest area, another ten to fifteen in another and a final one with room for only two or three steeds. It wasn't completely dark though as there were apertures set high up which let in the daylight and fresh air.

The animals moved restlessly as he came down, probably hoping for something to eat as they weren't being fed much with rations short at the moment. There was no one else there, however, which was exactly why Rhys had chosen it as a meeting place.

He waited by the stairs and when Arabella arrived, he took her hand and pulled her into the smallest room, out of sight. It was empty right now, the occupants outside being groomed perhaps. 'I'm sorry to bring you down here,' Rhys whispered, 'but I wanted to talk to you without being seen.' He was very aware of the overpowering equine smells and tried not to step in any manure.

245

'I don't mind. What is it?' Her eyes were anxious and the way she was looking at him made him wish he could just gather her close and never let go. Never have to leave her. But it wasn't his choice.

'Two pieces of bad news, I'm afraid. First of all, a messenger arrived from Oxford – Prince Rupert couldn't hold the town any longer. The man said the prince and about two thousand men left the town in orderly fashion yesterday. I'm guessing a lot of them will simply go home, while the rest will head overseas to try and find work as mercenaries. I'm sure Prince Rupert will anyway. He's a brilliant soldier.'

'And the second thing?' He heard Arabella's voice quiver ever so slightly, but she didn't comment on the disastrous news from Oxford. What was there to say, after all?

'I have to leave for a few days. We are running out of supplies so I'll need to go with some of Lord Charles's men to gather more.'

'Isn't that dangerous?' Her eyes grew even bigger and his heart squeezed tight.

'No, we'll be fine,' he lied. Of course there was a chance they would be seen and apprehended, but they had to take that risk or everyone in the castle would starve soon. And they had accomplices on the outside, men loyal to the marquis who'd been gathering supplies for them.

'How long will you be gone?'

He was still holding her hand and he noticed her fingers tightening on his as she spoke. 'Two days, three at most. I'll be careful, I promise.' He gave her what he thought was a reassuring smile, but he had a feeling she wasn't fooled.

She threw her arms around his neck and burrowed close. 'See that you are,' she whispered. 'Godspeed.' She lifted her face and stood on tiptoe to kiss him on the mouth.

'Arabella, *cariad* …' He shouldn't kiss her, but Rhys was afraid that it might be his last chance to do it properly, so he gave in to the urge he'd been suppressing for so long. There was no resisting her and as she had taken the first step, he was sure she wouldn't be frightened.

He tried to be gentle at first, caressing her lips with his own so as not to scare her with the desire that was welling up inside him. She followed his lead and appeared to accept his kisses without fear, so he deepened them, until finally his tongue sought entry. She gave a little gasp and he almost stopped, but then she tugged him closer and he understood that she wanted this as much as he did. After that, he didn't hold back. Their tongues stroked and sparred, caressing, tasting, while their hands learned the contours of each other's bodies until they were both trembling uncontrollably.

It was time to stop. Rhys could have taken her there and then, but what honourable man would do that to a woman when he might not be coming back from his mission? He couldn't. Biting his teeth together hard, he drew in several harsh breaths and just held her close. Their heartbeats slowed as one and then he looked down on her.

'I will do everything in my power to come back, I swear,' he whispered.

'You had better. I'm counting on it.' Her voice was soft, shy, but determined. 'Now I must go. I'll look for you in three days' time.' She gave him one last kiss and a tremulous smile, then she was gone.

He leaned his forehead on the stone wall and tried to slow his breathing further. If only they weren't in this infernal castle, stuck in the middle of a hopeless siege, he would have told her he loved her. If only ... But he would find a way to be with her. He must.

Chapter Twenty-Six

Josh was whistling to himself as he followed Bryn, carrying a rake. He was starting to love helping the old guy and didn't mind the hard work, especially since it meant he got to see more of Tess who was usually outdoors too or in her workshop.

They'd gone out for drinks again at the weekend, just a quick one in another country pub, but he felt they were getting to know each other pretty well. She'd relaxed around him since her confession about the weird dreams, but they hadn't discussed it further. Josh wasn't ready to tell her about his own psychic experiences yet, so thought it best to leave the subject alone for now.

He wondered whose spirit had invaded Tess's brain. A woman, she'd said, but who? He'd have to ask.

'Can you tidy this a bit, please?' Bryn stopped on the gravel drive that covered a large area in front of the main entrance to the house. 'I sprayed it with weed killer the other day so it just needs raking.'

'Sure.'

'Thank you. I'd better get back to young Louis.'

'How's he getting on?' Josh hadn't seen much of the boy, who spent most of his time with Bryn.

'Very well. He'll make a fine gardener, learns fast.' Bryn smiled. 'And he's a joy to have around. Great for me to have the company.'

As the old man walked off, Josh reflected that it must have been lonely for him here with no other staff, but he'd stayed on, loyal to the family. To Tess. Josh would make sure he was rewarded for that and that he had more help in future.

Raking the drive was an easy task that left his thoughts free to roam and they kept coming back to her – to Tess. She was really something and he was afraid he was seriously falling for her. Was that a bad thing? He hadn't decided yet, but his body was telling him not to think so much and just go with the flow.

He looked up towards the façade of the house and his gaze was drawn to the Norman tower and the window. Would Sir Rhys be there? Sure enough, the shadowy figure was back, gazing down at him. No courtly bow today, barely any movement at all, but Josh could feel the spirit's need, even at that distance. There was more to his story, much more, and he wanted to tell someone.

Josh knew he could walk away, refuse to listen, but then he'd never find out what was so important that this spirit had hung around here for hundreds of years. Perhaps he was the first psychic person to come into the shadow's orbit? The only one who had the ability to hear. With a sigh, Josh sat down on the steps leading up to the fancy front door and prepared himself.

Raglan Castle, 28th June 1646

The sense of relief Rhys felt on walking into the chapel at Raglan and seeing Arabella was so great he had to steady himself against the wall. He'd faced death many times on the battlefield, but it had never terrified him as much as the thought of what might be happening to her in his absence. Thank the Lord she was still safe.

'Stable after supper,' he breathed as he passed her on the way out and she gave him a tiny nod. He could hardly contain himself until the appointed hour arrived.

'You're back!' Arabella looked equally relieved as she

came down the steps. 'What happened? Did you manage to bring supplies? We've been on short rations for days now.'

Everyone was losing weight, especially the poor horses. Rhys couldn't bear to look at them. He took Arabella's hand and pulled her into the smallest stable, as before. A solitary horse was there this time, but once he'd established that they hadn't brought him any food, he went back to dozing in the late afternoon heat.

'Yes, we brought nearly three hundred bushels of corn and malt. The bailiff of Llantilio had gathered it for us, mostly from the town and manor of Monmouth who are still loyal to the marquis, and he helped bring it here. He's been pretending to help the enemy soldiers too, delivering some grain to them, so they weren't suspicious of him.'

'Oh, good, but ...' She hesitated. 'It would have been safer for you to stay outside.'

He let go of her hand and pulled her close for a blazing kiss. 'Did you really think I'd leave you in here? That would have been like leaving my soul behind.' He smiled at her and she smiled back, blushing. She was obviously too shy still to tell him how she felt, but he could see the emotion in her eyes.

'How did you sneak the provisions past the enemy soldiers?'

He shook his head. 'That would be telling and it's best you don't know in case we have to do it again.' He kissed her once more. 'Now, I can't stay long as I'm on duty soon, but I just wanted to hold you for a moment. Have you missed me?' He was teasing, certain that she wouldn't have been kissing him back with such fervour if she hadn't.

'You know I have.'

It had been three, interminable days while Arabella went about her duties in a state of apprehension so great she'd barely noticed the horrific sounds all around her – ordnance being fired at regular intervals, musket shots, the crashes when bits of the castle walls fell and the screams of those hurt by the splinters of stone that had shattered. She'd just tended to the wounded, served Lady Margaret and existed. Without Rhys, that was all life was – an existence without meaning.

But he had returned, thanks be to God.

She allowed him to kiss her for as long as he wished. As before though, he didn't go too far and she was both sorry and pleased. Sorry because her body was crying out for his, but pleased that he had such care for her.

'I have to go. There's been another summons from Colonel Morgan and he said General Fairfax himself is on his way here.'

'Oh, no!' That sounded ominous to Arabella. The general was said to be a great soldier and leader of men.

'Yes, and if we want to stand any chance at all of defeating the besiegers, it has to be done before he arrives. I've no doubt he'll bring reinforcements.' Rhys pushed his fingers through his thick hair, flicking it away from his face impatiently.

'I take it the marquis is still refusing to surrender?' Arabella was sure nothing would change the old man's mind, but had to ask.

Rhys sighed. 'Yes. There's been correspondence between him and the colonel, I understand, and the enemy are claiming the king has sent an order for us to give up and disband, but his lordship doesn't believe it because it wasn't addressed to him, only to some of the other garrison commanders. I hear he said that after all he'd done for the king, His Majesty would have mentioned Raglan specifically if the message was genuine, but since he didn't ... Besides, as he says, he wouldn't just be giving up a garrison – this is his home. Why should he leave?'

'Is there no way of ascertaining if the king's order is

authentic?' Arabella almost hoped it was. At least then they could all leave this place alive, their honour intact. And Rhys wouldn't have to do any more fighting. She suppressed a shudder at the thought of him sallying forth again later that day.

'The colonel apparently suggested that someone from Raglan should go to Oxford together with one of his men to find out for themselves, but I don't think the marquis would agree to that.' He sighed again. 'I really must go now, *cariad*, but we'll meet again whenever we can,' he promised.

All too soon he was gone, but at least they were both in the castle again. That was enough for now.

Merrick Court, 3rd July 2016

Tess loved her bedroom in the Norman tower, where she'd taken to sleeping the night after Giles's accident. She hadn't been able to face going back to the room she'd shared with him. The tower one was prettier anyway, with primrose yellow walls and a spectacular French rococo bed painted antique silver. There were windows on two sides of the room – both with deep sills as the walls were so thick – and a high ceiling with old roof beams painted white, making it a bright and airy space.

Coming into the room late in the afternoon, she glimpsed movement over by one of the windows and saw a shadowy figure leaning on the wall next to it as though looking out over the garden. She stopped on the threshold, putting a hand up to cover her mouth to stop the gasp from escaping. *Jesus!* A proper ghost this time? It had to be, because she could see the walls through his arms.

The figure was wearing a long waistcoat, loose trousers and huge boots with the tops turned down. And a plumed hat set on top of long, wavy hair. She drew in a sharp breath and whispered, 'Rhys!' The shadowy person turned towards her with a sad smile, then vanished.

Tess's legs gave way and she sat down where she was, in the door opening, and leaned against the frame. 'Ohmigod!' she muttered, blinking to make sure there wasn't something wrong with her eyesight. But she knew in her heart it had been him – Rhys, the man from Raglan Castle and also from the painting.

She and Louis hadn't been able to find out anything more about him or the woman. There didn't seem to be any records from the Civil War period and after – at least not from the parishes in this area; they'd been lost. So they were no further forward, and she'd been avoiding water and any old items around the house in order to escape being sucked into a vision. She didn't want to find out that way, it was too scary.

But now he'd come to see her here. Why?

His smile had been sad, which might indicate something horrible had happened to him and he wanted someone to know. To care. Perhaps to tell the world? Wasn't that what ghosts were supposed to be doing – drawing attention to past misdeeds? Tess had read stories where murdered people haunted someone because they wanted their killers caught and punished. Obviously this couldn't be the case here, but if Rhys had been killed, maybe he wanted the name of his murderer to be known to posterity?

She had to find out more. But how?

Maybe she needed to go back to Raglan Castle. That's where he'd first appeared after all. Had he been about to tell her something that day she'd met him down by the moat? But she wasn't sure she wanted to encounter him again for real, although if he was going to start haunting her at Merrick Court, it wasn't as though she had a choice in the matter.

No, she'd go to Raglan, but not on her own this time.

She'd bring Josh if he agreed to come. If the man she'd met showed himself again, Josh could scare him away, and if he didn't ... well, then at least she wouldn't be alone.

And maybe she'd wear the earring, just to see if it worked its magic somewhere other than at Merrick Court.

Raglan Castle, 4th July 2016

Josh had always loved the idea of castles, ever since his mother read him fairy tales as a kid. His grandfather had added to the allure by telling him stories about knights of old, quests and treasure hunts – all fuel for a boy's imagination. He'd been to quite a few during his world travels, but not one round here, so when Tess suggested a visit to Raglan, he was happy to agree. Especially if it meant he'd get to spend a whole afternoon with just her.

'Wow, this is pretty huge, huh?' He followed Tess towards the castle's main gate, while staring up at the enormous towers either side. They must have seemed intimidating to anyone not invited.

'Yes, but I'm sure it was much more magnificent in its heyday. Such a shame it's just a shell now. Come on, let's go inside.'

They entered the first courtyard – Tess told him there were two – and the muted sounds of traffic from the nearby main road faded into the background as the peace of the castle settled around them. Josh immediately felt an affinity with the place, some sort of visceral connection which took him by surprise, especially since he'd never been here. But then he remembered that he sort of had now – through Sir Rhys and the visions. And even before that, he'd felt drawn towards the castle on the morning when he'd driven to see Merrick Court for the first time.

Yes. Recognition, familiarity, belonging. *Weird.*

He found himself looking around for any details that might seem familiar. There was the kitchen over in the corner, the offices to the right. On the cobbles of the courtyard the men had drilled, polished their weapons, filled their little wooden gunpowder pouches to hang from a leather bandolier and ... *whoa!* How did he know that? He frowned. Maybe Grandad had told him?

But it was more likely Sir Rhys, messing with his mind again.

Josh shook his head. Were there other shadowy souls hanging around here too? He searched every corner but couldn't see anyone, which in itself was unusual. An old site like this where there had been warfare should have had dozens of departed spirits haunting it, if not heaps more.

He decided to ignore the strange memories and just followed Tess, concentrating on the lovely sight of her instead. She filled out a pair of jeans very nicely, and her strappy top gave tantalising glimpses of a pretty, lacy bra underneath in a colour-coordinated shade of lilac. He'd love to peel that off her and ... but she probably wasn't ready for that kind of thing yet. He'd kissed her goodnight again several times after going for drinks at various local pubs, but although she'd kissed him back, she hadn't given any indication that she wanted to take things further.

He'd have to be patient.

He saw something glinting on her earlobe and stopped next to her. 'Is that the earring you were telling me about? You're wearing it?'

'Yes, sorry, I brought it to show you, but then I got caught up in all this.' She swept a hand round to indicate the castle. 'I'll take it off later.'

'Okay, I'd love to have a closer look. It's beautiful in the sunlight.' The aquamarine-coloured stone reflected the sunshine, throwing out prisms of light. Josh felt as though it was calling out to him and itched to hold it in his hand, but he turned away. It could wait.

He dragged his gaze off Tess and back to his surroundings again. Wandering in companionable silence, gazing up at what was left of once magnificent walls, windows and fireplaces, Josh was mostly struck by the sadness of it all. 'What a waste,' he muttered.

She nodded. 'Yes, I know what you mean.'

'So what happened to it? A siege during the Civil War, did you say? Looks like whoever lived here lost big time.' Josh could almost hear the mighty boom of the cannon that would have made the walls come tumbling down.

'Not exactly. I read that the castle was still standing at the end of the war, but Cromwell's troops decided to destroy it so that no one else could use it against them. I guess in case of further uprisings? Wonder what the Royalists thought when they came back after the Restoration?' Tess trailed her fingers along smooth stone. 'If it had been me, I'd have cried.'

'The Restoration? That was, what, ten years later?' Josh tried to remember the few bits of English history he'd studied.

'More like fifteen.'

'I'm sure by then they'd got used to the idea.' Josh shrugged. 'And maybe the new king gave them other, better estates?'

'Yes, I think he did. Still ...'

They'd reached the Pantry and Buttery, according to the signs. 'Let's go down these stairs. It says that they lead to the wine cellar.' Josh set off and Tess followed him.

It was dark and cold, despite a window set into a wall that had to be almost two metres thick. He saw Tess shiver and something about that windowsill struck a chord in his memory. *That bastard Howell.* An almost primeval anger surged through Josh as he remembered the near-rape incident Rhys had shown him. This was the place where it had happened, he was sure.

'I don't like it down here,' Tess murmured.

Josh took her hand, his protective instincts going into overdrive. 'It's just a bit gloomy.' He didn't want to admit the shadows were affecting him too. He pulled her along into a roofless room. 'Look, this would be perfect for storing wine or beer. It would be chilled to perfection. I could do with one right now, actually.' He smiled at her and felt some of the tension leave her. Even so, she hurried him up the stairs on the way back and seemed relieved when they emerged into the sunshine again.

Josh was glad to get out of there too. Something dark and twisted had pushed for a foothold in his mind, but he refused to let it in. Whatever – or whoever – it was, could stay in that dark stairwell. And he wouldn't let anyone harm Tess, no matter what.

Tess breathed a sigh of relief. That underground space had given her the creeps and she was very glad she had Josh with her. He was reassuringly solid and she felt better when staying close to him. The castle was definitely affecting her and she could feel the pull of the past like a nagging headache at the edges of her mind. But should she let it in?

They walked through the former Great Hall and marvelled at the gigantic fireplace.

'This is really weird.' Josh went inside it, looking up. 'See? It's divided into two flues so they could have a window above it, in the middle. Why on earth would you design it that way? Doesn't make sense.'

'Maybe it was a stronger construction this way?' She joined him inside the fireplace, which was big enough to allow at least fifteen people to stand in it. 'Gosh, it wouldn't be difficult to have an actual Yule log in here!'

The enormous oriel window next to the fireplace had no

glass in it, but was otherwise intact. Tess could barely see out of it though, as the bottom of it started at about chin height. 'I wish I could have seen this glazed,' she murmured, although she could actually picture it quite vividly in her mind. She sat down on a bench while Josh wandered round.

Birds flitted about high above them, tweeting, chirping and cooing. They seemed at home, the jagged tops of the towers perfect for their nests. There were a few tourists wandering around as well. Most of them looked solemn, awed by what had been lost here, and everyone seemed to be speaking quietly as if they didn't want to disturb the former inhabitants of the place. The very air felt heavy, like a forlorn blanket draped over the castle. Tess let her thoughts roam ...

Chapter Twenty-Seven

'Can you see to that man in the corner, please, Arabella. He's got a slight wound to the thigh and it needs washing.' Mrs Watson pointed to a mattress in the far corner of the room and Arabella's heart sank.

Glyn. Who else?

She debated whether to tell Mrs Watson that she didn't want to treat Glyn and ask for someone else to do it, but she could see his mocking gaze from where she was standing and she wasn't a coward. She'd face him, damn him, and if he accosted her here she'd scream for all she was worth. Besides, telling Mrs Watson would involve explaining *why* she didn't want to do this task and it was far better to keep that a secret.

'Well, well, my luck must be in.' Glyn had a gloating expression on his face as she approached with a bowl of water and some rags for cleaning with. 'Your lover not around to beat people senseless today? Has he been killed, perhaps? Wouldn't that be a shame.'

Arabella didn't reply. She knew Glyn was just goading her and she didn't want to speak to him at all. She'd just finish her task and leave.

'I suppose you're disappointed I'm not more severely wounded,' he commented as she rolled the leg of his breeches up to expose the wound.

She *was* but then she'd known he wouldn't be killed in any of the skirmishes. He had the devil's own luck and Rhys had told her Glyn feigned illness most of the time so didn't do much actual fighting. He'd always been a coward and a cheat. It wouldn't surprise her to hear that he always hung back, skulking at the rear whenever he was forced to take part. No, the small cut she was looking at must have been just an accident. Or something to lull the Royalists into thinking him one of them. Either way, he was despicable and she wished she could plunge her own little knife right through his heart.

She dipped her cloth in the bowl, slightly shaken by the force of her anger. She'd never been a violent person and the thought of killing anyone in cold blood hadn't ever entered her head before. Glyn had that effect on people though and he didn't care. She took a deep breath and began to clean his wound.

'Nothing to say for yourself today, then?' he sneered. 'You were in good voice the other night, more's the pity. Brought that whoreson to your rescue. But don't you worry, I'll get rid of him, then we can finish what we started.'

A cold feeling settled in the pit of Arabella's stomach at the thought of Glyn harming Rhys. But he was probably just bluffing and she'd tell Rhys to be on his guard.

She cleaned his leg and bound it up without adding any wound powder or other poultice. She probably should have done, but if it became infected and killed him slowly, so much the better as far as she was concerned. He didn't seem to notice the omission as he was becoming more and more frustrated at her refusal to speak to him.

'Act the high-born lady if you want to,' he hissed. 'But once we are safely married you'll be dancing to my tune and you'll damn well answer when I speak to you, understand?'

He grabbed her arm and pulled her towards him, much too close for comfort. Arabella tried to control the shivers of panic skimming through her and reached a hand inside her pocket. She threw a quick glance across her shoulder to check that no one was watching, then brought out the knife and pushed it against his chest so that he could feel the lethal tip against his lower ribs.

'Touch me again and I'll kill you myself,' she whispered back through clenched teeth. '*Understand?*'

His eyes widened and he let go of her before swearing most foully. 'Bitch!' he spat and shoved her away from him. 'If it wasn't for your damned possessions, I wouldn't *want* to come anywhere near you.'

'See that you don't.'

She picked up the bowl and walked away, still shaking but pleased that she had stood up to him. Now all she had to do was warn Rhys.

⚜

Raglan Castle, 4th July 2016

'Tess? Are you okay?'

Tess blinked and found Josh crouching in front of her, concern in his eyes. The images of wounded men, bandages and bowls full of blood faded and were replaced with a surge of relief that she was here, with Josh, and the horrors of that long ago summer were gone. 'I'm fine. Just, you know, channelling a bit again. Sorry.' She shivered, despite the sunshine.

'No worries.' He pulled her to her feet and headed for the Fountain Court. It was a grassy expanse covered with daisies and with some flat stones in the middle where presumably a fountain had stood. As they descended some steps, a man came sauntering over from the South Gate, his ginger hair stubble glinting in the sunlight, his suit incongruous in these surroundings.

Tess drew in a sharp breath. 'Not again!' she hissed.

Josh looked up and stiffened. 'Bloody hell,' he muttered.

'We meet again.' Marcus smiled as he came closer. 'Lovely day, isn't it?'

Tess nodded, but alarm bells were ringing inside her head

and she had the urge to run. The feelings of loathing and revulsion she'd experienced in her vision just now returned with a vengeance, and for a moment the two men – Marcus and Glyn – became one, their faces blurring into each other. Tess repressed a shudder. There was something about the controlled way Marcus held himself that terrified her, as if he was keeping violent emotions tightly leashed. She cleared her throat as some sort of response was clearly expected. 'So you fancied a bit of sightseeing then?'

Marcus nodded. 'Yep. Friend of mine recommended this place. Said the sights were spectacular.' But he wasn't looking at the castle ruins. Instead his gaze travelled over Tess and the implication was clear – she was the sight he'd come to see.

She pushed her hands into her pockets to stop them from shaking.

'Listen, mate—' Josh started to say, but Tess interrupted him.

'Sorry, but we must get on.' She plastered on a fake smile and gave Josh a little push towards a staircase leading underneath the castle. She didn't want a confrontation just then. It would ruin everything and that was clearly what Marcus wanted. Why give him the satisfaction? 'There's so much to look at. Enjoy the rest of your day.'

Josh hesitated for a second and threw Marcus a death glare, but then he shrugged and walked down the steps. Tess followed him into what looked like an underground storage area and sagged against a cold wall as soon as they were out of sight. Thankfully Marcus hadn't followed them but she heard him start to sing in a low but penetrating voice – a Def Leppard song, 'Two Steps Behind', and something in the chorus about 'you can run, but you can never hide.' She shivered violently.

'Why did you stop me?' Josh's eyes flashed. 'He needed to be taught a lesson. The guy is stalking you, for Christ's sake!'

'I just wanted to get away from him. Show him he can't rattle me.' Although he had, definitely.

Josh let out a huffing breath. 'Yeah, like that's going to work. His type need to have things spelled out for them in more forceful ways.'

Tess put a hand on his arm. 'Next time, okay? If he does it again, I'll let you deal with him. For today, can we please just pretend that didn't happen? Not let him spoil things?'

'Okay, fine.' Josh looked around and seemed to make an effort to calm down. 'What is this? Storage space?'

'No, I read about it. I think they used it as a sort of makeshift stable during the siege. Poor horses! It's so dark down here.'

She'd been skimming through the books about the castle that she'd found in the library and she'd learned quite a bit about the siege.

'Not that dark.' Josh pointed to several openings high up in the walls that allowed daylight to penetrate the gloom. 'But, yeah, I don't suppose they liked being down here much. Me neither. Come on. Let's see if that bastard's gone yet.'

There was no sign of Marcus so they went up a staircase to access the bridge to the Great Tower, which Josh insisted on climbing. Tess waited for him at the bottom, remembering how terrified she'd been the previous time. When he came back, all enthusiastic about the amazing views, she led the way down to the moat. At almost exactly the same place where Tess had sat the last time, Josh sank down onto the low stone wall and patted the place beside him. 'Let's enjoy the sun here for a while.'

The stones were slightly uneven, but pleasantly warm. Around the base of the tower the grass had been flattened by all the visitors, but a few daisies still managed to thrive. It was peaceful here, with the heavenly scent of newly mown grass drifting in.

'So can I see that earring then?' Josh smiled at her.

'Oh, yes, sure.' Tess took it off and handed it to him.

'Wow, that's quite something, huh?' He held it up to the light and studied the intaglio. 'Can I try it on?'

'You've had your ear pierced?' She didn't know why she was surprised.

'Sure, why not? I was a rebellious teenager once.' He managed to put the earring on and turned his head for her to see. 'So what do you think, does it suit me?' He grinned.

'Actually, it does!' Tess didn't add that the sight of him wearing it also made her stomach flutter and she thought she heard that Welsh word again – *cariad*.

Josh had gone quiet and was staring out across the moat with a faraway look in his eye. Was the earring having a weird effect on him too?

'Josh?' She gave his shoulder a little push. 'Hey, you can give it back now.'

'What? Oh.' He blinked. 'I … that was strange. I felt almost dizzy there for a minute.'

'That's how it makes me feel too sometimes.' She held out her hand and he gave her back the little jewel.

Tess fingered the earring. A tingling feeling surged through her and she looked at the water in the moat, which was completely still today with a thick tangle of green waterweeds almost choking it. She had that weird sensation of the water rising up towards her, sending her head into a spin. A voice washed over her, as if from far away, and she turned to look into a face that was familiar. Rhys.

Her heart started to beat triple time. It was happening again.

'*Cariad, don't ever leave …*' he whispered, the Welsh word as always washing over her, soothing her fears.

A part of Tess was aware that he wasn't really talking to her, but the woman he'd loved. She closed her eyes, waiting for his touch, but the world tilted again and she had to open them in order to stop the nausea from taking over.

She found herself still looking into mesmerising green eyes fringed with thick, dark lashes, but there the similarities ended. Instead of the long-haired Rhys, she was staring at Josh. Josh, with questions in the depths of those eyes, asking permission to do the same thing the Cavalier had wanted. She blinked in confusion and he took that as a yes.

As his mouth moved over hers in a kiss that was in a whole different league to those they'd shared before – fiery, sensual, electrifying – she gave herself up to the pure enjoyment of the moment. She'd been hallucinating just now, her imagination working overtime, but it didn't matter. She was safe. She was with Josh. This was who she wanted to kiss, not centuries-old dead Cavaliers.

When they came up for air, he murmured, 'Whoa! I didn't think you were ready for that.' There was a teasing note in his voice, the lovely Kiwi accent every bit as enticing as that Welsh one. No, more so.

She sent him a mock glare. 'I guess you're just too irresistible.'

'Yeah? Music to my ears.'

She pushed him away, jokingly, and stood up, ready to leave this place which was confusing her. Josh didn't seem to mind, even though they'd only just sat down. He took her hand, twining his fingers with hers and it felt so good. She relished even this small connection between them and couldn't deny it any longer – she was in love.

Tess and Josh lingered for a while outside the South Gate on a grassy terrace overlooking the A40 in the distance. Beyond some trees the hill sloped down towards Raglan village and the fields where the besieging army had apparently camped. Josh could picture them in his mind, their scarlet coats vivid against the dusky green background, with tents and campfires spread out over the field some five hundred yards away. He had no idea why he imagined their coats were red. Possibly because he'd heard the British Army always wore scarlet later during other wars. When he blinked, the image disappeared and all he could see was the tranquil, rural scene in front of them. Although it was clouding over now, the air was very clear, and on the faraway hills were squares of light green fields divided by darker green hedges, a beautiful sight.

He kept hold of Tess's hand, plaiting his fingers with hers. He wanted to be patient, but at the same time he was desperate to repeat that spectacular kiss. Out here wasn't really the place though and he thought it best to let her dictate the pace. If anything more was to happen between them, it should be because she wanted it as much as he did and he wasn't sure of that yet.

'I think it's going to rain,' Tess commented. 'We'd better go.'

'What? Oh, yeah, you're right.' Josh looked at the sky and saw that the dark clouds had turned menacing.

As they headed back into the courtyard, thunder rumbled above them and within minutes the heavens opened. A veritable curtain of rain slashed down, pelting them as they ran towards the former private apartments, which would lead them to the main gate. They sheltered in a doorway at first, watching as the Chapel and Great Hall turned into impromptu swimming pools in a short space of time. But they were getting very wet and Josh became impatient.

'Let's find somewhere drier. In here?' He pulled Tess into a tiny exhibition room just before the main gate. It must have been a guardroom at one point as it was so small, but there were a couple of chairs and some glass cases with a few exhibits. 'We might as well wait for a bit. I bet the rain will stop as quickly as it started.'

He shook his head, sending droplets of water sparkling through the air, and Tess laughed. 'That's what Vince does.' She bent over and shook her own hair out, dripping onto the floor.

'Are you comparing me to a dog? You'll pay for that.'

Josh grabbed her from behind, putting his arms round her waist and pulling her down onto his lap as he sat on one of the plastic chairs. Tess squealed in mock outrage, but she was smiling when she squirmed around so she was sitting sideways instead and her eyes were shining. 'Oh, yeah?' she challenged, but he was sure she knew what her pretend punishment would be.

They were alone in here, all the other tourists presumably having fled to other parts of the castle, and Josh didn't waste the opportunity. He captured her luscious mouth with his and kissed her with all the pent-up desire he'd been holding in check outside. It was even more spectacular and as they didn't have a possible audience, he allowed his hands to explore as well. He cupped the enticing behind he'd been eyeing up earlier and it was exactly as perfect as he'd thought it would be. After a while, he dared to roam higher up.

Tess gasped, but he continued to kiss her, not giving her a chance to push him away now. He wanted her to be as hot for him as he was for her, even if they couldn't do anything about it here. He felt her quivering with desire as he caressed her, and his own jeans were being strained to breaking point.

It was time to stop.

Josh was breathing heavily, as was Tess, and he pulled her close, holding them both still. 'I think we need to get a room,' he joked feebly. 'A better one than this anyway.'

'Mm-hmm. One with a closed door and a lock would be good.'

A glow spread through him at her words. They were on the same page, at last.

Josh looked out the window and noticed the rain was slowing down. 'We'd better go back to Merrick Court then.' He tilted her chin up and gave her a long, slow kiss, before looking into her eyes. 'And just so you know, you decide what happens when we get there. No pressure, okay?'

He was trying to be a gentleman because he sensed this was too important. This wasn't about having a bit of fun; he'd gone way beyond that. And if he slept with her, he wanted it to mean something to both of them. But, hell, he wished he could just take her right here, this minute …

She nodded. 'Okay.' She kissed him back and smiled. 'Thank you.'

But when they got back to Merrick Court and walked into the kitchen half an hour later, they weren't just greeted by Louis and Vince – who should both still have been in the garden as it was only mid-afternoon and the rain had stopped. There was also a teenage girl sitting at the table and as she caught sight of Josh she looked up and glared.

'Hi, Dad. Nice of you to be at home when I come to visit. But then again, if you'd wanted me around, I guess you wouldn't have moved to England.'

Chapter Twenty-Eight

Merrick Court, 4th July 2016

Tess let go of Josh's hand and glanced between him and his daughter, trying to swallow down her disappointment that their afternoon hadn't ended quite the way she'd envisaged. Although perhaps it was for the best? They had been rather carried away and so quickly. She shouldn't have gone along with that, but the very air at the castle had seemed charged with desire and she'd been caught up in the moment.

But his daughter! What on earth was she doing here? It was clear from the shocked expression on his face that he hadn't been expecting her.

'Shayla? What the hell …? I mean, how did you get here?'

'Er, hello? Airplane? Bus? It's not the Middle Ages, although you kind of wonder around here.' The girl glanced at the kitchen with a frown.

She seemed to have plenty of attitude and from what Tess could see Shayla wasn't particularly fond of her dad, just as he'd said. So why had she come then? Wearing a low-cut top that must have had Louis's eyes nearly popping out of their sockets, she was dressed to provoke any parent. The top ended just below her bra and showed a flat stomach with a navel piercing above minuscule shorts. To be fair, she was wearing black leggings underneath the shorts, so her legs weren't on display, but somehow that just made the outfit worse, especially as they were teamed with biker boots. Tess looked at Josh – would he go ballistic?

To his credit, he didn't. Instead, he seemed to take a deep breath and start again. 'Yeah, fair enough. Airplane. But did your mum send you? Because she sure as hell didn't tell me you were coming.' He was scowling now. 'It would've been nice to have some warning.'

Shayla shrugged. 'No, Mum didn't send me. I came by myself.'

'What, she doesn't know?' The girl gave a small nod and this time Josh did go nuts. 'Jesus, Shayla, she's going to kill me! And you. What were you thinking? And where does she think you are now?'

'So many questions, Dad. It's great to see you too.' Shayla took a sip of a Coke that Louis must have found for her.

The boy had been quiet up till now, but he stood up and shoved his chair in, almost matching Josh's scowl. 'I'm going back outside. Coming, Vincent?'

The dog followed him out the door and Tess stared after them. What was that about? Had the girl annoyed Louis? Or perhaps he'd noticed Tess and Josh holding hands and taken offence? She hadn't thought he'd mind if she moved on, but she could have been wrong. Giles had been his uncle after all.

'Tea? Coffee?' she asked Josh, trying to defuse the tension a little.

'Coffee, please.' He sat down opposite his daughter. 'Okay, can we stop with the attitude and just tell me why you're here? Then I'd better call your mum.'

Shayla's mouth took on a sulky pout. 'It's the holidays. I just wanted to spend some time with my dad. Is that so wrong? Most kids of divorced parents do.'

'Cut it out, Shayla. You've never wanted to visit me before.'

'That's because you lived on a smelly sheep station. Who'd want to go there? But this is England, that's way cooler. And Louis said this house is yours. Was he having me on?'

Josh shook his head as if he couldn't quite believe what

he was hearing. 'Yeah, it's mine. For now. And actually, it's in Wales, but anyway ... So all I had to do to spend time with my kid was to move here? Great. Wish someone had told me that a long time ago.'

'Hah! You just didn't want to be bothered with me.' Shayla crossed her arms, pushing her breasts up perilously high. Again, Josh didn't comment, although Tess would bet good money he was biting his tongue. But maybe he was used to Shayla's fashion sense, or lack of it.

'Is that what your mother told you?' He copied her and crossed his own arms over his chest. 'Because if so, it's a big fat lie. I asked to be allowed to have you for visits, at least once a month and for longer during holidays. Your mum got the court to give her sole custody and decided not to allow me access because I wasn't paying her enough maintenance. Her words. So don't give me that crap.'

Shayla opened her mouth and closed it again, as if she didn't know what to say. Tess almost smiled. That was obviously a first.

'Here's your coffee, Josh.' She put a mug in front of him and looked at Shayla. 'Hi, I'm Tess. Are you okay with that Coke or can I get you something else? If not, I'm going upstairs for a bit.'

'Nah, I'm fine. Thanks.' Shayla added the last word almost reluctantly but Tess pretended not to notice.

Josh glanced at her, his eyes sending her a message – apology for Shayla's intrusion and behaviour, intense frustration that their afternoon had been cut short, but she also thought she glimpsed a promise that he'd get back to her, to what they'd been contemplating, as soon as he could. She nodded at him. This wasn't his fault, but right now, he needed to be alone with his daughter.

'So, welcome to Wales then. Although you weren't far off as we're just across the border from England.' Josh pushed his fingers through his hair and tried to think rationally. Shayla, here? Who'd have thought?

When he and Tess had arrived back, he'd been fizzing with anticipation, sure the afternoon was going to end exactly like he'd been hoping. They'd been holding hands for much of the way, making it difficult to change gears, but that only made them laugh. The desire had been simmering, an electric current between them, just waiting to erupt again.

Damn it, why had Shayla chosen today of all days to arrive?

But she couldn't have known, of course, and it wasn't fair to blame her for her bad timing. He sensed there was more to her arrival than she was letting on, but decided to take things one step at a time.

'Are you going to send me back?' Shayla had found her voice again, and the attitude. She reminded him so much of himself at that age. Cocky on the outside, hurting on the inside. Was that his fault? He wasn't sure, but Isla had made it very difficult for him to have any kind of relationship with his daughter.

'That depends.'

''Cause if you do, you'll have to pay for the ticket. Mine was a one way.'

'How did you even buy it? You have that kind of money?' She was sixteen. Did they allow sixteen-year-olds to travel by themselves?

'No, I used Mum's credit card. I'll pay her back. Eventually. Or maybe you can?'

'Jesus.' Isla really *was* going to kill him. 'You do realise your mum is going to blame this on me? What did you do, leave her a note to say I wanted you to come live with me?' He wouldn't put it past her. She was obviously a shit-stirrer. He'd noticed she had already pissed Louis off, which wasn't an easy thing to do as the kid was so laid-back.

'No, I just said I was visiting.' Shayla bit her lip. 'Actually, I told her I had a right to see my dad occasionally because I'd heard her telling her best friend that she'd put a stop to your visits.'

'Ah, so you knew it wasn't my fault? Well, thanks for trying to make me feel bad then.'

'I just wanted to test you, see if it was true. I guess it is, since you said the same thing.'

Josh sighed. 'Yeah, well, I think your mum thought it was better for you not to see me. It's not like I know anything about teenage girls.' He glanced at her outfit. Christ almighty. He was way out of his depth here as he'd never done much parenting. But she probably wanted him to comment, so he wouldn't.

Shayla took another sip of Coke. 'So can I stay? I mean, I'm here anyway ...'

'I suppose, but you'll have to square it with your mum or she'll be on a plane over here faster than a missile. If she's not already on her way. And I won't have her shouting at me again, not even for you.'

Shayla smiled at that. 'You're scared of Mum?'

'No, I just don't like being told off for something I haven't done. So will you call her? You can use my phone if you like.' He fished his mobile out of his pocket and held it out to her. An olive branch of sorts.

After a slight hesitation, she took it. 'Okay. How long can I stay? Just so I know what to tell her.'

'I don't know. When does school start again?'

Shayla wouldn't meet his eye and fiddled with her Coke can. 'I'm not going back. It's so boring and I don't want to study any more.'

Josh took a deep breath and counted to ten in his mind. 'Okay, let's save that discussion for another day. Just call her and say you'll be here for a couple of weeks to start with. Then we'll see.'

Shayla smiled and she was actually very pretty under all the make-up she'd plastered on herself. She stood up. 'I'm going outside, so you won't have to hear the shouting.'

He grinned back, relaxing a little at last. 'Deal. Actually, you'll have to climb to the top of the hill behind the house. That's the only place around here you can get reception. Sorry, I keep forgetting.'

'Hah, you're just trying to make me go even further. Mum's voice isn't *that* loud you know.'

He shook his head after her retreating back. So she had a sense of humour. Good. Perhaps he'd survive a couple of weeks with her. He had to admit it would be wonderful to finally get to know her a bit better. But it would sure as hell put a dampener on his budding relationship with Tess.

Shit.

Raglan Castle, 4th July 1646

'Are you well, my dear? You look a little pale, but then I expect we all do.' Lady Margaret leaned back on her bed where she was resting during the worst of the afternoon heat.

Arabella had been sitting next to her, doing some sewing while dwelling on her encounter with Glyn. Despite having the courage to stand up to him, she'd been left feeling scared and anxious. Could he hurt Rhys? He was devious enough to try.

'Arabella?'

She looked up to see the concerned expression on her ladyship's face and was touched that there was someone here who really cared what became of her.

'It's no wonder if we're all a bit frayed, is it, my lady? This siege seems never-ending, but then I'm not sure what we expected.' Arabella suppressed a sigh. She couldn't tell her ladyship the real reason she was looking peaky. Rhys continued to ride out with the others and even without Glyn's threats, the constant anxiety about his well-being was wearing Arabella down. Not to mention the fears for her own safety.

A loud crash made them both jump, but neither commented on the fact that it had sounded a bit too close for comfort.

'Yes, this situation is affecting us all, to be sure, but I couldn't help noticing that you've not been your usual self these past few days. Is there something on your mind? Or should I say, someone?' Lady Margaret smiled gently as if to show that she didn't mean to pry.

Arabella shook her head, but smiled inwardly. She should have known she couldn't fool her ladyship. 'Well ... there is someone I am a bit worried about but I'm sure he can take care of himself. And all of our fates are in God's hands. We can but pray and hope for the best.'

'Aha, I knew it!' Lady Margaret's smile widened. 'I've never known you to be distracted before. Quiet, certainly, but always efficient and capable, but lately it's been as though you were here in body, but not in spirit.'

'Oh dear, have I been that transparent? I do beg your pardon!' Arabella was aghast to hear this. She'd thought she had hidden her preoccupation well, but obviously not.

Lady Margaret held up a hand. 'No, don't fret. I'm sure I'm the only one who's noticed and that's because I know you so well. Everyone else will have been too concerned with their own worries. But, please, won't you tell me who it is that has captured your heart?'

'I'd rather not say for the moment, my lady, as I don't know if anything will come of it. What with the siege and the men fighting every day ...'

'Very well, it shall be your secret for now, but I want you to promise to come to me if you want help in any way.'

'Thank you, my lady, I will.'

'Good, that's settled then. Now please, will you read to me for a bit? Perhaps then I'll fall asleep.'

Not very likely, Arabella thought, as another loud bang was heard and the windowpanes rattled. But perhaps her ladyship had the right idea and sleeping through the siege would be the best thing? Then at least it would be over quickly.

***

Merrick Court, 4th July 2016

Tess hadn't gone upstairs, but into the library. She'd sat down in one of the comfy armchairs that flanked the fireplace and sipped at the cup of tea she'd made herself at the same time as Josh's coffee. The beverage was too hot so she blew on it and stirred it with the spoon. The milky liquid swirled into a tiny vortex and she became mesmerised by the perfect pattern ...

'Tess?'

She was brought back to the present by someone calling her name and swore quietly. Those damned spirits had been about to get into her head again. Couldn't she even drink tea now without this happening? It was too much.

'In the library,' she called, taking a deep breath.

Josh poked his head round the door. 'Ah, there you are. Sorry to disturb, but I have a favour to ask.'

Tess could guess what it was so she nodded. 'You want a room for Shayla? No problem. I think the one Emilia uses is made up already. I'll go and check.'

'Cheers, that would be great. We'll be in the kitchen.'

He disappeared and Tess rubbed her eyes to try to kick-start her brain. It was ridiculous, him having to ask for his daughter to stay in his own house. It really was time

Tess did something about moving out. She'd told Josh end of July, but it would be much better if she left sooner. He didn't seem in any hurry to sell the house now so she wasn't needed to show prospective purchasers around. No, she should go. She needed a plan.

Houses were cheap in this part of the country so she'd considered renting a cottage and continuing with her furniture business. With a degree in graphic design, she could try to find freelance work as well. She'd have to start checking for jobs online. If she could work part-time and keep going with her own business for the rest, maybe she'd make ends meet? It wasn't like she had an expensive lifestyle.

And she'd like to stay in this area. *At least for as long as Josh does.* But what did he want?

One thing was clear, if she didn't stick around, their budding relationship would never even get off the ground and she very much wanted to see if it could lead somewhere, even though she was afraid of making another mistake. Josh was so different to Giles. Chalk and cheese. Giles had been temperamental, always on edge, while Josh was totally laid-back and much harder to read. What if all he wanted was a short-term fling? It wouldn't be Tess's preference, but maybe it would be worth it?

She smiled to herself. He'd certainly wanted her today at the castle even though he'd been gentleman enough to insist it should be her decision how far they went. Her insides melted just thinking about what being in his arms had felt like. She'd wanted him too, definitely. And was that so bad? They were consenting adults with no strings.

Things had definitely moved a little too fast though so it was probably a good thing that Shayla had arrived, giving Tess time to think it over a bit more. If Josh was serious about wanting her, surely he wouldn't mind waiting for a while longer. He had said it was up to her.

Chapter Twenty-Nine

Merrick Court, 5th July 2016

The following morning Tess was teaching Louis how to scramble eggs to perfection. Bryn's hens had started to lay several a day so they were eating a lot of egg dishes. While Louis did his best to follow her instructions, they chatted. He seemed to have reverted to his normal, sunny self and Tess didn't know whether to bring up his bad mood of the day before. In the end, as Shayla was still asleep, she decided she had to tackle it.

'So, uhm, Josh and I had a good time at Raglan Castle,' she began, wondering if he'd take the hint. He did and grinned at her.

'Yeah, I noticed. You were kind of shining when you came through the door.'

'You don't mind? I mean, if I … if we should happen to …'

Louis shook his head, while scraping the now cooked eggs onto two plates. 'No, why would I? It's nice to see you happy.' His expression clouded over and he added in a near whisper, 'Although that little bitch sure killed the mood, didn't she?'

Tess added already cooked bacon to the plates and carried them over to the table. 'Yes, but that was just bad timing. Not her fault.'

'Huh.' Louis just grunted and started shovelling food into his mouth.

'What happened when she arrived? You seemed a bit … cross? Did she interrupt you and Bryn in the middle of something?'

'No, it wasn't that.'

Tess frowned, seriously curious now. 'What then?'

Louis put down his fork and sighed. 'I shouldn't tell you really, because I like Josh and it's not his fault he has a bitch for a daughter, but ... promise you won't mention it to him?'

'No, of course not.'

'Okay, well, she walked in here and started mouthing off right from the word go. She went on about what a bastard her dad was, how she hated rich people like us who live in huge houses, how English transport sucked, how school sucked ... I mean, jeez! I tried to be friendly, but I didn't get a word in edgewise. And then she told me I'm dressed like a nerd.' He indicated his clothing, normal torn jeans and a faded T-shirt. 'What the hell is wrong with this? Just coz I'm not wearing the latest fashion like her.' He huffed.

Tess felt her eyes widen. 'Wow! She did seem to have a bit of an attitude. I'm sorry you had to look after her for a bit.'

Louis shrugged. 'Not your fault. I just feel sorry for Josh.'

'I'm sure he can deal with it. For what it's worth, I think it was all a front and her mission in life is to provoke and grab attention any way she can. If you got to know her, she might not be so bad underneath all that bravado.'

Somewhere behind the attitude had been a scared and sad little girl, Tess was sure. One who wanted attention at any cost. She was obviously going the wrong way about it though.

Louis looked thoughtful and nibbled on a piece of toast. 'Yeah, maybe you're right. I'll give it a try, for Josh's sake. And yours.' He sent her a teasing glance. 'Maybe she'll be your stepdaughter. Then you'll have to deal with her.'

'Whoa, not so fast! Josh and I were just holding hands.' Although they'd been thinking of doing a lot more than that, but that wasn't something she wanted to share with Louis right now.

'Mm-hmm.' He grinned. 'Well, I'm going outside. You coming?'

'In a minute. I'm just going to put some breakfast in the warming oven for Shayla. See you later.'

Josh grabbed Tess the instant she walked through the door to her workshop and pulled her hard up against him. She gasped with surprise, but he cut the sound off with a searing kiss. He'd spent a damned uncomfortable night thinking of nothing else but kissing her again. Now he made a thorough job of it, behind the door to make sure they weren't seen. She seemed a bit hesitant at first, but soon melted into his arms as if she couldn't resist. Good.

When she'd been kissed to within an inch of her life, he stopped for a breather and buried his nose in her silky hair. 'God, Tess, I'm so sorry about yesterday. I just didn't know what to do ...'

She looked up and put her hand on his cheek, rasping through his stubble with a couple of fingernails, making him shiver. 'It's okay, wasn't your fault.' She stood on tiptoe and gave him another kiss, but then, to his intense frustration, she pushed him away. 'Maybe this isn't such a good idea right now? I mean with Shayla just arrived and everything ...'

'Yeah, she has seriously bad timing, my kid.' He took one of her hands and plaited their fingers, not wanting to lose the contact between them entirely.

'Well, perhaps she did us a favour. We did kind of go from naught to sixty in about three seconds flat. I ... you seem to have a strange effect on me.' Tess gave a shaky laugh and looked away, her cheeks turning slightly pink. 'We should maybe take it a bit more slowly?'

Josh almost groaned out loud. He wanted to turn her around and lift her onto a workbench, continuing where they'd left off just now, but he had told her she could dictate their pace and he had to stick to his word. It was torture, but he'd survive and hopefully when she did feel ready, it would be even more amazing. He swallowed a sigh and nodded. 'Yeah, you're right.'

They heard voices outside and reluctantly he let her hand go. Damn it, were they never to get a moment's peace?

His daughter and Louis walked through the door. Louis smirked at them, so Josh gathered the boy had put two and two together, but he didn't let on, just nudged Shayla and directed her attention to one of the pieces Tess was working on at the moment. 'See? That's the kind of thing my aunt does.'

'This is so cool.' Shayla had turned to Tess and the words seemed to have been dragged out of her almost against her will. For the first time since her arrival, her eyes were shining with something that looked like enthusiasm. 'I love art. It's the only thing I'm good at in school, but Mum said I should concentrate on other stuff too.' She threw her dad a look, as if wanting to see his reaction to her words, but Josh kept a straight face. He was so not getting into that discussion. Not until he'd talked to Isla first, and at the moment she was refusing to take his calls. He'd gathered she was blaming him after all, despite what Shayla had told her. Well, tough. Nothing new there.

'You can help me if you like?' Tess offered, and Josh wanted to give her a massive bear hug when he saw the look of joy on Shayla's face.

'Really?' Shayla glanced at him again. 'But Dad said yesterday I had to help out in the garden, to "earn my keep". Apparently you can't just be a guest around here even when your dad owns a castle.' She made a face that told him exactly what she thought of that.

'If you help Tess, that's the same thing,' Josh said. 'Fine with me.'

Shayla smiled again, transforming her face from sulky

teenager to pretty girl. Josh saw the startled look Louis threw her and almost smiled himself.

'Ace,' Shayla declared. 'When can we start?'

'How about right now?' Tess turned to Josh. 'We can maybe continue with the knot garden later? I really have to get these pieces of furniture finished first, sorry. But you said you needed help with lifting those heavy paving stones, right?'

Josh caught on. In the knot garden they could at least be alone together. 'Yeah, okay. Later's good. Come and find me when you're ready.' He was looking forward to it already, even if all she wanted to do for now was kissing.

'Is this the right colour for the stool?' Shayla held up a pot of fuchsia-coloured paint with a look that said she was sure Tess would hate it.

'Up to you. Use your artistic judgement. Whatever you think looks pretty.'

'Oh, okay.'

Tess hid a smile and picked up her own paintbrush, while daydreaming about Josh.

'He's already taken, you know.'

Shayla's voice cut into Tess's thoughts. 'What? Who?' She frowned at the girl who was now smirking.

'My dad. He's got a girlfriend back home. Her name's Pam and they've been together for years. Can't keep their hands off each other.' Shayla rolled her eyes. 'But then, most of the women seem to like him. No idea why. I mean, he's so old!'

'You think?' Tess tried not to show that the girl's words were affecting her in any way. She might just be stirring it, but then again, Josh *was* extremely good-looking so of course he wouldn't have lived like a monk.

'I just thought I should warn you so you don't fall for him. No point. I met Pam just the other week and she said he'd told her he'll be home by the end of the summer.'

Shayla grinned and added in a whisper, 'And he'll be bringing a ring.'

Tess dredged up a smile from somewhere and affected nonchalance. 'How nice!'

Shayla continued as if Tess hadn't spoken. 'Of course, Pam'll be even more excited when she hears about this house. She's going to love being the mistress here. Like you used to be?'

She emphasised the words 'used to' and Tess gathered she'd been pumping Louis for information. Not that it mattered. It was the truth after all.

'Well, she might be disappointed then,' she replied. 'He's going to sell it and buy another sheep station. He just can't keep away from the smelly beasts. Even helped our neighbour with the shearing. It'll be lovely for you to visit him out in the country though, won't it?'

Shayla's expression turned sulky. 'Why would he want to do that? No sane person would swap a mansion for a bunch of sheep.'

Tess smiled. 'Who said he was sane? Now did you want to try another colour or are you happy with that one?'

She felt she'd won that round, but inside she felt sick. Josh was just too handsome. How could she be sure he wasn't toying with her? She didn't really know him that well after all. Was he a player? The certainty she'd felt the previous day was fast evaporating.

She decided to make an excuse not to meet him in the knot garden that afternoon as she needed time to think.

<hr>

Raglan Castle, 15th July 1646

All through the hot month of July the siege continued – boring, relentless, claustrophobic. Arabella became used to the sharp smell of gunpowder, the stench of too many humans in one place; of horses, manure, leather and wood smoke. The clanging of smiths working at their anvils, the tooth-jarring sound of weapons being sharpened and the constant hiss and steam of cannonballs and shot being manufactured in moulds. The garrison was more or less self-sufficient militarily, as they had a mill within the defences which could produce up to three barrels of gunpowder a day, but at some point they would run out of shot. It was only a question of time.

It was purgatory to look out over the surrounding fields, gardens and orchards, where fresh fruit and vegetables were growing just out of reach. Even the fishponds, with their bounty of carp, were inaccessible, and the daily diet became monotonous in the extreme. There was an air of tension throughout the castle. Everyone had heard the rumours of what had happened in other places to those who'd found themselves besieged and eventually defeated. There were tales of rape and murder, horror stories no one wanted to hear but everyone was whispering. It all added to the atmosphere of anxiety, apprehension and strain.

The marquis continued to be defiant, even when a musket ball came through a window one day, bounced off a pillar and hit him on the side of the head.

'Gave me quite a fright, I can tell you,' Lady Margaret, who'd been present, said. 'But my lord Worcester is made of sterner stuff. Just laughed it off.'

Luckily he hadn't been badly wounded. And with such a fearless leader, how could anyone else inside the castle be less than brave in their turn?

Most of the women were listless, however, spending their time either sewing, looking after the wounded or trying to entertain fractious, bored children. Arabella preferred to deal with the injured as that kept her mind from dwelling too much on what was going on around them. But halfway through the month, the sight she'd dreaded became reality. Rhys, being carried in on a stretcher, covered in blood.

Her whole body began to shake as she hurried over, pretending she was just concerned over yet another casualty. 'Can I help? How badly is he wounded?'

Rhys opened his eyes, which were narrowed with pain but as sharp as usual, their clear mossy colour almost translucent. 'It's but a scratch,' he said, his voice hoarse. 'I'll be fine.'

But Arabella didn't believe him. 'Put him over there,' she directed the men carrying him. A straw mattress had just become free that morning when its occupant had died and she had put a clean sheet over it.

'What happened?' she whispered to one of the men who'd brought him in.

'Another sally but things didn't go our way.' The man shook his head, his mouth in a tight line. 'Major Price and some of the others were taken prisoner, while myself and the captain here only just escaped with our lives. A bad business.' He and the other stretcher-bearer bowed to her and left.

'Where are you hurt?' she asked Rhys after they'd gone.

'Shoulder. I swear, it's nothing. Don't look so worried, *cariad*,' he said quietly. 'I'll live.'

She still didn't dare believe him and the icy knot in her stomach refused to dissolve until she removed his shirt and started cleaning all the blood off him. As it turned out, he'd been right. He had a fairly deep cut, high up on his left arm, which had bled a lot, and a lump on his head which also needed her care, but once she'd washed both wounds and bound up his arm, she couldn't find anything else wrong with him.

He was sitting up, leaning against the wall as she tended him, his upper body naked. Arabella couldn't resist glancing at his magnificent physique. Not that she had much to compare with, apart from other men she'd treated here, but he seemed to her quite perfect. His broad chest was well muscled, his stomach taut. There was a smattering of hair in between his pectorals, which continued down in a line towards his breeches. She had an unladylike urge to discover what this dark arrow pointed at and felt her cheeks heat up. Such thoughts were not seemly.

As if he'd seen her looking, he took her hand under cover of her skirts. 'Do you like what you see?' he teased. 'If we were but alone, I'd show you more.'

'Rhys!' Her cheeks felt as though they were on fire.

He smiled. 'Forgive me, but I'm wishing I had the right to be with you in my natural state, the way a husband can.'

'Husband? You mean …?' Arabella held her breath, waiting for his next words.

He shook his head, his expression chagrined. 'I would love for you to become my wife, sweetheart, but I can't ask you. I have nothing to offer. All I own is a horse, my weapons, some clothes and a handful of coins. You're an heiress, Arabella. You deserve better.'

'To hell with that,' Arabella hissed, startling herself with such blasphemy, although with all the profanity being shouted daily from the enemy camp, everyone was becoming inured to such words.

He blinked. 'What?'

'Rhys, I'm not an heiress any more. Do you seriously think I'll be given back my estate once this siege is over? My uncle Howell has it well and truly in his grasp and with the Parliamentarians as victors, the only way I'd ever be mistress of Merrick Court would be by marrying Glyn. I'd rather die. So if that's the only thing holding you back … But perhaps there are other reasons?'

She looked down, brushing away a stray tear that threatened to spill over. There was nothing she'd like more than to be Rhys's wife, for richer for poorer. But if he didn't want her enough ...

'*Cariad*, look at me!' His insistent whisper made her turn back. 'If that is truly how you feel? I can't do this properly here, but imagine me on my knees right now, with a gold ring in one hand. Arabella, you are the only woman I will ever love – please will you do me the honour of becoming my wife?'

She felt a smile spread almost from ear to ear. 'Yes,' she whispered back, giggling at the absurdity of them doing this here, now, in hushed voices and surrounded by blood and gore. It didn't matter. 'I will, but let's concentrate on healing you first and ...' She threw a glance over her shoulder at Mrs Watson, whose hawk eyes were roaming the room, and pretended to adjust Rhys's bandage. 'We'll discuss it more later.'

The smile he gave her in return made her legs feel so weak she wasn't sure how she managed to carry the bowl of bloodied water out of the room. But despite everything that was going on around them, she wanted to dance and sing.

She was going to marry Rhys.

Chapter Thirty

Tess was woken by the burglar alarm in the early hours of the morning and shot out of bed before she was fully conscious. The alarm had now been changed so she could have it on downstairs at night, which was great, but she hadn't given any thought to what she would do if it went off.

If the burglar hadn't been scared away by the noise, there was nothing she *could* do. She had no weapon or anything else to threaten them with, apart from Vincent.

'Vince!' She shook her head, trying to make her brain work better. He was barking like mad and she ran to the door with him on her heels. 'Come on, boy, you can bite whoever it is, right?'

They raced down the stairs and Tess held her hands over her ears to muffle the horrible shrieking of the alarm. She didn't want to turn it off until she was sure the intruder had gone. Louis appeared, just like last time, doing the same, closely followed by Shayla.

'Jeez, that's loud!' he complained.

'Is there a fire?' Shayla shouted.

'No, burglars,' Louis called over his shoulder.

'Shit!'

Vincent didn't go to the library this time but headed for the Victorian drawing room, a very formal room that was only ever used for special occasions. Apart from all the huge Gothic windows, it had double French doors leading onto a terrace and as soon as she turned the lights on, Tess could see that a pane of glass had been skilfully cut out of the left-hand door allowing the intruder to just open it from the inside. Nothing else had been disturbed though as far as she could make out.

'Looks like whoever it was got scared when the alarm started up. Good.' Tess walked around, checking the room. 'I can't see that anything's been touched, can you?'

'Nope.' Louis was right behind her, which was comforting.

Tess sat down on one of the silk brocade-covered chairs, a bit wary of its spindly legs, while Shayla wandered around looking at all the knick-knacks dotted around the room. 'So he's not giving up then,' Tess commented, leaning her head in her hands. 'Damn it all!'

'Bastard,' Louis muttered while continuing to pace the room. 'You've got to call the police this time. The window's broken.'

'Yes, I know. I'll do it in the morning.'

'Are you going to turn that off?' Louis waved a hand to indicate the still blaring alarm. 'It's doing my head in.'

'Yes, sorry.' Tess went and found the panel and stopped the noise. A blessed silence fell on the house, but it felt oppressive somehow. She found herself listening for any sounds that shouldn't be there, like footsteps or breathing …

'You know who did this?' Shayla had come over and looked at Tess, frowning.

'I think so. It's someone who's trying to scare me into giving them a lot of money.'

'Why?'

Tess almost sighed. The girl was persistent, but then again, she would have been curious too if she'd been her. 'It's a long story, but it's someone to whom my late husband owed a huge sum.'

Shayla nodded, as if absorbing this. 'Hadn't you better give it to him then?'

'I wish I could, but I don't have anywhere near enough.'

'And the douche won't believe her,' Louis added, clenching his fists.

Tess shivered. It certainly didn't look like it. 'What time is it?'

'Four-ish.' Louis yawned. 'I'm going back to bed. I don't think they'll come back but you could always leave Vince down here for the rest of the night?'

Tess shook her head. She was keeping the dog right next to her as he made her feel safe. 'I'll just reset the alarm.'

Returning to her room, she locked her door for good measure. When she turned around, she noticed a shadowy shape over by the window and jumped. 'You again!' she breathed, her heartbeat kicking up a notch.

She glanced at Vince, who was staring intently at the shadow, his ears alert. He emitted a low rumbling growl, but it was half-hearted and soon he gave it up and headed for his bed. Tess gathered he didn't consider the apparition a threat, which was reassuring.

Its shape was rather indistinct this time, as if it didn't have the energy to quite materialise. Perhaps producing a human form took it out of him? Tess was surprised to find she wasn't scared, merely curious. There was also that strange feeling of safety, as if she was being watched over, protected. She walked slowly towards the window and the shadow disappeared.

'Thank you,' she whispered, then felt silly for talking to someone who wasn't there. At least, not really.

She had the feeling the ghost had come expressly to show her she wasn't alone. It seemed crazy, but why else would he have shown himself now of all times?

Bristol, 16th July 2016

'You didn't even go inside? What the bloody hell do you think I'm paying you for?'

Marcus glared at Archie. Maybe it was time to retire the guy? He was obviously turning into a wuss of epic proportions – not a good trait for someone in his line of business.

'I couldn't, could I?' Archie was scowling, clenching and unclenching his big fists in agitation. 'The rich bitch'd had a burglar alarm installed. Made one hell of a racket the minute I stuck my hand inside. There were probably cameras and all. I wasn't going to take any chances as I figured you wouldn't want me on film. Hadn't brought me balaclava, had I?'

'For fuck's sake …'

'And there was someone in the room coming towards me too. A shadowy figure, like some damn ghost guarding the place.' Archie shuddered. 'I felt it breathing down my neck when I left.'

Marcus stared at the man. 'A ghost? You're losing your marbles, man.'

'I know what I saw.' Archie looked mulish, obviously sticking to his story.

Marcus decided to let it go. If the man was going to get spooked each time he did a job, he'd definitely have to get rid of him. For now, he needed to deal with the problem at hand. 'So we can't get into the house to search it.' He drummed his fingers on the desk. 'That must mean there *is* something to find. She's holding out on me, Lady Merrick. I'll have to deal with it myself. Damn it all, this wasn't supposed to take so long! Her idiot of a husband's been dead for ages.'

He waved at Archie to leave. Useless bastard.

'Bollocks!' Marcus slammed the palm of his hand down onto the shiny surface of his desk, trying to find an outlet for the rage that filled his brain to overflowing. He wondered if he was going through some sort of male midlife crisis as he'd never felt this out-of-control before. But it only seemed to happen when he thought of Lady Merrick. Therese. What was it about her that triggered such a violent reaction? Such intense lust?

Damned if he knew.

One thing was for sure though, he had to get this sorted, and soon, because he couldn't stand the waiting. And he hated loose ends – this one needed tying up before it got out of hand.

<hr />

Merrick Court, 16th July 2016

'Another attempted burglary? Shit! Did they take anything?'

Josh felt his stomach muscles clench at the thought of an intruder. Tess could have been assaulted, raped, murdered ... And so could his daughter. It didn't bear thinking about. He calmed down a bit when she told him what had happened.

'Well, I'm glad we had the alarm rerouted, but still ...'

'I've reported it to the police but as nothing was taken this time either they're not too bothered. They said the alarm obviously did its job.' She drew in a deep breath. 'Damn it, I'm scared.'

Josh tried to put his arms around her but she resisted and slipped away to stand by the Aga. 'Don't. Not now.'

'Why?' Josh frowned. They were in the kitchen, where he'd gone to find her the minute he heard about the break-in from Louis, and there was no one else around. She'd been avoiding him for over a week now and he was getting seriously frustrated.

'I ... I just don't think it's a good idea. I had a little talk with Shayla and, well, I think we should cool things a bit.'

'What's Shayla got to do with it?' Josh didn't understand. What could his daughter possibly have said?

Tess just shrugged and Josh let it go for now. He'd have

a chat with Shayla himself later to find out what was going on.

'Well, I think I should sleep here in the house after all. With you,' he added jokingly, and tried out his most flirtatious smile on her but she barely noticed. What the hell was going on here?

'I don't think so. What would Bryn say? And Shayla?'

'I'll just tell them you didn't want to be alone here. I'm sure they'll understand.' He moved closer to her, but she flitted away to fiddle with the kettle. Something was up, but he had no idea what. He was damned well going to find out though.

'I don't know, Josh. I'm not sure ...' She glanced at him and must have seen the determination in his eyes. 'Okay, fine, it's your house. I can't stop you. And it's not like we're short of space.'

'Damn right.' Josh didn't want to force his presence on her, but this was serious. Both she and his daughter could be in danger; he had to be here to protect them.

He swallowed his disappointment at her reluctance to be near him. He got the message – she was getting cold feet. Seriously freezing. His body was crying out for him to just scoop her up and carry her upstairs. But something was wrong and until he'd found out what it was, he wouldn't push her. 'I'll go and get my stuff.'

Tess was in her workshop, half-heartedly doodling some flower sketches for a pretty little cupboard, when she heard a car drive into the stable yard. Shayla hadn't come to help today so she was all alone. When asked if he knew where Shayla was, Louis had just shrugged.

'Probably gone shopping or something. Didn't say anything to me. Or maybe she's with her dad, he's not here either.'

She didn't even have Vince for company as he was

somewhere outside with Louis. Tess stood up slowly and went to see who'd arrived. She sincerely hoped it wasn't Rosie again. It was so much more peaceful without her. But the car she spotted wasn't her sister-in-law's Chelsea tractor, it was a black BMW.

Marcus. Again. *Shit.*

No sooner had the thought whizzed through her brain than the man himself stepped out of the car. He was dressed casually, but still expensively. Designer label everything, if Tess wasn't mistaken, from his dark jeans to the crisply ironed shirt. Even his sneakers looked brand new. She walked forward, wiping her hands on the back of her own, rather disreputable, jeans.

'Hello, I wasn't expecting you.' Tess tried not to sound as shaken as she felt on seeing him. Had he come to threaten her properly now?

'Lady Merrick, or can I call you Therese this time?' The dimpled smile appeared as he came towards her, both hands outstretched. To Tess's surprise he grabbed her shoulders and air-kissed her cheeks, as though they were friends of long standing. She tried not to pull away.

'I ... yes, I suppose ...'

'Another lovely day.' He squinted up at the sun. 'I thought you might want to come for a pub lunch, but you look like you're busy.' His gaze travelled the length of her, no doubt taking in the dusty jeans and paint-stained shirt, but there was still an appreciative look in his eyes as if he more than liked what he saw.

'Yes, I'm working I'm afraid, but ... uhm, nice thought.' Tess wondered why on earth he'd imagined she would want to go out for lunch with him and why he hadn't at least called to ask.

'I was just passing and thought I'd drop by on the off chance. No worries, another time, eh? But perhaps we can have a little chat at least? Take a five-minute break?'

Tess nodded somewhat reluctantly. 'Sure. Shall we go and sit in the garden?' She felt safer talking to him out in the open. Although he seemed different today, less threatening, she didn't want to take any chances She led the way to a bench outside the front of the house and they sat down.

'So, I spoke to your solicitor after all,' Marcus began. 'He says you're personally responsible for Giles's debts, not the person who inherits the estate, and claims your assets are virtually non-existent.' He put one leg on top of the other and turned so he was facing Tess.

'Yes.'

'Well, it's just not good enough, Therese. I hate to be persistent, but I really need the full amount. I've got other people breathing down *my* neck and a debt's a debt. Have you thought about what I said? Decided to sell a few trinkets maybe?'

Irritation swirled inside Tess. Which part of 'I have no assets' didn't he understand?

'Look, Marcus, I don't know why you don't believe me or the solicitor, but I really, *really* don't own anything apart from a few bits of furniture and stuff. When I leave here, I'll be renting a cottage or something like that as I can't afford to buy. I have no money, no jewellery, no property – nothing! The only thing of value is my car and even that's not worth much now.' She spread her hands. 'How am I supposed to come up with half a million pounds when I can barely afford to eat?'

The dimpled smile appeared again. 'Oh, come on, it can't be as bad as that. Giles must have provided for you somehow, lovely woman like you. Life insurance?'

Tess shook her head. 'No, he didn't have any, and if you must know, we were about to get divorced.'

That made him frown. 'Really? He didn't mention that. Kept telling me he had to have a big win for your sake.'

Tess snorted. 'I doubt he was thinking of anyone other

than himself.' She sighed. 'If you insist on claiming this money back from me, I'll have to declare myself bankrupt so you'd only get a small sum anyway.'

'Not happening, Therese.' He took one of her hands in both of his and looked her in the eyes. 'But maybe we can come to some sort of arrangement? I could let you pay in instalments, perhaps? I'm sure the bank will let you borrow some money, then you can develop your little business.' He smiled. 'I looked into it. Pretty things you produce. Should do well once you're established properly. I could even help you get back on your feet, if you like? I know people.'

His fingers were playing with her hand and Tess kept still, fighting the urge to pull it away. What was he implying? She was afraid she understood all too well what the 'payment' for helping her would entail and the 'arrangement' between them. No way. The mere thought of it made her skin crawl, but she knew she'd better not let him see that.

'Thank you, but I'd rather manage on my own. Instalments would be good though. I'll speak to the solicitor again, see what he thinks.' She finally managed to free her hand and it was as though she'd released it from a trap. 'And now, if you'll excuse me, I think I'd better crack on with some work.' She stood up and he followed suit, although more slowly.

'Okay, I'll expect to hear from you soon then. And if you change your mind, you know where to find me.' He pulled out his wallet and handed her a business card. 'Here, give me a call in the next couple of days.'

'Right.' Tess had no intention of calling him, but thought it best not to say so. She'd send him an email.

'Nice seeing you again.' They'd reached the stable yard and he grabbed her for another air-kissing session, although this time he managed to actually kiss her cheeks. It wasn't an unpleasant experience, but Tess still had to suppress a shudder. She just didn't want him anywhere near her.

She watched him drive out of the yard and headed for the house. It was time to talk to Mr Harrison about bankruptcy procedures. No way was she taking out any bank loans to pay Marcus bloody Steele. And she was *so* not paying him in kind either.

Chapter Thirty-One

'And I now pronounce you man and wife. May God bless your union and be with you always. Amen.'

It was just after midnight, and Arabella thought for a moment it was all a dream, but the man standing beside her in the near darkness – her husband – was holding her hand so tightly she couldn't possibly be imagining this.

They had agreed to marry in secret for various reasons. Firstly, because the marquis, although giving his blessing, had urged them to keep it to themselves for now.

'There are scores of men here without their womenfolk and if they get wind of your nuptials, there could be jealousy and discontent. I'd rather you were discreet.'

Rhys and Arabella could see the sense in that. There was also the fact that they wanted to keep it a secret from Glyn. Although the man had been prevented from coming anywhere near Arabella again, both by Rhys and some of his friends who kept Glyn under constant surveillance, he'd made several veiled threats.

'Better to keep him in the dark,' was Rhys's opinion, and Arabella agreed, hence the furtive wedding so late and with only four people present.

Rhys had persuaded an Anglican minister from the soldiers' side of the castle to come and marry them in the chapel. The only witnesses were Lady Margaret and a man called Matthew Emrys, who Rhys said was a friend of his. Arabella had decided to take Lady Margaret into her confidence, since she'd said to come to her for help if ever it was needed, and the lady had been delighted for her.

'You are right to grasp happiness while you can, my

dear,' she'd said. 'I won't breathe a word, you know that, and I will stand witness with pleasure.'

The minister had brought paper and a quill and wrote out a statement to prove they had been married this day. 'For we don't have access to the usual church ledgers here,' he muttered. 'With this, you can have the marriage entered later.' Emrys and Lady Margaret both signed it, after the bride and groom, and Rhys gave it to Arabella.

'Keep it safe somewhere,' he whispered. 'We may need it as proof.'

She nodded and pushed it into a pocket inside her skirt for now. Later, she would sew it in securely.

The minister and witnesses melted into the night, and Arabella was left with her new husband, who took her hand and pulled her towards the stairs leading up to the Long Gallery.

'Come, I have a surprise for you.'

'Where are we going?' A little breathless, both from the speed with which he was walking and the effect his smile had on her, she followed, intrigued.

They didn't go to the Long Gallery, however. Instead, Rhys pulled her through a small door on the first floor and into the Minstrel's Gallery. 'Here we are. Your wedding feast, Lady Cadell.'

Arabella gasped. The light from the moon shining in through the huge windows of the Great Hall showed a blanket on the floor with several cushions and a trencher with bread and cheese. There was also a bottle of wine and two tankards.

'No glasses, I'm afraid, but I'm sure it will taste the same whatever we drink out of,' Rhys said. He spread his hands in invitation for her to sit, and she did.

'This is amazing! But, why here?'

She had been wondering how they would spend their wedding night, but had assumed the best they could do would be to share the dirty straw with the horses. There was no privacy to be had anywhere in the castle.

Even Lady Margaret had been stumped. 'Every nook and cranny is filled with people,' she'd said with a worried frown. 'I don't know that I can ask anyone to forsake their beds for a night, not without telling them the reason.'

'Don't worry, my lady, I'm sure we'll … uhm, find a way.' And Arabella had counted on it, but she'd never dreamed of coming here.

Rhys chuckled. 'I was looking up one day and it occurred to me that this space wasn't being used for anything at the moment. I doubt anyone else will come here, so provided we're quiet, we will be undisturbed. Now, would you like some wine, my love?'

They shared the food and wine, taking their time. 'We have all night,' Rhys assured her. 'I'm not needed on guard duty until tomorrow.'

Arabella was nervous, but the wine helped and when Rhys eventually took her in his arms and pulled her down onto the blanket, she knew everything would be all right. His kisses were exciting, intoxicating, firing her blood and he seemed to know just what to do in order to put her at ease. Being all alone here, they were able to shed their clothes completely, and he allowed her to explore the contours of his battle-scarred body, while he caressed every inch of hers.

'You are so beautiful, my lovely.' He trailed kisses across her shoulders, breasts and down her stomach. 'I can't believe I'm this lucky. Whatever happens, this night will be the one thing I'll always remember.'

'I'm the lucky one.' Arabella was becoming impatient, her body yearning for his. 'Show me what to do, Rhys, please. I want to be yours in every way.'

'All in good time.'

His fingers continued their soft touches, seemingly

knowing exactly what she craved. The yearning inside her built until she was sure she couldn't stand it any longer. Then and only then did he enter her, carefully at first, but with longer, firmer strokes as she began to moan and writhe with the pleasure of it. He kissed her so that her cries were muffled, but she was so caught up in the moment she wouldn't have cared if the whole world heard her screaming his name.

Pleasure exploded inside her, radiating out into every fibre of her being, and she felt Rhys shudder with his own release. Then he gathered her close and they lay there entwined, as one, man and wife in every sense.

Arabella had never felt so content in her life.

*

Merrick Court/Home Farm, 18th July 2016

Josh was pleased to find his daughter on her own in the kitchen and decided it was time to confront her.

'What have you been telling Tess about me?' he asked, sitting down opposite Shayla at the table and folding his arms.

'What?' She looked up, her spoon halfway to her mouth. Her eyebrows came down. 'I didn't say *anything*,' she snarled. 'Why? Is she making stuff up about me?'

'Well, you must have said something to make her back off from me. She and I were friends, but now she can't wait to get me out of the house each day.'

'Friends, huh? She fancies you, you know, just like all the older women. Mum says you always were a player.'

'Is that what you told Tess?' Christ, he hoped not. He may never have had any long-term relationships, apart from Isla, but Josh wasn't a player. And 'older women'? He wasn't *that* ancient. Jesus.

'No, of course not! Why would I?'

Shayla gave him that wide-eyed, innocent stare that told him she was hiding something. 'Shay,' he growled. 'If I find out that you're lying you'll be on the next plane out of here, is that clear?' The little madam had done *something*, he could feel it, so he put some steel into his voice.

Shayla squirmed a bit. 'You like her that much, huh?'

'Yes, I do actually. Tess is special.'

'I see.' She looked down, then sighed. 'Okay, fine. I just told her you were getting engaged to Pam when you go back to New Zealand.'

'What?' Josh sat up straight. 'Who the hell is Pam?'

'Uhm, some woman I made up.' Colour flooded Shayla's cheeks and she wouldn't look him in the eye.

'For Christ's sake, what were you thinking?' Josh stood up. 'No wonder Tess is avoiding me.'

'I'm sorry,' Shayla muttered. 'I just wanted you to myself for a bit, now we're finally, like, talking and stuff.' She hung her head.

Josh took a deep breath, then walked round the table and pulled her up for a hug. 'Idiot,' he murmured. 'We can still have time together no matter what happens.' He pretended to knuckle the top of her head. 'Just don't pull stunts like that on me, okay?'

'Okay. I promise.' She smiled and a warm feeling spread inside Josh. He didn't want to lose her either. She was precious – he'd never known how much before. But she had to learn that there were limits to what he'd put up with.

'Good. I've got to go now. See you later.'

Josh tried to tamp down on his frustration as he drove up the long lane leading to Fred Williams's farmhouse. He'd wanted to find Tess immediately to tell her about Shayla's lies and sort things out between them, but he had an appointment with Fred and couldn't let him down. The matter with Tess would have to wait. When he reached the Home Farm a measure of peace settled over him. The old-fashioned house, the huge barn and a series of neatly kept storage sheds and stables, all felt welcoming. There were no shadows here, nothing to disturb him. And the buildings looked to be in good repair and would be the perfect base for Merrick Court's flock of sheep, although he'd need to build another barn probably as he wanted to double the number of animals Fred currently had. His plans were coming along and now he had to discuss them with Fred.

Mair came out the minute he'd parked his car. Small and round, she smelled of baking and gave him a wide smile. 'Welcome, Josh, how lovely to see you again. Fred was ever so grateful for your help with the shearing. You should've let him pay you ...' She chattered on as she led him into the house. 'Here, sit yourself down. You will have some tea and cake, won't you?'

'Yes, please.' Josh definitely wasn't averse to eating a piece of the newly baked cake whose aroma filled the cluttered farmhouse kitchen. He settled down at the table just as Fred came in from the sitting room to join them. Characteristically, the man got straight to the point.

'Josh, welcome. So you're looking to buy the Home Farm then? I'm glad you've decided to stay on.'

'I thought I'd at least give it a try, but I haven't told anyone else yet so can you keep it to yourselves, please?' Josh didn't want to tell Tess or Bryn until he'd sorted everything out. 'And it all hinges on whether you'll accept my offer for the farm. Without it, I won't have enough land for what I want to do.' Josh helped himself to a generous slice of the cake Mair passed around. She didn't seem to have cut any small pieces, but that was fine by him. The moist carrot cake melted in his mouth, one of his favourites.

'And what's that then?' Fred followed suit.

'Sheep, lots of them. It's what I know best, so the cattle

would have to go. If you were to sell to me, I'd be willing to buy your existing flock and I'm aiming to double it for next year. I think the combined land of Merrick Court and Home Farm can sustain that number. Would you agree?'

Fred thought it over for a moment, then nodded. 'I do. But you'll need help. That's a lot of work.'

'Of course. I'll hire some people and I'd need a foreman. I was thinking he could live in this house so he's on site for any emergencies. And I'll probably build another barn. There are cottages on the estate if needed for other workers.'

'Sounds like a good plan.'

'Perhaps you could advise me as to who'd be the best person for that job? You know the people hereabouts and I think a local man would be good.'

Fred rubbed his chin. 'Well, there's Pete who helped with the shearing. The fourth and youngest of the Powell boys, he is, so doesn't have land of his own. The older brother bought out everyone else's share when their da' passed away. He's a good man, experienced, steady.'

'Okay. I'll have a chat with him.' Josh took a sip of his tea then looked Fred in the eye. 'So what do you think, would you like to sell me this place? I've made an offer but I can raise it if you don't think it's enough. I'm not asking for any special favours.' He thought briefly of Rosie and her demands, but he wasn't like her.

Fred smiled and looked to Mair, who nodded. 'Yes, it seems fitting somehow that Home Farm should go back where it came from, seeing as our son doesn't want it. And your offer was fair, the estate agent said so.' He stuck his hand out and they shook on it. 'You've got yourself a deal.'

'Excellent, thank you. I've got to sell some property I own in New Zealand, but hopefully that shouldn't take long, then we can finalise things. Do you mind waiting a month or two?'

'Not at all,' Mair chimed in. 'That'll give us time to sort

everything out for our future. Find somewhere to move to and clear out this place. Forty years is a long time to live in one house; we've got a lot of things we won't need.'

Josh knew it would be a wrench for them to leave, so he smiled and said, 'You're welcome to stay up at the Court any time. I think I can find you a bedroom or twenty somewhere.'

Fred and Mair laughed. 'We might just take you up on that.'

'But remember, let's keep this to ourselves for now, okay?' Josh didn't want to jinx the deal by having anyone know about it until it was done.

'You've got our word.'

* * *

Merrick Court, 18th July 2016

Tess blinked through a curtain of water and realised that her expression was fixed into a smile of joy. She was sitting on the floor of her shower with her back against the wall, water streaming down onto her head and body. She'd gone into some kind of trance just from the sound of the water and her legs must have given way. This was getting ridiculous.

But what did it matter? Rhys had married her.

'No, not me – Arabella,' she hissed at herself and stood up, reaching for the soap. The memory was clear in her mind even now, the ceremony itself distinct even though she didn't recall much else.

The strong emotions, the pure love she'd felt, that was all there, running riot in her veins. One thing was crystal clear – Arabella and Rhys had lived for the moment, grasped what happiness they could while there was still time, and Tess knew she should do the same.

She'd been keeping Josh at arm's length, avoiding him as much as possible. It was just too difficult to be around him and not throw herself into his arms, craving those amazing kisses. Shayla's words had stopped her, but she couldn't deny the strong attraction between them. Why hadn't Josh mentioned the woman waiting for him in New Zealand? Maybe he wasn't as serious about her as Shayla had made out?

Tess would have to ask, because she wanted Josh. Badly. And if Shayla was wrong, it was time to take a chance on happiness.

'Okay, she is *so* grounded. For the next ten years at least.'

'What? Who?' Tess had come into the knot garden to continue the work there and found Josh waiting for her. He was standing with his arms crossed over his chest, but he was smiling so she assumed he was joking.

'Shayla! She told you a pack of lies, didn't she? About someone called Pam? She confessed.'

'Well, yes, but … Lies?'

'Too bloody right. It isn't true, any of it. There's no such person. She made it up.'

Tess blinked. 'Pam doesn't exist?'

'Nope. Never met anyone by that name and I'm *definitely* not marrying her. The little ratbag … I came *this* close to putting her on the next flight home.' Josh held up his thumb and forefinger to show a millimetre's space between them, but his green eyes were shooting sparks of amusement so Tess knew he wasn't really angry. Or not any more. 'Honestly, kids!'

'Oh.' Tess was almost giddy with relief, but then another thought struck her. 'Did she get the name wrong? I mean, do you have anyone waiting for you in New Zealand? I … I should have asked before, I guess.'

'No, no one.' He stepped closer. 'Is this the only reason

you've been keeping me at arm's length? Seriously, I wouldn't pull a stunt like that. I'm a one-woman-at-a-time kind of man.'

'Uhm, yes. She kind of made me doubt you ... and myself.' Tess looked away. She should have just challenged him about it instead of letting the girl's words fester.

'Well, no more, okay? I swear, I don't have any ladies waiting for me anywhere. And as for Shay, she was just scared of losing me to you.'

'Okay.' Tess was shaking, whether with relief or something else, she wasn't sure. In the next moment she found herself swept into a fierce embrace behind a clump of bushes, kissed so thoroughly her legs turned to mush. She was glad Josh's arms were around her or she might have had to sit down. She put a hand on his chest and could feel his heart going ballistic. Her own was just as bad.

'This is crazy. We're acting like a couple of naughty teenagers.'

He laughed. 'I know, right? But the real teenagers around here seem to be everywhere and they've caused enough damage. Now I just want you to myself for five seconds!'

'Is that how long it's going to take?' Tess teased. 'In that case, I'm not sure it'll be worth it.'

'Why you ...' He kissed her again, fiercely, punishingly. 'You'll be the one who won't last more than five seconds. Just you wait.'

Tess smiled. 'That's a dare, if ever I heard one. You'll have to prove it.' She looked up at those amazing eyes, seeing her own desire reflected in their depths. 'Come to my room tonight? Louis won't be here – he's going back to his school this afternoon for some leaving ceremony or something – so let's hope Shayla sleeps like a log. Although her room is at the other end of the house, thank goodness.' She stood on tiptoe and bit his bottom lip, softly, gently. 'I'll be waiting.'

Josh stared at her, his eyes shining now as if she'd given

him the most amazing treasure. 'Seriously? You're inviting me to … tonight?'

'Well, yes. I don't fancy a tumble in the grass. There may be ants.' She laughed at his expression. 'What? You didn't think a woman could take the initiative? Or have you been teasing me and you don't actually want to sleep with me at all? You're just trying to drive me insane with lust.'

Josh pulled her close, his hands on her bum pushing her against him. 'Does that feel like I'm not willing?' he whispered, caressing her neck with his mouth. 'I've been waiting weeks for this, for you. Wild horses won't keep me away tonight, I can promise you that. And I don't just want to sleep with you, I want to make love to you.'

Tess shivered with anticipation. The evidence of his desire was hard to ignore. 'I believe you. But maybe we'd better try to concentrate on something else until then? If those pesky teenagers come and look for us right now, you'll be in trouble.'

He let go of her with a sigh and pushed his unruly hair out of his eyes. 'Yeah, you're right. I wish that fountain was working; I could do with a cold shower. Let's get started on those paving stones. Maybe hard labour will help, although just being next to you is going to be tough.' He shook his head. 'Come on. I'll try to get a grip.'

Chapter Thirty-Two

Merrick Court, 18th July 2016

Tess was pacing her bedroom. How long would it be before Josh arrived? And did she have time to change once more? She'd debated what to wear for hours, unsure what he'd be expecting. She wasn't used to playing the seductress and hadn't wanted to tempt anyone into her bed for a very long time. In the end, she'd settled for a pretty bra and knickers set in black lace, with a thin kimono style bathrobe on top. Men were supposed to like feminine underwear, weren't they? Or was that just a cliché?

'Decisions, decisions.' She was probably over-thinking it.

Vincent lifted his head and growled softly, but this changed swiftly to tail-thumping on the floor. Tess went to the door and saw Josh coming up the stairs, his smile when he caught sight of her making her blood fizz.

'Hey, you,' he said and bent to give her a quick kiss, before greeting Vincent who'd come over to sniff him. 'Good boy. You didn't bark, eh?' Satisfied that there was no threat to his mistress, the dog padded back to his bed and went to sleep. Josh turned to Tess and looked her up and down. 'Silk. Nice. Do I get to undo the belt?'

He moved to stand close to her and when she nodded he tugged at the belt until it came away, allowing her robe to fall open. Josh drew in a sharp breath. 'Even better,' he murmured, trailing a couple of fingers along the top of one breast. Tess shivered.

'I wasn't quite sure how to dress for the occasion. I see you dressed up,' she joked. He was wearing tracksuit bottoms and a T-shirt, but his feet were bare.

'Camouflage,' he said. 'If Shay sees me going back to my

room early in the morning I'll pretend I've been for a run. And they're easy to take off, should you wish to.' His grin was infectious and Tess smiled back, relaxing a bit.

'I can't imagine why I'd want to do that,' she murmured, putting both hands on his hard chest and running them downwards.

He pulled her close then and kissed her, slowly, languorously as if he was memorising the taste and feel of her. He stroked her back, pushing the silk robe off her shoulders so he was touching her naked skin, and cupped her bottom, rubbing his thumbs in lazy circles that sent shafts of desire streaking through her.

His mouth became more demanding and he walked her over to the nearest wall, pushing her up against it while reaching for the clasp on her bra. He made short work of taking it off, his fingers stroking her breasts, touching, teasing, making desire pool in her stomach and lower.

Tess wanted to touch him too and tugged at his T-shirt, pushing it up and over his head. He was so beautiful, so perfect, the hard ridges of his chest and abdomen covered with silky tanned skin and a dusting of dark hair. She traced the outline of his tattoo with her fingertips, resolved to ask him about it later, then kissed his shoulder and neck. He smelled clean and citrusy, but all male. Gorgeous. His hair was soft, but messy as always, and she ran her fingers through it, pulling him down for more delicious kisses. Then she allowed her hands to roam further down, across his stomach and to the waistband of those tracksuit trousers, where she hesitated.

Josh stopped kissing her for a moment and looked down at her with a teasing smile. 'You're not shy, are you? I thought you were going to seduce me. I'm all yours.'

'How about we seduce each other?' She dared to dip her fingers inside his waistband and caressed the tip of him which was straining to escape confinement. She pulled his trousers down a bit and took the whole length of him into her hand. 'Like this?'

He sucked in a harsh breath. 'Good idea. But if you're going to do that, you may have been right about the five seconds.'

He backed them up until they fell onto the bed, then took charge again. His mouth and fingers were everywhere, stroking, licking, caressing, and Tess thought she would explode any second. 'Josh, please ...'

'Do I need protection?' he whispered.

'No, I've got it covered. Just ... yes! Oh, God ...'

She'd barely said the words before he was inside her, his strokes deeper and harder, while his fingers continued to caress her. Tess felt herself dissolve into a giant explosion of pleasure and cried out his name. Josh soon followed, before slowing down, the aftershocks making them both quiver uncontrollably.

'Jesus,' he muttered as he collapsed beside her and pulled her to lie with her head on his chest. 'That was intense! In the best possible way.' When she looked up, he kissed her tenderly. 'You are one amazing woman, Tess!'

'You weren't so bad yourself. In fact, I think you're pretty much perfect.'

The smile and kiss he gave her promised that she hadn't seen anything yet.

***

Raglan Castle, 7th August 1646

The mighty stone foundations shook as 'Roaring Meg', an enormous mortar with the fattest barrel Rhys had ever seen, sent yet another cannonball their way. Dust and stone splinters rained down on a few unfortunates and there were screams of agony from others, with people running in search of cover. The siege surely couldn't last much longer, but the marquis gave no sign of wanting to surrender yet.

Damn the old man. Had he no thought for the women and children in here? For Arabella? Rhys knew it was fatal to think too much about the woman he loved as he could lose his concentration, but he wanted to stay alive now, more than ever before.

He wanted to grow old with Arabella, not fight in this infernal war.

They were still making short forays out of the castle, but he'd sensed that the men were becoming disheartened and the bravado was forced. The capture of Major Price and many others dampened the spirits of those left behind considerably. No one believed they could win any longer and no matter how many enemy soldiers they killed, more arrived daily.

Even worse was that Colonel Morgan had brought with him an engineer by the name of Hooper, who was rumoured to be very skilful at his job. He'd begun by building a battery from which the enemy managed to disable quite a few of the defenders' cannon, which was a blow. Bad news arrived as well when they were reliably informed that Goodrich Castle had been taken on or around the last day of July and had surrendered to the enemy.

'So we're the last to stand,' Rhys had muttered to his friend Matthew.

'Save Pendennis down in Cornwall, I believe. And maybe Harlech? At least I haven't heard as how they've fallen yet.'

The situation seemed truly hopeless and still the marquis continued defiant.

The month of August saw the arrival in the Leaguer field of General Fairfax himself and he seemed to galvanise the Parliamentarians into even more action.

'Damn it all, they're digging all the time.' Rhys and Matthew were on guard duty at the highest point of the castle, on top of the Great Tower, where they had uninterrupted views of the surrounding area. There was no doubt the enemy's siege works were coming ever closer, the efficient Hooper bringing up mortar batteries, heavy cannon, to within sixty yards of the defensive walls. 'We cannot possibly withstand this.'

Matthew shrugged. 'You tell his lordship. He won't listen to the likes of me.'

But Rhys didn't think the old man would listen to him either, so there was no point even asking to speak to him. 'The General sent him a summons this morning, I heard tell.'

'Oh, aye? What did it say? Apart from the obvious.'

'The usual, give up the castle to him or else ...' It was the 'or else' that worried Rhys the most. Not for himself, but for Arabella and the other women and children. He'd seen first-hand what a victorious army could do to innocent people caught up in this war and it wasn't pretty.

'I'm guessing his lordship sent the messenger back with a flea in his ear?' Matthew's grin was a bit forced, but Rhys admired the man for being able to smile at all.

'I think he's a bit cannier than that. I believe he asked for reassurances.' The question was, would Fairfax give them?

As it turned out, the general did offer a fair deal. The marquis gathered the officers together to tell them about it, Rhys among them.

'General Fairfax has written to me to offer fair terms for you all, on condition that I give myself into the hands of Parliament.'

There were murmurs of protest and the marquis held up his hand for silence. 'Surely it's better to sacrifice one man for the sake of everyone else? I see that as reasonable.'

But the men wouldn't have it. 'No, my lord,' someone called out. 'The terms should be the same for all of us or we'll die with you.'

'Hear, hear ...' A chorus of agreement echoed round the Great Hall and Rhys thought he saw the old man blink as if to dispel a sudden tear from his eyes. He was clearly touched by such loyalty.

'Very well, so be it. I will write back accordingly.'

Rhys managed to steal a moment with Arabella in the Minstrel's Gallery that night. They'd continued to meet there whenever they could and so far no one had found them out. In the aftermath of their lovemaking, he told her about the meeting.

'Yes, I heard,' she replied. 'Lady Margaret mentioned it, but ... I don't like it, Rhys.'

'Neither do I, *cariad*, but it's true we are all in this together and it was the path we chose. Now we have to see it through.'

'Do you think there is any chance we can emerge unscathed?'

He heard the fear in her voice, although she was clearly trying to be brave. 'Yes, I've heard that Fairfax is a man who lives up to his name – fair. I'm hoping he will at least protect the womenfolk and the little ones.'

'If, by any chance, we both get out alive, will we go to France?'

'That seems the best option, yes.' Rhys didn't want to admit it was the only option for him. There was no way he'd be going back to his brother's house to beg for shelter, despite the fact he had a wife to think of now. He'd find some other way of surviving and providing for Arabella and any children they might have. But if he didn't make it out alive ... 'Just in case something goes wrong, though, I want you to go to my family up in the Black Mountains. Show them our marriage lines and ask them to take care of you. My brother, Gwilum, and I have never seen eye to eye, but you're family and he won't refuse you. Promise me?'

She did and he told her how to find her way there.

Arabella had another thought. 'What about if something happens to me? I should make a will so that you can petition Parliament for my estate.'

Rhys frowned. 'That shouldn't be necessary. We're married so all that belonged to you is now mine.'

'Yes, but I have the marriage certificate and there is but the one copy. If I make a will, you can keep that and we'll be doubly sure.'

'I suppose that makes sense.'

'I'll ask the chaplain to help me. He and Lady Margaret can witness it and then I'll sew it into your jacket.'

'Very well.' Although it was a dispiriting conversation, it did take a weight off his mind.

All they could do now was to wait and hope for the best.

Chapter Thirty-Three

Merrick Court, 7th August 2016

'Tell me about your tattoo – does it mean something special?'

A part of Tess had been afraid to ask in case it had something to do with a former girlfriend, but they'd been sleeping together for a couple of weeks now and she was curious. And as far as she could make out there was no name on it or anything. Now she was half lying on top of Josh's chest and the swirly design was right in front of her eyes.

'What, this? It was a gift from a friend.'

'A gift? You mean someone paid for you to have it done?'

Josh chuckled. 'No. I had a Maori friend at school and I helped him out with a couple of things so he designed this for me as a thank you. You can't buy something like this, it has to be given to you. They have all these rules about stuff like that. It's hard to explain.'

'I see.' Tess was just relieved the friend had been male. 'Well, I like it. It looks great on you.' She couldn't resist running her fingers over it and the taut muscle underneath the ink, then snuggled up closer to him and breathed in his unique scent. She didn't think she'd ever get enough of being with him like this. It was bliss.

'Did I tell you Shayla has decided she wants to stay here in Wales with me? And apparently it's all your fault.' Josh kissed Tess's ear, then moved on to her neck, which was very distracting.

'Why?' Tess pulled away slightly so she could concentrate on what he was saying. 'What have I done?'

'Helping you with the furniture stuff has encouraged her to believe she can have a career doing art. She said you think she's good. And you'd been telling her about your studies so she and Louis googled art colleges around here and found one in Hereford. She's even rung them to ask how to apply and it seems it might be possible. All we need is her mother's approval and some paperwork from New Zealand, although she might have to go to a sixth form college first for a while.'

Tess snorted. 'Well, there goes that plan then. Isla isn't likely to agree to that, is she?' Josh's ex-wife was still blaming him for their daughter's trip to the UK and seemed to be as furious with him as Rosie continued to be with Tess. They were both cast as villains of the piece, despite being mostly innocent of any wrongdoing. 'Wasn't she demanding Shayla's return only a couple of days ago?'

'Yes, but Shayla can be *very* persuasive when she sets her mind to it.' Josh rolled his eyes. 'As I've found to my cost. Also incredibly stubborn. She might wear Isla down in the end. She got her own way over staying a bit longer anyway.'

'Hmm, and what are your thoughts about it? Have you definitely decided to stay in Wales then?' Tess almost held her breath, waiting for his reply. Their relationship was still very new and she wasn't sure how serious he was about it. The chemistry between them hadn't abated and each night was as exciting as the first. Tess was afraid to jinx it so hadn't dared to raise the subject of the future.

'Yeah, I'm staying. At least for a while. You were right in saying I shouldn't be too quick to make a decision about this place so I'll take my time.'

'Right.' Tess's spirits plummeted. 'A while' didn't sound as though he was thinking 'forever' like she'd been hoping. But it was better than nothing and it would be up to her to persuade him to stay. She'd do her best.

He kissed her and passion flared up between them again and it was a while before they were able to hold a conversation, but as Josh gathered her close to his chest for a spooning session, he brought up the subject of his daughter again. 'So yeah, about Shayla – I have to admit I'm kind of pleased that she *wants* to stay with me. Not in a gloating way, although a small part of me can't resist thinking it's payback for Isla not allowing me access. I guess I wouldn't be human if I didn't think that. Still, I love my daughter and I'm getting the feeling she might love me too, which is fantastic. I never thought I'd have that kind of bond with her, you know?'

'I'm pleased for you. And, yes, you're entitled to a bit of gloating, I'd say.' Tess hugged his arm, which was wrapped around her. 'If I'd had kids, I would have hated not to be part of their lives.'

'Would you like children?'

Josh's question was a natural continuation of their conversation and Tess was pretty sure he didn't know about her issues with Giles and his wish for an heir. It made her think, though, and she came to the rapid conclusion that she did want kids. Very much so. She wanted them with Josh. It would feel right, the way it never had with her late husband.

'Yes,' she replied. 'I would.'

'Oh, good.' He pulled her to him even tighter. ''Cause I'd love a whole brood. Can we have six?'

'Six! That's a bit excessive. I'd compromise on four.'

'Okay then. We'll need time for ourselves too, after all. We can get big sister Shayla to babysit while we have some private time ...'

Tess wasn't sure how serious he was being, but it was fun to daydream. And a future with Josh sounded like the best thing in the world.

He went quiet and she assumed he'd fallen asleep, one arm wrapped around her. Tess smiled into the semi-darkness of the room, cherishing the moment. She was just about to drop off when she saw something moving over by the door. A shadowy figure with funnel-top boots and a plumed hat.

Rhys.

Her eyes opened wide and she stared at him intently, wondering again why he was here. She sensed no menace, rather the opposite. A warm feeling invaded her senses, contentment, security, happiness. She thought she saw him smile at her, then he doffed his hat to perform a sweeping bow, and disappeared. It was as though he'd given his seal of approval and left. Tess thought she understood.

She had Josh to protect her and didn't need the Cavalier any longer. His task was done.

'Does he always do that to you too?'

Josh's sleepy voice startled her and she turned to blink at him. 'What? You saw him?'

'Mm-hmm. I didn't think you would though. I'm usually the only one but I noticed you reacting to his presence.'

'What do you mean? You see ghosts?' Tess was fully awake now and leaned on one elbow to stare at Josh.

'Yeah, I guess that's what they are. Shadows, people's souls, whatever it is that's left behind if they don't pass on.' He closed his eyes for a moment, then regarded her almost warily. 'I've seen them all my life. My grandmother did too – I told you she was psychic, right? – and she said it was a gift. I'm not so sure. I never talk about it because the few times I've mentioned it to someone they've told me I'm weird.'

'Of course you're not! Or if you are, then I am too, what with all those visions or whatever they are. This ghost is the only one I've ever seen though and at first it spooked me a bit. Literally. I thought I was going crazy.'

'Ha ha, very funny. But no, you're not crazy.' He pulled her tight again. 'Or maybe we can be crazy together.'

She snuggled back down under the duvet. 'Sounds great to me. I think his name is Rhys.'

It was Josh's turn to sit up. 'How do you know that?'

'Because I'm pretty sure he's the man I see in my visions *and* he's the spitting image of the man in that portrait Louis and I found.'

'Shit!' Josh raked a hand through his hair and shook his head.

'What's wrong?' Tess's heart skipped a beat as he sounded very serious.

'That ghost has sort of been communicating with me, or trying to. Showing me things, kind of like your visions, I suppose. I wondered if the two were connected. He did say his name was Rhys ... or rather, other people called him that.'

'What have you seen?'

'A siege at a castle – Raglan, I think – Rhys fighting, falling in love, protecting a woman called Arabella.'

'No!' Tess stared at him. 'I ... that's my name in those visions. What does she look like?'

'A bit like you – honey-gold hair and blue eyes, pretty in an old-fashioned sort of way.'

Tess got out of bed. 'Come with me, please, I want to show you something.'

'Now?' But Josh did as she asked and threw on a pair of boxers while she put on her dressing gown.

He followed her upstairs to the gallery where she and Louis had left the old portraits and when he'd helped her to turn them round, he whistled. 'Yep, that's her.'

'Arabella Dauncey,' Tess whispered, then her eyes flew to his. 'Do you think we are them reincarnated? Is that why ...?'

He put his arms around her and pulled her close. 'No, I don't. They've been telling us something, but it's got nothing to do with what's going on between you and me except maybe in the sense that they were trying to get us together.' He turned to stare at the portraits again. 'I wonder what happened to them?'

Tess felt tears well up in her eyes. 'I'm not sure I want to know.'

'That's it. I think the marquis has finally realised it's hopeless to resist. I mean, look out there. It's only a matter of days, if that.'

Rhys pointed. He and Matthew were once again on guard duty, this time above the South Gate. Hooper's trenches now came even closer to the castle, perhaps only some ten yards or so at some points, and soon he'd be in a position to blow up the walls from underneath.

'Yes. There isn't much left of some of the walls anyway,' Matthew agreed, his expression as gloomy as Rhys's must be. 'Some of the cannonballs they've been sending our way are as big as fifteen or twenty pounds, I'll swear. Even walls this thick don't stand a chance against that.'

It wasn't just the walls that were crumbling. Some of the tops of the towers and turrets had been destroyed too, even if the Great Tower itself still stood strong. And there was absolutely no hope of relief. It seemed they really were the last Royalists in the whole of England and Wales. Even if they weren't, and Pendennis and Harlech castles were holding out as well, what good would it do them? They were hundreds of miles apart.

Rhys proved to be right. The marquis sent out a message to Fairfax that afternoon, asking to have 'commissioners' negotiate on his behalf, and a meeting was agreed for the fifteenth of the month. The general insisted no more than six men and their servants should come, then he would promise they'd be returned safely to the castle afterwards. And there would be a ceasefire from nine in the morning until two in the afternoon.

The marquis had no choice but to agree.

Rhys, who'd been one of the men chosen to go, finally found a moment to tell Arabella about it two nights later. 'Well, I believe it's done at last. We met at the house of a

Mr Oates, about a mile and a half from here at Cefntilla, and the articles of the treaty are now agreed.' He refused to call it the 'Articles of Capitulation', the way the Parliamentarians did, as that sounded much too depressing and demeaning.

'You don't sound happy about it. Are the terms that awful?' Arabella had obviously picked up on his bad mood and stroked his cheek.

He captured her hand and leaned into it, feeling unutterably weary and yes, angry. 'No, but everything we've fought for these past ten weeks has to be given up without exception. We're to hand it all over intact, including every last thing inside the castle. The ordnance, what's left of the provisions, all the marquis's possessions ... We have to march out on Wednesday with only our horses and personal items, although they will allow us to be armed and fly our colours as we leave.'

'That doesn't sound so bad,' Arabella soothed. He could still hear the fear in her voice and she was probably wondering, as he was, whether Fairfax would keep to those terms.

'No, but we don't get to keep the weapons. We have to go to some appointed place and hand them over, while swearing we won't bear arms against the Parliamentarians ever again. Then we go home, if we have a home.'

'So, France for us then?'

Rhys nodded. 'The general has promised passes for those who wish to go overseas, as long as we do it within three months.'

'Well, I shouldn't think it will take us that long. I, for one, can't wait to leave.'

Rhys couldn't either, but he still had a bad feeling about this. He didn't tell Arabella, but he made love to her that night as if it was the last time.

Chapter Thirty-Four

'Hey, where're you off to this morning? You don't look like you're dressed for painting.' Josh was in the stable yard when Shayla came round the corner of the house. He pulled her in for a hug, glad that she was still here despite everything. He'd never thought he'd be lucky enough to spend this much time with her, at least not until she'd become an adult and left home.

'Louis and I are taking the bus to Abergavenny. There's a new film he wants to see and I said I'd go with him.' She seemed torn between wanting to pull away and hug him back. In the end she opted for the latter and clung on fiercely.

'Then I guess you'll need some money for popcorn.' Josh fished out a couple of notes from his wallet. 'Here, treat Louis too.'

She smiled. 'Thanks, Dad. You're not as bad as Mum made out, you know.'

'High praise indeed,' Josh joked, but inside he was warm and fuzzy. And somehow he'd make Isla see that they could both have their daughter's love. He was sure she had enough for two.

He needed to tell Shayla about him and Tess though. They were still sneaking around, which felt totally wrong, but it was all very new for both of them. He'd sit Shayla down soon and just come right out with it, that would be best. He really hoped she wouldn't mind as it would be much worse losing her now that he'd finally managed to establish a rapport with her. And as he'd told her, he was sure they could still have quality time together.

Damn, why was life so complicated?

❦

Merrick Court, 17th August 2016

'Tess, come here a sec, would you?'

They were in the knot garden, working on the final part of the paving behind the fountain. The stones they'd reset so far looked beautifully even and as they were free from moss and weeds, it was all much neater and tidier. Soon the garden would be more or less back to its former glory.

'What is it?' She went over to where Josh had lifted one of the smaller stones. 'Oh my goodness!'

They both kneeled down as she brushed the earth off an object that was partly uncovered. It glinted and sparkled like a thousand sunbeams when she pulled it out and blew on it to remove the remaining dust and dirt. It was a necklace – a large golden cross on a long thick chain, with pink, blue and lilac gemstones. It looked very old and precious.

'Wow! That's really something, huh?' Josh held out his hand and Tess gave it to him to examine.

'The Merrick treasure?' she guessed. 'Or what's left of it. So the old family legend was true after all.' A part of her felt sad that Giles would never get to see this, but at the same time she was glad because he would only have sold it to fund his gaming. Or maybe not? He'd kept the earring after all.

'Merrick treasure? I didn't know there was any.'

'Yes, well, I thought it was just an old wives' tale so I didn't tell you about that.' Tess had never really believed in the story, and yet here was proof that it existed. 'Is there more?'

Josh dug around a bit, then shook his head. 'No, that's it.' He held up the cross to the light again. 'It's more than

324

enough though! Looks like it should be in a museum or something.'

'That's up to you to decide. It's yours.'

He looked at her. 'We'll have to check on that – maybe it could be classed as "content" of the house or Giles's personal possession?'

'No! I don't want it. You should have it,' Tess said firmly. 'It belongs to this place, to you. I have no right to it.' She frowned at the jewel, wondering what would have happened if the cross had been found before Giles died. Would it have stopped him from going off the rails? No, she didn't believe that. And it wouldn't have changed anything between them.

She definitely didn't want it now, though, as she'd only have to sell it and give the money to Marcus Steele. What a waste that would be.

Josh didn't reply, but handed the cross back to her and turned away. 'You'd better go and show Louis and Shayla. I can finish up here.'

Tess thought it strange that he didn't seem as excited any longer. She hesitated before rushing off to find the teenagers. 'Are you okay, Josh?'

'Yeah, sure.' He glanced up from placing another paving stone in the right position. 'Why wouldn't I be?'

'You just seem a bit ... distracted?'

'Nah, I'm fine. Want to get this done.'

But he bent down again and wouldn't look her in the eye. Tess took a deep breath, wanting to find out what was the matter – because something was, she was sure – but at the same time not wishing to push him too far. She decided to leave it for now.

'Okay, I'll be right back.' She put on a cheerful voice, but only received a grunt in reply and as she walked off the worries started up. Had she said something wrong? What if she were to lose him now? She didn't think she could bear it.

* * *

Josh watched Tess disappear in the direction of Bryn's potting shed and stood up, closing his eyes. She'd scared him just now, with that emphatic denial of ownership. It was like she didn't want anything to do with things belonging to Merrick Court or its owner. From what he'd gathered, she had so many bad memories of this place, but he'd thought they were just connected with Giles. What if it ran deeper than that?

And, if so, how could he ever hope to erase them? Make her stay?

Most women would have jumped at the chance to own something like that jewelled cross and yet she'd looked as though it was poisonous. Did she really hate it here that much?

He'd thought he could persuade her to live with him here, to share his dream of sheep farming on Merrick's land and raising a brood of kids. She wasn't afraid of mucking in and together they'd make a great team. But they hadn't discussed the future except jokingly. Hadn't even said the L-word yet. It was as though they were both scared of mentioning it out loud in case that made what they had disappear. Jinxed it.

He had to talk to her, find out where they stood. Because he could see now that if she wasn't part of his future here, he didn't want it. Any of it. He might as well sell up.

———

Raglan Castle, 19th August 1646

They were gathered in the Pitched Stone Court with their belongings in bags or tied into shawls – everyone except for the sick and wounded, who would be allowed to stay behind.

Arabella stood with the other women, looking up at

the great oriel window on the right hand side. Through the glass there were glimpses of General Fairfax inside the Great Hall, come to oversee the departure of the defenders. He'd arrived with his officers, all surging into the courtyard like a dam that had burst, in good spirits. *A pox on them!* The marquis had received them – in his usual unflappable way, Arabella guessed – and then left. She imagined Fairfax must be feeling pleased with himself as he'd accomplished what he'd set out to do. But it was his job, so perhaps it was only one of many such occasions for him, whereas for Arabella it was the end of a part of her life.

It was much worse for others, the poor marquis for one. Arabella had heard that he wouldn't be allowed to leave with everyone else and the 'articles' Rhys had talked about didn't apply to Lord Worcester.

'The men were all for standing by him again,' someone had said, 'but he would have none of it this time. Said that it didn't matter as he's so old, whereas the rest of us mostly have our lives before us. Such a noble man, insisted the articles should be accepted ...'

It made Arabella want to cry as she knew first-hand what a kind and considerate man the marquis was. He didn't deserve to be treated so shabbily, his home and possessions taken away, and himself at the mercy of the enemy. What would happen to him? Surely they wouldn't imprison a man of such great age? But who could tell? She sent up a swift prayer for him.

The crowd of people began to move towards the main gate. She looked up one final time at the impressive row of library windows in the apartments above the gate and wondered what would become of all the amazing books housed there. She hoped the general would have the sense not to destroy them, but that had happened in other places.

Through the massive gateway they filed for the last time, their footsteps echoing under the vaulted ceiling. One gate, two – both standing wide open with the portcullises raised – and outside, the enemy soldiers massed, waiting to watch them surrender, probably gloating. Would they be shouting 'Royalist whores' at them yet again? The epithet had much less power to hurt now they'd heard it so many times.

Sixteen steps – Arabella counted silently – and then she was outside the castle for the first time in months. The moat was on her right and beyond it the Great Tower, forlorn against the summer sky, the windows dark and empty as if the soul of the place was already gone. As the marquis had left, it was true – he *was* its soul. It felt strange to be outside and she concentrated on the view so as not to become disorientated, staring at what was left of the village straight ahead in the distance down the hill.

Rhys was already out there somewhere, the many hundreds of soldiers having gone first with drums beating and their flags held high. They'd been preceded by the marquis, Lord Charles, Lady Margaret, Dr Bayly – Lord Worcester's faithful friend – and some of the more important neighbours who'd taken refuge in the castle.

'Meet me over by the trees where you collected your horse on the night you went to Merrick Court,' Rhys had said. 'That's the only place I know where I'll be able to find you.'

Arabella had agreed but it would take her a while to get there.

She'd said her goodbyes to Lady Margaret. 'I promise to retrieve your jewels and bring them to you abroad,' she'd whispered.

'Thank you. There's no hurry as I shall go and join my husband in Ireland first,' Lady Margaret had told her.

It was a big responsibility, those jewels, but both Arabella and Rhys were determined to deliver them to their owners safely somehow. Perhaps in return they'd be offered employment of some sort. Anything would be preferable to

Rhys having to become a mercenary. He'd had enough of fighting and Arabella wanted him to stay in one piece.

As she made her way past the enemy soldiers who were remarkably well behaved, she was still in a daze, clutching her small bundle of possessions. She reached the edge of the throng and was just about to head towards the trees, when someone grabbed her arm and pushed it up behind her.

'At last. You took your sweet time.'

Arabella tried to turn around to stare at her assailant, but there was no need really. She'd recognise that voice anywhere. Glyn. How had she forgotten about him?

'I've a sharp knife pointed straight at your heart, so unless you do exactly as I say, you'll die right here,' he snarled. 'Now walk this way.'

He shoved her in the opposite direction to where she wanted to go and she threw him an angry glare over her shoulder, noticing that he was wearing a bright red jacket. A Parliamentarian one.

'Well, there's a surprise,' she spat. 'Finally showing your true colours? You dare to be brave now your side has won, I see. Coward!' She tried to jerk out of his hold and kick him on the shin, but he was too strong and held her in a tight grip.

'Shut your mouth.' He pricked her with the knife and she felt a sharp pain in her back. 'I'll stick it in deeper next time,' he threatened.

Arabella thought it best to stay silent for now, but her mind was trying to come up with some way of escaping from him. Could she cry out? Call to someone for help? But she didn't recognise anyone here and she doubted they'd believe her. Where was Rhys? Surely he'd be looking out for her? She couldn't see his familiar features anywhere. Glyn was now holding onto her as though she was his wife and they were walking companionably. The knife was hidden from sight.

Soon they reached a large horse and Glyn threw her bodily onto its back before climbing up behind her. He dragged her into a sitting position and gathered up the reins.

'I've still got the knife, so one sound out of you and you're dead, understand?'

As they trotted off, Arabella scanned the crowds one last time, looking for the man she loved. She had no way of letting him know where she'd gone. Would he guess what had happened? Or would he think she'd simply decided not to go with him?

She sincerely hoped the former was true. He must know by now how much she loved him.

Rhys paced among the trees for what seemed like hours, but as the throng of enemy soldiers and the former inhabitants of the castle dispersed, little by little, there was still no sign of Arabella. Where was she?

He'd seen her in the courtyard before leaving, but outside in the chaos he'd been unable to get close enough to watch the women and children march out. 'Keep moving,' he'd been told, someone shoving him out of the way, and then they'd closed ranks so that he was forced to stay on the outskirts of the crowd.

He was just about to set off on another walk round the area when a group of men rode up to him. They jumped off their horses and advanced on him, their expressions menacing. Two of them had knives, the others clubs or broken off pikes.

'What the hell ...?'

'Say your prayers, Sir Rhys Cadell. You won't be leaving this place alive,' one of the men snarled before they set upon him.

Rhys registered that they knew him by name and had obviously come specifically to find him, which was ominous. He had nothing worth stealing so the only conclusion he could reach was that they really were going to kill him. It wasn't an empty threat.

He still had his sword as he hadn't yet been to hand it over as agreed in the Articles, and started to defend himself as best he could, nearly cutting one man's arm off so that he screamed with pain and shock, while wounding another in the abdomen. But there were just too many of them and he didn't have eyes in the back of his head.

'The treaty stated that none of the castle's defenders were to be harmed while leaving,' he shouted, in the midst of parrying a blow from a large club. 'The general will punish you for this.' It was true. Fairfax had promised safe passage to everyone and that they wouldn't be robbed or injured in any way as they left. These men either didn't care or weren't part of the Parliamentarian army. Rhys guessed the latter.

His assailants merely laughed. 'He won't know, will he? You'll be long dead afore he knows anythin' about it.'

'Who do you work for?' he panted, wounding yet another man while receiving a blow to the shoulder that sent him staggering.

'The next lord of Merrick Court.' One of the men chortled. 'And he don't like you much.'

'Shut your mouth, fool,' someone else snarled. 'We weren't to speak about that, were we?'

'Who cares? It's not as if he's going to tell anyone, is it? Unless it's St Peter.'

That brought more laughter, which Rhys barely registered. The next lord of Merrick Court. That couldn't be anyone other than Glyn Howell. Why hadn't he thought to look for him today? He should have guessed the man would try something now his friends were victorious. Damn it all, what had he done with Arabella?

Rhys fought on, desperation at the thought of her in Glyn's clutches spurring him on to almost heroic efforts, but it still wasn't enough. He received a blow to the head that made his ears ring and it was through a haze of pain he heard a voice ring out. 'You there, what do you think you're doing? I gave orders no one was to be harmed and I keep my word!'

Fairfax? But before Rhys could look up to verify this, another blow to the back of his head made the world go black.

Chapter Thirty-Five

Merrick Court, 19th August 2016

'Therese, I understand you've finally got something to give me in payment of those IOU's.'

Tess almost dropped the phone when she heard the smooth voice of Marcus Steele. 'Wh-what do you mean?'

'Your little find from the garden. I know all about it. News travels fast. I'm so pleased for you. Now you won't need to go ahead with that bank loan, eh? Although I hear you weren't planning on going down that route anyway.' He tutted. 'You really should listen to me, you know.'

'But how...?' Tess couldn't believe this. Very few people knew about the cross and they hadn't even told Rosie yet.

'I have friends in the area, I told you, didn't I?'

'You mean you've had someone spying on me.' It wasn't a question as Tess knew she was right.

'I wouldn't use that word.' Marcus chuckled. 'Actually, I'm seeing one of them tomorrow so I can come and collect the little bauble in person. Nine a.m. suit you?'

Tess was momentarily lost for words, but soon found her tongue. 'But it's not mine to give you. It's the heir's and—'

'Sod Owens!' He laughed. 'Yes, I know it's your "handyman" we're talking about. Wasn't hard to figure out. But come on, there's no need to tell him about it. What he doesn't know and all that ... And you can always tell him it was stolen. You've had break-ins before, I understand.' Another chuckle. 'I'll see you tomorrow, nine sharp. Look forward to it. And make sure you're alone, yeah? We wouldn't want an audience to our little transaction, now would we?'

He hung up and Tess stared at the phone, her legs shaking. Her first instinct was to run and tell Josh, but he'd gone off to London and wouldn't be back until tomorrow night. He had some business to attend to, he'd said, so she didn't want to disturb him. Besides, it wasn't his problem, it was hers. She sank down onto the floor with her back against the wall.

What was she going to do?

Louis found her like that when he stuck his head round the door to say he'd finished his lunch and was heading out into the garden. 'What's the matter? You seen a ghost or something?' he joked.

Tess just shook her head. If only. Marcus was much scarier than any ghost. He'd been spying on her. Listening in on her phone conversations? How else did he know so much? Friends in the area wouldn't know about the cross. No, someone had been watching them. She shivered.

Louis frowned and came into the room. 'What then? Are you okay?'

'No. I've just been talking to Marcus Steele. He said he's coming tomorrow to take the Merrick cross, in payment of your uncle's debts? Wanted me to make sure I was alone.'

'Shit!' Louis sank down onto a chair near her, scowling. 'He can't, it belongs here. We've got to do something. Tell the police?'

'No, I'm pretty sure involving the cops would make things worse. He might do something to hurt me ... I get the feeling he could be violent if he doesn't get his way. Oh, Louis, I don't know what to do! I told him it's not mine to give, but he just laughed. And I think he's been spying on us. He knew lots of things.'

'The bastard! Let me think about it. I'm going to talk to Shayla, she might have some ideas too.'

'Oh? I thought you didn't like her.'

Louis flushed and Tess had to hide a smile at this sight. She'd noticed that the two teenagers were getting on much better now.

'She's not as bad as I thought. Or rather, she's improving,' Louis admitted.

'I see. Well, I'm glad.'

'Oh, yeah? Maybe because she's going to become your stepdaughter?' Louis teased, recovering his composure.

It was Tess's turn to flush and she felt her cheeks grow hot. 'Ah, you've noticed.'

'Kind of hard not to. You guys aren't fooling anyone, to be honest. The way Josh looks at you is ... well, he's hot for you.'

'Louis!'

'Just saying. And the stairs creak.' Tess narrowed her eyes at him but he just laughed. 'It's okay. I'm glad for you. Later.'

Tess sat for a while digesting his words, relieved to have her secret out in the open. She supposed it was inevitable that someone would have noticed. As Louis had said, the heated glances she and Josh exchanged were difficult to hide, even if they'd managed to keep their hands to themselves in public. And she should have remembered about the stairs.

But that was a minor thing compared to the problem she now faced. What on earth was she to do? She didn't want to hand over the Merrick jewel. She couldn't. There must be a way of stopping Marcus. Could she ask the police for advice without him knowing? Not if he was listening to her phone calls.

She wanted to talk it over with Josh, but again that wasn't an option if Marcus was monitoring her calls. Maybe she could go to the village and borrow a phone? But he'd know if he was watching her.

'Damn it all! I can't let the bastard win.'

In the end, she went to do some painting in order to calm her tightly strung nerves. It was great for thinking about knotty problems and the work freed her mind, but she still couldn't come up with a way forward. Louis and Shayla found her there an hour later, and they came bouncing in, almost jumping up and down with excitement.

'What's up with you two?' Tess felt it was a bit disloyal of them to look so happy when she was in such a fix.

'We've got it! The solution to your problem.' Shayla smiled and threw herself down onto the floor next to Tess.

Louis followed suit. 'Shhh, someone might hear.' He continued in a whisper, 'Yeah, we're going to trick the bastard into telling the police himself.'

'Telling them what?' Tess was confused.

'That he's making you give him the cross illegally to pay a debt instead of going through the proper channels,' Louis clarified.

'How?' Tess put down her paintbrush and stared at them.

'Wait.' Louis went to turn on the tap in an old sink which Tess used for cleaning her brushes. 'I've seen in movies how the sound of running water makes it so anyone spying on you can't hear.'

'Okay, double-O-seven.' Tess lowered her voice even more. 'So what's the plan?'

'It's this – you're going to be in the library when the guy arrives, sitting behind the desk with your laptop in front of you, like you've been typing emails or something while you waited for him.'

'Right and ...?' Tess didn't see how that would help.

'I'll put a webcam at the top and it can be turned round so it's filming whatever's on the other side,' Louis continued as if she hadn't interrupted him. 'It will be filming him. Steele.'

'I see.'

'No, you don't,' Shayla put in, smiling in that superior way teenagers did when they were trying to explain technical things to their elders. 'The thing is, he'll be talking to you and all the time we'll have set up a live video link to that police guy who Louis said you dealt with after the accident.'

'Inspector Houghton?'

'Him, yeah. We'll contact the inspector via Bryn's computer first – Dad told me he has an ancient one, but it should still work for something simple like that. We don't think Steele will have thought to hack into that. Why would he? Bryn's just the gardener. So all you have to do is get the bugger to talk, explain what he's doing and then the police can come pick him up. Easy!'

Tess made a face. 'You think? How on earth am I supposed to do that? It's not like I can just demand that he talks to the camera. And is it really grounds for arrest? They could just as well arrest me for giving away something that doesn't belong to me.'

'Nah, we'll explain all that to them. And, yes, they can arrest him for dealing in stolen goods. You don't think he'd sell it on the open market, do you? He couldn't, not without a proper receipt. Now, come on, you can do this.' Louis gave her an encouraging push. 'Just get him talking. Smarmy types like him love to brag about what they've done when they think no one can do anything about it. He'll want to show you he's in charge and he's got you beaten. So bat your eyelashes at him and act all feminine, fluttery and scared. I swear it'll work.'

Tess wasn't so sure. 'I don't know. I think it would be better to try and get hold of your dad, Shayla. It's his cross, he should deal with it. Can't we email him from Bryn's computer?'

'We can try but he told me he wouldn't be checking his phone much today as he's meeting up with some old mates.' Shayla mimed drinking. 'It could be a long night.'

'Damn it all,' Tess muttered.

'Come on, you'll have to follow our plan. It's the only option,' Louis said.

Tess sighed. 'I can try I suppose. At least it would be good to have it on camera that I've been forced to hand over the jewel. Can you keep a copy of the film so I can prove to Josh I didn't steal it?'

'Yeah, no problem. Not that he'll believe that for a second, but anyway.' Louis jumped up. 'Come on, Shay, let's go set it up.' He turned back towards Tess. 'Oh, and make sure you wear something sexy that shows a lot of your boobs.'

'Louis!'

'No, he's right.' Shayla nodded. 'That'll distract the guy from looking at the laptop too closely. Seriously low cut and lots of mascara so you look like Bambi. Want me to help you choose a top?'

'Er, no thanks, I think I can manage.' The thought of receiving fashion advice from Shayla was mind-boggling. Tess was sure she could figure out a sexy look by herself. All she had to do was wear something she thought would make Josh's eyes light up. Although, come to think of it, that was pretty much everything at the moment. Or it had been until they'd found that jewel. Since then he'd been very subdued, but she didn't want to think about that now.

Tess had to stay sitting on the floor for a while after they'd gone. She felt like she'd been steamrollered, but at least she now had a glimpse of hope.

⟡

Merrick Court, 19th August 1646

'I can't marry your odious nephew because I'm already married. That would be bigamy.'

Arabella took some satisfaction from being able to say those words to her uncle-by-marriage, who had greeted her with a gloating smile that matched Glyn's as they walked into the great hall at Merrick.

Huw Howell shook his head, as if he was looking at a

deluded child. 'We thought that might be the case as Glyn reported that you were overly friendly with a certain man. When you would have contracted such a marriage, I've no idea, but just in case, we have taken precautions, girl. In fact, if all has gone as planned, you should already be a widow. So prepare yourself to be wed on the morrow. Your mourning period will be somewhat short.' He laughed, the sound grating on her ears.

'What? No!' As his words sank in, Arabella felt her legs begin to buckle and there was a buzzing noise inside her head. Coupled with the terrifying experience of being abducted by Glyn, Huw's assured statement was just too much. They had killed Rhys?

No, it couldn't be.

'Catch her, you fool. She's about to faint.' Huw, impatient as always, directed his nephew, but Arabella barely heard him. She pulled herself together and shoved Glyn away with both hands.

'Bastards! Whoresons! What have you done? I'll tell General Fairfax himself. I'll—'

A blow across the mouth cut off the rest of her sentence. 'Shut. Your. Mouth! Hell's teeth, but you don't learn very fast, do you?' Glyn picked her up and slung her over his shoulder like a sack of grain. 'Where do I put her?' he asked his uncle.

'The tower room. It has a stout lock and it's too high up for her to escape out the windows. Just leave her there to stew until tomorrow, then we'll send in your aunt to pretty her up for the wedding service.'

'But can't I—'

'No! I know you're eager for her, boy, but best to leave it till you're legally married. No one can say anything about you beating her black and blue then if you want. For now, we play by the rules.'

As Glyn deposited her on the bed in the tower room,

Arabella was grateful for the small reprieve. But it was only temporary and the following day the purgatory which was the rest of her life would begin.

She felt numb and couldn't even begin to comprehend how things had come to this pass. She should have been more vigilant, should have told Rhys to be on his guard ... But it was too late now. And if Rhys was truly dead, she didn't care what became of her. In fact, what was the point of staying alive? Taking her own life would be preferable to submitting to Glyn and giving him the power to do with her whatever he wished. Indeed, *anything* was better than that.

And then she'd be with Rhys again.

<hr />

Abergavenny, 20th August 1646

Rhys opened his eyes and blinked to clear his sight. He was staring at something white with black lines across, but he couldn't focus because they were undulating. Nausea rose up in his throat but he swallowed it down and blinked again. This time he succeeded in ascertaining that he was looking at a ceiling with dark roof beams at irregular intervals. After a little while longer, they stopped moving in front of his eyes and the queasiness receded.

'Ah, you are awake. Here, let me give you some ale.' A soft voice speaking Welsh turned out to belong to a stout, middle-aged woman, who came into his line of vision holding a cup.

'Thank you,' he said, replying in the same language when she lifted his head and shoulders and held the cup to his lips so he could slake his thirst. His voice was hoarse as if he'd been doing a lot of shouting, but the ale helped. 'Where am I? What happened?'

'At the Lion Inn outside Bergavenny. General Fairfax's

men brought you. Said you were dying and paid my husband handsomely to take care of you until then. But I have some skill at healing and it seemed to me your heartbeat was much too steady for someone about to depart this world, albeit you have a nasty lump on your head. I had you carried up here and I've been tending your wounds.' She smiled. 'Couldn't let a Welshman die unnecessarily, now could I?' As if answering his unspoken question, she added, 'You muttered something in Welsh when I bandaged your head.'

'Again, I thank you for your kindness, mistress …?'

She smiled. 'Mistress Davy. Now just you rest and I'm sure you'll feel better tomorrow.'

'And I'm Sir Rhys Cadell.'

At the mention of his name, a sudden onslaught of memories flooded Rhys's mind and he drew in a sharp breath. 'What day is it, pray? Was it today I was brought to you?'

'No, it was yesterday. Today is the twentieth day of August, I believe.'

'So the day Raglan Castle surrendered and everyone marched out was yesterday?'

'Indeed. I'm assuming you were one of them, although why the general should worry about you in that case, I don't know. But you do have the look of someone who's not been fed properly for a while, like all those poor souls what came out of the castle. Never fear, I'll bring you some victuals shortly.'

Rhys sat up, trying to ignore the pounding in his head. 'I'm sorry, but I have to leave. My wife is in terrible danger!'

'Your wife?' Mistress Davy frowned and looked disapproving. 'I've not seen hide nor hair of her.'

'That's because she was abducted, just before I was assaulted, I believe. And I must rescue her before it's too late.' He pushed the blanket covering his legs and torso away and swung his legs over the side of the bed. 'In fact, it could be too late already.'

'I really don't think that would be wise, Sir Rhys. You'll be no use to anyone in the state you're in.'

'I'm sorry, but I must. The matter is urgent in the extreme. I'll manage somehow.'

She sank down on a chair next to the bed. 'Now wait a moment. Why don't you tell me what you think has happened and I'll see if my husband can help? You shouldn't go anywhere on your own.'

Rhys debated with himself whether to trust her or not, but in the end decided he had no option. And if she'd wanted him dead, she could have killed him earlier, so he didn't think she was in cahoots with the men who had attacked him. 'Very well,' he said, and gave her a quick version of events.

Mistress Davy clasped her hands together and smiled at him as he finished his tale. 'My, what a wonderful love story, to be sure. But I see what you mean. Now just you rest a bit more while I fetch you something to eat. You'll need sustenance. And in the meantime, I'll have a word with my husband. He knows the place, that Merrick Court, and I'm sure when I explain, he'll go with you. The present owner isn't much liked hereabouts.'

She was as good as her word and after he'd had some bread and nourishing broth Rhys felt better. His head still hurt, but it wasn't pounding as fiercely as before. And best of all, when he made it downstairs he found Mistress Davy's husband and a group of other men waiting for him, all with horses and weapons of some sort. Someone handed him a sword, which looked like it had been looted from a cavalry officer.

'We reckoned you'd need a bit of back-up, like.' The landlord gave him a small smile. 'I wouldn't send anyone to Merrick Court on their own, not even my worst enemy.'

'Thank you.' Rhys bowed to them all. 'I'm much obliged to you. If only we're not too late.'

Chapter Thirty-Six

Josh woke with a pounding head and stared at the unfamiliar surroundings. A hotel room. Stark, clean, featureless. But where? He'd stayed in so many this past year, they all looked the same and blurred in his mind. Then it came to him – London.

He'd been out with some mates from New Zealand who'd come to work in the UK for a while. They'd had dinner and a few beers, then moved on to a cocktail bar because the other two guys were on the pull. Bad mistake. Cocktails and beer so didn't go together. He checked the time – 5.42 a.m. Christ. No wonder he felt like death warmed up. He'd only slept a couple of hours.

As he groped on the bedside table for a glass of water, Josh became aware of something over by the window. A shadow. No, a spirit. He sat up and rubbed his eyes to clear his vision. Was he seeing things? But no, the shape was still there and he recognised it.

Sir Rhys.

'What the hell …?' he muttered. 'You're a long way from home, mate.'

The spirit moved as if it was agitated about something and seemed to be beckoning Josh forward. 'What's the matter?' He frowned. 'You want me to come with you? Where?'

Sir Rhys either couldn't or wouldn't tell him.

Josh took a deep breath. Something was very wrong, he could sense it. At Merrick Court, maybe? Why else would the spirit follow him here? As far as Josh knew, Sir Rhys had no connection with London whatsoever. He checked his phone, but the battery was dead.

'Damn it! Okay, you're going to have to spell it out, Sir Rhys,' he whispered. 'Talk to me.'

He ignored the pain in his skull and cleared his mind, trying to open his senses. It was as though he was reaching out towards the shadowy figure by the window, meeting him halfway. The effort made him feel nauseous, but he kept at it until at last he was rewarded with one word.

'*Tess!*'

'Shit!' He was galvanised into action and barely noticed the shadow disappear. He had to get back to Wales. Had to leave now, this minute. He never should have left her alone in that big house.

Merrick Court, 20th August 2016

Tess fiddled with everything on Giles's desk, nervous beyond belief. She really wished she didn't have to confront Marcus on her own, but there didn't seem to be any choice. As she rearranged a pile of papers for the umpteenth time, she knocked over the pencil pot and a USB pen rolled out, together with all the pens and a ruler. Tess frowned. She'd forgotten all about that.

'Maybe there's time to look at it now?' She glanced at her watch – a quarter to nine.

She put the pens back and plugged the USB into the laptop, where a window opened showing the saved files. There were lots of different ones, but a particular heading stood out. 'Black Rose?' All the air hissed out of Tess. Had Giles saved his IOU's himself? Perhaps she didn't owe Marcus as much as he said?

She was just about to click on open when she thought she heard the crunch of tyres on the gravel outside. 'Shit.' She quickly opened her email account and sent a message to Louis. '*Please have a look at attached file. Might help today? T x*' She prayed Marcus wouldn't be able to hack into her emails from his mobile or he'd see this message too.

As Louis was monitoring Tess's actions via the webcam, she said the words out loud as well. After quickly shutting down that screen, she pulled out the USB pen and threw it back into the pencil pot and not a moment too soon as there was a knock on the door.

Marcus's head appeared round the door frame. 'Ah, there you are. So I'm allowed into the nicer part of the house this time, not the servant's quarters? Glad to know I've gone up in your estimation.'

Marcus's joking comment had Tess itching to slap him, but she concentrated on controlling her breathing. 'I thought it best if you came in the front way. I've locked my new dog in the kitchen,' she said. 'He doesn't like strangers much.' Although she wished she could have had Vincent with her, she'd agreed with Louis that it was a bad idea. The dog could ruin their plans if he got too protective of Tess. She'd put a note on the back door for Marcus to go round to the front and left the door there unlocked.

'Good. I don't like dogs much.' He flashed her a smile, but she didn't reciprocate.

Instead, she got up from behind the desk as calmly as she could and gestured for him to take a seat in a chair by the fireplace. It had been placed so that he'd face the camera and thankfully he didn't seem to notice as his eyes were – predictably – on her.

Tess wished Josh had been here, but so far there was no word from him. It would seem she was alone in facing Marcus and she'd have to manage somehow. Following the teenagers' advice, she was wearing a low cut top with a push-up bra underneath that made her cleavage twice as eye-catching as normal. She'd decided against teaming this with a miniskirt, as she felt that would be too much and possibly suspicious since Marcus must be well aware she wasn't happy about this meeting. Instead, she'd opted for a tight pair of black jeans which hugged her bum. Open-toe sandals with a bit of heel completed the outfit and showed off newly varnished pink toenails. Her face was carefully made up with maximum effect mascara in case she needed to flutter her eyelashes as Louis had instructed.

She wasn't sure she could do it, but took the seat opposite Marcus.

'The "heir" not around?' He was smiling so Tess guessed he already knew she was alone in the house.

'No.'

'Nice of him to let you continue to live here. I suppose you've been … nice to him.'

Tess suppressed the urge to throttle him. 'Actually, I'll be moving out soon.' That wasn't quite true. She *had* found a suitable cottage to rent, but hadn't discussed it with Josh yet.

'So you've decided to be reasonable.' Marcus crossed one leg over the other, making himself comfortable.

'I don't seem to have much choice.' Tess glared at him. She figured being friendly towards him would give the game away. Far better to act affronted.

'We always have a choice, Therese.' His vulpine smile said otherwise. 'Like Giles did.'

'Giles? He was suffering from an illness. You shouldn't have taken advantage of him.' Tess dared to add, 'Your croupiers probably cheat. I know it happens, I've worked in places like that myself although I refused to do it.'

Marcus's smile dimmed. 'Never throw accusations like that around. That's exactly what your dear Giles did and look what happened to him?'

Tess couldn't help it, she gasped. 'Wh-what do you mean? He had an accident.'

'Mmm, yeah, but what if it wasn't just an accident?

346

Tampering with his car would have been rather too easy, I'm afraid. He was so fond of it, he always asked to leave it in my personal garage for safety.' He laughed. 'Ironic, wouldn't you say? And it was only a measly Porsche, not even a Lamborghini or McLaren.'

'You k-killed him?' Tess was shaking now, terror beginning to creep through her veins. This man was seriously ruthless.

He shrugged. 'Might have done.'

Tess tried to pull herself together. If the police really were watching this exchange, they'd want a proper confession. 'You're bluffing,' she said. 'I don't think you'd have the guts to kill anyone. You're just trying to scare me now.'

His expression turned ugly. 'I sure as hell do! If the police weren't so incompetent, they'd have noticed something wasn't right with the Porsche's engine. But you'd have to look hard to find the fault and I'm not stupid enough to leave fingerprints. Anyway, he did us both a favour and drove home drunk, didn't he, so chances are he'd have died either way.' He took a deep breath as if he realised he'd told her too much. 'Now where's that new jewel of yours?'

Tess dug her fingernails into her palms to stop herself from losing it completely. 'Why should I give you the Merrick jewel? You won't be able to sell it as it's quite distinctive. I'm sure the police will keep an eye out for it on the black market. And the new Lord Merrick won't buy a story about another break-in.'

Marcus sent her a pitying glance as if she was a stupid child. 'I know several private buyers who will keep it hidden in their collections. And as for why you should give it to me, I thought I'd made myself clear.' He leaned forward in his chair, his eyes glacial. 'If you don't, you won't live beyond the end of the week.'

Tess didn't have to fake the trembling in her hands as she got up to take a box from the desk. He really was scaring her and she was terrified that something might have gone wrong with the Skype link or whatever it was that Louis and Shayla had set up and connected to Inspector Houghton. They'd assured her it would work and wouldn't go live until just before Marcus arrived so he'd have no inkling of what was going on even if he was monitoring the internet usage at Merrick Court.

'Here you go.' She almost threw the box at him. It genuinely annoyed her to have to let him hold it even for a short time. He had no right to it whatsoever. It was Josh's.

Marcus grinned and opened the box, pulling out the cross. He dangled it on its chain and watched the sparks shooting off the various gemstones. 'Hmm, quite a beauty. Yes, that should do nicely for now, thank you.' He stood up and walked towards her. 'Although, that won't fetch nearly enough so I do believe you owe me a little more than that. Something a bit … extra, shall we say?'

'What? No!' Tess backed away as he reached out to grip her arms, pushing her against the desk.

'Come on, this is the part I've been waiting for. It's you I've wanted all along, didn't you guess? I have plenty of money already. Don't fight me, Therese, or I might just have to squeeze that beautiful throat of yours a little too hard while I'm pleasuring you.'

'No! Get off me! Why, you … aaargh!' Tess screamed and tried to kick him, but her sandals were useless and only made her lose her balance.

He pulled both her arms behind her and gripped the wrists with one hand, holding her fast. Then he put his other hand over her mouth, hauled her in close and started to kiss her neck, moving his mouth down towards her cleavage. She fought to get away from him, wriggling furiously and trying to lash out, but he was very strong, his sheer bulk pinning her down.

Her only hope was Louis and Shayla, who'd promised

to watch from a safe distance, and the police who were probably even further away. Tess hadn't wanted the teenagers in the house, in case they gave the game away, but Louis had said they'd be monitoring the situation. So where were they?

As if in answer to her frantic telepathic messages, the door opened and a furiously barking Vincent came hurtling into the room. Tess felt Marcus jerk as Vince sank his teeth into the man's behind. Marcus let out a howl of rage and turned to aim a kick at the dog.

'No! Vince!' Marcus had let go of her mouth and she screamed at the dog who seemed to be a blur of teeth and flying fur.

In the next instance, someone else came rushing into the room and Marcus had a different problem to contend with.

'Josh! Oh, thank God …' Tess had never been so glad to see anyone in her life.

'You bastard! Get your hands off her.' Josh was in the grip of an almost feral fury and although Marcus was undoubtedly bulkier and possibly stronger, Josh landed some heavy punches to the other man's face, head and abdomen that had him staggering.

'Sir! *Sir!* We'll take it from here. Leave him be! Come on, easy now.'

What looked like an entire troop of police officers were suddenly swarming into the room, closely followed by Louis and Shayla. One of the policemen restrained Josh, whose eyes were still blazing with emerald fire, while Marcus wiped blood from his mouth and nose and stared at them. 'I warned you not to tell anyone about our meeting, bitch,' he hissed at Tess. 'You've got nothing on me and they'll have to let me go. Then you'll be sorry.' He pointed at Josh. 'And I'll sue you for assault and all.'

'I think you may find you're wrong there, Mr Steele.' Inspector Houghton had walked into the room and flashed his badge at the now handcuffed Marcus. 'Thanks to the lady's enterprising nephew, we've got you on Candid Camera, confessing to murder.' He pointed at the laptop and Tess saw the exact moment when the webcam registered with Marcus.

He let out an animalistic roar and tried to head-butt the nearest police officer. 'Fucking devious bitch! I should've killed you too when I had the chance. It won't hold up in court, you tricked me—'

'Shut up, Mr Steele. Whatever you say now can and will be used against you. And we'll have the evidence from the Porsche, remember? We've still got it. Plus, the late Lord Merrick appears to have saved a file showing your croupiers cheating. I've just seen it. Now why would he do that, I wonder?'

Tess glanced at Louis, who whispered, 'The file you sent me.'

'I deleted that! I made sure his computer was wiped clean. I—'

Marcus's tirade was cut short when Tess fished the USB pen out of the pencil pot and held it up. 'Guess he was smarter than you thought.'

As Marcus snarled out his anger yet again, Houghton nodded at the officers holding his arms. 'Get him out to the car, please.'

Josh had shrugged off the policemen holding him by now and came over to pull Tess into his arms. 'Are you okay, hun? I'm so sorry I left you alone here. Sir Rhys came and warned me. I've driven like a maniac ...'

'Sir Rhys?' Tess was stunned. So the ghost was still protecting her. 'I'm okay, really.'

'You sure? Christ, I thought I wasn't going to make it on time. Nearly drove me nuts!'

'It's all right, you're here now.' Tess breathed in the familiar smell of him and burrowed her face into his shoulder.

Josh hugged her so hard she was sure she heard her spine crack. 'Seriously, he didn't ...?'

'No, he didn't get that far. But I'm going to need several baths to get rid of the smell and feel of him.' Tess shuddered. 'Urgh!'

'Mr Owens, might we have a moment to take your statement, please? Lady Merrick, you'll be next.' One of the inspector's men led a reluctant Josh outside and Tess sank down into a chair, her legs still shaky.

Shayla came over and demanded to know if she was okay, while Inspector Houghton directed his men to seize the laptop and jewel as evidence.

'Yes, I'm fine, thanks. Or I will be. But, goodness, it's like Piccadilly Circus in here!' She frowned at the sight of the Merrick jewel leaving the room.

'Don't worry, you'll get it back, Lady Merrick,' Houghton assured her. 'We'll keep it safe.'

Into this melee walked a perplexed Rosie with George in tow. 'Louis! What on earth is happening? I knew it! We should never have let you stay here with that ... that ...'

'Rosie!' George nudged her and nodded towards the police.

'It's nothing, Mum. At least, everything's okay now. The police have just caught Uncle Giles's murderer thanks to us and now they're gathering evidence, right, Inspector Houghton?'

The inspector gave him a smile. 'Just so, young man.'

'M-murderer? But I thought ... the accident?' Rosie's face turned pale.

'Turns out the car had been tampered with.' Houghton nodded at Rosie. 'You should be proud of your son, madam. Very clever, he is.'

Louis beamed, but magnanimously confessed, 'It was half Shayla's doing too, actually. We came up with the plan together.'

Rosie looked Shayla up and down. 'And where did she spring from?' Rosie's expression indicated it might have been from a sewer.

'She's Josh's daughter,' Louis explained.

'I see. I suppose he has a whole brood of children back in Australia, a beach bum like that.' Rosie made a face.

Tess sent her sister-in-law an irritated glance. 'For the last time, Rosie, he's from New Zealand. And he's no more a beach bum than you are.'

'Yeah, he's a sheep farmer,' Shayla added, sending Rosie a death-glare in defence of her dad.

'Whatever. Good riddance to him. I just hope he accepts our very generous offer for Merrick Court before he goes home.'

'What's that supposed to mean? He's not leaving yet.' Tess stared at her. Since when did Rosie know anything about Josh?

'I think you'll find that he is. I was in Mr Harrison's office in London yesterday afternoon, waiting for an appointment with my own solicitor. I don't think he saw me. But I heard him talking to Harrison and I definitely heard the words "sell" and "property". I've contacted all the major estate agents and they'll let me know which one of them is handling the sale.'

Tess opened her mouth to deny this. Josh hadn't told her he was leaving, but he hadn't said he was going to visit Mr Harrison either. A sense of unease rippled through her. Had Josh changed his mind? Was he selling up after all and just hadn't got round to breaking the news to her? That would mean their affair – or whatever you wanted to call it – was a summer fling, nothing more. He'd taken advantage of her utter infatuation with him. The bastard.

She swallowed hard, suddenly engulfed in misery. The rosy future she'd been envisaging with him tumbled in her mind like a broken Lego tower and she felt like a fool. Yet again, she'd apparently fallen for a man who didn't show his true colours. How could she have been so stupid?

Chapter Thirty-Seven

Arabella stared straight ahead of her, refusing to look at her aunt Elizabeth, Huw's wife. Her mother's own sister.

'How *could* you be a part of this?' she hissed at the older lady. 'I hope my mother comes back to haunt you at the very least.'

'Tut, tut, you always were a touch melodramatic. I don't know why you can't behave like a sensible girl. But your mother spoiled you and that's the truth. Far too headstrong, you are.'

'You're wrong and what you're doing is against the law.'

Aunt Elizabeth didn't reply to that. She had always coveted the estate and had been furious when it was all left to Arabella, as her mother's heiress. The woman hadn't had any surviving children of her own so instead she'd doted on Glyn, who'd been left motherless at an early age. She'd spoiled him and thereby helped to turn him into the unbearable brute he was. And now she obviously wanted Arabella's possessions for him, which meant Arabella had to marry him.

I'd rather die.

The good thing was that none of them would inherit when Arabella died. Just before taking her own life, she would tell them about the will she'd made in Rhys's favour. If he really was dead, someone would have found it and anything belonging to him would go to his brother, Gwilum.

But how was she to accomplish a suicide? Despite an extensive search of the room, she'd found nothing with which to take her own life. There weren't even any bed sheets and she could only assume her uncle had been afraid she'd tie them together in order to escape. And he was right about that.

She was sure Glyn would carry some sort of weapon though, even in church. Perhaps that nasty-looking knife he'd pricked her with the day before? She'd have to try and snatch it out of his belt while the minister performed the service and then she could turn it on herself. She must. The alternative – having to submit to Glyn later – was too awful to contemplate.

'Sit still, for heaven's sake! I do wish you'd try to be a bit more amenable. It's all your own fault anyway, you silly girl,' her aunt scolded, while tugging a comb through Arabella's long hair. 'If only you'd done as you were bid all those years ago, Glyn wouldn't be in such a foul mood now. He'll make you a fine husband, so long as you treat him right.'

Arabella just snorted. They would never agree on that subject.

Aunt Elizabeth had lent her a silk jacket in deep red and Arabella had put it on over her own clothes. It didn't really matter what she wore and the colour would match the stains she'd be adding to it later. Her stomach muscles clenched at the thought of taking her own life. It was a terrible sin and she risked not seeing Rhys in the afterlife at all, but she believed God could hear those in need so surely He would understand she had no choice?

She swallowed hard and hoped it wouldn't be too painful. That she'd have the strength to see it through. For Rhys, she would, but she didn't want to think about him right now. It would make her cry and she was determined not to break down in front of her aunt. She'd maintain an icy silence from now on and never speak to the evil woman again.

'Come now, you're ready.' Elizabeth took her by the arm none too gently and led her down the stairs and out into the courtyard.

Glyn and Uncle Huw waited there with servants and other members of the household. They all stared at Arabella, but she lifted her chin in a defiant gesture and walked past them. They were *her* retainers really, but it was clear they had forgotten that fact. Or, more likely, they were afraid of Huw.

The church was in the village, just outside the entrance to the estate. It wasn't a long walk and Arabella managed it with her head held high. Glyn kept pace with her, but she didn't look at him. Only once did she glance his way and that was merely to ascertain that he did indeed have the hateful knife tucked into his belt. It glinted in the sun, promising a swift death. Arabella prayed it would be so.

Inside the little church it was dark and gloomy, the candles smoky because of their poor quality. Arabella's steps faltered as she walked down the aisle. Glyn was right next to her, but still she refused to acknowledge his presence. She could tell it was annoying him, as he was muttering to himself. He'd soon be even more cross, as would Uncle Huw.

There was shuffling behind them as everyone filed into the church. The minister began the service, droning on about something Arabella shut her mind to. It didn't concern her. She took a deep breath, gathered her courage and prepared to carry out her final act of defiance right now, before it was too late.

'... and if anyone knows of any lawful impediment, speak now or —'

In that moment, the church door crashed open and someone shouted, 'Yes, I do! The lady has a husband still living and is committing bigamy.'

Arabella spun around, her eyes taking in the sight of Rhys standing just inside the door, very much alive. She drew in a hissing breath, her whole being flooding with joy. She wanted to run down the aisle and throw herself into his arms, but her legs seemed frozen to the spot and she started to tremble with emotion. She was also stopped in her tracks by his expression, which was colder than the north wind. He didn't so much as look at her as his gaze was fixed on Glyn, his eyes narrowed and shooting sparks of hatred.

Glyn swore most foully, causing the minister to send him a shocked look. 'You can't prove it,' he snarled. 'There's no one left at Raglan to bear witness to your nuptials, whether you actually had a ceremony or not.'

Rhys looked at her then. 'Arabella?'

She blinked, still so shocked she was having trouble assimilating what was happening. 'What? Oh. Yes.' At last, she caught his meaning, and fumbled inside her skirt, ripping up the neat stitches that held their marriage lines in place. She pulled out the piece of paper and showed it to the minister. 'Here's the proof, signed by Lady Margaret, no less,' she said, but she didn't let go, in case he or Glyn would snatch it out of her grasp and destroy it.

After a quick look, the minister cleared his throat and sent Glyn a nervous glance. 'Well, then, it would seem the lady is indeed married, so I—'

'Not for much longer,' Glyn growled and sent Rhys a menacing stare.

Arabella saw his hand move towards his belt, but before he had time to grip the knife, she lunged towards Glyn and snatched it away.

'Give me that, you foolish woman!' He tried to take his knife back, but Arabella jumped out of the way and, picking up her skirts, sprinted down the aisle. Glyn followed, with a howl of rage, but came to an abrupt halt as a group of men moved to stand next to Rhys.

'Get behind me,' Rhys hissed, and Arabella hurried to comply.

It wasn't a moment too soon, as Glyn apparently threw caution to the wind and launched himself at Rhys. 'You whoreson! I won't let you take what's mine again, do you hear?' he yelled.

'It was never yours in the first place,' Rhys replied.

The two men tumbled out through the open church doors and onto the path outside. Everyone else followed, including Arabella who watched the ensuing fight with her heart beating so fast she thought she would faint. Glyn's sudden attack must have taken Rhys by surprise, because he had dropped his sword and the two of them were fighting with nothing but their fists. Arabella was terrified on her husband's behalf, especially since he seemed to have a head wound, as witness the bandage round his head. But she soon saw that he was still capable of holding his own.

The men he'd brought shouted encouragement and offered help.

'No, stay back. I can handle this,' Rhys grunted in between blows. But his companions looked ready to intervene if it should prove necessary, which reassured Arabella somewhat.

She should have guessed that Glyn wouldn't fight fair, however, and after a while he pulled back slightly before drawing a small knife out from inside his boot. He went on the attack, brandishing it in a maniacal way, and Rhys couldn't do more than jump out of his path.

'Here, Rhys, catch!' Arabella threw the knife she'd been holding towards him, hilt first, and to her relief he caught it. The surprise of suddenly seeing his opponent with a longer, sharper weapon made Glyn take a step backwards. He caught his heel on the verge of grass that surrounded the graves in the churchyard and stumbled, falling backwards and hitting his head on a tombstone. There was a loud crack, then he slumped to the ground, his eyes rolling up so that only the whites showed before they closed.

Everything went quiet.

'Is he … dead?' someone whispered.

One of the men who'd come with Rhys bent down to feel for a pulse. 'Yes, he's gone.'

A wail of despair sounded behind them and Arabella turned to see the horror-struck expressions of her uncle and aunt as they came out of the church and took in what had happened. Elizabeth looked distraught and threw herself onto her husband's chest, but he passed her on to a serving-woman, never one to put up with female histrionics.

Arabella sank down onto the grass herself, her legs not able to hold her any longer. She heard Huw shout, 'You'll pay for this, Cadell!'

'It weren't his fault,' someone else said. 'We all witnessed it. An accident, pure and simple.'

'And you're the one who'll pay,' Rhys shot back. 'Don't think you'll get away with stealing my wife's estate for much longer. You may have friends in high places, but so do I and remember this, I'll be waiting for an opportunity to take you down. You'll never be safe from now on.'

Arabella looked up in time to see her uncle's face turn white, then Rhys was there, pulling her up.

'Come. It's time to go.'

She was lifted onto a horse, this time more gently, and sat sideways in front of Rhys with his arms around her as they rode off. The men who'd come with him followed and she was grateful for their escort as she didn't trust Huw not to come after them with his henchmen.

Rhys was silent for a long time, then he asked quietly, 'How could you agree to marry that bastard a mere day after I was presumed dead? Have you so little faith in me?'

Her eyes shot up to his. 'What?' It hadn't even occurred to her that he would assume her complicit. 'I most certainly hadn't agreed! In fact, I was just about to take my own life. I had planned to snatch Glyn's knife and ... well, I saw no point in living without you and death was definitely preferable to being Glyn's wife.'

Rhys's eyes widened in shock. 'Arabella!' He shuddered, as if he didn't want to even think about such a thing. 'So if I'd arrived just a few moments later, I would have been too late?'

'Yes. I'm sorry, but they told me they had killed you. I had no reason not to believe them. I've witnessed first-hand what they're capable of and I didn't think they'd dare a church ceremony unless they were sure you were dead. I see now that I should have asked them to show me your body, but that didn't even occur to me …' She trailed off, horribly aware of how close they had come to disaster, one way or another.

His arms tightened around her. 'No, I'm the one who is sorry. Please forgive me for doubting you. I shouldn't have, but seeing you standing there so calmly next to Howell, it was just …'

She put her own arms round his middle and squeezed hard. 'There's nothing to forgive. Just know this, I will never love any man other than you and I will follow you into the very mouth of hell, as long as we're together.'

'Oh, sweetheart, I love you more than life too. From now on, nothing and no one will come between us, I swear.'

He gave her a fierce kiss, which she returned in full measure until she remembered something. 'Wait, stop!'

'What is it, my love?'

'The jewels,' she whispered so that the other men wouldn't hear. 'We have to go back for them. I promised Lady Margaret.'

She held her breath, hoping he wouldn't be too angry, but to her surprise he just chuckled. 'Very well, a promise is sacred. Let's go. Merrick Court gardens is probably the last place they'd look for us right now.'

Chapter Thirty-Eight

'Stirring things again, Mrs Edmonton?'

Josh walked into the room and gave Rosie a hard stare, having obviously caught at least the tail end of what she'd been saying.

She raised her chin and glared back. 'Just informing Therese of what I saw. She has a right to know, especially if she's been taken in by your ... charm.'

'That makes a change then, you being concerned about Tess.' Josh's smile was mocking. 'I thought you said she'd corrupted your son and you couldn't wait to see the back of her?'

'She *has* put some silly ideas into his head ...'

'Rosie.' George's warning growl made her sigh.

'... but perhaps it will be good for Louis to try things his way at first, then when it doesn't work out, he'll see that he should've listened to us.'

'Yeah, like that's going to happen,' Louis muttered, but didn't otherwise rise to the bait.

'Anyway, you'll soon tire of working in the garden, Louis,' his mother continued. 'Surely you won't want to stay the whole summer? Daddy and I came to ask you to accompany us and Emilia to the Riviera. We've taken a villa for the rest of August and beginning of September. Won't that be fun? The Fletchers are coming too, with their boys and that nice daughter of theirs, Olivia.'

'I hate Olivia, she's worse than Em,' Louis said. 'So thanks, but no thanks. Shay and I were thinking of going round Italy by train for a couple of weeks. She's always wanted to go there, haven't you?' He threw Shayla a smile and she grinned back and took his hand, causing Rosie's frown to deepen to epic proportions. 'And anyway, I'm not leaving here until Josh says I have to. It's his call.'

'Well, that'll be soon then.' Rosie looked smug.

Tess had only been listening half-heartedly while she tried to figure out what to believe about Josh and his secrets, but now she'd had enough. Rosie was welcome to this place. Tess never wanted to see it again. 'If anyone's tried to manipulate Louis, it's you! I'm glad he'll be the ultimate owner of this place – at least he's not a crushing snob,' she snarled before rushing out of the room and into the garden. The last thing she saw was the shocked expression on Josh's face, but she ignored it. If he couldn't be honest with her, they had no future together.

'Lady Merrick? We need your statement!'

Inspector Houghton's voice followed her along the path, but she just waved a hand at him and shouted, 'In a minute!'

She didn't stop until she was in the knot garden and could sink down onto the old stone bench by the fountain. Her entire body was trembling. How had it all gone so wrong? Why hadn't Josh told her of his plans? But he'd acted strange when they found the Merrick jewel and then he'd gone off to London, apparently to see Mr Harrison ...

'Tess! What's going on? You surely don't believe anything that über-bitch says? She was just stirring things ... Tess?'

She was crying, tears trickling down her cheeks, but she swiped at them with her knuckles, more angry than sad at the moment. 'Why didn't you tell me you were selling up after all? Or were you planning to leave without saying anything? If all you wanted was a summer fling, you should've said ...' She couldn't go on; her throat was too choked.

'Tess, look at me.' He cupped her face with both hands, giving her no choice but to stare into his eyes. 'Do you really believe that I could give this up now? The house, the history, but most of all, you?' He shook his head. 'I'm Joshua Owens Cadell, Earl of Merrick, and I'm staying right here. With you, if you'll have me.'

She opened her mouth to say something, but he didn't give her a chance.

'Look, I know you hated being Lady Merrick the first time and this place has some pretty bad memories for you, but I was really hoping we could make better ones. You were the one who told me it meant something to own this place because it had been in the family for a thousand years. So I was kind of hoping to persuade you to become Lady Merrick again, except as *my* lady, which would be a totally different thing, I swear. Perhaps together we can make this a happy home with those six kids we were planning to have?'

'F-four.'

He gave her a lopsided grin. 'Okay then, four.'

She closed her eyes. His nearness was too distracting and she didn't want to be won over by charm. She wanted cold, hard facts before she could make up her mind. 'Why did you go and see Mr Harrison then? What are you selling?'

'Property I own in New Zealand. I need the money from that to buy Home Farm. Remember, I told you about having a huge flock of sheep? We'll need more land.'

'Oh. Right.' Tess felt silly now for jumping to conclusions, but he hadn't told her his plans were definite. 'So you want me to stay here with you? And ... marry you?'

'Exactly. I love you and I want to spend the rest of my life with you. If you're dead set against this place, I'll give it up, but ideally, I want us both to stay.' He got down on one knee in front of her and pulled a little box out of his pocket. 'I bought this in a local antique shop before I went to London. It called out to me and I was going to ask you when I got back, but ... yeah, that didn't quite work out. Anyway, I'm asking you now – please, will you be my wife?' When he opened the box, a beautiful gold ring was revealed, studded with tiny sapphires and diamonds that were embedded in a design of leaves.

Tess's eyes welled up again, but this time the tears were happy ones. 'You really want to marry me? After your experiences with Isla I thought you'd been burned for life.'

He smiled. 'So did I, but this time I'm asking of my own free will, not because I have to.'

She smiled back and held out her finger for him to slide the ring onto. 'Then, yes, please, I'd like that very much. I love you too, Josh, and I was prepared to go and live with you on a sheep station in New Zealand, if that was what it took.' She looked back at the house. 'I'd be happy to continue as custodian of this place and hopefully provide it with some more heirs. You're right, we'll make our own memories. Good ones.'

'Thank God for that!' He swept her into a fierce hug, then kissed her with all the pent-up emotion of the past few hours.

Some time later, he leaned his chin on the top of her head and chuckled. 'So do you fancy learning all about sheep?'

'Sounds brilliant! I can't wait.'

'Now you're just being sarcastic. Sheep aren't so bad, really. And not stupid, just introverted.'

'Introverted?' Tess laughed. 'And I was being serious. As long as I can spend every day with you, I don't care if we run a pig farm or whatever. I'm going to enjoy every minute.'

'That's okay, then.' Josh nodded towards the fountain. 'Looks like they approve too.'

'What? Who?' Tess looked in that direction but couldn't see anything.

'Rhys and his lady. They're smiling at us.'

'She's there too? Oh, I can't see anyone, but I'm glad if they're pleased. And thank God he warned you this morning!' She suddenly remembered something. 'Did you say your name is Joshua Owens Cadell?'

'Of course. I'm directly descended from Rhys and Arabella, remember? I've just never used the surname Cadell as it was my father's. I ditched it as soon as Mum and I left him and changed to hers. But now I know where it came from, I'll be proud of it.' He nodded towards the bench. 'And I'm pretty sure that Rhys, the first man of that name to own Merrick Court, would want me to use it again. He got this place thanks to his wife, Arabella Dauncey, who seems to have inherited it from her mother, and his descendants have been here ever since. He was the one who set up the entail to make sure of that. Harrison gave me a family tree they'd drawn up when looking for me. And guess what?'

'What?'

'He and Arabella almost didn't make it out of that siege, although that wasn't the fault of the besiegers. They were okay in the end though. I've, uhm, had a few more mind visits from our friend over there ... I'll tell you all about it later.'

Tess smiled. 'Well, that's lovely. I hope they hang around and watch over us.'

Josh took her hand and pulled her up. 'Yeah, I hope so too. Now, how about we go and face the dragon, er, I mean Rosie, and tell her our good news? And there's a policeman waiting for you as well.'

'If we must. I'd much rather go somewhere with just you.'

'Don't tempt me. At least not right now. Later, I'll let you do whatever you want with me and that's a promise, my lady.'

Tess couldn't wait.

Epilogue

'Arabella, my dear, might I borrow you for a moment, please?'

Rhys took his wife's hand and pulled her out of the room where four of their five children were running around playing a noisy game of chase, while the youngest was attempting to walk with some help from the nursemaid.

Arabella followed him, promising to return soon. 'Where are we going?' she asked.

'For a walk.' He sent her an enigmatic smile, but didn't tell her where to.

He led the way out into the gardens of Merrick Court and along the paths to the knot garden, where the fountain presided over the quietest corner. A stone bench was placed nearby and Rhys pulled her down next to him. Arabella glanced at the paving stone that still hid the necklace Lady Margaret had given her. They hadn't needed to sell it so far and had decided to leave it where it was as insurance against future calamities.

'We were lucky the king listened to our plea and gave the estate back to us, even if there is much to do here to set it all to rights.' He shook his head. 'Good thing your uncle was already dead or I'd have made him pay for his mismanagement.' The gardens were overgrown and ill-kempt, but at least the surrounding fields had been looked after and the tenants had all seemed to welcome Arabella's return with her husband and family.

'I don't think luck had much to do with it.' Arabella smiled. 'Rather, it was your friendship with Prince Rupert and your loyal service to the king while he was in exile.

And I suspect Lady Margaret put in a good word for us too.'

They'd lived a peripatetic lifestyle for the last fourteen years, going wherever the exiled king went. They hadn't had to starve, but times had been hard and it was a relief now not to have to rely on others for employment or handouts. At last they could provide for their children properly.

'Well, it *was* kind of him to create me Earl of Merrick.'

'Hmm, and so much cheaper than giving you a stipend of any kind,' Arabella muttered sarcastically.

Rhys laughed. 'Yes, there is that. But don't forget the earring – just what I'd always wanted.'

'Liar. You hate wearing it.' She smiled and gave him a playful shove.

'True. But we don't need anything more from His Majesty, not when we have this magnificent place.' He swept a hand to indicate all the surrounding lands which were fertile and bountiful. 'I mean it. No gift could have been better and we've had a rich harvest, which is partly why I brought you out here.'

'What, to discuss our fields?' Arabella's eyebrows rose a notch.

'No, of course not, but the proceeds of selling some of our excess grain gave me the opportunity to do something I've wanted to do for a long time.'

He lowered himself onto one knee in front of her and pulled something out of his pocket which he held out on the palm of his hand. 'Arabella, I know that we are already married, but I wasn't able to propose properly or give you a ring, so this is for you. If I'd asked you to become my wife now, would you still say yes? I love you more than life itself and can honestly say I've never regretted a single moment spent with you.'

She took the gold ring set with tiny sapphires and diamonds in a design of golden leaves and pushed it onto her finger. It sparkled beautifully in the sunlight as she turned it this way and that. 'Oh, Rhys, of course I would! I'd marry you again tomorrow. Meeting you was the best thing that ever happened to me and the lack of a ring has never bothered me, as long as I have your heart the way you have mine.'

His green eyes shone with joy and love, which she was sure were mirrored in her own gaze. 'That you do, *cariad*. For all eternity, I can promise you that.'

As he took her into his arms and kissed her, the sparks between them more than matched those of the gems on her finger and Arabella knew it would always be thus, for as long as they lived. Perhaps even longer.

Thank You

Thank you so much for reading *The Velvet Cloak of Moonlight* – I hope you enjoyed spending time with my two couples as much as I enjoyed writing about them. To an author, the characters are very real and I'm always hoping they will feel that way to my readers as well and that I've made you care about them too.

I would really value your feedback so if you have the time, please leave a review on Amazon, a book review site such as Goodreads, or the retail outlet site – that would be amazing and much appreciated! Reviews really help other readers find the kind of books they like and they can definitely make an author's day!

Please do feel free to contact me any time, I'd love to hear from you, especially if you're a fellow fan of time slip novels. You can find my details under my author profile. And if you like this book, you might want to check out the others in the 'Shadows from the Past' series.

Thank you and happy reading!

Christina x

About the Author

Christina lives near Hereford and is married with two children. Although born in England she has a Swedish mother and was brought up in Sweden. In her teens, the family moved to Japan where she had the opportunity to travel extensively in the Far East.

Christina's debut *Trade Winds* was short listed for the 2011 Romantic Novelists' Association's Pure Passion Award for Best Historical Fiction. *The Scarlet Kimono* won the 2011 Big Red Reads Best Historical Fiction Award. *Highland Storms* (in 2012) and *The Gilded Fan* (in 2014) won the Best Historical Romantic Novel of the year award and *The Silent Touch of Shadows* won the 2012 Best Historical Read Award from the Festival of Romance. *The Velvet Cloak of Moonlight* is Christina's eleventh full-length novel with Choc Lit.

For more information on Christina:
www.twitter.com/PiaCCourtenay
www.christinacourtenay.com
www.facebook.com/christinacourtenayauthor

More Choc Lit

From Christina Courtenay

The Silent Touch of Shadows

Book 1 in the Shadows from the Past series

*Winner of the 2012 Best Historical
Read from the Festival of Romance*

What will it take to put the past to rest?
Professional genealogist Melissa
Grantham receives an invitation to visit
her family's ancestral home, Ashleigh
Manor. From the moment she arrives,
life-like dreams and visions haunt her. The
spiritual connection to a medieval young
woman and her forbidden lover have
her questioning her sanity, but Melissa is
determined to solve the mystery.

*A haunting love story set partly in the
present and partly in fifteenth century
Kent.*

The Secret Kiss of Darkness

Book 2 in the Shadows from the Past series

Must forbidden love end in heartbreak?
Kayla Sinclair knows she's in big trouble
when she almost bankrupts herself to
buy a life-size portrait of a mysterious
eighteenth century man at an auction.
Jago Kerswell, inn-keeper and smuggler,
knows there is danger in those stolen
moments with Lady Eliza Marcombe, but
he'll take any risk to be with her.

Forbidden love, smugglers and romance!

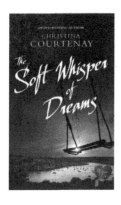

The Soft Whisper of Dreams

Book 3 in the Shadows from the Past series

Some dreams shouldn't come true ...
Maddie Browne thought she'd grown out
of the recurring nightmare that plagued
her as a child, but after a shocking family
secret is revealed, it comes back to haunt
her – the same swing in the same garden,
the kind red-haired giant and the swarthy
arms which grab her from behind and try
to take her away ...

In an attempt to forget her troubles,
Maddie travels to Devon to spend time
with her friends, Kayla and Wes. However,
it becomes clear that relaxation will not be
on the agenda after a disturbing encounter
with a gypsy fortune teller. Not to
mention the presence of Wes's dangerously
handsome brother, Alex.

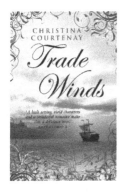

Trade Winds

Book 1 in the Kinross series

*Shortlisted for the 2011 Pure Passion Award
for Best Romantic Historical Fiction*

Marriage of convenience or a love for life?
It's 1732 in Gothenburg, Sweden, and
strong-willed Jess van Sandt knows only
too well that it's a man's world. She
believes she's being swindled out of her
inheritance by her stepfather – and she's
determined to stop it.

When help appears in the unlikely
form of handsome Scotsman Killian
Kinross, Jess finds herself both intrigued
and infuriated by him. In an attempt
to recover her fortune, she proposes a
marriage of convenience. Then Killian is
offered the chance of a lifetime with the
Swedish East India Company's Expedition
and he's determined that nothing will
stand in his way, not even his new bride.

Highland Storms

Book 2 in the Kinross series

Winner of the 2012 Best Historical Romantic Novel of the year

Who can you trust?

Betrayed by his brother and his childhood love, Brice Kinross needs a fresh start. So he welcomes the opportunity to leave Sweden for the Scottish Highlands to take over the family estate.

But there's trouble afoot at Rosyth in 1754. The estate's in ruin and money is disappearing. He discovers an ally in Marsaili Buchanan, the beautiful redheaded housekeeper, but can he trust her?

Marsaili works hard at being a housekeeper and harder still at avoiding men who want to take advantage of her. But she's irresistibly drawn to the new clan chief, even though he's made it plain he doesn't want to be shackled to anyone.

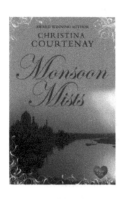

Monsoon Mists

Book 3 in the Kinross series

Sometimes the most precious things cannot be bought …

It's 1759 and Jamie Kinross has travelled far to escape his troubled past – from the pine forests of Sweden to the bustling streets of India.

In India he starts a new life as a gem trader, but when his mentor's family are kidnapped as part of a criminal plot, he vows to save them and embarks on a dangerous mission to the city of Surat, carrying the stolen talisman of an Indian Rajah.

There he encounters Zarmina Miller. She is rich and beautiful, but her infamous haughtiness has earned her a nickname: The Ice Widow. Jamie is instantly tempted by the challenge she presents.

The Scarlet Kimono

Book 1 in the Kumashiro Series

Winner of the 2011 Big Red Read's Best Historical Fiction Award

Abducted by a Samurai warlord in 17th-century Japan – what happens when fear turns to love?
England, 1611, and young Hannah Marston envies her brother's adventurous life. But when she stows away on his merchant ship, her powers of endurance are stretched to their limit. Then they reach Japan and all her suffering seems worthwhile – until she is abducted by Taro Kumashiro's warriors.

In the far north of the country, warlord Kumashiro is waiting to see the girl who he has been warned about by a seer. When at last they meet, it's a clash of cultures and wills, but they're also fighting an instant attraction to each other.

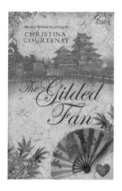

The Gilded Fan

Book 2 in the Kumashiro Series

Winner of the 2014 Romantic Historical Novel Award

How do you start a new life, leaving behind all you love?
It's 1641, and when Midori Kumashiro, the orphaned daughter of a warlord, is told she has to leave Japan or die, she has no choice but to flee to England. Midori is trained in the arts of war, but is that enough to help her survive a journey, with a lecherous crew and an attractive captain she doesn't trust?

Having come to Nagasaki to trade, the last thing Captain Nico Noordholt wants is a female passenger, especially a beautiful one. How can he protect her from his crew when he can't keep his own eyes off her?

The Jade Lioness

Book 3 in the Kumashiro Series

Can an impossible love become possible?

Nagasaki, 1648

Temperance Marston longs to escape war-torn England and explore the exotic empire of Japan. When offered the chance to accompany her cousin and Captain Noordholt on a trading expedition to Nagasaki, she jumps at the opportunity. However, she soon finds the country's strict laws for foreigners curtail her freedom.

On a dangerous and foolhardy venture she meets Kazuo, a ronin. Kazuo is fascinated by her blonde hair and blue eyes, but he has a mission to complete and he cannot be distracted. Long ago, his father was accused of a crime he didn't commit – stealing a valuable jade lioness ornament from the Shogun – and Kazuo must restore his family's honour. But when Temperance is kidnapped and sold as a concubine, he has to make a decision – can he save her and keep the promise he made to his father?

New England Rocks

Book 1 in the Northbrooke High series

First impressions, how wrong can you get?
When Rain Mackenzie is expelled from her British boarding school, she can't believe her bad luck. Not only is she forced to move to New England, USA, she's also sent to the local high school, as a punishment. Rain makes it her mission to dislike everything about Northbrooke High, but what she doesn't bank on is meeting Jesse Devlin …

A young adult novel

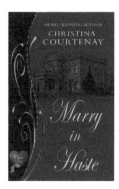

Marry in Haste

Book 1 in the Regency Romance Collection

'I need to marry, and I need to marry at once'
When James, Viscount Demarr confides in an acquaintance at a ball one evening, he has no idea that the potential solution to his problems stands so close at hand ...

Amelia Ravenscroft is the granddaughter of a earl and is desperate to escape her aunt's home where she has endured a life of drudgery, whilst fighting off the increasingly bold advances of her lecherous cousin. She boldly proposes a marriage of convenience.

And Amelia soon proves herself a perfect fit for the role of Lady Demarr. But James has doubts and his blossoming feelings are blighted by suspicions regarding Amelia's past.

Will they find, all too painfully, that if you marry in haste you repent at leisure?

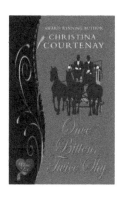

Once Bitten, Twice Shy

Book 2 in the Regency Romance Collection

'Once was more than enough!'
Jason Warwycke, Marquess of Wyckeham, has vowed never to wed again after his disastrous first marriage, which left him with nothing but a tarnished reputation and a rather unfortunate nickname – 'Lord Wicked'.

That is, until he sets eyes on Ianthe Templeton ...

But can Wyckeham and Ianthe overcome the malicious schemes of spiteful siblings and evil stepmothers to find wedded bliss? Or will Wyckeham discover, all too painfully, that the past has come back to bite him for a second time?

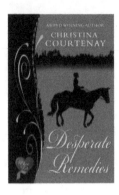

Desperate Remedies

Book 3 in the Regency Romance Collection

'She would never forget the day her heart broke …'
Lexie Holloway falls desperately in love with the devastatingly handsome Earl of Synley after a brief encounter at a ball. But Synley is already engaged to be married and scandal surrounds his unlikely match with the ageing, but incredibly wealthy, Lady Catherine Downes. Heartbroken, Lexie resolves to remain a spinster and allows circumstance to carry her far away from England to a new life in Italy. However, the dashing Earl is never far from her thoughts.

Can Lexie help Synley outwit those who wish to harm him and rekindle the flame ignited all those years ago, or will her associations with the Earl bring her nothing but trouble?

Never Too Late

Book 4 in the Regency Romance Collection

Can true love be rekindled?
Maude is devastated when the interference of her strict father prevents her from eloping with Luke Hexham. It is not long before she is married off to Edward, Luke's cousin – a good match in her father's eyes but an abhorrent one to his daughter.

Eight years later, Edward is dead. Maude, now Lady Hexham, is appalled to find his entire estate is to go to Luke – the man she still loves – with no provision for either herself or her young daughter. Luke has never forgotten Maude's apparent betrayal, but he has the means to help her.

Soon Maude and Luke realise that perhaps it is never too late for true love.

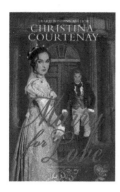

Marry for Love

Book 5 in the Regency Romance Collection

Trapped in an intolerable marriage?
Delilah cannot bear to watch as her twin
sister Deborah marries Hamish Baillie,
Fourth Earl of Blackwood. Not only
because she knows that her conniving
sister has manipulated the poor man into
marriage, but also because she has been in
love with the Earl since she first set eyes
on him …

Delilah is willing to make the ultimate
sacrifice to save Hamish from a life of
unhappiness – but will her plan work,
or will she have to accept that she is no
match for her twin's scheming ways?

Introducing Choc Lit

We're an independent publisher creating
a delicious selection of fiction.
Where heroes are like chocolate – irresistible!
Quality stories with a romance at the heart.

See our selection here:
www.choc-lit.com

We'd love to hear how you enjoyed *The Velvet Cloak of Moonlight*. Please leave a review where you purchased the novel or visit: **www.choc-lit.com** and give your feedback.

Choc Lit novels are selected by genuine readers like yourself. We only publish stories our Choc Lit Tasting Panel want to see in print. Our reviews and awards speak for themselves.

Could you be a Star Selector and join our Tasting Panel? Would you like to play a role in choosing which novels we decide to publish? Do you enjoy reading romance novels? Then you could be perfect for our Choc Lit Tasting Panel.

Visit here for more details...
www.choc-lit.com/join-the-choc-lit-tasting-panel

Keep in touch:
Sign up for our monthly newsletter Choc Lit Spread for all the latest news and offers: www.spread.choc-lit.com.
Follow us on Twitter: @ChocLituk and Facebook: Choc Lit.

Or simply scan barcode using your mobile phone QR reader:

*Choc Lit
Spread*   *Twitter*   *Facebook*